The realm of Rokugan is a land of samurai, courtiers, and mystics, dragons, magic, and divine beings – a world where honor is stronger than steel.

The Seven Great Clans have defended and served the Emperor of the Emerald Empire for a thousand years, in battle and at the imperial court. While conflict and political intrigue divide the clans, the true threat awaits in the darkness of the Shadowlands, behind the vast Kaiu Wall. There, in the twisted wastelands, an evil corruption endlessly seeks the downfall of the empire.

The rules of Rokugani society are strict. Uphold your honor, lest you lose everything in pursuit of glory.

T0112095

ALSO AVAILABLE

ARKHAM HORROR
   *Wrath of N'kai* by Josh Reynolds
   *The Last Ritual* by S A Sidor
   *Mask of Silver* by Rosemary Jones
   *Litany of Dreams* by Ari Marmell
   *The Devourer Below* edited by Charlotte Llewelyn-Wells
   *Dark Origins: The Collected Novellas Vol 1*
   *Cult of the Spider Queen* by S A Sidor

DESCENT: LEGENDS OF THE DARK
   *The Doom of Fallowhearth* by Robbie MacNiven
   *The Shield of Daqan* by David Guymer
   *The Gates of Thelgrim* by Robbie MacNiven

KEYFORGE
   *Tales From the Crucible* edited by Charlotte Llewelyn-Wells
   *The Qubit Zirconium* by M Darusha Wehm

LEGEND OF THE FIVE RINGS
   *Curse of Honor* by David Annandale
   *Poison River* by Josh Reynolds
   *The Night Parade of 100 Demons* by Marie Brennan
   *Death's Kiss* by Josh Reynolds
   *The Great Clans of Rokugan: The Collected Novellas Vol 1*

PANDEMIC
   *Patient Zero* by Amanda Bridgeman

TERRAFORMING MARS
   *In the Shadow of Deimos* by Jane Killick

TWILIGHT IMPERIUM
   *The Fractured Void* by Tim Pratt
   *The Necropolis Empire* by Tim Pratt

ZOMBICIDE
   *Last Resort* by Josh Reynolds

# *To* CHART
# *the* CLOUDS

### Evan Dicken

First published by Aconyte Books in 2022

ISBN 978 1 83908 122 4

Ebook ISBN 978 1 83908 123 1

Copyright © 2022 Fantasy Flight Games

All rights reserved. The Aconyte name and logo and the Asmodee Entertainment name and logo are registered or unregistered trademarks of Asmodee Entertainment Limited. Legend of the Five Rings and the Legend of the Five Rings logo are trademarks or registered trademarks of Fantasy Flight Games.

This novel is entirely a work of fiction. Names, characters, places, and incidents are the products of the author's imagination or are used fictitiously. Any resemblance to actual events, locales, organizations or persons, living or dead, is entirely coincidental.

Sales of this book without a front cover may be unauthorized. If this book is coverless, it may have been reported to the publisher as "unsold and destroyed" and neither the author nor the publisher may have received payment for it.

Cover art by Nathan Elmer

Rokugan map by Francesca Baerald

Distributed in North America by Simon & Schuster Inc, New York, USA

Printed in the United States of America

9 8 7 6 5 4 3 2 1

**ACONYTE BOOKS**

*An imprint of Asmodee Entertainment Ltd*

Mercury House, Shipstones Business Centre

North Gate, Nottingham NG7 7FN, UK

*aconytebooks.com // twitter.com/aconytebooks*

*To Inō Tadataka, Mamiya Rinzō, Takahashi Kageyasu, Gyōki, and all the dedicated cartographers who put Japan on the map.*

# CHAPTER ONE

Miya Isami stood alone atop Seppun Hill, grateful there was no one about to interrupt. The day had dawned overcast and humid, pale sunlight casting the usually vibrant colors of Otosan Uchi in a muted palette of grays and browns. Adjusting her spyglass atop its stand, Isami gazed down the gentle slope. The Imperial City spread around her like a faded watercolor painting, the carefully planned streets of the Inner Districts girded by the imposing breadth of the Enchanted Wall. Beyond sprawled the outer city, a riot of architectural styles crowding its winding thoroughfares.

Through her spyglass, Miya could see the outer city streets already full of people, the flow of traders, townsfolk, visitors, and low-rank samurai in marked contrast to the relatively empty streets of the Inner Districts. Servants moved along the wide, straight avenues, below the notice of their betters. Here and there, Isami spied a group of retainers shepherding a noble procession, their master's palanquin just visible through the press. It was but a fraction of the normal traffic, the morning heat having no doubt convinced many to remain home, sipping cool tea in the shade of their private gardens.

All of which suited Isami well.

As the spot where the divine siblings first touched down on their descent from the Celestial Heavens, Seppun Hill remained free of structures by imperial fiat. With its commanding view of Otosan Uchi, it was the perfect finish to Isami's survey.

Just as Hantei and his divine siblings brought their knowledge to the people of this land, so would Isami expand the bounds of cartography. She pushed down the unworthy thought, glancing around as if someone might have overheard. To compare herself to the gods was the height of arrogance.

With an absent smile, Isami unrolled a sheet of heavy paper marked with faint gridlines and affixed it to her drawing board. From the sleeve of her kimono she drew forth a small lead weight affixed to a string. After using it to determine the grade of the hill, she adjusted her spyglass atop its stand, sighting down the length of the Emperor's Road. Straight as a spear, it bisected Otosan Uchi, a series of grand torii arches spread along its length. Through careful measurement with the surveyor's chain provided to all apprentice cartographers, Isami had determined each arch was spaced exactly eighty-one yards apart – nine times nine, an auspicious number meant to represent the Emperor's everlasting rule.

Tongue pressed in the corner of her mouth, Isami inked a line across the paper, then used a carpenter's ruler to mark off equal sections to represent the arches. It irked her to use artisans' tools to achieve such precision, but Rokugani maps had always been more concerned with appearance than function.

Isami consoled herself that may very well change if today's evaluation went well. By nightfall, she might very well call herself an imperial cartographer, if only of the eighth and lowest rank.

It was all she could ever remember wanting. But, as Master

Tadataka said, wanting something was not the same as working for it.

With a shake of her head, Isami bent to her survey, sketching buildings and roads, careful to check their placement against the torii gates. The Inner Districts were easy, various temples, palaces, and clan embassies laid out along wide, straight roads. The outer city presented more of a problem. If the Inner Districts were a garden, carefully pruned and manicured, the outer city was a field grown wild, its jumble of buildings reminding Isami of weeds reaching for the sun.

"You there!" A shout from down the hill startled Isami. Her brush left an unsightly smear of ink upon the page, and, scowling, she turned to regard the interlopers.

Three people hurried up the thin gravel path that wound up Seppun Hill. Their armor and blades marked them as city guard.

Isami's frown deepened. They shouldn't be here, not for another half hour at least. She had spent three days at the Temple of the Seven Fortunes just below the hill, timing the frequency of guard patrols.

Stuffing scrolls into her satchel, Isami muttered imprecations concerning various guards and watchmen. It had been foolish of her to assume the patrols would remain static – the samurai who warded the inner city were some of the best in the Empire.

Isami glanced down the hill, stomach tightening as she realized there wasn't time to flee. She swallowed, throat suddenly dry at the thought of what the masters might think if Isami appeared for her evaluation in the custody of several city guards.

She straightened, adjusting her sash and smoothing the wrinkles from her kimono. As a member of an imperial family, however minor, Isami was technically allowed access to Seppun Hill. In practice, receiving *actual* permission would have required her to navigate a series of onerous bureaucratic requirements.

It had seemed more expeditious to ask forgiveness than permission. Isami was acting for the good of the Empire, after all.

"What are you doing?" The first guard to crest the hill was a broad-faced man, heavy-browed beneath his helm, a thick mustache tracing the downturned line of his lips. The golden lion's head crest on his helmet marked him as a member of the Lion Clan.

"Surveying the city, of course." Isami kept her tone light, as if the guards had surprised her on a stroll through the water gardens rather than atop a sacred landmark.

Noticing the Miya family crest on Isami's robes, the lead guard gave a quick bow, surreptitiously glancing back as his companions crested the hill. The second guard to arrive also boasted a lion crest below the imperial guard symbol on his armor. Isami cursed inwardly as she saw the third guard's crest was the chrysanthemum and bamboo symbol of the Seppun imperial family.

The Seppun guard, a sharp-jawed woman with suspicious eyes, slipped past her bowing companion. She took in Isami with a glance, then thrust her chin at the equipment arrayed along the hilltop.

"What is that?"

Isami tilted her head. "It doesn't really have a name."

"Looks like a spyglass on a tripod." The Seppun guard pushed roughly past Isami to glare down the barrel of the spyglass. She grunted, frown deepening as she straightened.

"Why are you watching the Imperial Palace?"

"It's the most prominent landmark." Isami gestured at the Emperor's Road. "And the main streets extend at perfect right angles from…"

She trailed off as the Seppun guard's eyes narrowed.

"Who are you?"

"I am Miya Isami, of the Imperial Ministry of Cartography." Isami nodded at her satchel, laying half open at the base of the tripod. "You can find my seal in there."

At the woman's nod, the broad-faced guard knelt to upend the sack, unleashing a cascade of inkstones, paper, measuring sticks, bits of angled steel, weighted strings, and other oddments. He sifted through the scattered equipment, coming up with a seal of carved jade incised with a stylized star marked with symbols representing the four cardinal directions.

The woman fixed Isami with an appraising stare. "You are a master cartographer?"

Isami considered lying, but the guard already seemed likely to probe at any perceived falsehood.

She lowered her head. "I am a copy clerk."

"Well, Clerk Miya, it seems you have some explaining to do."

For a wild moment, Isami considered unwinding the weighted surveyor's chain belted about her waist. It was unlikely any of the guards had trained against such a weapon, but surprise would be little use against three armed samurai. Even if she managed to flee, they already had Isami's name and face. The damage was already done, escape would change nothing.

It was as if a silken cord had wrapped around Isami's chest, drawing tighter with each breath. She had known the risk, but had so wanted to prove herself at the evaluation. She had dreamed of presenting the masters with a map of the inner city more accurate than any before.

Even Master Kageyasu could not fail to note such a feat of measurement.

Isami shook her head. "Send a missive to Master Tadataka. He can explain everything."

"I am sure he can. In the meantime, we shall escort you to the district barracks, Clerk Miya." The woman offered a slight bow, then thrust her chin at Isami's tools. "Captain Kuroda will be very interested to examine your spying equipment."

"It's not–" Isami took a quick step back as the broad-faced guard stepped forward.

"Lady Miya, please allow me to accompany you." Although phrased humbly, there was steel below the Lion samurai's words.

"Pardon me." The call came from farther down the hill. Isami tried to see, but the guard blocked her view.

"Who's this, another spy?" The Seppun guard cocked her head.

The speaker finally stepped into view. Although he was bent in a low bow, even in profile she recognized the high cheekbones and thin nose of Otomo Kazuya, one of her fellow clerks at the Ministry. They had often exchanged friendly words in passing, but Kazuya's research did not involve Isami, and his appearance on Seppun Hill was unexpected.

"Honored wardens, please forgive my companion's rudeness." Kazuya held his bow for a long breath, then straightened, his face a study in embarrassed contrition. "Master Tadataka wishes to draw a new map of Otosan Uchi to present at Winter Court, and bade us survey the Road of the Most High."

The Seppun raised an eyebrow, glancing from Isami to Kazuya. "She is with you?"

"Yes, lady." Kazuya clasped his hands in supplication. "We were meant to come together, but in her excitement to do Master Tadataka's bidding, Isami left early to set up the equipment."

"Is this true?" the woman turned to Isami.

"Yes," Isami lied. Although she had no idea what Kazuya was playing at, anything was better than the district barracks.

The woman gave a brusque nod, and the Lion guards stepped back.

As Isami bent to collect her scattered papers, the woman turned back to Kazuya. "And I suppose you have the proper approvals to ascend Seppun Hill?"

"Of course." Kazuya reached into the sleeve of his kimono, only to come up empty-handed. Reddening, he searched the other sleeve, then made a show of patting the front of his robe. With a strangled moan, he dropped to his knees, forehead pressed to the grass.

"A thousand apologies, noble lady. It seems in my haste to catch Isami, I have forgotten the papers back at the Ministry. Please forgive my foolishness. I have done the masters a terrible disservice. Here, upon Seppun Hill, no less."

The woman's lip curled as Kazuya continued to heap abuse upon himself. She glanced to the other guards, who watched the display with narrowed eyes, their expressions unreadable. Higher in standing than even the Seppun or Miya, Kazuya's family, the Otomo, carried the blood of emperors, and it was rare to see one debase themselves so.

"Get up, before you embarrass us all." The Seppun guard bent to assist Kazuya to his feet.

Eyes downcast, Kazuya straightened his robes. "I beg you to overlook this. If you would but accompany us back to the Ministry, Master Tadataka will–"

"Enough." The Seppun guard gave a quick chop of her hand. "Gather your equipment and go."

Hardly daring to breathe, Isami retrieved her spyglass and drawing board as Kazuya bent to collect his satchel.

"Next time, be sure you present yourselves at the district barracks before ascending the hill." The Seppun guard spoke loudly, as if more to her fellow guards than Isami and Kazuya. "We wouldn't want another misunderstanding."

Unable to believe her good fortune, Isami hurried down the hill, hardly daring to look back lest the guard change her mind. Kazuya fell in beside her, an easy smile on his face.

"That was close."

Isami glanced over. "How did you manage that? I thought she was going to drag us both back for questioning."

"It was easy enough." Kazuya shrugged. "Seppun, Miya, Otomo – an embarrassment to one imperial family is an embarrassment to all. She couldn't risk further awkwardness, especially with those Lion brutes watching. I'm sure I'll hear about it later, but that is later."

Isami blew out a long breath, her anxiety replaced by a sudden flash of envy at how Kazuya had so effortlessly manipulated the guards. A middling cartographer at best, Kazuya seemed always on the verge of being removed from the Ministry. In Isami's experience, he was a pleasant enough fellow, possessed of a quick tongue and easy manner she often envied, but there was no doubt it was the Otomo name that kept Kazuya on the Ministry rolls.

Isami swallowed the uncharitable thoughts – he had just rescued her, after all.

"Thank you." She offered a low, and heartfelt, bow.

"You would do the same for me." Kazuya gave a dismissive wave. "You're just lucky Master Tadataka sent me to find you."

"My evaluation isn't until the Hour of the Horse."

Kazuya tilted his head. "That was a half hour ago."

Isami glanced at the sky, panic washing over her as she realized how high the sun had risen. She had become lost in her work again, hours slipping like sand through her fingers.

Red-faced, Isami doubled her pace, Kazuya hurrying to keep up with her longer strides. If Master Tadataka had managed to stall the others, there might still be time. Fortunately, Kazuya had found her when he did.

The thought made Isami frown. How had Kazuya located her?

"I told no one where I was going." She cast an appraising look back at the small noble.

"I may have looked through your things." He massaged the back of his neck, his grin turning embarrassed. "What choice did I have?"

Isami grunted. She ought to have been furious, but Kazuya's imposition was an understandable one. Even so, it was troubling his first instinct had been to search her private effects.

"You could have asked around the grounds."

"You said it yourself – you told no one." He stopped in the middle of the street, forcing Isami to pause or leave him behind.

"I was worried you would miss your evaluation," Kazuya replied.

"I still might." Shaking her head, Isami sighed.

They hurried along the wide streets of the inner city, pausing only to make way for the procession of a high noble. Fortunately, the late summer heat had become truly oppressive, and the avenues remained mostly clear.

Isami was sweating through her robes by the time she stumbled into the broad courtyard of the Ministry of Cartography. A small town to itself, the Ministry's low walls contained buildings ranging in size from the sprawling, multi-tiered Imperial Cartographic Archives, to the individual masters' villas, to the small, peaked structures that housed the clerks' quarters. Raised wooden walkways ringed a large central courtyard, its rolling expanse sculpted into a stylized replica of Rokugan by the Ministry's legion of gardeners.

"May the Ancestors watch over you." Kazuya offered an encouraging smile as he returned Isami's satchel. With a nod of thanks, she hurried into the garden.

Master Tadataka awaited Isami in the shade of the Carpenter Wall, the massive Crab Clan bastion reduced to a low stone rise that snaked along the lower portion of the courtyard.

"You are late." A frown deepened Master Tadataka's normally somber expression. Despite the heat, his graying hair was neatly combed, not a fold of his kimono out of place. Kneeling before the wall, with his high cheekbones and dark, deeply set eyes, Tadataka looked like the statue of a Fortune enshrined in some ancient mountain temple.

"I have no excuse, master." Isami's bow was spoiled by her satchel, which threatened to spill its contents over the small replica of Hida Palace.

"I have managed to keep the other masters engaged," Tadataka said. "Although Kageyasu has drunk two pots of my finest silver nettle tea."

Isami withered beneath the weight of his mild disappointment. Miya Tadataka was not only her master and patron, but family as well. Isami's parents were both imperial heralds whose duties often took them far afield. In their absence, Tadataka had seen to her education and upbringing.

"I am ready, master."

Tadataka rose, two servants hurrying from the shadow of the wall to see his robes did not become disarrayed or soiled. He sent them back to their alcoves with a gentle wave. Like most Miya dress, Tadataka's kimono was cut for form over function, its fabric thicker and more serviceable than the light, layered garments favored by other noble families. Even the Miya family colors seemed to have been selected not to stand out – a combination of ochre and muted greens that, while pleasant to look upon, would never turn heads.

"One last thing." Tadataka nodded to a third servant Isami hadn't even seen. In his hands he carried a long silk-wrapped bundle bearing the Miya crest. With a bow to Tadataka, he knelt to place the parcel at Isami's feet before retreating a discreet distance.

All other thoughts seemed to fade as Isami dropped to her knees. The bundle contained a length of polished cedar about as long as a walking cane. Adorned with brass fittings and incised with a webwork of diagonal lines, the staff was beautiful, but Isami's breath caught in her throat as she beheld what was affixed to the top.

It was a small thing, a flat cylinder of polished bronze barely big enough to fit in the palm of one hand. Its glass face was inlaid with golden symbols representing the four directions, below which a thin fleck of jade lay upon a disc of shining silver.

"A geomantic compass." Isami whispered the name as she lifted the small staff. The first had been a gift by Hantei himself to the progenitor of the Miya family, so that no matter how far Miya traveled, he would always know the way home.

"Only master cartographers are awarded these." Turning it in her hands, Isami watched, spellbound, as the needle steadfastly pointed toward the Emperor's Palace.

"Consider it a loan," Tadataka replied. "Until you receive one of your own."

Isami turned the compass to see Tadataka's name engraved on the bottom. Throat tight, she held it out to her master.

"I cannot accept this."

"And yet you will." Tadataka's warm tone belied the harshness of his words. He waved a hand in front of his face. "It has been years since I have left the capital, even longer since I required the compass."

"I shall endeavor to be worthy of this gift." Isami held the relic with care, hardly believing the trust her master had placed in her.

"I have no doubt you will."

Isami straightened, holding the compass as if it might sprout wings and fly away.

"Take a moment to collect yourself." The ghost of a smile flitted across Tadataka's severe expression. "You look as if you've sprinted across half the Inner Districts."

As Tadataka departed, Isami regarded herself in the long thin pool sculpted to resemble the contours of Earthquake Fish Bay. She looked a sight – hair wild, her cheeks flushed from exertion and anxiety. The sleeves of her kimono were damp with sweat. She would have very much liked to change robes, but decided promptness, however overdue, was more important than presentation.

Isami had lost her hair pins on the run across the city, and had to do with the string from one of her lead weights. She was not high enough rank to warrant the attentions of servants, so she did her best to straighten her sash and smooth her robes.

Forcing her breath into a steady rhythm, Isami fought to center herself. She focused upon the sun glittering from the water, the soft earth beneath her feet, the low breeze hissing through the garden branches. The sensations blended within her senses, swallowing her concerns like a rising tide.

There was nothing left but to act.

Isami gathered up her equipment and the geomantic compass. Normally she paid little attention to guards and servants, their furtive scurryings an ever-present facet of life in the capital. Now, she was painfully aware of their gaze upon her. With as much poise as she could manage, Isami made her way across the courtyard, from Crab lands to Scorpion, then Lion and Unicorn, and finally across the bridge that marked the ends of the Empire.

Her calm lasted almost to the evaluation chamber.

# CHAPTER TWO

The room was surprisingly small to carry such weight. A framework of broad cedar beams supported a high peaked roof in the old imperial style. The heavy screens that formed the chamber's walls were painted with intricate cartographic murals ranging from roads to temple complexes to highly stylized representations of entire regions. The screens along the far wall had been drawn back to reveal in the courtyard with a stone garden. It had been carefully sculpted to resemble the sea beyond the capital, stones representing various coastal islands, with whorls of raked sand to show the tides and currents flowing around them.

Any other time, Isami would have paused to enjoy the thoughtful artistry of the scene, but at the moment, she had eyes only for the three masters who knelt upon the raised dais to her right.

They sat in order of rank. The first, Miya Naotora, had been an old woman for as long as Isami could remember, her pinched and wrinkled face conveying that peculiar sense of agelessness that occasionally settled upon those of advanced years. Although clearly woven of costly materials, her plain robes were cut in a style that had not been popular for decades, adorned with little more than the Ministry and Miya crests. Naotora's bearing and dress made a simple yet effective statement – namely that she cared little for the frippery of court life.

It was a sentiment Isami wholeheartedly embraced.

Next to Naotora, Doji Kageyasu knelt upon a silken mat, a cup of Master Tadataka's tea steaming on a tray near his right hand. Like most Crane Clan nobles, Kageyasu's hair was the color of driven snow, drawn back from his high forehead by a tie of azure silk. In keeping with his artistic inclinations, Kageyasu's robes were pale blue, embroidered with a spray of white plum blossoms in deference to the season, their petals stirred as if by the beat of passing wings.

Last, sat Miya Tadataka. Although his face remained stern, there was an encouraging cant in his posture that gave Isami the strength to enter.

She moved across the woven mats, eyes downcast, careful to take the small, shuffling steps that showed deference to the three upon the dais. Naotora and Tadataka remained motionless as Isami dropped to her knees, but Kageyasu nodded to a nearby servant. Although the master's cup was already full, the man hurried forward to make a show of pouring more.

The insult was plain enough – Kageyasu considered Isami to be on the level of a mere house retainer. Isami bore the affront without response. Although Kageyasu was of the Great Clans and ranked lower than a member of a noble family, even one as small as the Miya, he was nonetheless a master cartographer.

Tadataka's jaw tightened, and he seemed about to speak when Naotora waved a dismissive hand at the servants.

"Leave us." Although soft, her voice carried the authority of an imperial command. As the servants turned to go, she nodded at Kageyasu's tea. "And take that with you. Wouldn't want to spill anything on the maps."

"Thank you." Kageyasu offered the senior master a stiff bow, his eyes cold as a winter sea. "The tea had grown stale anyway."

It was an obvious lie, but allowed Kageyasu to save face in light of Naotora's admonishment.

With a soft sigh, the elder master turned her steady gaze upon Isami. Although they shared the same ancestor, Naotora had never shown Isami anything resembling familial affection.

"I am told you are here to be evaluated."

Isami bowed again. "Yes, Master Naotora."

"And whose work have you chosen to reproduce?"

Isami drew in a slow breath to steady herself. This was the moment she had prepared for – hundreds of sleepless nights, days spent poring over ancient mathematical texts in the imperial archives, calculations and theories inked upon page after page.

Naotora glanced toward Kageyasu. "Have I gone deaf?"

"No, venerable one." The Crane courtier did not bother to conceal his smile. "She has yet to reply."

Isami glanced to Tadataka, who returned the slightest of nods.

Isami's body felt like a mooring line, drawn tight by a storm wind. Nonetheless, she bowed once more.

"No one, masters."

Silence stretched between them, charged as the breath between lightning and thunder.

"That is …" Naotora cocked her head. "Highly irregular."

Kageyasu leaned forward. "You have nothing to present for evaluation?

"I do, master." Isami drew a half-dozen scrolls from the satchel at her side, carefully spreading them upon the floor before the masters.

"What is this?" Kageyasu asked.

"Otosan Uchi, master," Isami replied. "The streets and landmarks."

"These look like a child's scrawl." Kageyasu frowned down at the scrolls. "Where is the artistry? The color? There are no forms, no life, no sense of balance."

A flush crept up Isami's neck. Tadataka had warned her it would be difficult, but she hadn't expected such a vehement reaction, even from Kageyasu. Although she could see from Tadataka's bearing he wished to respond to Kageyasu's accusations, as her patron it would be unseemly for him to voice direct support. The pretense of impartiality was but one more fiction that supported the foundations of polite society.

"These are measurements, master." Isami lifted a map detailing the inner districts. "Accurate down to the foot. Once I realized the Road Most High bisected Otosan Uchi at a right angle, I was able to divide the city into equal quadrants and use the torii arches to calculate precise distances. After that, it was just a matter of reducing everything to scale. Initially, I couldn't find the proper tools, but by the Ancestor's grace, I happened to be passing by a newly erected teahouse when I noticed the strings and marked rules the carpenters used for measurements. I realized they could be applied to cartographic representation with just a few modifications, so I…"

Too late, Isami realized she was rambling. Naotora and Kageyasu stared at her with undisguised surprise. Even Tadataka seemed taken aback by the outpouring of words.

Thankfully, Naotora spoke first. "These maps; why did you

choose to create them instead of replicating a traditional work as was expected?"

"I believe they may be of great use to the Empire." Isami fought to keep her voice level. "We have accurate maps of Otosan Uchi and its surrounds, but as one travels farther from the capital, precision suffers. The extreme reaches of the Empire are barely mapped at all. More accurate surveys would help with tax collection, more accurate road maps would aid trade and travel, terrain maps would assist in military–"

"I've heard enough." Disdain whetted Kageyasu's tone to razor sharpness. "To disregard the past is to spit upon the work of the masters of old. I, for one, will not sit here and be lectured by some amateur with pretentions of glory."

Kageyasu made to rise, only to pause as Naotora cleared her throat.

"You used the torii to measure distance within Otosan Uchi, but they reach only to the city walls. Surely you don't expect the Empire to erect such measures across Rokugan?"

"No, master. There is another way." Isami's fingers felt loose and wooden as she grasped Tadataka's geomantic compass.

Kageyasu frowned down at the relic, but Naotora looked toward Tadataka.

"Is this your doing?"

He gave a quick nod, face betraying nothing.

"A beautiful treasure. But of what use is this relic?" Kageyasu asked.

"My technique relies on an old principle, first developed by a third-generation disciple of Shinsei, Master Hui."

"Hui was a mathematician," Naotora replied. "To my knowledge, he created no maps."

"That is true, master. But many of his formulations can be applied to cartography." Isami drew another scroll from her satchel, this one inked with various triangles and numbers. It was tempting to launch into an explanation, but, wary of her past overstep, Isami bit back the urge.

"Simply put, Master Hui proved that if we know the length of the base of a triangle, as well as the angles where the base meets the other two sides, we can determine the lengths of all sides of the triangle."

Master Naotora's face was studiously blank, but Master Kageyasu's scowl seemed etched in stone.

"We use the surveyor's chain to measure fields and roads." Cheeks burning, Isami forged on, unwinding the chain from around her waist. "But I can also use it to measure the baseline of a triangle, then use my spyglass to sight a distant location. Since the geomantic compass always points toward the Imperial Palace, it can be used to determine the angle of each side. From those measurements, I can calculate exact distances."

Naotora rocked back on her heels. "Your theories are interesting, but–"

"They are not theories. I will show you." Isami didn't remember standing, but somehow she was on her feet, the embarrassed prickle on the back of her neck washed away by a flood of determination. Isami was correct, they would see.

Kageyasu gave a choked gasp as Isami stepped from the room, hurrying through the open screens and down into the rock garden.

She laid the chain upon the sand. Moving to first one end, then the other, she held up the compass, then sighted down her spyglass at a rock on the other side of the garden. Jotting down the angles on a bit of paper, she quickly ran through Master Hui's formula.

Distantly, she heard Naotora talking, but Isami couldn't make out the words over the pounding of her heart. It was as if she were looking down upon herself from a great distance, her limbs seeming to move of their own accord.

"Isami!" Tadataka's voice cut through the haze of calculation.

Isami turned, seeming to snap back into her body. "Sixteen feet!"

The three masters' expressions ranged from shock to undisguised anger.

"You forget yourself, clerk," Tadataka continued, his tone measured despite his rigid bearing.

The admonition hit Isami like a thrown stone. She looked around the trampled sand, dropping to her knees as the full implication of her transgression settled on her like a physical weight.

"You have made a mockery of these proceedings, of the Ministry of Cartography, and of us." Kageyasu spoke as if passing a death sentence.

Naotora folded her hands in her lap, looking down at Isami through eyes gone hard and cold as river rocks.

"To study greatness is the first step toward achieving it," she said. "The purpose of this evaluation is to judge a candidate's ability to replicate the works of the ancient masters. How can we judge your fitness to be an imperial cartographer if we cannot compare your work to those who came before?"

Isami drew in a breath, but could find no words.

"Despite your… rather lively demonstration, it is my decision you have not met the criteria for evaluation," Naotora turned to Kageyasu. "What say you?"

"A shameful display." He almost spat the words.

"And you, Master Tadataka?"

He regarded Isami for a long moment. She searched his eyes for the familiar flicker of kindness.

Master Tadataka's expression betrayed nothing as he looked away, then slowly shook his head.

Isami blinked back tears as Master Kageyasu stormed from the chamber, already calling for servants to attend him.

Master Naotora lingered for a moment. "Take time to reflect upon your conduct, Isami. Determine how word and deed may better match your aspirations."

She turned away, robe hissing across the woven mats as she walked from the room.

Then Isami was alone with Tadataka.

Worse than the shame at having embarrassed herself was the pain of having failed her master. It coiled like a serpent within her stomach, cold and venomous.

At last, Tadataka spoke. "Kageyasu's response was expected, but I thought we could sway Naotora. If not for your... outburst, we might have.

"The Ministry may seem like a mountain," he continued. "A grand thing, imposing, sharp, and obstinate. This is not so." He inclined his head toward the garden. "It is more like this garden, composed of stone and sand, but representing something greater."

Isami blinked back tears. "Master, I–"

Tadataka held up a hand. "What is the best way to move sand, Isami?"

"I- I don't understand."

He stood and stepped from the dais, no hint of warmth on his face. "One shovel at a time."

And with that, Master Tadataka left her alone.

Isami moved as if in a dream, collecting her scrolls, chain, tripod, and compass. It seemed impossible that she had failed. Just this morning her path had been so clear. She would travel the Empire; village, mountain, forest, castle, road, and shore all reduced to lines inked upon a page, all things measured and assessed, circumscribed by the breadth of her art.

It had been all Isami could ever remember wanting.

She had always believed maps were more than art, more than the lands they represented; they were tools, they were *language*. And like language there was room for both beauty and function. What use were words if they could not be understood, could not be used? This impulse had occupied Isami's thoughts since she was a little girl, sketching maps of her parents' journeys on bits of discarded paper. Until mere moments ago, it had seemed an almost elemental truth, so sharp and clear it felt impossible others could not recognize the rightness of Isami's path.

She clutched her satchel to her chest, head bowed to conceal the tears that cut shining tracks down her cheeks. She had doubted her ability, her dedication, but never her purpose – not until now.

Two servants waited by the chamber entrance, rakes in hand, ready to set the garden right. In an hour, it would be as if the whole affair had never happened.

If only Isami could make it so.

# CHAPTER THREE

Paper rusted beneath Isami's questing fingers, one of a score of scrolls and books laid across the large table. Normally, the sight would have excited her, to have such knowledge within easy reach was a heady draught, but even the comforting smells of ink and ancient pages couldn't untie the knot in Isami's chest.

Flickering lamplight cast the room in autumn tones, Isami's hunched shadow like a mountain tengu come to steal naughty children from their beds. For weeks, she had labored, as summer aged to fall.

She pored over stacks of rustling maps, pausing only to refill the oil lamps, careful of the flame. Like all raised in Otosan Uchi, Isami had seen her share of fires, terrible affairs contained only through great effort. Many in the Inner Districts paid priests skilled in invocations of fire and water to keep constant watch. But the wild tangle of the outer city seldom had such protections. It was why arson was one of the few crimes punishable by the more brutal forms of execution available to the courts.

After checking the lamps, Isami bent back to her work. It was long after sunset, and most of the copy clerks had either retired to teahouses or wandered off to their tiny rooms in the Ministry dormitories. Isami should have left with them, but dreaded spending another night tossing on her futon as the evaluation replayed in her mind.

Only through work was she able to press down the shameful memories. So Isami worked – her fingers stained with ink, her eyes tired and vision blurry, her hands trembling with fatigue – and still she would not leave the Ministry archives, as if by copying map after map, text after text, she could somehow erase the stain of her failure, somehow show the masters that they had been incorrect, that Isami *could* be a dutiful scribe, a humble apprentice.

But the masters were not watching.

Even Tadataka had been distant, his schedule suddenly full of appointments that took him away from the Ministry grounds. As her patron, Isami's outburst had disgraced Tadataka as well. He had risked much for her, supporting her new ideas, even entrusting her with his geomantic compass.

The rip of paper snapped Isami from her dire contemplation. With a start, she realized her hands had tightened into fists, tearing a long gash in the delicate scroll – part of a series of ancient maps of the northern Spine of the World mountains by an obscure fourth century cartographer named Gyōki.

Isami snatched back her hands as if the scroll had burned her. Her first instinct was to attempt to conceal the damage. Gyōki was considered somewhat of an eccentric, his work seldom referenced, and almost never copied. This dearth of reproductions had left a hole in the Ministry archives, one which Isami hoped to rectify, and thereby show her commitment to the work of past masters, even those as unconventional as Gyōki.

The archives were almost empty. If Isami simply rolled up the scrolls and returned them to their alcove, it was unlikely the tear would be noticed for some time. It was not as if she could fall any further in the masters' esteem.

She sighed. Just because Isami had embarrassed herself did not mean she could behave like some backwoods rogue. She was a Miya, after all.

Isami picked up the scroll, intending to take it to one of the archive guards, but paused as the torn portion curled down. Through the gap in the scroll she saw the other maps spread across the table, Spine of the World mountains faint as clouds in ancient, faded ink.

Throat dry, she laid the ripped scroll atop another map, flipping the torn portion back and forth as if turning the page of a book. Mountains overlaid mountains in perfect replica.

The maps appeared to match.

Hardly believing her eyes, Isami knelt to rummage through her satchel. Considered impossible to measure, mountains were often sketched freehand, varying widely in scale and size even within the same map. For Gyōki to have replicated exact measurements across multiple representations was nothing short of unbelievable.

Although many cartographers still preferred to pace out distances, the surveyor's chain allowed for more accurate measurements of fields, streets, villages, and the like. Still, it was useless for larger maps, which meant long distances were often estimated, or represented by the time it took to travel from one place to another. Apart from a few landmarks like Beiden Pass, the Spine of the World Mountains were largely unmapped, the rendering of their vast expanse given broad artistic license.

Isami retrieved her carpenter's rule and applied it to the maps, jotting down measurements as she went. At some point, a bell rang announcing the Hour of the Rat. Isami barely noticed, so engrossed was she in her notation. Only when the morning sun crept through the screens did Isami sit back, blinking in the sudden brightness. She could hear the other clerks outside, their banter painfully loud after a night of silent scrutiny. Soft sandals whispered across the halls as they spread through the archives, ready to begin their day's work.

Isami straightened, pressing a hand to the small of her back. It felt like a bent bow, strung too long and refusing to return to shape. She wanted to continue studying Gyōki's maps, but even the slightest motion left her feeling faint.

Isami stood, leaning on a nearby wooden column as her head began to spin. Even her faint call was enough to bring a servant hurrying down the long hall.

"I am retiring, but my work is not yet done," she told the man. "Let none disturb this room."

He gave a low bow, muttering his assent. It was not uncommon for clerks to spend weeks or even months copying a particular map. Normally, Isami would have been worried some other scholar would request the maps, but Gyōki was a rare enough name she was confident none would miss them.

After a quick breakfast of rice gruel, she stumbled back to her small room, barely able to unroll her futon before exhaustion overcame her.

It was late afternoon when Isami rose, awakened by a gentle scratch on the screen that served as her door. A servant carried a tightly wrapped letter and a light lunch. Mouth full of rice and pickled vegetables, Isami unfolded the letter, surprised to see her mother's angular hand. The writing covered barely half the page, and consisted largely of a description of the far northern coast, to which she and Isami's father had been sent to oversee the dispensation of the Emperor's Blessing – a project to rebuild the Phoenix Clan's docks after a spring storm had reduced several of the larger wharves to flinders. Isami's mother went into detail concerning the delicacies they had sampled at the behest of their Phoenix Clan hosts, but made no mention of Isami's evaluation, for good or ill.

It was possible they had not received word of her failure, but equally likely they simply did not wish to broach the subject. So it always was with her parents. Utterly committed to delivering truth to all corners of the Empire, they found it seemingly impossible to conscience ill news within their own house, as if by ignoring something they could somehow consign it to the void. Although this was often a source of irritation for Isami, she found her mother's descriptions strangely comforting, if only because Isami didn't think she could bear another round of condemnation.

As always, her mother promised to write again when she could, which, from experience, Isami knew meant it would be weeks, months, or even a year before she could expect another letter.

It used to sting that Isami was merely an afterthought to her parents, but she had grown used to their benevolent neglect. They had never wanted a child, but nobles, even minor ones, must produce heirs. With an absent shake of her head, she set the letter with the others. It was good they weren't close, better to shield her family from the stain of Isami's failure.

Bolting down the rest of her meal, she returned to the archives to continue her work.

Night blurred into day, then night again. Like some Shinseist ascetic, Isami slept and ate only when she must, drifting like a restless spirit as she compared Gyōki's maps with recent imperial surveys to determine if they had replicated his representation. But she found no indication of measurement, the mountains' sizes varying wildly, even within maps drawn by the same cartographer.

Columns of figures filled the cramped pages of her notebook, sketches of mountains girded with lines of measurements and calculations. More than once Isami collapsed into her bed, suspecting her most recent discovery had more to do with fatigue than insight. But something drove her on.

At last, she breathed deep, eyes wide as she reviewed the maps spread before her.

Either Isami had gone mad, or somehow Gyōki had managed to capture the height and breadth of each mountain in relation to one another. Given the Spine of the World's size and inaccessibility, there could be no other answer short of divine intervention:

Gyōki had used Hui's triangle.

Even the imperial surveys depicted little more than a wall of forbidding peaks speckled with the occasional river or village, but if Gyōki's maps were to be believed, the northern expanse of the range was much larger than previously thought.

And yet, something was wrong.

Checking her calculations, Isami examined the edge where the original torn map met the next in the series. If she was correct, there should have been more mountains, but instead there was only a blank space. It seemed strange Gyōki had measured all of the nearby peaks, only to leave a small portion unmapped. Isami couldn't believe he had made more maps of the region, but failed to return to finish this one. Perhaps it was truly impassible, or shielded from view by the surrounding peaks.

Isami sat back as the realization struck her like divine thunder.

Perhaps it wasn't a mountain at all.

She returned to the imperial surveys, but found nothing of use. The lands depicted were owned by the Scorpion Clan, part of a stretch bordering territory claimed by the Lion Clan. If there was a hidden valley, there might be more in the Scorpion or Lion archives. But even if Isami managed to travel such a great distance, it was unlikely the clans would open their records to a mere copy clerk. If only she were an imperial cartographer, she could mount an expedition and survey the range herself.

But alas, that was not to be.

Isami sought information on Gyōki, but there was frustratingly little written about the man.

She wanted to tell someone, but even Tadataka would not see her.

"Isami? What are you still doing here?"

The question brought Isami to her feet like a startled squirrel. She looked back to see Otomo Kazuya leaning against one of the door columns. Although his robes were in disarray and his cheeks flushed, Kazuya's smile was wide as a crescent moon.

"Working yourself to death won't put you back in the master's good graces," he said. "The Empire has martyrs enough already."

Isami cocked her head. "Are you drunk?"

"Of course not." Kazuya stepped into the room, his movements betraying only the slightest unsteadiness. He knelt next to her, sighing. "Perhaps a little. My evaluation is tomorrow."

"Then you should be resting."

"Could you sleep the night before?" He chuckled. "I figured I might as well spend the time doing something useful."

Isami looked him up and down. "Drinking with the other apprentices?"

"Drinking with Master Kageyasu's and Naotora's apprentices." Kazuya waved at the pile of scrolls. "That's what you never understood, Isami. Maps aren't important, *people* are. A few cups of sake and some kind words, and they told me everything I needed to know to win their masters' approval."

"Grains of sand," Isami muttered to herself.

"What was that?"

"Nothing." She shook her head. "So now I suppose you've come to learn how to impress Master Tadataka?"

Kazuya glanced away, reddening.

Isami fixed him with a searching look. She had seen Kazuya's work, and it was poor at best. Master Tadataka would tear him to ribbons. Thoughts of torn maps made her glance back to the table.

"What have you got here?" Kazuya asked.

"Ancient charts by Gyōki."

"I've never heard of him," Kazuya replied.

"Few have."

"It's late, even for you." He leaned in to peer at the maps. "What is so interesting that it would chain you to this table?"

Isami bit her lip, considering. Kazuya hardly qualified as a clerk, let alone a colleague, but he had found Isami before the evaluation; although perhaps things might have gone better had he let the guards arrest her.

"This looks like the Spine of the World?" Kazuya shook his head. "Nothing there but bandits, beasts, and boulders."

"Not if these maps are to be believed." Isami drew in a deep breath. Truthfully, apart from Master Tadataka, Kazuya was the closest thing she had to a friend in the Ministry. In the end, though, it was less about trust than the fact Isami simply needed to tell *someone*.

"What do you mean?" he asked.

Isami told him.

When she had finished, Kazuya rocked back on his heels. "Ancient maps, hidden valleys – that is quite a lot to base on very few facts."

"I triple-checked my calculations. It may not be a valley, but there *is* something." Isami hated the note of desperation in her voice. Was Kazuya right? Was this merely a false hope, her feet planted not on mountains, but clouds?

"I don't doubt you." Kazuya laid a gentle hand on her shoulder. "You look half a ghost, Isami. There is nothing here that won't wait until morning."

"I wouldn't be able to sleep."

"Then come out with me," he said. "There are teahouses open even at this hour. If you are right, then this discovery is worthy of celebration. If not, commiseration."

Isami regarded him. She wanted to keep working, but what else was there to do? Gyōki's maps were like a single island, alone amidst a sea of breaking waves. It would be nice to forget her troubles, if only for a moment.

She gave a quick nod. "I will come."

"Excellent!" Kazuya clapped his hands, rising to his feet. "There's a wonderful place near the Southern Gate. It's owned by a woman from the Islands of Silk and Spice. You wouldn't believe the sorts of spirits she brews."

Isami hesitated.

"I'm happy to pay." Kazuya grinned down at her. "After all, it's not every night I lure a hermit out for a drink."

With a start, Isami realized Kazuya's was the first smile she had seen in days. Despite herself, she found she was grinning back.

She couldn't believe he was so confident, especially the night before his evaluation. As with many things, that species of easy self-assurance had always been foreign to Isami.

Following Kazuya out into the hall, Isami glanced back at the maps one last time. Nodding, she slid the door shut.

Kazuya was right, they would be here tomorrow.

For now, it simply felt good to smile.

# CHAPTER FOUR

Isami rolled over with a soft groan, knuckling her eyes. Her head felt as if someone had filled it with wadded silk, and her mouth tasted of old vinegar. She blinked up at the maps and sketched surveys that adorned the walls of her tiny room. They tracked the history of her fascination, the earliest little more than a child's scrawls. Isami's first memory was of drawing maps. Her parents were often gone, but they would return with such tales – of delivering missives to the Carpenter Wall or the vast grassy plains of the Unicorn Clan, of crossing Beiden Pass into Scorpion lands, or winding up into high mountain abode of the Dragon Clan.

Isami had drawn maps of the places they described. An exercise of her young imagination, they hardly resembled reality, and yet sketching her parents' journeys had always made Isami feel as if she traveled with them.

A stab of pain from her head punctured the warm haze of Isami's childhood recollections. Memories of last night came like a series of woodcut prints, still scenes laid one after the other. Isami recalled a smoky room filled with laughter and music, too loud at first, but gradually more welcoming. Isami had taken but a sip from each drink Kazuya passed her, but even that had been enough to set her lips buzzing. She remembered laughing at Kazuya's foolish jokes, although she could not recall a single one. Still, his good humor had been infectious, and for the first time in weeks the tangled knot in Isami's stomach had begun to loosen.

The late evening breeze had been cool against Isami's cheeks as Kazuya walked her back to the Ministry. He left her at the gate with an easy grin, his mock bow deep as a palace courtier's as he thanked her for a fine evening, then flitted off to his own quarters.

Isami sat up to slide open one of the window screens, raising a hand to shield her eyes from the afternoon glare – the sight a dipper of cold water dashed across her face.

Isami lurched to her feet. With no time to change, she smoothed her robes with nervous hands. Kazuya's evaluation was scheduled for the Hour of the Horse – long past if the sun was any indication. Isami clenched her jaw against an upswell of sick anxiety that accompanied the realization she had overslept.

Her cheeks burned as she hurried along the wooden walkway leading to the courtyard. After Kazuya had worked so hard to fetch Isami for her evaluation, she had not even come to wish him luck.

What if their late night had cause Kazuya to miss his appointment?

Barely able to maintain a sense of proper decorum, Isami practically dashed after the first servant she saw.

"Otomo Kazuya," she asked the stoop-shouldered woman, "how fared his evaluation?"

"Well, mistress." Beaming, the servant patted her on the hand. "All three masters approved."

Such was Isami's relief she didn't even bother to chide the woman for her over-familiarity. Although the day remained hot, the breeze seemed to lighten Isami's steps as she crossed the central garden. Feeling better than she had in days, she exchanged her outdoor sandals for slippers and entered the branching corridors of the Ministry archives.

Most of the rooms were empty, the clerks having retired for lunch – no doubt followed by a leisurely cup of cool barley tea on account of the early autumn heat. The archives were stifling, shuttered as they were to prevent any humidity from creeping into the maps, but it hardly bothered Isami. The musty scent of ancient scrolls was as comforting to her as the sacred incense Master Tadataka burned on the Emperor's birthday.

Isami's smile wilted as she slid open the screen to her study.

Gyōki's maps were gone. Not only that, her work had vanished as well – three books full of notations, as well as the mountain maps she had been working on.

Surprise blossomed into confusion. Drifting to her knees, Isami called for a servant. Soon enough, a round-faced man in a light kimono came hurrying down the hall.

"Where is it?" She nodded at the disarray.

"Mistress?" The man flinched as if he expected a slap.

"My notes."

He dropped into a low bow, forehead pressed to the floorboards. "Otomo Kazuya, mistress. He came by earlier this morning to collect the documents."

"Why?" Isami forced the question through gritted teeth, already fearing the answer.

"He explained you were working together," the servant replied. "At the behest of Master Tadataka."

Isami cocked her head, confused. What business would Kazuya have with any of it? He had little understanding of the calculations involved and no inclination as to what the maps represented.

Isami let out a slow breath. No. That wasn't right. She had explained everything to him last night when he came asking for a way to impress–

It was as if some invisible force gripped Isami by the throat. Her words came as a soft rasp.

"Where is Kazuya now?"

"The garden, mistress," the servant answered, without rising from his bow.

Isami rose without bothering to dismiss the man. Fury lent speed to her steps, the soft soles of her slippers hissing across the polished wood. She did not even stop to exchange them for wooden ones as she stepped onto the gravel path that wound through the rows of gnarled dwarf pine representing the Shinomen Forest and past the stand of blood-red camelia trees that marked the entrance to the portion of the garden sculpted to resemble Scorpion Clan lands.

She found Kazuya relaxing near a bed of flowers – red spider lilies intermixed with the dark, almost black blooms of kuroyuri to form the crest of the Scorpion Clan. He sat in the shade of a broad umbrella, two servants fanning him as he dangled a lazy hand in the water of the rocky stream that twisted through the garden.

"It is fitting I should find you here." Isami cast the words at him like a spear.

"Come out of the sun." Kazuya turned, arching one thin eyebrow as Isami stood over him. He patted the grass beside him. "Have a cup of tea."

Isami wanted to slap the smile from his face. Instead, she knelt upon the grass, back straight as a spear shaft, her hands clenched inside the sleeves of her robe. Although no one of note was nearby, servants saw everything. If Isami lost her temper, word would spread faster than a summer fire.

"I am told you removed the Gyōki maps from the archives."

"They were exactly what I was searching for." Kazuya offered a grateful bow. "I am in your debt for bringing them to my attention. Master Tadataka was quite impressed. Although I did leave out that nonsense about a hidden valley."

Isami bit back the urge to shout, taking several deep breaths to calm her racing heart. She had made a grave error in coming here. To accuse Kazuya openly of theft would bring all manner of unfortunate consequences upon them both. Even were Isami able to prove his guilt, Kazuya's shame would reflect upon the entire Otomo family, and by extension all imperial families, the Miya included. It was the same maneuver he had used to silence the Seppun guard.

Far better for Isami to approach Master Tadataka behind closed doors and deal with the matter privately. Her anger and hurt had led Isami right into Kazuya's hands. For her to cause a public scene would only confirm the masters' belief she was ruled by emotion rather than propriety. All that remained was for Isami to try and salvage what little she could.

"I am… glad to be of assistance." There was nothing else she could say. "When will the Gyōki maps be returned to the archives?"

"Presently, I am sure." Kazuya gave a companionable nod.

"And my notes."

"I don't understand." He frowned, seemingly bemused. "There were no notes."

Isami's hands bunched the fabric of her kimono. Of course Kazuya had stolen her notes; they represented the only physical proof of his crime. Yes, people would talk, but the words of servants and guards were little more than wind against the reputation of a high family such as the Otomo.

It felt as if a thick cloak had been thrown over Isami's shoulders, heavy and smothering.

"Why?" Her question was barely a whisper.

"For both of us, of course." Kazuya's grin was a knife pressed to Isami's throat. "Look at your future, Isami. After that regrettable display at your evaluation, did you think you would ever become an imperial cartographer?"

He gave a sad shake of his head. "You were killing yourself in those dusty archives. And for what? A master who had abandoned you, a career shallow as a garden pond. You are a fine scholar, Isami, perhaps the best I have ever seen. But you lack the understanding to capitalize on your talents. That is where I can help."

Kazuya leaned forward, voice low and conspiratorial. "I received the highest marks from all three masters, and am now an imperial cartographer of the eighth rank. With the reputation of my family behind me, it shall not be long before I rise higher. When that happens, I will rescue you from this tired old place. We shall roam the far reaches of Rokugan together, travel wherever you wish. With your knowledge and my talents, no gate will be closed to us."

Isami's light summer kimono suddenly felt too tight, the air close and stifling. "You would make of me a servant."

"I would make of you a *partner.*"

"And yet, it would be your name upon all the maps."

"At first." Kazuya waved a dismissive hand. "But once the stain of your evaluation has faded, we can work to restore what should have been yours."

Isami reached for words, but her thoughts were a jumble of helpless recrimination.

Apparently mistaking her silence for consideration, Kazuya beckoned to a servant bearing a tea tray. Holding back the trailing sleeve of his robe, he poured two small cups, then held one out to Isami.

"Only fools paint with a single brush. Come with me and we can both have what we want." He grinned. "Surely you must see this is the only way."

Isami slapped the cup from his hand.

For a moment, Kazuya's smile became something terrible, his dark eyes flashing like flecks of obsidian beneath lowered brows.

"It astounds me you have survived as long as you have in Otosan Uchi." He leaned close, words ground between gritted teeth. "Blundering about like a drunken ox, you were lucky it was I and not some other who took advantage."

Before Isami could draw in a startled breath, Kazuya was already leaning back, chuckling as he wiped at the growing tea stain on the front of his robe.

"Oh dear, I seem to have broken my cup." He waved one of the servants over, then glanced at Isami. "No matter, there will be others."

Lips pressed into a tight line, she rose to her feet, turning from Kazuya without even the slightest of bows.

"Tonight, we celebrate my successful evaluation," Kazuya called after her. "I hope you will attend. It would do you good to get out more."

Isami knew that if she paused to so much as glance back, the sight of him would drive her to blows. Then her career truly would be over.

With an effort of singular will, Isami walked from the garden, forcing herself to take slow measured steps when every part of her shrieked to run and never look back. Had Kazuya said but one more word, she would have cast everything to the wind just to see him bleed.

Seemingly, he possessed enough wisdom to let matters lie, for nothing accompanied Isami from the garden save her own wounded pride.

Only when she passed beyond the camelia trees did Isami realize she had nowhere to go. Her room offered no solace, and the Ministry archives felt sullied by her memories of Kazuya.

She walked the garden paths, drifting across the Empire in miniature. From the delicately cultivated pine and wisteria of Crane lands to the tawny beds of azaleas and daffodils meant to represent the unswerving duty of the Lion Clan, her feet took her along the roads she would never walk in life.

Without a plan, or even a conscious thought, she found herself kneeling before the door to Master Tadataka's study. It was a futile gesture. Sooner or later a servant would come by to gently guide her away. For the moment, though, it calmed her to even look upon the place where she had spent so many happy hours.

Isami was so lost in thought, she hardly noticed when the door slid open, glancing up only as Tadataka's shadow fell across her. Her master looked down from a mere three steps away, and yet the gulf between them seemed insurmountable.

"You should not be here," Tadataka spoke softly.

"I know."

He seemed to sense something in her words, for a shadow of concern flitted across Tadataka's sharp features.

Isami's breath seemed to linger in her chest. She swallowed against the knot in her throat, wanting to speak, but afraid words would give way to sobs.

"Leave me."

Isami half-rose before she realized Tadataka was speaking to his servants. They hurried from the study, not even daring a backwards glance.

Nodding, Tadataka beckoned to Isami. "Come."

She practically ran into the study.

Tadataka followed her at a slow pace. Isami knelt on a cushion, fingers worrying the hem of her robe as she waited for Tadataka to prepare and pour two cups of the bitter silver nettle tea he seemed to prize so much.

She opened her mouth, only to swallow her words at a reproving glance from Tadataka. Slowly, he lifted the cup and breathed in the pungent steam, nodding at Isami to do the same.

The tea smelled of grass and winter pine. The rich scents seemed to curl inside Isami's lungs, gentle steam relaxing the tightness in her throat. The day was hot, but not uncomfortably so in the shade of Master Tadataka's study. A small flock of shrikes chattered in a nearby stand of bamboo, their calls rising above the whisper of wind through the leaves.

"They impale their prey, you know," Tadataka said at last.

Isami frowned, confused.

"Shrikes." He inclined his head toward the bamboo. "Lizards, insects, even small crabs – they spear them upon thorns, then leave them to die. Some call it cruel." He took a long sip. "I say they only act according to their natures, helpless before the will of Heaven."

Isami watched the little birds flit amongst the leaves, hands tightening around her teacup.

"So, Kazuya has tricked you."

She glanced over, surprised. "You knew?"

"Do you think I cannot recognize my own student's work?"

"And you did nothing?"

"The Otomo are a powerful family, the blood of Emperors flows through their veins." Tadataka shook his head. "I could have Kazuya cast from the Ministry, make enemies of his patrons and allies. What would that gain us?"

"Justice," Isami replied.

"Children and peasants cry for justice. The rest endure what we must." Tadataka's reproach came sharp as a wasp's sting. Seeming to notice the effect it had on Isami, his expression softened. "I promised your parents I would protect you, but it seems I have gone too far."

He sighed. "The court is full of men and women like Kazuya. I am not sure if they are born into their cruelty or if society makes them so, but it is the natural order in which we live. Better to remain below the notice of such shrikes."

"You would let Kazuya walk free?" Isami asked.

"I would see him whipped through the streets of Otosan Uchi like a common thief," Tadataka spoke in a sharp whisper. "But I understand that to do so would cast everything I care about to ruin."

"I am sorry, master." Isami bowed her head. "I should have come to you first."

"You must bear this betrayal," Tadataka replied. "See you do not shoulder the burden of guilt as well."

His words should have been balm to Isami's conscience, but they changed nothing.

Tadataka fixed Isami with a steady look. "Can Kazuya replicate your calculations? Does he truly understand the import of your studies?"

"I do not believe so, master."

He grunted, a faint smile nestling at the corner of his lips. "Then all he has stolen from you is time."

"Kazuya has Gyōki's maps."

"Then request them back," Tadataka said. "He must comply."

Isami nodded, shoulders rounding at the thought of having to replicate all her calculations from scratch.

"Worry not." Tadataka broke protocol by reaching out to give Isami's hand a comforting pat. "Kazuya is unfit for the role he covets, sooner or later he will fail. You will see."

Isami very much did not see, but she bowed nonetheless. "What shall I do now, master?"

"I must attend Kazuya's celebration, but I shall draft some urgent fiction to send you out into the city." Tadataka set down his cup. Straightening his robes, he stood. "Have a good meal, visit the theater, get some rest. You appear as something washed up upon the beach."

Isami forced a smile. "May I have leave to visit Seppun Hill?"

Tadataka regarded her for a long moment, then chuckled,

shaking his head. "You truly are a wonder, Miya Isami. If that is what you wish to do, then go, bearing my writ."

Isami bowed. The prospect of continuing her survey of Otosan Uchi buoyed her mood more than kind words.

Perhaps the day would not be a complete loss.

# CHAPTER FIVE

Isami saw the smoke long before the Ministry itself came into view. Long streamers threaded the night sky, delicate as dragons' tails against the full moon's silvery light. The braziers were all lit, lamps in every alcove and lanterns hanging from seemingly every eave. Isami had remained out into the late hours, not wanting to sup from the bitter dregs of Kazuya's stolen triumph.

Even so, the celebration should have been long over by now.

She paused, surprised to see Otomo samurai rather than Ministry guards stationed outside the main gates. Beyond, shadows moved through the flickering light – servants bearing paper lanterns, small groups of clerks and administrators walking together, their heads bent as they whispered to one another.

Curious, Isami approached the gate.

A stocky, broad-shouldered guard bearing the Otomo crest on his breastplate walked out to meet her.

"Who are you?"

"Miya Isami, a copy clerk and disciple of Master Tadataka's." Isami presented Tadataka's writ. "What has happened here?"

"A tragedy for the Empire, noble lady," the man replied. "Otomo Kazuya is dead."

Isami took an unconscious step back. "How?"

"The captain is still questioning those present, but it appears a bit of eel became lodged in his throat." The guard frowned, shaking his head. "In the midst of the celebration, no one noticed until he collapsed. Alas, he had passed before the healers could arrive."

Isami's thoughts were a confused whirl. Kazuya's betrayal loomed so large he had taken on almost demonic proportions in her mind. In her anger and hurt, Isami had conjured a dozen terrible fates for him. It seemed impossible Kazuya should succumb to a mere accident.

The ground seemed to shift beneath Isami's feet, her legs suddenly unable to bear her weight. The guard reached out a hand to steady her.

"Are you well?"

"Sorry." She shook her head to clear it. "Kazuya and I were… friends."

"My apologies, lady." The samurai gave a knowing nod. "I should have been more tactful."

Isami's first thought was to correct the guard's assumption of intimacy, but she bit back the words. If Kazuya had taught her anything, it was to never surrender a potential advantage.

"He had some things of mine." She raised a hand to her face as if to conceal a blush. "I wonder if I might retrieve them."

The samurai bowed. "My condolences, lady, but that would be–"

"Quite embarrassing for the Otomo," Isami spoke over him. "Should they be discovered, of course."

The samurai glanced back at his companions, who seemed intent on events unfolding within the Ministry.

"Surely no one would think it untoward if you were to

accompany me to Kazuya's quarters," Isami said. "It would take but a moment, and spare the Otomo significant difficulty."

The samurai winced, his warrior's sternness replaced by genuine distress. Although sworn to the Otomo, he was but a house warrior, and Isami an imperial noble.

After a moment, he bowed. "As you command, lady."

She led him along the edge of the garden, keeping to the sheltered walkways that would shield them from view.

Kazuya's quarters were much larger than Isami's – composed of a small suite of rooms with a private garden. The Otomo samurai stood near the entrance, face reddening as he watched the corridor for passersby.

Isami made for the study. Despite his relaxed attitude, Kazuya had not struck Isami as a disorganized person, and yet the mats of his room were strewn with all manner of scrolls and papers. She searched amidst the jumble, finding many of Kazuya's lackluster maps, but no evidence of her notes or the Gyōki surveys.

The Otomo samurai shifted near the entrance. Isami blanched, cursing herself for a fool. Kazuya must have hidden them elsewhere. Casting about the room, Isami noticed a small brazier, its brass bowl full of ashes.

Throat tight, she approached it, blinking down at the burned paper within. Although the flame had gone out, the ashes were still warm. A scrap of paper lay near the edge, partially burned, the familiar outline of mountains just visible amidst the char.

Isami pressed a hand to her mouth. Even in her deepest well of hatred, she had not believed Kazuya so petty as to destroy the maps rather than see them returned to her. Cold fury blossoming in her chest, Isami prodded the ashes, revealing the remains of her notes and calculations.

Lips pressed into a thin, pale line Isami returned to the entrance.

"Did you retrieve it, lady?"

"Yes." Isami's voice simmered with barely concealed fury as she leaned in close to the guard. "Speak of this to anyone and I will be forced to reveal Kazuya's shame."

"You have my word."

"It might be best if we are not seen together," Isami said. "Wait a few minutes after I depart, then return to the gate."

The samurai gave a relieved nod.

Isami crossed the courtyard as if in a dream, the muttered gossip of those around her lost beneath the wild roar of her thoughts. The Gyōki maps were gone, burned in what appeared to be a fit of pique, and with them an irreplaceable bit of the Empire's history.

"Isami." Master Tadataka's voice cut through the aggrieved babble in Isami's head.

She turned to see him hurrying down the gravel path, robes in uncharacteristic disarray. Tadataka stopped a few paces from her, apparently reading the truth in her face.

"So you have heard."

She gave a slow nod.

"It is unexpected, to be sure. Fortunately, the Otomo have ruled it an accident, and you were far from the Ministry, so no suspicion can be placed upon–"

"He burned the maps." It was beyond rude to interrupt her master, but Isami was beyond caring. "My notes, as well,"

"The insolence!" Tadataka reddened. "I will see his name stricken from the Ministry records."

"And what would that gain us?" Isami cocked her head. "You

said to wait, master, but it appears the Fortunes did not heed your advice."

Tadataka stiffened.

"It seems justice is not only the provenance of children and peasants." Isami gave a low bow. "My apologies, it has been a long day and I grow weary, master. With your leave, I would return to my room."

Tadataka looked as if he wished to say more, but instead only waved her away.

Bowing once more, Isami departed. She had not spoken false, the day had been long, and exhaustion draped her like a heavy robe. There would be time enough to talk later – once Kazuya's body had been blessed and prepared for the funeral. Priests would exhort the honored ancestors, chanting sutras to speed Kazuya's journey to the Realm of Waiting. There would be incense lit, poems read, and offerings made.

Isami vowed she would be there for it all.

If only for the pleasure of watching Otomo Kazuya burn.

# CHAPTER SIX

The pyre had dwindled to ashes, the last thin trails of smoke lost against the overcast sky. Most of the onlookers had long since departed, propriety requiring they remain only to pay their respects. Some did this with stacks of golden coins, discreetly wrapped in silk so they might be passed hand-to-hand with minimum fuss. Others offered poems or songs to commemorate the loss – odes comparing Kazuya to the imperial chrysanthemum or peony blossoms scattered upon a lake. With all personal details planed away by embellishments and court propriety, the performers might as well have been reading the same verse over and over.

Isami weathered the funeral rites, a serene expression on her face even as her legs cramped from kneeling. Through it all, she was aware of the glances, the simpering smiles, the fluttering fans raised to conceal wagging tongues. Isami's presence no doubt fanned the fires of speculation concerning her relationship to the deceased, but she did not care. The courtiers moved like wind about her, no more substantial than spirits.

Shinseist priests came forth to rake the ashes into sacred

urns, one to be interred in the temple, the other placed within the Otomo family vault. And still Isami watched, waiting for the shroud that had hung over her these last few days to lift. She had hoped the sight of Kazuya's charred remains would untangle the snarl of her thoughts.

It did not.

"You two were close?" The question came as lightning from a clear sky.

Isami glanced over to see a man had knelt next to her.

He was small and long-faced, with high cheekbones and cold, sharp eyes. His gray hair was tucked under the wide brim of his peaked minister's cap, his slight frame seemingly awash in a sea of courtly robes. He held a closed fan in one hand, the other resting gently upon his knee. Two samurai in Otomo colors knelt a step behind at his right and left, a small village of servants arrayed beyond them.

Even without the entourage, Isami would have recognized him as a high noble. Instinct took over, and she turned to bow, the muscles in her back stiff as she pressed her forehead to the ground.

The man gestured for her to rise with a wave of his fan. "You were a friend of my nephew?"

"Yes, my lord." It was not quite a lie.

"You are a copy clerk at the Ministry of Cartography?" He touched the fan to his chin as if recalling something. "One of Tadataka's students?"

"It is as you say, lord." Isami made to bow again, but paused as the man gave an irritated flick of his fan.

"No need for formality. This is a funeral, not the Winter Court."

Isami inclined her head to hide her surprise – a funeral was *exactly* the place for formality. Even so, to dispense with ceremony was the prerogative of the highly ranked.

"I am Otomo Shinpachi, Fourth Assistant to the Chief of the Imperial Treasury, Second Intendent for Regulation of Taxation and Tribute, and so on…" Shinpachi made circles in the air with his fan. "But I have not come to bore you with titles. I am told you worked closely with Kazuya, is that so?"

Isami's hands tightened in her robes. Although Shinpachi spoke off-handedly, his question cut to the root of her anxiety. It seemed impossible he was asking about anything other than the Gyōki maps. Master Tadataka had spoken of Kazuya having friends in court, could Shinpachi be one such patron? If so, Isami needed to choose her words carefully lest she lose what little she had left. A man as highly placed as Otomo Shinpachi could crush her with the stroke of a brush.

"Are you familiar with my nephew's work?"

"Not as such, lord." Isami raised a hand to cover her lower face, glancing away as if embarrassed. "Kazuya and I were friends, but we did not share notes."

"I see." Shinpachi sat back on his heels. "And yet, you took something from his quarters, did you not?"

"A scrap of poetry, nothing more." Worry made a hard pit in Isami's stomach. Of course the guard had talked. How could she have been so foolish as to visit Kazuya's quarters?

"Truly?" Shinpachi sniffed. "I did not take my nephew for a poet."

"He was not, lord." Isami swallowed, unable to believe she was lying to a high lord. Although convinced Otomo would see through her stammering falsehoods at any moment, she could not but forge ahead. "I am sorry for the deception, but it would have been awkward had it been discovered."

"Infatuation oft drives young men to attempt things they ought not." Shinpachi's smile was a thin thing, brittle around the edges. "And where are these poems now?"

"I burned them, lord."

"Excellent." Shinpachi nodded. "It is bad fortune to speak ill of the dead, even the words come by their own hand."

He regarded Isami, gaze sharp in the waning afternoon light. Silence stretched between them, tight as a drumhead. After a long moment, Shinpachi grunted, seeming to nod to himself.

"I heard of your evaluation."

"Your interest does me great credit." This time, Isami's chagrin was not an act.

"I very much doubt that," Shinpachi chuckled. "And yet, it may be of some use to you. Come by my manor once the funeral has finished. There are other matters I would discuss."

"Of course, lord." Isami bowed to hide her concern. It was one thing to speak in public, protected by the rituals and formalities of polite society, but anything could occur behind the walls of a high lord's manor.

"Gorobei here will see you do not get lost." Shinpachi nodded to the samurai to his right, a scruffy-looking man with a broad, peasant's face and pale brown eyes. His dark hair was gathered in a warrior's topknot, but although he wore robes of deep green, the Otomo crest was noticeably absent.

Jaw tight behind her smile, Isami acknowledged Gorobei's bow. She had hoped to speak to Master Tadataka about her encounter with Shinpachi, but the samurai's presence would make that impossible.

"I shall expect you presently." Shinpachi stood and swept off, servants trailing behind like a dragon's tail.

"Mistress." With another bow, Gorobei took up position on Isami's right, one step behind.

It seemed impossible Shinpachi could blame her for Kazuya's death. And yet, if he had seen through her stumbling lies, he might suspect her of withholding information. As much as Isami tried to quell her burgeoning anxiety, the fact remained that one did not assign a guard to individuals one did not wish watched.

Gradually, the priests finished their chants, a group of somber burakumin workers dealing with the less savory aspects of the pyre. As much as Isami wished to draw out these final moments, she did not dare risk Shinpachi's ire.

As the final nobles filed out of the temple courtyard, she turned to Gorobei.

"Lead the way."

"Yes, mistress." His grin was overly familiar, although not unkind. He ushered her from the temple grounds and onto one of the broad thoroughfares of the Inner Districts.

Isami felt as if she were marching to her own execution.

"Have you eaten, mistress?"

Isami blinked, taken aback by the question. "Not since this morning, no."

With a nod, Gorobei produced a small bundle from the sleeve of his kimono. From it, he drew a pair of leaf-wrapped rice balls, offering one to Isami.

"With respect, you look about to faint."

It was untoward for Gorobei to speak to her in such a manner, let alone offer food, but Isami had moved beyond any concern with social niceties.

Gingerly, she took the proffered rice. Although stale, it seemed the best thing Isami had eaten in days. Only when she sucked the last stray grains from her fingertips did Isami realize how hungry she had been.

"You needn't worry, mistress," Gorobei said as they walked. "If my master wished you ill, you would have never seen his face."

Isami glanced over, strangely reassured by the samurai's rustic bravado. "What kind of a man is your lord?"

"Harsh, but fair." He scratched at his scruff of beard, frowning. "Certainly not a man to concern himself with pleasantries."

Isami nodded. "If I may ask – you wear Otomo colors, but you are not a family retainer?"

"I was a rōnin, mistress." He shrugged. "Lord Shinpachi is powerful, but even he cannot raise mountains."

"And how did you come into Lord Otomo's service?"

"That is a long story, perhaps one for a different time." Gorobei gestured ahead with one calloused hand. "We have arrived."

Otomo Shinpachi's manor sat back from the road, warded by a high stone wall. Two Otomo guards stood at the gate, backs as straight as their spears. They stepped aside at Gorobei's easy nod, and the heavy doors swung open to admit Isami into a small but tasteful garden.

It was composed in a classical style – carefully pruned trees framing neat flower beds. Although most of the summer blooms had fallen, early hints of autumn bellflower, carnation, and clover were just visible through the greenery. Barely a sliver compared to the vast garden of the Ministry, it spoke to Shinpachi's rank that he was able to have a garden at all, especially within the confines of the Inner Districts where space commanded a premium.

Gorobei led her across a small arcing bridge and up the steps into a sitting room that had been opened to let in the night breeze. Although pillows had been set upon the mats, Shinpachi was nowhere in evidence. Isami settled onto the one indicated by Gorobei, who retired to kneel in the packed earth of the garden.

Before long, servants arrived with tea and red bean cakes. Isami was once again grateful for Gorobei's food, as it would have been embarrassing for her to do anything more than nibble at the offered sweets.

The air hung heavy with the scents of cut leaves, the low babble of the city reduced to a distant hum by the intervening wall. From somewhere else in the manor, Isami heard the faint strains of a biwa, the high, quavery voice of a woman accompanying the plucked chords. All of it combined to make Isami feel how well and truly alone she was.

"I trust you were not waiting long." Shinpachi swept into the room with a rustle of layered silks.

"Time passes quickly in surroundings so lovely." Isami had summoned a dozen more vague pleasantries before she remembered Gorobei's advice. "But we are not here to speak of gardens."

"Indeed." Shinpachi gave a quick nod, then glanced about as if he had reason to be cautious. "Truth be told, I find myself in need of your assistance."

Of all the things Isami had expected from Lord Otomo, a plea for aid was beyond her imagination.

"But say it, lord."

He waved an irritated hand. "This is not an order, nor would I be able to compel you even if it were. The Bureau of Taxation has no claim on the Ministry of Cartography. Though, as with all things in the Empire, it is best they work harmoniously."

Isami took a sip of tea, both to wet her suddenly dry throat and give herself time to think.

"Among my many duties is the formalization of borders between the great clans," Shinpachi continued. "It behooves the Bureau to be aware of from whom to collect the Emperor's taxes and tributes. In this capacity, we have oft relied upon the Ministry of Cartography for cadastral surveys and the like."

"I have great respect for such endeavors," Isami said, and meant it. Tax surveys demanded a level of accuracy often absent in other maps. "But how can a mere copy clerk be of assistance in this capacity?"

"I am not interested in what you are, but what you can become." Shinpachi gave his fan a brusque tap against his knee. "What I am about to tell you could cause great harm to the Empire if revealed. Do I have your word you will repeat nothing you hear tonight?"

"You do." There was no other answer Isami could give. Not that her word mattered, especially when measured against the will of a high noble.

"There is a strip of land north of the Spine of the World Mountains, nestled between the Lion and Scorpion Clans. It is known as Stone Willow Valley. It holds perhaps a dozen villages, but its true value lies in its strategic importance, namely that it provides the Scorpion a foothold north of the mountains." Shinpachi sighed, shaking his head. "For as long as anyone can remember, this land has been administered by the Scorpion. But it seems some Lion Clan busybody has unearthed a number of old maps proving the land actually belongs to them."

Isami gave a sympathetic tilt of her head. Of all the great clans, the Lion and Scorpion were perhaps the most disparate, the Lion's blunt forthrightness often clashing with the Scorpion's penchant for more discreet endeavors. It would take very little to set them at each other's throat.

"As you can imagine, both sides have already dispatched parties intent on pressing their respective claims," Shinpachi said. "I do not care who ends up with the land, only that they reach a peaceful accord. Bloodshed tends to have a deleterious effect on tax receipts."

"Thank you for entrusting me with this information, lord," Isami replied. "But I am still at a loss as to how I may be of service."

"I cannot resolve this matter myself, as the Otomo name is somewhat suspect among the great clans. Nor do I think it would be wise to send a Seppun to bully them into submission." Shinpachi fixed Isami with a level gaze. "Which brings me to you."

"Lord, I–"

"If I wish your opinion, I shall ask for it." Shinpachi slapped his fan against his palm to punctuate the point. "The Miya family are well regarded through the Empire, your kin are often accepted in places where the presence of other imperial families would be suspect."

Isami bit back her reply. What Shinpachi meant to say was that the clans did not view the Miya as a threat. Which was true enough.

"I would have you go as an imperial representative, see if you can smooth this ruffled fur and set matters right between the clans before blades are drawn."

"I am no diplomat, lord."

"But you *are* a cartographer," Shinpachi replied. "Examine these Lion maps. If they are as the Ikoma say, then award the lands to the Lion. If not, let them remain in Scorpion hands."

Isami drew in breath to speak, but Shinpachi raised a hand.

"Do this for me and I shall see to it you are awarded the rank of imperial cartographer. Although the Bureau and Ministry are separate, my word carries much weight in the lower courts."

A glimmer of surprise slipped through Isami's polite mask. After suffering the depths of Kazuya's betrayal, it seemed impossible to have such a reward set before her. Even so, it was the belated realization of another facet of Shinpachi's offer that caused her to stiffen.

"This contested land, you said it was north of the Spine of the World?"

"In the very foothills." At Shinpachi's wave, a map was brought forward and unrolled. One of Master Kageyasu's, it displayed sharp, angry peaks gradually giving way to hills and valleys, pale watercolors gently tinging the land either Scorpion crimson or the Lion Clan's tawny gold.

As much as Isami disliked Master Kageyasu, she could not but admit the man was a true artist. Still, it was all she could do not to gasp as Shinpachi gestured at the disputed area. Although Kageyasu's drawing could not match the accuracy of the Gyōki surveys, Isami was nonetheless sure: the contested land was directly east of the blank spot on Gyōki's map, but where Gyōki had left a tantalizing void, Kageyasu's map boasted only more elegantly rendered peaks.

"I shall go." The words slipped from her lips seemingly before her mind could articulate the thought.

"Excellent." Shinpachi nodded. "The journey will take several days, even at speed. So you must depart quickly. Be prepared to leave at first light."

Isami could only bow. It seemed only this morning she had lamented her fate. Now, everything she could hope for had been offered to her on a gilded tray.

"I shall make all the arrangements – servants, horses, provisions," Shinpachi said. "And Gorobei shall serve as your bodyguard."

"That is not necessary, lord. As our duties often take us to dangerous places, all in the Miya Cartography School receive martial training."

"These are not rebellious villagers or mountain goblins, but great clans you face." Shinpachi tilted his head. "It would put my mind at ease to have a dependable sword at your back."

"As you wish, lord." Isami turned to Gorobei, who bowed low.

"Until my mission is complete, I shall put your life before my own."

Isami returned the former rōnin's bow, happy the deepening shadows hid the blush coloring her cheeks. She never had anyone willing to die for her. The thrill was tempered by discomfort, as Isami had done nothing to deserve such loyalty.

"Return to the Ministry, collect what you need." Shinpachi stood.

Before Isami could voice her thanks, Lord Otomo departed, leaving her to stare, wide eyed, at the empty room.

"Mistress," Gorobei called softly from the garden. "We should hurry."

Isami nodded, afraid to speak lest Shinpachi rescind his offer.

It was as if she moved in a strange dream, the world around her no more substantial than passing clouds. Smoothing her robes, Isami rose and made her way back through the garden, Gorobei a step behind.

If this were truly a dream, then she had no wish to wake.

# CHAPTER SEVEN

"Have you gone mad?" Tadataka's question came like a slap.

It took a moment for Isami to gather herself. "I thought you would be pleased."

Uncommon anger clouded Tadataka's thin face. He had been out late on Ministry business, unable to respond to Isami's urgent requests until the early hours of the morning. Even now, he wore loose bed robes, his normal straight-backed poise weighed down by apparent exhaustion.

"By the Ancestors, Isami." He ran a hand through his unbound hair. "You fall prey to one Otomo plot only to walk blindly into another."

"Shinpachi has need of my expertise."

"Shinpachi has need of your name," Tadataka replied. "Lords such as he have scores of agents to call upon. Did you stop to consider why he chose a mere clerk over someone better suited to the task?"

Isami cast her gaze down. In truth, there had been no time to think. Or perhaps she just hadn't wanted to think about it.

"You are deniable, Isami." Tadataka took a slow breath. Edging closer, he continued in a softer voice. "If you succeed, Shinpachi will claim all the credit. If you fail, it will leave no stain upon his reputation. More likely he will blame me for improperly preparing you."

"Shinpachi will have me named an imperial cartographer."

Tadataka was silent for a long moment. "This is not the way."

"Then what is, master?" Isami's question came sharp as broken glass, the anger in her tone surprising even her.

"You have failed, but you are not a failure." Tadataka did not rise to Isami's fury. "Continue as you have been; follow the requirements, copy the old masters' work and in a year, perhaps two, we can try again."

"I worked my whole life for this, every day, every night spent at the archives, studying while the other clerks drank at teahouses or attended poetry readings." Although Isami spoke in a softer tone, her words carried a desperate urgency. "I believed you when you said dedication and diligence would see me succeed, but now I know it will take more than mere devotion."

Isami met Tadataka's eyes, seeing in them a mirror to the anger and sadness that roiled within her own heart.

"You spoke to me of the natural order, of cruelty and balance." She knew her next words would wound Tadataka deeply, but the decision had already been made. "If the Empire's natural order allows men like Kazuya to steal and lie with impunity, protected from all consequence by the hand of their patrons, then it is clear I need a more powerful benefactor."

"I see." Tadataka straightened. Like ice creeping across a winter pond, the old master's emotions were covered by a mask of icy civility. "Then it appears we have nothing more to discuss."

He turned away. "I shall relay this change in circumstances to your parents. Please keep the geomantic compass as a token of my past regard."

"Master, I–"

"I am your master no longer, Isami." He spoke without glancing back. "May the Ancestors favor your new endeavor."

A thousand replies welled up inside Isami, all jostling to get out. She wanted to apologize, to throw herself at Tadataka's feet and beg forgiveness for failing him, to let him cradle her as he had when she was a little girl and she had come running with a skinned knee. She wanted him to stroke her hair and whisper that everything would be all right. She also wanted to shout at Tadataka, to ask why he had done nothing when Kazuya had stolen her work, when the other masters had berated her? Was his advice about bowing before the natural order simply cowardice masquerading as caution?

In reality, Isami said nothing, hands bunched in the folds of her robe as if to strangle the life from this moment. As Tadataka departed, for the first time she saw the weight of years upon him – his hair more white than gray, the lines on his cheeks like the creases on an ancient map. Without his courtly attire, swathed only in a light sleeping robe, the old master seemed frail as a plucked flower.

Isami bowed low to the empty room. She had made her choice. Words would not heal the rift between them, only success.

She crossed the garden to the Ministry archives, gliding through the halls like a wayward spirit. The other scholars avoided Isami, as if acknowledging her presence might somehow subject them to the stain of her failure. At any other time, their coldness would have wounded her, but Isami was beyond caring.

If anything, it made what she had to do far easier.

The imperial surveys were stored in a large chamber near the front of the archives, stacks of logbooks arrayed along low shelves in the center of the room, the walls set with row upon row of niches, each housing a carefully rolled scroll.

Isami knew where the map of the Northern Spine of the World mountains was located, she had consulted it often enough. The scroll was a little longer than her forearm, its outer surface protected by wrapped fabric. With a glance about the chamber, Isami drew it from its niche and placed it within her satchel, before quietly slipping from the room.

The map was a copy, the real survey being far too important to allow into the hands of mere clerks. Scrolls occasionally went missing or were lost to the wear of regular use. Isami knew it would be replaced, and yet she could not help but feel a sense of wrongness, creeping through the shadows like a common thief.

Outside the archives, she straightened, scowling. It was not as if her reputation in the Ministry could sink any lower. Despite its failings, the map would be invaluable to Isami in her coming task.

Gorobei awaited her at the Ministry gates, along with a small palanquin borne by a half-dozen strong men and women. Although mounts awaited at the Eastern Gate, it was considered untoward for imperial nobles to travel by horseback in the inner city.

Isami allowed herself to be helped inside, reflecting on the strangeness of the situation. Mere weeks ago, she had watched such elaborate processions from the top of Seppun Hill, and now she herself was being borne as court noble. Isami had ridden in palanquins before, although not often enough to have accustomed herself to the rolling movement of the bearers.

The hour was early and the streets mostly clear. Sunlight glittered from the golden characters inlaid into the eastern portion of the Enchanted Wall – the names of brave warriors who had died in the war against the dark elemental spirit Fu Leng. Heroes of the Empire, all, the wall had always made Isami feel as if she were being weighed against their sacrifice.

She steadied herself as Gorobei paid the bearers. Beyond the gate, a small group of servants awaited with two mounts. They bowed as Isami and Gorobei approached, proffering the horses' reins with the care usually reserved for offerings of sacred incense. Most of the bearers were loaded with supplies, but Isami was relieved to see her tripod and equipment had been carefully wrapped and packed.

"The promise of a new journey stirs the blood." Gorobei grinned as he and Isami mounted up.

Isami returned a hesitant flicker of a smile, unsure if the flutter of her heart came from excitement or regret. She was far more familiar with horses than palanquins, having been trained in riding from an early age, but hunting trips and jaunts to nearby temples were little preparation for a ride across the Empire.

"Ah, mistress, I almost forgot." Reaching into the front of his robe, Gorobei produced a jade seal embossed with Lord Otomo's personal chop.

With a nod, Isami took it. Although things were not as she might have wished, she was nonetheless leaving Otosan Uchi as a servant of the Empire.

Isami kicked her horse into a trot, the servants falling in behind at a steady jog. A moment later, hooves clattered on stone as Gorobei joined her. They rode through the Kanjo district, the Emperor's Road cutting through the barely restrained chaos of the outer city. A few hours saw Otosan Uchi gone from sight. Although it still weighed heavily in her thoughts, Isami did not look back.

Her future lay ahead.

The day was warm, but not uncomfortably so, the first breaths of true autumn slipping through summer's oppressive grip. Rice paddies spread to either side, the backs of farmers visible as they stooped to cut drooping stalks. Those closer to the road stopped their work at the sight of Isami's entourage, dropping to their knees to press foreheads to the muddy dirt. The attention made Isami uncomfortable, and she did not begrudge those who did not stop their work – the harvest was more important than propriety.

Several days' ride saw paddies give way to wheat fields as they moved from the manicured order of Crane lands into the rolling plains of the Lion Clan. Normally, it required travel papers signed by the local lord to pass from province to province, but Shinpachi's seal was sufficient to see them through the various gates and waystations scattered along the Emperor's Road. At each, they were supplied with fresh mounts, puffing servants handing off their packs to fresh bearers. Men and women tanned the color of burnished oak by the summer sun, their muscles hard as tree roots. They shouldered the burden without complaint, running along behind the horses with heads down, intent only on the road in front of them. Isami made a note to have Gorobei reward the bearers well for their service.

Her first choice came as the Emperor's Road snaked north toward Loyalty Castle, the ancestral seat of the Lion Clan. Although the quickest route, she was concerned that passing through the castle lands could give the Lion warning of her arrival. An advantage the Scorpion Clan would no doubt resent.

She put the matter to Gorobei. "The backroads will make for a harder journey – camping outside rather than in comfort."

"It will not do to start the negotiations with one clan on the back foot," Isami replied.

"Hard earth, with only the starry sky for a blanket." Gorobei's tone belied his somber scowl. "Not the bed I would choose, but one I have slept on often enough."

Truth be told, Isami was grateful for the chance to rest her sore muscles. Unused to the rigors of long rides, her legs and back burned with an ache that seemed to have settled in her very bones. Isami tried to conceal her discomfort as the servants set up camp near a stand of spreading pine, but Gorobei only clucked his tongue. Fussing over her like a mother hen, the former rōnin plucked needles from the nearby trees, stewing them with camphor and tea leaves to create a poultice.

"It will draw out most of the ache." He set the concoction at her feet with a gravelly chuckle. "A hot bath would be better, but a few days of this and you'll be hard as granite, mistress."

It was not quite as Gorobei described. As the rutted road wound up into the foothills of the Spine of the World, Isami found herself dreaming of the Emperor's Road, its flat, gentle expanse dotted with waystations and inns. As it was, Isami was not sure if her pains had lessened or she had merely become used to the constant throb of overtaxed muscles. She did not complain, even as blisters made it difficult to close her hands. It felt improper to show such softness in front of Gorobei and the bearers, all of whom seemed inured to the petty hardships of travel.

Although they passed several small villages tucked amidst the wooded hills, Isami did not tarry. It was a testament to the Lion Clan's strength that, even in the less settled parts of their domain, travelers had little to fear from bandits and strange spirits. Isami was more nervous they would encounter a Lion patrol, for while she could not be compelled to reveal her mission, she did not want to begin talks by deceiving one of the clans.

Fortunately, Gorobei seemed intimately familiar with the blinds and rocky backtrails, guiding them past the better guarded routes with almost preternatural skill.

"How do you know the land so well?" Isami asked of her bodyguard, as he led them down an almost invisible goat path.

"More than once, these trails have been the only thing that kept my head upon its shoulders." Gorobei scanned the brush ahead with a practiced eye before urging the bearers forward.

"The patrols hunted you?"

"The Lion are many things, but discerning is not one of them. They make little distinction between rōnin and thieves." Gorobei grunted. "Although, truth be told, they are often right."

"Is that how you came to serve Lord Otomo?"

"In a way," Gorobei replied. "We had been hired by a village, myself and a few other rōnin. A gang of bandits had taken up residence in an ancient mountain fort and set about bullying the surrounding land. This was wild land, hard land – high up in the Spine of the World where even the Lion's claws found no ready purchase."

Gorobei sat back in his saddle, gaze distant. "The villagers were half-bandits themselves, but we trained them, helped to construct barricades. When the thieves came to collect their tribute, we ambushed them. It was a hard-fought battle. A number of my comrades fell, villagers as well."

Gorobei drew back the sleeve of his kimono to reveal a long scar running down the length of his upper arm. "I escaped with this."

Isami shook her head. Gorobei's story had all the makings of a warrior tale. "And did you defeat the bandits?"

"Sure enough. But it was the villagers we ought to have worried about." He gave a rueful chuckle. "They turned on us as soon as the battle was over."

"Cowards," Isami said.

"Perhaps." Gorobei shrugged. "When the choice is between betrayal and starvation, honesty often suffers. To pay us would have left the villagers little better off than had the bandits made off with their winter stores. Truth be told, I should have seen it coming, but I was young and foolish."

Isami gave a sympathetic nod, the sting of her own imprudent decisions still fresh in her mind.

"Fortunately, Lord Otomo happened along with a score of well-armed guards," Gorobei continued. "He was a mere regional assessor back then, but had heard of the bandit's predations. Although the villagers tried to spin the tale, the remains of the battle spoke for themselves. Lord Otomo cut us free, then he hanged the village headman and forced the rest to pay what was owed. My companions departed quickly, but I begged Lord Otomo to take me into his service." Gorobei slapped his thigh, giving voice to a gravelly chuckle. "Fool that he was, Shinpachi agreed."

Isami shook her head, smiling at the former rōnin's story. To leap from starving warrior to the retainer of a great lord was something few managed. Truly, this journey was proving an education in more ways than Isami had imagined.

They rode along a wooded ridge, afternoon sunlight slipping through the high branches overhead to cast the path in shifting shadows. A cool breeze blew from the mountains to the west. Isami knew the wind would grow teeth as the season deepened, but, for now, it was pleasant after a long day of travel. She sat back in her saddle, head slowly drooping toward her chest, gently rocked by her horse's slow amble.

A grunt from Gorobei snapped Isami from her half-doze. The samurai had brought his horse to a stop to gaze down the slope. Isami kicked her horse into a trot, coming up beside him.

The sight ahead snatched the question from Isami's lips. Perhaps a mile ahead the trees thinned, giving way to a rocky escarpment that marked the beginnings of true mountains. Girded by willow and larch, the Spine of the World appeared like nothing so much as a row of jagged blades thrust up from the ground itself. Waterfalls tumbled from broken cliffs, the higher slopes dotted with patches of snow, rising higher and higher until the peaks were lost amidst the clouds.

There had been many times in Isami's life when she had felt small – standing in the shadow of the Enchanted Wall; gazing at the high peaked towers of the Imperial Palace; or even deep within the Ministry archives, a map of Rokugan spread before her. And yet, all the great works of human hands seemed but pale shadow when set against the impossible vista that stretched before her.

"Mistress, we are but a few hours from the Scorpion border, just east of–"

"I know where we are." Isami glanced away to conceal the tears pricking the corners of her eyes. She would have known this place in her sleep, each cleft and crag burned into the hollows of her memory through long days of study.

It was all there, exactly as Gyōki had drawn it.

Isami bit back the urge to call for her equipment as a swell of bitterness bubbled through the cracks in her amazement. Even if Isami charted the mountains, Gyōki's maps were gone, destroyed by a spoiled courtier in a blaze of temper.

With a nod to Gorobei, Isami started down the hill, jaw tight, her former excitement like a bit of parchment tossed into a bonfire. Even dead, Kazuya still had the strength to wound her. The realization sat like a stone in the pit of Isami's stomach.

Kazuya, Tadataka, the Ministry; Isami's fondest memories of Otosan Uchi had become as broken glass, jagged and liable to cut.

She straightened in her saddle. Although she could not yet see the Scorpion or Lion forces, she knew they lay ahead. The days to come would bring more than sharp words, and Isami could ill afford to let the past distract her. The fact remained that she had been sent as a diplomat, not a surveyor. There would be time for reconciliation later, but only if Isami succeeded.

She did not dare think what would happen should she fail.

# CHAPTER EIGHT

The Lion claimed the high ground.

Isami swept her spyglass over the camp. A score of tents in a tight circle sat atop a low rise overlooking the river valley. Soldiers shouted and strained as they surrounded the camp with a small berm of piled earth and stone. Tawny pennants snapped in the breeze, the display of martial discipline overtopped by a banner bearing the snarling torii arch of the Ikoma, one of the four great families that made up the Lion Clan's elite.

By contrast, the Scorpion camp seemed an almost careless affair. Situated along the river, several crimson tents had been erected near a large pavilion draped in red and black silks, a flag emblazoned with the Bayushi scorpion hanging just above the entrance. Roughly half the size of the Lion contingent, those few guards Isami could see seemed intent on observing the Lion samurai. Leaning on spears and hooked polearms, they peered at the bustle of activity atop the hill, appearing by turns fascinated and amused by the ongoing construction.

"The Ikoma look to have stolen a march on their rivals," Isami said, as they trotted down the hill.

"I am not so sure, mistress." Gorobei gave a quick smile to

soften his disagreement. Over the journey, the former rōnin had grown familiar in his speech, but there were still lines that could not be crossed.

At Isami's nod, Gorobei continued. "Both camps are on the east side of the river. The Lion's is more defensible, but they must pass through the Scorpion to fetch water."

Isami gave a thoughtful frown. She would do well to remember the great clans played a dangerous and ancient game, each seeking advantage amidst the shifting web of alliances and rivalries. Isami's rank would afford her little protection against manipulation or trickery.

The Lion were the first to spy Isami's party. A small contingent of samurai quickly assembled at the makeshift gate, jogging down the hill as Isami rounded the base of the low hill. Although the Scorpion were slower to respond, the fact their camp was nearer meant the Lion arrived only moments before their rivals.

An Ikoma samurai in carefully polished armor approached Isami's horse. Despite the apparent quality of his arms, the man moved as if unused to the weight of battle kit. Dropping to his knees, he swept off his helmet to reveal a long, sharp-chinned face, dark auburn hair bound in a tight topknot.

"Noble lady." He stood to regard Isami, eyes bright and curious behind a practiced warrior's scowl. "I am Ikoma Shinzō, Warden-Captain of the High Histories and Personal Archivist to Lord Ikoma Hanbei."

Isami gave a gentle tilt of her head, both to acknowledge the greeting and hide her blush of surprise. The Ikoma commander seemed to snap into focus – voice, dress, bearing, even the cut of his hair.

It was uncommon, but certainly not unheard of, for women

to become men, and the reverse. So long as they could continue to perform their duties to clan and empire, such transitions were not remarked upon. In Rokugan, rank and status carried far more weight than gender.

"We are honored to have an imperial representative come to oversee our humble petition." Although Shinzō's words had been phrased meekly enough, they hid an unstated question: why had an imperial noble traveled so far to handle a minor land dispute?

In truth, Isami wasn't sure herself.

"I am Miya Isami." Propriety required Isami also state her rank and title, but she wasn't sure how to proceed. As Shinpachi's representative, she could rightly claim she acted on behalf of the Imperial Treasury, but she also remained a member of the Ministry of Cartography.

Possibly mistaking Isami's reticence for arrogance, Shinzō's jaw pulsed. As he bowed again, Isami noticed the beginnings of a flush creeping up his neck.

"Allow me to welcome you to Lion lands."

"A bit hasty, aren't we, Ikoma?" The Scorpion contingent rattled up, squaring off against the Lion. At their head stood a rather unassuming man in robes of black and crimson. Round-faced, with wide, dark eyes, he wore his hair long and loose, drawn back from his forehead by a cloth band bearing the Bayushi family's scorpion crest. The lower half of his face was concealed by a small mask of black silk trimmed with gold. Unlike Shinzō, the man was unarmed and unarmored, but seemed untroubled by the nearby Lion guards.

"Such is always the way with the Lion." He offered Isami a low bow, the hint of a smile on his boyish face. "As if repeating a lie over and over imbues it with some measure of truth."

"Fine words from a Bayushi." Shinzō glared down at the Scorpion courtier. At least a head taller, he looked as if he dearly wished to spit upon the little man.

The Scorpion calmly stepped around the armored samurai, leaving him to glare at his back as he approached Isami.

"I am Bayushi Keisuke." His bow pushed the limits of courtesy. "Sub-Intendant for Noted Records of Scorpion Clan archives in Journey's End City."

"Miya Isami, of the Ministry of Cartography." After a bit of thought, Isami had decided it was best she not mention Lord Otomo until she better understood the situation. Although both Shinzō and Keisuke held positions within their clans far in excess of Isami's humble role; as an imperial noble, they were expected to treat her with respect. In practice, however, Isami was well aware such courtly distinctions mattered less and less the farther one traveled from Otosan Uchi.

"They have sent us a surveyor?" Keisuke looked positively jubilant. "Such wisdom. And here I had expected an Otomo courtier accompanied by a regiment of Seppun guards."

Shinzō gave a satisfied nod. "All the better to confirm the truth of the Lion claim."

"Oh indeed, friend Ikoma," Keisuke replied. "We have all come seeking the truth."

Shinzō regarded the Scorpion courtier for a long moment, frowning as if the words contained some verbal trap. With a dismissive shake of his head, he turned back to Isami.

"Lady, would you allow me to host you and your entourage in my camp? It is large and well defended."

"And yet *so* dry." Keisuke spoke as if to himself. Bobbing his head, he gestured toward the large pavilion. "I humbly offer accommodations more in keeping with the status of our honored guest."

Shinzō's scowl deepened. "So you may pour poison in her ear, Bayushi?"

"Have a care. A less discerning man might mistake such words for an insult." Keisuke made a show of studying his fingernails. "One which I, as a Bayushi noble, would be bound to avenge."

"A Scorpion speaks of integrity?"

"It is not my own I'm worried about." Keisuke gave a mock frown. "Bloodshed is best avoided, especially when such conflict would be of great concern to our lords."

"You are welcome to crawl back to Lady Kaede," Shinzō replied. "Lord Hanbei places more trust in his retainers."

"Is that why he sent so many samurai to keep watch on you?" Keisuke nodded at the Lion guards.

"If we have come in force, it is only because the Scorpion have let these lands run wild with bandits," Shinzō said. "And *I* command these warriors."

"Of course you do," Keisuke said. "Tell me, is there much call for archivist generals among the Lion?"

Shinzō's hands curled into fists, then slowly relaxed. When he spoke again, his voice was flat as a winter pond. "If you want to test my skills, Bayushi, you have but to ask."

"Fortunately, I am a broad-minded man, not easily given to offense." Keisuke gave an airy wave, like a monk dispensing absolution. "I forgive you."

Shinzō took a step forward, his guards bristling. Keisuke's own warriors moved to surround the Scorpion courtier, hands on their weapons.

"I think it would be best if I made my own camp," Isami said before the matter could escalate further. The two commanders had obviously been sniping at each other for some time. "My people and I are tired from the long ride. I would ask that you give us time to wash the dust of the road from our throats. Shall we reconvene tomorrow morning at the Hour of the Dragon?"

"As you command, lady." Although Shinzō bowed, his gaze never left Keisuke.

"Nothing would please me more," Keisuke added.

Riding away from her first encounter with the Scorpion and Lion, Isami felt as if she had gone a night without sleep. Realizing she held the reins in a white-knuckled grip, she forced herself to relax and slowed her breathing.

"Quite a pair, mistress." Gorobei rode up beside her.

"What do you make of them?" she asked.

"That Bayushi bears watching." He frowned. "And I would have mistaken that Ikoma for a Matsu berserker, the way he snorts and stamps."

Isami nodded. Shinzō's dourness was at odds with the Ikoma bards and storytellers she had seen back at the capital, and yet, he had not been provoked to violence by Keisuke's barbs. "One does not rise to the rank of personal archivist to a high lord without some measure of self-control."

"As you say." Gorobei seemed thoughtful. "It is likely Bayushi Keisuke has been prodding him for days."

"To what end?" Isami asked.

"Anger has been known to cloud judgment." Gorobei dismounted, moving to help Isami from her horse.

She paced along the riverbank, the swirling water below reflecting the twisting gyre of Isami's thoughts. The precariousness of her situation seemed to settle about her like a fog.

No matter Isami's status and family, she was in contested lands with only a single bodyguard and a dozen servants standing between her and two sizeable contingents of clan samurai. Imperial agents had been known to go missing in such circumstances, their disappearance blamed on bandits or mountain goblins. From the look of it, Stone Willow Valley seemed wild enough to host either. If Isami disappeared there would be questions, but in the absence of tangible proof, no one would raise a formal inquest over the life of a mere copy clerk.

Although she had come to rely on Gorobei, ultimately it fell to Isami to walk the knife's edge between these two proud and fractious clans. It was not that she couldn't decide, it was that her decisions had never mattered before. Suddenly *everything* mattered, from the words she spoke, to the way she carried herself, to the place she chose for her camp.

"Just over there will do, I think." Isami nodded to a relatively flat spot roughly halfway up the rise. "It would be more convenient nearer the river, but I suspect that might offend our Ikoma friend."

With a quick bow, Gorobei turned, already calling for the servants to set up camp.

Just beyond the river, the Spine of the World mountains rose like the teeth of a fallen dragon. The setting sun slipped behind the high peaks, painting the land with jagged shadows.

Isami stared up at the mountains, breathing deep of the cool air that swept down from their rocky sides. Somewhere, concealed within the crags and cliffs, lay Gyōki's hidden valley – she was sure of it. But without the maps, Isami had only a vague approximation of its location. Back at the Ministry, it had seemed possible to draw on her memory of Gyōki's surveys to find the valley. Now, confronted with the vast and immeasurable breadth of the ancient peaks, she wasn't so sure.

Isami drew Tadataka's compass from a loop on her horse's saddle. The sight of it conjured a sharp pang within her chest. The old master's words came rushing back, a litany of careful advice she had tossed aside in pursuit of her dreams.

For better or worse, Isami was here.

"One shovel at a time." Gripping the compass like a walking staff, she moved up the hill, seeking the pack that held her surveying equipment. Isami had spoken true when she said she desired rest, but she was under no illusions about being able to sleep tonight.

Distant but intent, guards from both camps watched as Isami assembled her tools. The surveyor's chain was a reassuring weight in her hand as she measured a straight baseline. Three links to a foot, ten feet in all, she laid the chain end-to-end along the little plateau, charting and subdividing, losing herself in calculations as she pushed the sharpened tip of Tadataka's compass into the ground, using it to draw angles to the nearest peak.

As it always did, the act gave structure to Isami's muddled thoughts. She retreated into the comforting simplicity of measurement, free from the maddening complexities of obligation and status that seemed to underpin even the simplest social interaction.

Mountains cared nothing for rank.

Set against the backdrop of such natural majesty, all mortal concerns became trivial, borders and boundaries little more than clouds passing over the land, come and gone in the blink of an eye. Even the sweep of history dwindled to nothing before the ageless weight of these ancient peaks.

Isami imagined herself upon the shrouded summit, gazing down upon the miniscule squabbles playing out below. It seemed strange that so many were willing to fight and die over something so ephemeral. And yet, Isami knew every border in the Empire had been drawn in blood.

"Mistress." Gorobei's soft call drew Isami from her thoughts.

She glanced around, blinking. When had it become so dark?

The former rōnin knelt at the edge of Isami's lamplight, head bowed to soften his intrusion.

"Dinner is … was ready." He rose at Isami's nod, gestured back toward camp. "It is not right for us to eat before you, but I fear the servants may devour me whole if I hold them back any longer."

"By all means." Isami bobbed her head, thankful the evening shadows hid her reddening cheeks. "Please don't wait on my account."

"Yes, mistress." Bowing, Gorobei turned away.

Isami ran a hand through her hair, watching the former rōnin disappear into the gathering dark. It would not do for her perspective to become so wide she lost sight of the smaller things. Borders might shift like clouds, but they were real enough to those who died defending them.

Gathering her equipment, Isami followed Gorobei into the night. Although her task was no less daunting, for the first time since accepting Shinpachi's offer, Isami's path appeared clear.

In order to succeed, she must learn to chart clouds as well as mountains.

# CHAPTER NINE

Isami sighted along the river. Marking the position of a distant village, she used compass and spyglass to fix its position on her growing map. The survey was still a rough thing – mountains, towns, and river little more than vague outlines, but drafting a map of Stone Willow Valley provided Isami with the perfect pretext to meet Shinzō and Keisuke on her terms.

Isami had dispatched a pair of servants just before daybreak, each carrying a missive. Rather than flood her tiny camp with fractious samurai, it seemed better to invite the two representatives to accompany her as she familiarized herself with the contested territory.

To understand the situation, she must first understand the land.

"Lady Miya." Keisuke was the first to arrive. Although Isami's letter had commanded the clan nobles to bring only one bodyguard, Keisuke was flanked by a pair of hulking Scorpion samurai, their faces concealed behind grinning oni masks.

"What a fine morning. Truly, the gods smile upon your endeavors." Keisuke's mouth was covered, but his eyes held an audacious glint – almost as if he were daring Isami to mention his flaunting of her orders.

She regarded the Scorpion guards. Although Isami kept her expression neutral, her thoughts twisted like snakes. To make a point of Keisuke's impudence would be an inauspicious start to the meeting. All knew Isami had no actual way to force the Scorpion courtier to comply, but to say nothing would be to admit her weakness.

Fortunately, Gorobei saved her the trouble. "You were to bring only one guard, my lord."

"Ah, but I have." Keisuke nodded at the samurai on his left. "This is Okita, my bodyguard."

"And who is that?" Exasperation tinged Gorobei's gravelly voice.

"This is Masaru." Keisuke bobbed his head. "Okita's bodyguard."

The Scorpion noble leaned forward, his voice dropping to a conspiratorial whisper. "If my Ikoma colleague is to be believed, this valley is *crawling* with bandits. In such dangerous times, even bodyguards require bodyguards."

"Tell Okita not to fear." Isami gave a thin smile. "You are both under my protection."

Keisuke hesitated. Despite Isami's obvious inability to guard anyone, to refuse her offer would be a dire insult. Isami's authority might be a polite fiction, but it was a useful one.

"Your strength is equaled only by your wisdom, noble lady." Bowing, Keisuke waved Masaru away, and not a moment too soon, as Shinzō cantered down the dirt road, a single guard in tow.

The Ikoma archivist had exchanged his armor for loose robes, gathered around the waist with an embroidered sash. Despite the swords belted at his side, Shinzō seemed more comfortable in scholar's attire than battlefield kit. The archivist bowed low in the saddle, his voice taking on the high cadence of a court recital.

> *"The wind carries us.*
> *Sunlight pierces racing clouds.*
> *Fine day for a talk."*

Isami stiffened, pleasant smile frozen upon her face as the two clan nobles watched expectantly. Isami had come expecting more argument and sniping, not poetry.

A burgeoning realization tickled up Isami's spine; she had gravely misjudged Shinzō. In his way, the Lion archivist was just as dangerous as his Scorpion counterpart. To compose such verse showed the Ikoma had wit as well as scholarly acumen. Belatedly, Isami gathered her thoughts. It had been years since she attended a poetry competition, and then only at Master Tadataka's insistence.

> *"It is a rare sky,*
> *that contains both sun and moon.*
> *Still, they are not foes."*

There was a moment of silence, then Shinzō dismounted with a polite nod. "Well put, lady."

Keisuke's words cut the air like a sword.

> *"Such fine sentiments.*
> *Leaves scattered by autumn wind.*
> *Shall any see spring?"*

Isami gritted her teeth, forced to acknowledge the Scorpion's barb. Keisuke had followed the rules, if not the spirit of the exchange.

"Let us not stand on ceremony." She gave a dismissive wave, trying to imbue the words with all the gravity she could muster. Authority came so easily to nobles such as Naotora and Shinpachi, but Isami felt as if she stood upon spring ice, liable to give way at any moment.

Better move to safer ground.

"You may address me as Isami." She turned away. Looking into the spyglass, Isami turned back to the low camp table to make a few more notes on the map. Her hand was shaking so badly the characters came out as inky blurs. Fortunately, neither Shinzō nor Keisuke seemed to notice.

"What is this?" Keisuke stepped to her side, gazing down at the equipment.

"A map of Stone Willow Valley," Isami replied. "The beginnings of one, at least."

"And these?" Shinzō leaned to gently trace the outline of a triangle on the map face. Although the two clan nobles stood within striking distance of one another, neither appeared to notice.

Isami did not let her surprise show. Amidst all the glares and harsh words, she had forgotten both Shinzō and Keisuke were scholars. Perhaps this might even provide a way past their mutual hostility.

Smiling, she explained the work, even going so far as to demonstrate her technique by calculating the distance to the top of a nearby rise.

"Interesting." Keisuke nodded. "But a map is not the territory."

"Nature seldom draws straight lines," Shinzō added, seemingly unaware he had just agreed with his rival. "How do you account for hills and valleys?"

"I haven't worked that out, quite yet," Isami conceded. "There were some ancient surveys in the Ministry archives drafted using the same principles, but they are... gone, now."

Isami glanced away, memories of Kazuya's betrayal surfacing like corpses bobbing on a dark sea.

"Be that as it may, this survey is unnecessary." Shinzō crossed his arms. "What matters is ownership. And I have documents clearly proving this land belongs to the Lion Clan."

Keisuke gave a sharp bark of laughter. "Documents he refuses to show to anyone."

"I was merely waiting for the proper authority."

"Well, here she is," Keisuke replied.

Isami swallowed the urge to sigh. It had perhaps been too much to hope the clan commanders would remain civil.

"Lady Miya, the documents are under close guard in my camp," Shinzō said. "I would be happy to–"

"Have us at your mercy?" Keisuke said.

"You are already at my mercy, Scorpion." Shinzō's scowl seemed etched from granite. "Your force numbers barely half mine."

"And what a glorious battle it would be." Keisuke spread his hands, fingers wide as if he were a teahouse drunk recounting a warrior tale. "So did the noble Ikoma Shinzō bravely engage a token Scorpion garrison, bathing the land in the blood of its rightful owners."

Shinzō reddened. When he spoke again, his words came low and hard. "This is not your land."

"Centuries of Scorpion rule beg to differ," Keisuke replied, seemingly unconcerned by the unstated threat in Shinzō's tone. He turned to Isami as if for support. "As you can see, the Lion are as unreasonable as ever."

"I would like to see these documents," Isami said.

"Of course," Shinzō replied. "Allow me to escort you."

"At *my* camp." Isami fixed the Lion archivist with what she hoped was a steady stare. The Scorpion and Lion commanders' animosity seemed wide as the sea, its tides both personal and political. Isami would need to bridge those troubled waters, lest the waves turn crimson.

"With respect, lady, these maps and records represent the only documentation of our claim." Shinzō's reply came tinged with concern. "I am reticent to place them in jeopardy."

Isami did not waver. "Although your reputation is impeccable, in matters such as this it is best to avoid any appearance of impropriety. Don't you agree?"

"Wholeheartedly," Keisuke nodded.

Shinzō leveled a withering glare at the Scorpion courtier before turning back to Isami. "May I at least detail guards to watch over the maps?"

"I think it would be best if I reviewed them alone." Isami knew she was pushing the Ikoma archivist, but there was nothing else for it. If she had Lion guards standing over her shoulder, the Scorpion would be quick to contest any decision. Isami's gaze flicked toward Keisuke, but the courtier gave no hint to his thoughts. Surely even he would not be so foolish as to attempt to steal the maps, especially knowing the act would lead to bloodshed.

"I shall have the documents delivered to your camp." Shinzō

spoke as if every word had been dragged from him. "But I *will* post guards around the Scorpion." He leveled an accusatory finger at Keisuke. "If one of your people so much as glances at Isami's camp, there will be consequences."

"And now you would stop me from walking my own clan's territory?" Anger flared in Keisuke's eyes. "You act as if the matter were already settled, but do not forget the Scorpion have ruled these lands for years. We will not be bullied by a band of thieves wearing clan colors."

Shinzō took a step toward the courtier, hand tight on the hilt of his blade. The move was mirrored by Okita, Keisuke's bodyguard. Steel hissed against wood as Shinzō's own bodyguard drew her blade.

Gorobei laid a hand on Isami's arm, but she shook free of his grip, a hot flash of anger boiling away her better judgment.

"Enough!"

Apparently surprised by the outburst, the guards and their masters took a step back.

"Lord Shinzō, you will deliver the maps to me by noon." Isami waved her spyglass like a general's fan. "And you will *both* remain in your camps until I have finished my review. Is that clear?"

The moment stood balanced upon a knife's edge. If either Keisuke or Shinzō took offense, Isami could not prevent the violence. Just like that, her anger guttered, replaced by a sudden surety the commanders would order their guards to strike her down. Isami's hands drifted to the surveyor's chain wrapped about her waist. There was no choice but to forge on.

"To assuage any concerns, you may each post ten samurai near the other's camp."

Shinzō looked about to argue, but bit back his words, settling for a stiff bow, muscles tight as corded rope.

"Of course." Keisuke clapped his hands, former animosity apparently forgotten. "The Scorpion are nothing if not reasonable."

"You may have three hours to review the documents. After which, my warriors will come to collect them." Teeth bared, Shinzō mounted up and rode off, Okita jogging behind.

"I am truly sorry you had to witness that, lady. Unfortunately, such displays of temper are all too common among the more brutish clans. When all you have is blades, everything appears a battle." Keisuke's voice dripped with sympathy. "I am only glad you intervened when you did."

With a bow, Keisuke departed. Although the Scorpion courtier's face remained covered, Isami was sure he was grinning beneath his mask.

"That one doesn't speak so much as conspire." Gorobei stepped to her side, watching Keisuke depart through narrowed eyes.

"You will need to be on your guard when the documents arrive."

"I have not forgotten my duties, mistress." Gorobei's tone held only the merest hint of reproach.

"My apologies," Isami replied. "Recent events have left me somewhat fatigued."

"Think nothing of it."

Isami turned back to her equipment, but even the familiar lines and measures provided little solace. All she could think of was the Lion maps. It seemed unlikely they would hold anything more than the imperial surveys of the region, but if they truly were as old as Shinzō believed, there might be some clue as to the location of Isami's hidden valley.

She shook her head, irked by her own wild ambition. Only a fool thought of winter when there were wolves at the door. Isami had barely kept the clans from coming to blows, triangles and hidden valleys would do her little good once blades were drawn. She needed to focus on the issue at hand. And yet, the prospect of recapitulating some of Gyōki's work echoed through her thoughts like a half-remembered song.

With a sigh, she straightened, waving for the servants to pack up her equipment.

Isami's thoughts buzzed like cicadas, she would get no more work done this morning. Best to return to camp and prepare to receive Shinzō's messenger. Back straight against the crushing weight of expectation, Isami started back toward camp. Whatever the maps held, it was likely to determine the course of events not only for the Scorpion and Lion, but Isami as well.

She only hoped she was up to the task.

# CHAPTER TEN

True to his promise, Shinzō delivered the documents – several large chests full of ancient parchments carried by a small army of servants with a delicacy usually reserved for imperial relics. Shinzō himself led the procession, flanked by no fewer than forty Lion samurai in full battle kit. They surrounded Isami's tiny camp like a besieging force before the Ikoma commander finally rode forward.

"Do not expose the scrolls to sunlight, and keep them from moisture." All hint of deference had fled from Shinzō's bearing. Still atop his steed, he gazed down at Isami like a field general surveying the heads of his defeated foes. "You alone shall handle them."

Isami nodded her consent. "I have experience with delicate papers."

Shinzō waved the bearers toward Isami's tent, watching the chests disappear from sight as if each were a dagger drawn across his flesh. When the servants reappeared, he turned to Isami once more.

"It is not too late for me to post guards. Despite his preening and posturing, Bayushi Keisuke is a dangerous man."

"I am confident in my retainers." Although the noon sun was bonfire bright, Isami forced herself to meet the Ikoma commander's gaze without blinking.

"Then upon your head it shall be, Lady Miya." With a click of his tongue, Shinzō turned his horse away, a column of samurai falling in behind. As if to punctuate Isami's helplessness, they rode around her camp once before snaking back up the hillside to the fortified Lion position.

Gorobei took up his post at the entrance to Isami's tent as if a whole legion of Seppun guards stood at his back. At his reassuring nod, Isami ducked inside, four great chests of documents open before her. There were far too many to review in three hours, as Shinzō had no doubt intended. Even so, Isami was confident she could chart her own course through the dusty records.

At long last, she was back in her element.

Old bindings creaked in the shadowed confines of Isami's tent as she sifted through the stack of genealogies, deeds, and battle descriptions. Collected from a variety of sources, they were accompanied by several sheaves of notes in Ikoma Shinzō's sharp hand. Although his writing style seemed almost deliberately harsh, his scholarship was impeccable. Isami glanced at the books spread on the carpet around her, moving from one to another as she followed the thread of Shinzō's arguments.

The claim seemed to be largely based on lineage. The last Lion lord to rule the contested territory, Ikoma Kentarō, had lived in the early seventh century.

Although Kentarō had married a Scorpion Clan wife, Bayushi Saihoku, the union produced no offspring. Normally, the couple would have adopted from a branch family of the Ikoma, thus securing Lion ownership of the land, but it seemed Kentarō had little interest in hereditary politics. In truth, he seemed a poor lord indeed. Flitting from obsession to obsession like a fly on spoiled fruit – architecture, exploration, painting, even cartography. Kentarō appeared to have no constant save his affection for his Bayushi wife, leaving the rule of Stone Willow Valley to her whenever he departed on one of his frequent expeditions into the Spine of the World.

It was only when Lord Kentarō failed to return from one of his journeys that ownership of the valley came into question.

In modern times, the land would have returned to the Ikoma family, but the ancients tracked ownership matrilineally so as to guarantee all property and title were passed to an heir of the blood. Lady Saihoku took advantage of this by quickly remarrying, this time to a Scorpion of high rank. The noble's name had been lost to history, but the marriage provided Saihoku with the opportunity to rejoin her old clan, taking with her all the lands belonging to her former husband.

Although a barefaced manipulation of inheritance customs, Saihoku's gambit secured the Scorpion Clan's claim for centuries; until Shinzō's diligent research into the High Histories of the Ikoma unearthed the fact Lord Kentarō had declared an heir – a child with Saihoku who had died shortly after birth. Even buried and unnamed, the child represented a clear link to the Ikoma. By right, the land should have passed to a cousin or other member of the family, rather than Bayushi Saihoku.

Fascinated by the interplay of ancient code and custom, Isami delved deep into the records, reading all she could about Lord Kentarō. Despite being instrumental in the collection and preservation of the original High Histories, Kentarō seemed to have been ostracized by the Lion nobility. Isami could not help but feel a twinge of sympathy as she read through unflattering reports by Lion generals, elaborating on the numerous slights Kentarō delivered to his betters, but Isami's heart truly leapt into her throat when she unfolded the remnant of one of his land surveys.

It lay like a pressed flower, nested between two pages of a tax ledger. The paper was brittle and thinned by age, brush strokes little more than pale shadows upon the page. Still, Isami leaned close, hardly believing her eyes as she ran her fingers along the faint outline of gridwork overlaying the river and peaks.

Isami leapt to her feet, ignoring the stab of pain from legs forced to move after so long kneeling on the carpet. Hurrying to her personal effects, she drew forth her unfinished survey of the valley, almost throwing herself down beside Kentarō's map in her haste to lay the two side-by-side.

Although the villages had changed and the river's course shifted over the intervening centuries, the peaks remained the same.

The air in the tent suddenly felt close and thin. No matter how quickly Isami breathed, she seemed unable to fill her lungs. Kentarō had been lord of these lands in the seventh century, long after Gyōki had begun his survey of the Spine of the World. Still, the Ikoma Lord had been a scholar. Could it be possible he had been familiar with Gyōki's work?

Kentarō's survey appeared to be a fragment of something much larger, perhaps one that stretched into the mountains themselves. Carefully as she dared, Isami paged through the Lion documents, searching for other maps of the region. She found sketches amidst the pages of Kentarō's journals, notations scrawled in the margins of reports and letters. Although there were no other maps, it was clear from the old lord's work that he had ventured deep into the mountains.

Amidst notes detailing the construction of a new dam, she found reference to a path that led amidst the peaks to somewhere Kentarō referred to as: "The Gilded Scar" . Isami recognized some of the peaks from Gyōki's survey, the directions and location roughly coinciding with the blank spot on the ancient map.

Isami rocked back, one hand pressed to the ground to keep from toppling over.

It was real.

She forced herself to take slow breaths, but the calming exercise did nothing to quell the whirling maelstrom of her thoughts. Surely this could not be the only reference. In her efforts to press the Lion's claim, Shinzō had gathered dozens of the old lord's journals. If Isami could find even a vague mention of the valley's location, she could compare Kentarō's maps to her own to determine how the river had once flowed and where along its ancient banks lay a path to the Gilded Scar.

If only she could find the valley. Not only would it prove Isami correct, it would show master Naotora that the ancients *did* employ more precise techniques than previously thought. Kentarō and Gyōki were considered eccentrics, yes, but they had been right – at least they *would* be proven right once Isami located the Gilded Scar. Then, even Master Kageyasu could not deny the scholarly lineage of her work.

At last, Isami wasn't alone.

Hands shaking, she reached for the next journal, only to

flinch back at the sound of a gentle scratch from the front of her tent. She looked over her shoulder to see Gorobei kneeling at the entrance.

"Mistress." Gorobei's voice was soft but insistent. "Shinzō has returned for the Lion documents."

"Tell him I need more time." The words tumbled from Isami's lips.

"Apologies, mistress." Gorobei gave an uncomfortable tilt of his head. "He is quite insistent."

A soft moan worked its way up Isami's throat. It seemed the Fortunes toyed with her once again.

From outside the tent, there came the creak of harness leather, punctuated by the impatient stamp of horses upon rocky soil. Isami bent like windswept bamboo, her shoulders high and guarded.

Once again, she stood helpless before the desires of others.

"Mistress." Gorobei twisted to glance at something behind him, concern coloring his cheeks.

Isami squeezed her eyes shut, hands clenched into fists. "Let them in."

# CHAPTER ELEVEN

Isami gripped the edge of the table, careful to not to betray her trembling hands. She was thankful for the bit of furniture, borrowed from the headman of a nearby village. After reviewing Shinzō's documents, Isami had personally gone to request the table as a show of favor, despite her embarrassment over the villagers' reverence, which had taken on a character almost akin to worship when they realized she had traveled from Otosan Uchi. If visitors of rank were rarer than summer snow this far into the hinterlands, imperial nobles were almost unheard of.

The headman had strutted about his little village, showing Isami everything from their waterwheel to the terraced fields. All the while, she was practically besieged by other peasants, who approached on hands and knees to pay respects. Isami had been enjoined to lay her hands upon the brow of a colicky baby, or stand, sweating in the sun, as some village elder recounted how his grand-aunt twice removed had once carried the sandals of a long dead noble.

At the time, the attention had made Isami uncomfortable.

Now, with the broad expanse of the table sitting like a shield between her, Keisuke, and Shinzō, Isami reflected that the journey had been well worth the trouble. Together with the carpets and umbrellas, the table gave the meeting a civilized air, as if they knelt in some well-appointed pavilion, rather than upon a grassy stretch of willow-shaded riverbank.

Most importantly, the table prevented the two clan nobles and their bodyguards from getting within striking distance of one another.

Keisuke sipped at his tea, covering his mouth with one hand such that, even as he moved his mask, his lower face remained hidden. The Scorpion courtier carried himself with a calm that struck a spark of anger in Isami's chest. Kazuya had possessed much the same smugness – as if confident the world would conform to his desires.

In contrast, Shinzō regarded his cup with the suspicion one usually reserved for unpleasant insects. When Isami's servants had brought the pot, he had taken a single sip so as not to give offense, then left the cup to steam upon the table, untouched and unremarked.

"A fine blend." Keisuke broke the uncomfortable silence. "Quite complex for such a rustic brew. But I have found even remote regions can conceal unexpected surprises. Is that not correct, Lord Ikoma?"

"Foreboding peaks conceal fine gems." Shinzō returned a thin smile. "All they require is someone with the determination to wrest them from the earth."

Keisuke gave a wry tilt of his head. "I suppose that depends on whose earth we are speaking of."

Isami took a slow breath to quell her anxieties. Courtesy

forbade the clan nobles from broaching the topic of the Lion documents directly, but it did not stop them from dancing around the issue.

"I have reviewed Shinzō's notes," Isami said. The two nobles' gazes snapped to her as if she had suddenly brandished the Emperor's personal seal.

"And?" Although Keisuke's tone was flippant, Isami could not help notice his hands tighten around his cup.

Isami took a long sip of tea. Since her time with the Lion documents, the question had weighed upon her thoughts. Her only glimmer of hope lay in resolving the conflict – the Lion had a clear, if tenuous, claim. Perhaps if she ruled in Shinzō's favor the Ikoma would grant her access to the High Histories?

Isami beat back the dishonest impulse. She had come expecting to confirm or deny the veracity of the Lion's evidence, but despite Shinzō's documents, the true ownership of the land remained murky. Could a deceased heir exercise rights over land they had never truly ruled? This was a matter for an emerald magistrate, not a cartographer.

Isami was an imperial representative. Her duty was to the Empire, not personal ambition. If she gave the land over to the Lion in order to advance her own goals, she would be no better than Kazuya. Even so, had not master Tadataka said the Empire was full of people like Kazuya? It would be only just for Isami to take back what had been stolen from her.

Perhaps there was a way to regain her standing without compromising her integrity. It was a long gamble, but Isami's tour of the village had also confirmed her suspicions concerning the imprecision of the imperial surveys. Her plan was just as likely to enrage the clan representatives as lead to a resolution.

And yet, Isami knew, despite how much she stood to gain, she could never act as Kazuya had.

"The Ikoma documents are valid." She held up a hand to forestall Keisuke's objection. "But the matter of ownership remains uncertain."

"The line of succession is clear," Shinzō said. "My research clearly points to Kentarō's heir."

"Only if ghosts can inherit." Keisuke slashed a hand through the air as if to cut the throat of Shinzō's argument. "The child may have been named heir, but he *never* ruled these lands."

Shinzō half-rose, cheeks reddening. "He had more claim than his traitorous Scorpion mother."

"I believe she was a member of the Lion at the time." Keisuke clucked his tongue. "Inauspicious, to speak ill of a clan ancestor."

Isami slapped a hand down on the table, causing the cups to rattle.

"Lord Keisuke," she spoke into the momentary lull. "How is it you know of Kentarō's heir when you have never seen Shinzō's research?"

"Despite their wish to the contrary, the Ikoma do not have a stranglehold on history," Keisuke replied. "Is it too outlandish to believe the Scorpion may have kept our own records?"

Shinzō glared at the Scorpion courtier through narrowed eyes. "All this time, and you said nothing?"

"The fact that you assumed I knew nothing is to your discredit, not mine," Keisuke replied. "Why share my knowledge when you refused me access to yours?"

A low, angry growl worked its way between Shinzō's clenched teeth, but before the Lion commander could act on his anger, Isami spoke again.

"These Scorpion records, where are they?"

"Do you think I would be foolish enough to expose them to harm?" Keisuke said. "The records are back at the clan archives in Journey's End City, along with the adoption papers."

"How very much like a Scorpion," Shinzō replied. "He claims proof, but neglects to bring it."

"Are you calling my word into question?" For the first time, an undercurrent of anger colored Keisuke's tone. "You are more than welcome to accompany me back to Journey's End City if you wish to check the veracity of my claims."

"You would enjoy having me at your mercy, Scorpion."

Keisuke leaned forward, a dangerous glint in his eyes. "Oh, very much."

Isami wished she could take the clan nobles by the neck and shake them like petulant children; but she must remain politic, even if they seemed intent on goading each other.

"You spoke of adoption papers," Isami said.

Keisuke seemed taken aback by the question, but quickly recovered.

"Why, yes." He turned to Isami, brows arched in something akin to delight. "With Lady Saihoku's marriage into the Bayushi family, it seemed only right her new husband posthumously adopt her dear, departed child."

"They had no right!" Shinzō surged to his feet.

"They had every right." Keisuke did not raise his voice. "Lady Saihoku was the child's only remaining blood relative, after all."

"Be that as it may." Isami's gaze flicked between the two angry clan samurai. As her hope of peaceful resolution began to crumble, she pulled at the only thread of authority remaining to her.

"As imperial representative, it falls to me to make a ruling." Isami forged ahead. "Would you each say the other's claim to this land is tenuous?"

"Of course, lady." Keisuke cocked his head, eyes suspicious.

After a long moment, Shinzō grunted his agreement, slowly drifting back to his knees beside the table.

"Then it is in your best interest to reach some manner of compromise."

"Lady Kaede will not be pleased to hear I have handed away Scorpion lands," Keisuke said.

Shinzō scowled. "And Lord Hanbei bid me reclaim that which had been stolen."

"Such wise lords as Bayushi Kaede and Ikoma Hanbei must recognize it is better to lose half a purse than all of it," Isami continued. "What would you say to an agreement that gained land for the Lion, but cost the Scorpion nothing?"

"I would first ask if you were a god," Keisuke said. "To conjure earth from void?"

"Not void. The land I speak of has always been here," Isami replied. "The map is not the territory, remember?"

Shinzō and Keisuke exchanged a wary look.

"It costs you nothing to listen," Isami said. When neither of the clan nobles raised an objection, Isami gestured for the servants to bring forward her unfinished survey.

"I have just begun surveying, but already found territory in excess of that shown on the imperial maps. Ikemura, for instance." Isami indicated the village she had visited earlier in the day. "The imperial surveys record barely half the fields and don't even mention a waterwheel. I suspect we shall find similar oversights in other areas."

Keisuke gave a thoughtful hum, scratching at his chin under the mask. Although Shinzō's scowl relaxed not at all, the Ikoma archivist raised no argument.

"I am proposing a rectification," Isami continued. "A new survey that will map the true extent of Stone Willow Valley. Per Shinzō's claim, the Lion may rule all lands currently depicted on the imperial map, with the newly surveyed territories remaining under Scorpion control."

Shinzō shook his head. "What is to stop the Scorpion from waiting until the survey is complete then claiming all the land for themselves?"

"The Lion army." Isami smiled. "You speak for both your clans in this matter. Any agreement you sign will be binding."

"Audacious." Keisuke brought his hands together. "But far better than war."

Shinzō sat back. "Lord Hanbei will not be happy to learn the Scorpion still hold land east of the river."

"It is not as if it will let them steal a march," Isami said. "Any forces would still have to come upriver from Beiden Pass. And with new territory nearby, you will be able to keep a closer eye upon them."

The Ikoma archivist massaged the back of his neck, expression turning almost pained as he considered Isami's proposal. After a long moment, he gave a grudging nod.

"A good idea, in principle. But I would see how much the Lion gain before I agree."

Keisuke bobbed his head in agreement. "And I, how much my clan stands to lose."

"We can discuss specifics once the maps are complete. I shall begin tomorrow." Isami fought to keep the excitement from her voice. She hadn't dared hope her plan would convince the two clans, let alone give her time to survey the valley – perhaps even the mountains beyond. "Of course, you may both watch the survey in person or send a representative."

Appearing almost surprised by the outcome, Keisuke and Shinzō regarded each other, then offered a slight bow.

Isami almost spilled the pot of tea in her haste to wave servants over with brush and paper. In less than an hour, the broad strokes had been arranged. Just like the survey itself, Isami understood the specifics would require much diligence and patience, but she allowed herself a small measure of satisfaction as Keisuke and Shinzō's names joined her own at the bottom of the last page.

It was not an accord by any means, but it bought time for her to forge a more lasting agreement.

With a final exchange of pleasantries, the Scorpion and Lion contingents returned to their respective camps. Hardly daring to believe she had accomplished her initial goal, Isami ran a hand over the burnished wood of the table.

It was a shame she would repay the headman's kindness by increasing his village's taxes, but such costs were far preferable to the devastation of clan border skirmishes. The peasants would complain, but their fields would remain unburned, their children alive.

In that, at least, Isami could find some solace.

The sun was just beginning to dip behind the mountains when she finished planning the survey route. Although still early, Isami felt as if she could sleep for days. She drifted back to her tent, Gorobei in tow. On Isami's order, the former rōnin had remained silent for the delicate proceedings, but as he held the tent flap for her to enter, Gorobei gave her a respectful nod.

"You have done the Empire proud this day, mistress."

Although courtesy forbade that she acknowledge the grizzled warrior's words, Gorobei's praise buoyed Isami's spirits more than it should have. It seemed she had finally begun to chart the clouds.

The servants brought Isami's meal, but she waved them away, already half asleep upon her pallet. The hard work was done, all that remained was to survey the valley and settle the agreement. With that in place, she would have achieved Lord Otomo's goals. Once she was an imperial cartographer, Isami would have access to the High Histories of the Ikoma.

The hidden valley in Gyōki's maps had to be Kentarō's "Gilded Scar", Isami was sure of it. Mind awash in dreams of promise and redemption, Isami drifted off to sleep. She dreamt of battles that would never be, now that Scorpion and Lion had forged a tenuous peace. So real were the images, Isami first mistook the shouts and clatter of steel for some wild conjuration of her dreaming mind.

Only when Gorobei burst into the tent, hair wild, sword in hand, did Isami rise from her pallet. Still rubbing sleep from her eyes, she was unable to muster more than a questioning murmur.

"Mistress." He dragged her from the pallet. "The Lion are coming down the hill, we must–"

A sword bisected the tent's entrance flap, revealing a Lion samurai in full armor. Screaming like an oni, he charged Gorobei, who released Isami to meet the man's rush.

She fell back, staring open-mouthed as the two men

struggled. From all around came shouts and screams, the air thick with smoke cut by the sharp smell of blood.

As if cut by a blade, the last vestiges of Isami's dreams fell away, leaving her surrounded by nightmares.

# CHAPTER TWELVE

Isami kicked at the attacker, acting more from reflex than conscious thought. Her bare foot struck the back of the Lion samurai's ankle, spoiling his swing. Gorobei was quick to take advantage, stepping in as the Lion samurai fought to retain his balance. His dagger slipped into the gap beneath the man's breastplate and shoulder armor, and Gorobei gave it a rough twist, driving up and into the samurai's chest.

The Lion warrior dropped his blade to sweep Gorobei up in a massive hug. For a moment the two men were face-to-face, close as lovers as they strained and grunted. Then the strength seemed to drain from the Lion. His arms fell limp, head lolling back. Gorobei shoved the man away and he sprawled back over Isami's sleeping pallet. The samurai tried to rise, only to slump back, his expression almost surprised.

"Are you hurt, mistress?" Gorobei helped Isami to her feet.

She shook her head. "What has happened?"

"I don't know." Panting, Gorobei scowled down at the dead samurai. "The Lion came boiling out of their camp just after midnight, no warning, and no reason I could see. We need to flee, mistress."

"They would lay hands upon an imperial emissary?" Despite sounds of battle from beyond the tent, Isami still couldn't bring herself to believe this was truly happening.

"They would do more than that by the look of it." Gorobei knelt and began to untie the Lion samurai's armor straps. "Fortunately, the Scorpion are keeping them busy. Despite the theater masks, those Bayushi can fight."

Isami snatched up her satchel, stuffing the bag with equipment, maps, and notebooks. She might flee, but she would not lose her research, not again.

"Mistress, there is no time." As if to punctuate Gorobei's point, there came a scuffle from outside the tent. A grunt of pain was followed by the thud of a body hitting earth. Gorobei stood, quickly retreating into the shadows of the tent.

A spear tip poked through the ruined entrance flap, the Lion samurai behind leveling it at Isami.

"You are to accompany us, lady. For your own protection."

"Who are you to give me orders?" Isami straightened, trying to imbue her words with every scrap of outrage she could muster. It was a struggle not to look at Gorobei, his back pressed against the canvas wall as he edged closer to the samurai.

The Lion's gaze flicked to the body on the floor of the tent, and his expression hardened.

Fortunately, Gorobei moved before the man could make a decision. Grabbing the samurai's spear with both hands, he dragged the man into the tent.

Even off balance, the Lion samurai reacted quickly, dropping his spear to draw his sword in a quick upward slash.

Twisting to avoid the blow, Gorobei snatched at his own blade, only to have the hilt tangle in the trailing sleeve of his kimono.

The Lion samurai raised his katana for another strike. Even Isami could see the former rōnin would never get his sword free in time.

She snatched up her surveyor's chain, the weighted links familiar in her hand. There was no room to swing, so Isami simply threw the chain at the Lion samurai, keeping hold of one end as it tangled around his sword and armor.

Like a fisherman hauling in a prize catch, Isami wrenched at the chain. The links bit into the flesh of her palms, and the man pitched backward. They tumbled down in a tangle of flailing limbs and rattling chain. The man weighed as much as a temple statue, his armored bulk threatening to crush the air from Isami's chest. He tried a wrestler's twist, but she kicked at his leg, driving it out from under him and preventing the turn.

The samurai might be stronger, but Isami had his back.

She looped a length of chain around the man's throat. He bucked and rolled, pawing at the chain, but Isami held tight, even as it felt like her arms might be ripped from her shoulders. His helmet smashed back into Isami's face, blossoms of light bursting amidst the shadows of the tent. She tasted blood, her nose and lips buzzing from the pain.

The samurai worked a hand up under the chain. He drew in a whistling breath, slowly dragging the chain away from his neck through sheer brute force. He tried another headbutt, but Isami had tucked her face low into his shoulder, instincts drilled into her over long months at the Miya dojo finally coming to the fore. She tried to hook her legs around his for more leverage, but the samurai shifted to block the maneuver.

Breath rasping in her throat, Isami fought to keep her grip, but the Lion samurai's strength seemed inexorable as the tide. With a grunt of effort, he pulled the chain down.

A shadow loomed over them.

Gorobei knelt to drive his blade into the hollow of the man's throat. Isami could feel the samurai shift to block the blow, but with his hands still tangled in her chain, there was little he could do.

Hot blood splashed across Isami's face as the man toppled forward, his strength bleeding away. A few moments, and it was over.

Arms shaking, Isami crawled out from under the samurai.

"That was a good bit of work there, mistress." Gorobei nodded at the body. "And here I thought you were all research and records."

"Imperial cartographers oft find themselves in far corners of the Empire." Isami winced, trying to rub some feeling back into her hands. "We long ago learned the value of being able to defend ourselves."

"If your surveying career doesn't work out, I may be able to find you work as a bodyguard." Gorobei gave a raspy chuckle.

Isami just stared at him, unable to understand how the former rōnin could joke at a time like this.

"Apologies, mistress." He rubbed the back of his neck, moving to peer out of the ruined tent flap. "It appears clear."

"Good." Isami bent to untangle her chain from the body, although she hoped not to need it.

Gorobei moved quickly to the first Lion samurai. Cutting away several more armor straps, he drew the breastplate and shoulder guards from the body.

"Put these on, mistress." He tossed them at her feet. "Helmet, too."

Isami frowned down at the dead man's armor.

Gorobei didn't wait for an answer. "In the chaos of combat, warriors rely on armor and flags to tell each other apart. Looking like Lion samurai may buy us the time to win free."

Although distasteful, Isami was forced to concede the former rōnin's point. The armor was far too big for her, and Gorobei had cut all but the lower straps, causing the breastplate to hang off Isami like a cape. She slipped the sweaty helmet over her head and secured it as best she could, sure the slightest jostle would tear the plates free. She felt like a child parading in their parents' dress armor.

She coiled her chain at her waist, then made sure she had spyglass, compass, imperial survey, and her maps. By the time Isami had finished, Gorobei had donned the other samurai's armor, leaving just enough of the straps to keep it in place.

Nodding, he took his helmet and stepped out into the night.

Isami followed, sure the shaking of her legs would rattle her armor loose. A servant lay spread across the earth outside of the tent. Isami wasn't sure if he had died trying to prevent the Lion from taking her unawares, or if he had simply been in the wrong place at the wrong time. Either way, she bowed to him, ashamed she could not remember the man's name.

Fortunately, the other servants seemed to have fled into the night, sparing Isami the pain of having caused more deaths.

Beyond her tent lay a waking nightmare. At the base of the hill, the Scorpion camp was in flames. Isami could see samurai fighting amidst the chaos, their struggling forms limned by firelight. Fallen bodies spread across the grass, half submerged in flickering shallows along the edge of the river. Despite being outnumbered, the Scorpion fought as if possessed by vicious demons.

Isami saw one masked warrior atop a pile of smoking crates, the curved blade of his naginata weaving a tapestry of steel as three Lion samurai stabbed at him with long spears. Another Scorpion leapt from the shadows to hurl himself at a mounted Lion warrior, dragging the man bodily from the horse. But despite their wild fury, numbers were beginning to tell.

Isami searched for Keisuke among the firelit shadows, but the Scorpion courtier was nowhere to be seen.

She did spy Shinzō, however.

The Ikoma archivist sat atop his horse, hacking down at a pair of Scorpion samurai, his expression more fearsome than the howling oni masks worn by his opponents. Helmetless, he swore and snarled at his foes, seeming driven by fury alone as he hammered his blade down in blow after crushing blow.

Isami drew back at the sight. The Ikoma archivist possessed a temper, but Isami could not believe him capable of such treachery. What had occurred to drive Shinzō into a blind rage?

"Mistress," Gorobei's soft call snapped Isami from her dire contemplation. With a shake of her head, she followed him through the camp. By the Ancestors' grace, the horses remained on their leads. Although the poor beasts' eyes shone white in the reflected firelight of the burning Scorpion camp, Gorobei was able to calm them with quiet words and sweet wheat cakes from the pouch at his belt.

They mounted quickly, kicking the horses into a canter – fast enough to put some distance between them and the fighting without appearing as if they were fleeing over the hill.

Isami's concern doubled as a trio of Lion samurai galloped past. She glanced away to hide her face, sure the warriors would see through her and Gorobei's clumsy disguises. They passed with barely a nod, thundering down the hill to join their companions. Isami watched them go, surprised.

"All this blood." Gorobei leaned over in his saddle to nod at Isami's stained breastplate. "They probably think we've been wounded."

The Lion samurai rode not toward the Scorpion camp, but toward Ikemura. Glancing toward the village, Isami was surprised to see torches in the distance. Strangely, the lights moved not with the confused panic of peasants in flight, but as if possessed by a singular purpose. They formed an ordered column, advancing quickly toward the battle. It seemed impossible the villagers would come to the defense of the Scorpion, and yet they advanced in haste. Isami squinted into the dark, trying to make out the torch-wielders. For a moment, she saw the glint of lacquered armor reflected in the light, then Gorobei reined up beside her.

"We must go, mistress. Before Shinzō receives word of our escape."

Fighting the urge to kick her horse into a gallop, Isami followed Gorobei around the hill. Although this hid the battle from view, it did little to silence the roar of conflict, sounds Isami was sure would haunt her dreams for weeks to come.

Once beyond the battle, they gave their horses a bit of lead, letting their long strides carry them down along the valley and into the sheltering trees.

Isami slumped from her horse. Wriggling free of the armor, she tossed it aside, glad to be free of its uncomfortable weight. Blood from the slain Lion samurai covered the front of her robes. Although the deep ochre and brown of the Miya colors hid the worst of the rusty stains, Isami was painfully aware of the stiffness marked by the dried blood.

"Take a moment to breathe," Gorobei said. "I'll water and brush the horses. Shinzō is likely to send riders after us, and we'll need the mounts at their best."

Leaning against a nearby tree, Isami almost collapsed as the night's events washed over her.

"How could this have happened?"

"Our Ikoma friend must not have liked the deal." Gorobei began to tend to the horses. "Or thought he could win a better one at sword point."

"That doesn't make sense," Isami said, remembering the look of abject fury upon Shinzō's face as he hacked at the Scorpion. "The Lion do not break their word."

"You must not have met many Lion, mistress." Gorobei chuckled as he brushed the shivering horse. "They are the same as any other clan – some good, some bad. I have seen many unconscionable acts performed in service of Akodo's Code."

Isami looked to her hands, bruises beginning to show where the chain links had dug into her flesh. It seemed impossible that Shinzō could have launched such an assault. How had she misjudged the Ikoma archivist so badly?

Slowly, Isami's shock drained away, replaced by a sudden upswell of anger.

"We will need to ride most of the night," Gorobei said. "Upstream if possible, to hide our tracks. Hopefully, we can find a cave or shelter before daybreak. These are Lion lands, and their patrols are likely out in force. If we can but reach Crane Clan territory, we should be able to–"

"We are not bound for Crane lands," Isami said.

"Mistress?"

"You think like a rōnin, Gorobei, scuttling about like a mouse."

Isami pushed to her feet, surprised by the sharpness of her tone. She had believed Shinzō negotiated in good faith, when all the time the Ikoma commander had been waiting for the chance to strike. Trusting fool that she was, Isami had fallen for the Lion ruse.

She turned away from Gorobei, thankful the night hid the bonfire-hot flush of her cheeks. Anger was easier than embarrassment, and Isami embraced the sentiment.

"We could run, hide, yes. But it is far better to think like a noble." Her hands made tight fists in the sleeves of her robe. "We shall find safety in the exact place Shinzō would never look – Sacred Watch Palace, the seat of the Ikoma family."

"You would have us ride into the lion's jaws, mistress?"

"It will not bite." Isami moved to help Gorobei with the horses. "I do not believe Shinzō acted according to his lord's wishes. Even if he did, the Ikoma would face serious repercussions for endangering the life of an imperial representative."

"All the more reason to make you disappear."

"There is a difference between killing me out in the hinterlands with no one to see, and disposing of me in open court." Isami's nod was more for herself. "We shall make such an arrival at Sacred Watch that none shall be able to deny our presence. Then Lord Hanbei must either move openly and risk imperial censure, or decry Shinzō's betrayal and cast the traitor adrift."

Gorobei sucked air through his teeth. "That is quite a gamble, mistress."

"I shall not run back to Lord Otomo like some frightened hound, tail between my legs."

Gorobei cocked his head. "Better a tail between your legs than your head in a basket."

"Spoken like a true rōnin."

"As you say, mistress." Gorobei's smile did not reach his eyes. "As you say."

# CHAPTER THIRTEEN

The Lion patrol moved in a staggered line. Two bow-armed samurai ranged through the brush on either side of the packed earth road ahead of four more with spears. They wore light armor, breastplates, helmets, and greaves – a far cry from the full battle kit of Shinzō's warriors. This, more than anything, convinced Isami she had made the right choice. Even so, the closeness of so many warriors gave Isami pause.

She pressed herself deeper into the tall grass covering the ridge overlooking the road, as if earth and leaves might shield her from the decision she had to make.

"Are you sure, mistress?" Concern edged Gorobei's normally gruff tone. The former rōnin had been a true asset these last few days, leading Isami through the Lion hinterlands with an almost preternatural skill. He seemed to know every stream and blind, every copse and ridge – at least those far from the beaten path.

"Those are not Shinzō's warriors." Isami nodded toward the somber Lion's face emblazoned upon the patrol leader's breastplate, marking him as an Akodo samurai. Although Shinzō had sent riders after them, Isami and Gorobei had been aided by the poor quality of the roads on the Lion borders. The roughness surprised Isami, until Gorobei had explained the Lion Clan purposely left the roads untended so as to make it more difficult for an invasion force to march across their outlying territories.

Although the speed of their journey left little time for surveying, Isami had recorded the routes and footpaths as best she could, marking their direction with Tadataka's compass. She had told Gorobei it was so they could more easily find their way back if necessary, but, in truth, the mapping calmed Isami. With so much beyond her control, she needed something tangible to focus on – even if it was only the twists of a few scattered trails.

"They may have changed armor." Gorobei squinted down the ridge, careful not to move any of the long grass he and Isami sheltered behind. "After what happened on the hill, I wouldn't put anything beyond Shinzō."

"Your caution does you justice." Isami chewed her lip, considering. It was not impossible Shinzō sought to entrap them. During the negotiations, the Ikoma commander had displayed a remarkable talent for forethought. Still, Isami thought it unlikely Shinzō would expect his quarry to flee into the center of Lion power.

The lead scout picked her way up the ridge. A few more moments, and Isami's choice would be made for her. She and Gorobei could still crawl back down the hill to where their mounts waited in a copse of trees. There was yet time to make for Crane lands and beyond to the safety of Otosan Uchi. A small part of Isami counselled such caution, but to do so would be to admit she had failed. She would be adrift in the capital, without prospect or patron, her future little more than smoke from a funeral pyre.

Jaw tight, Isami pushed up from the ridge, using her most commanding voice. "Noble wardens."

The Lion scout had her bow up in a heartbeat, arrow aimed at Isami's chest.

"Don't shoot." Isami walked several paces down the hill, hands high to show she held no weapons.

"State your business." The scout remained ready to fire. Behind her, the Lion warriors fanned out in a rough semicircle, advancing up the hill, spears at the ready.

"I am Miya Isami, of the Imperial Bureau of Taxation," she replied. "And I have come to speak to Lord Hanbei."

"You do not look like a noble." The scout regarded Isami with a suspicious frown. "Where are your traveling papers?"

"The last few days have been… difficult." Isami gave an embarrassed tilt of her head. Truth be told, they had been some of the worst in her life, living on river water, tubers, and what scraps of game Gorobei had been able to snare; the nights spent shivering in some cave or stand of trees, afraid to light a fire lest they give warning to Shinzō's scouts. The only consolation was that the blood on Isami's clothes had been thoroughly covered by mud and grass stains.

"I know I must look a sight. But if you will allow me to retrieve something from my robes." Isami continued as the Lion captain jogged up, sword in hand. He was a wide-faced man with heavy brows, his weak chin hidden by a short, trimmed beard.

The scout glanced at her captain, who returned a straight-faced nod.

"Slowly," the scout said.

Taking care not to let the trembling of her hands betray her, Isami reached into the front of her kimono, drawing forth Lord Otomo's seal.

"Place it on the grass, then back away." The Lion captain

maintained his position as the rest of his squad fanned out to surround Isami.

She did as requested, and the captain sent one of his warriors forward with a thrust of his chin.

"That is the personal chop of Lord Otomo Shinpachi, Second Intendent for Regulation of Taxation and Tribute for the Imperial Treasury." Despite her regrettable state, Isami sought to imbue the name with authority. "I believe that should suffice for travel papers."

"Where did you get this?" The captain turned the seal over in his hands.

"From Lord Otomo's hand."

"Captain, she speaks as a noble," the Lion scout said. "And those are Miya colors."

He frowned, heavy brows furrowed.

Isami could almost see him weighing his choices. If she were masquerading as an imperial noble he would look a fool for believing her; but if Isami *was* who she claimed and he gave insult – samurai had been cast down for far less.

The captain shook his head as if unable to believe the situation. "Either you are a noble, or you the most audacious thief I have ever encountered." He turned to the other guards. "We shall escort Lady Isami to Sacred Watch Palace. Show her all due courtesy."

"My apologies, lady." Dropping to her knees, the Lion scout offered a low bow.

"It is a poor lord indeed who takes offense at a retainer's diligence." Isami waved a hand to mask the fact she seemed finally able to draw breath again. "Rise, with my gratitude."

The scout stood, head low.

"My name is Akodo Kihei, warden captain in southern Gunsho Province." The captain sheathed his sword. "Lady, how have you come to be in such distress?"

"I would prefer to reserve my explanation for your lord," Isami replied. "Merely know that my bodyguard and I travel in some haste."

"Bodyguard?"

Isami turned back up the hill. "You may show yourself, Gorobei."

The former rōnin rose from the grass in which he had been laying, to the sudden consternation of the Lion scouts.

"Your retainer is quite skilled at concealment." Kihei did a good job of hiding his surprise. "Toshi and Masako here can usually spot a sparrow in the bullrushes at two hundred paces."

"He is quite talented, as befits an imperial retainer." Isami offered a tentative smile, hoping to elevate Gorobei so as not to slight the scouts' reputation. Although the Lion samurai would do their duty, things would proceed more smoothly if Isami did not offend her escort.

"There is a village perhaps three miles down the road." To her relief, Captain Kihei seemed placated by the gentle praise. "They will have clothes and food – far better than the humble rations we could provide."

Isami nodded her thanks. "Our horses are behind the hill."

"Of course, lady." Kihei waved two of his guards forward. The rest fell into a loose formation around Isami and Gorobei as they started down the hill.

Although much of the strain of the last few days had vanished, Isami could not release her anxiety. The guards seemed unaware of Shinzō's attack. And yet, Isami could not be sure of the welcome that awaited her in Sacred Watch Palace. Guests could easily become prisoners. Isami had placed much trust in the reputation of Lord Ikoma Hanbei, a man whom she knew very little about.

It was pleasant to travel on roads again, even more so after the Lion samurai requisitioned a hot meal and a change of clothes from the nearby village. Unlike the villagers in contested lands, these were more used to travelers of rank, and thus Isami was subjected to only the most polite scrutiny as she and Gorobei ate. Although tempted to move on immediately, Isami realized matted hair and travel-stained clothes were unlikely to make a good impression on the Ikoma lord.

The Lion guards kept the locals at a distance as Isami washed herself in a large wooden tub. A far cry from even the more modest bathhouses of Otosan Uchi, the tepid water seemed the height of opulence after so long on the road. Afterwards, Isami found her robes freshly cleaned and dried. Only the barest shadows of blood remained upon the earth-toned fabric.

If only Isami's memory could be scoured so easily.

The village headwoman offered them accommodations in her tiny inn. Although Isami felt as if she could sleep for days, she worried about what would happen should Shinzō reach the castle first.

With Gorobei's help, she set a brisk pace, Captain Kihei's squad jogging beside. In many ways, they reminded Isami of the bearers who had helped escort her to Stone Willow Valley – dedicated and tireless, their muscles hardened by long travel. She considered saying something to Kihei, but discarded the thought. Although Isami meant the words as a compliment, the samurai would take insult at being compared to common laborers.

They moved through the night, dismounting to walk or water the horses as necessary. Morning found them within sight of Sacred Watch Palace.

The Lion city might have been considered large by any who had not grown up in Otosan Uchi. Prior to the blustery return of the Unicorn Clan, Sacred Watch Palace had been built to provide warning of invasions from the west. In keeping with this role, the palace itself was a spartan affair, its high, sloping walls and peaked parapets designed for battle rather than beauty.

It seemed impossible such an unlovely edifice might hold one of the most complete historical records in Rokugan. But somewhere behind those foreboding walls lay the Ikoma Archives. Isami's arms prickled at the thought of what secrets she could unearth. Shinzō's research had been thorough, but focused on genealogy. Perhaps there were more maps of Stone Willow Valley, perhaps even of the mountains themselves.

Scowling, Isami pushed the thought down. The histories were closely watched, warded by a legion of warrior-archivists like Shinzō. What use was there in Isami torturing herself with things that could not be?

As with many castle towns in Rokugan, a large urban area had sprung up before the palace gates, the sprawl of buildings crowding the streets almost as if the castle had vomited them forth upon the plain. Like the outer regions of their territory, it seemed the Lion Clan had deliberately designed the city roads to frustrate potential invaders. Riding through the wild tangle of streets, Isami could not but feel pity for any surveyor tasked to chart such a morass.

Although Captain Kihei offered to secure them rooms at a local inn, Isami was keen to enter the castle. Trusting in the rank of her patron to secure her entrance, she presented Shinpachi's seal to the gate guards. True to his word, Kihei did not leave her side until the messengers had returned, bidding her enter the castle complex.

"May the Ancestors guide your steps, lady." Kihei's bow was echoed a moment later by his warriors.

"Your diligence is a credit to your clan," Isami replied.

"You are too kind." The broad-faced captain seemed to visibly swell at Isami's praise, cheeks reddening beneath his beard. "Should you need anything more, you have but to ask."

"I shall fondly remember the name, Akodo Kihei."

With that, the Lion wardens departed, leaving Isami and Gorobei before the castle wall. The great gates stood open, several samurai waiting to escort them inside. The sight of the Ikoma crest upon their armor gave Isami pause, but she consoled herself even as Gorobei gave a nervous mutter. Shinzō did not represent all Ikoma, nor did he stand for the clan.

At least, that was what Isami hoped.

Whispering a prayer to the Fortunes, she crossed the bridge, Gorobei a nervous presence at her back. The guard captain, an officious woman with a long scar across her forehead, took their names and escorted them through the palace grounds. Towers and outbuildings barred their path, numerous gates and guard posts arranged to provide concentric bastions if the outer walls were breached. Even the castle garden seemed cultivated to frustrate attackers, with narrow paths to allow for flanking maneuvers, stands of trees and closely planted bamboo arranged almost like ambush blinds. The stream was wide and deep, more moat than winding river, its bridges set to serve as choke points.

Although there was a simple martial beauty about the place,

Isami could not shake the oppressive feeling that followed her through the castle gates. As if any moment Shinzō might leap from behind a tree, blade in hand, calling for Isami's head.

"Lord Ikoma is reviewing recent graduates from the Sacred Watch Dojo." The guard captain spoke as if reciting from a scroll. "You may wait here, lady." She indicated a small pavilion, its screens painted with battle scenes. At Isami's acknowledgment, the woman hurried off. There were tea and refreshments waiting in the pavilion, several servants hovering in the wings.

"What do you know of Ikoma Hanbei?" Isami asked Gorobei, voice low so the servants did not overhear.

"Only that he despises bandits and rōnin." Gorobei scratched his chin. "I have taken great pains not to make his acquaintance."

They sat in silence for some time, the soft whisper of wind through bamboo a muted accompaniment to the distant clatter of weapons practice. Despite her hunger, Isami could not seem to stomach the thought of eating. The pot of tea sat untouched by her side, quickly replaced by another as it grew cold. She tried to calm her churning thoughts, but, again and again, anxieties rose through the murky babble.

Shinzō might be entering the castle even now, might have been here for days if he had ridden straight from the conflict. Any moment, she expected guards to collect her. The Lion could not simply make Isami disappear, but there were other ways of removing a threat. Gorobei was right, she had been a fool to come here, to think she could set right what Shinzō had torn asunder.

"Lady Miya!" A voice called from the path below.

Isami glanced up, startled from her thoughts.

Lord Ikoma Hanbei was a large man, wide-shouldered and

broad of chest, the swell of his belly just beginning to strain the front of his robes. Perhaps sixty years of age, he had the easy swagger of a lifelong warrior, if somewhat tempered by castle living. He wore simple robes emblazoned with the Ikoma crest, his graying hair still damp from washing. It seemed Lord Hanbei had done more than oversee the recent graduates. Many lords and ladies exercised with their samurai to keep their reflexes sharp and their waist tight.

An honor guard of four Lion samurai in full armor accompanied Hanbei. Although their weapons were sheathed and their posture more stiff than threatening, the crested helms and battle masks made for an imposing sight. With the ease of one accustomed to being surrounded by warriors, Lord Ikoma affected not to notice as they took up positions around the pavilion.

Hanbei paused at the bottom of the steps, fixing Isami with an appraising glance. For a moment, she thought he might order the guards to seize her, but the lord merely mounted the steps to kneel upon the pillow that had been prepared for him.

"My apologies for the wait." Hanbei did not bow, but such was not expected of him. Although Isami's rank required courtesy, in a Lion castle in Lion lands, Lord Ikoma's standing far outstripped the agent of a high court noble.

"Is my tea not to your liking?" He glanced at the untouched cup.

"No, lord." Isami bowed. "Urgency overwhelms my stomach."

"Well, then." He sat back, picking up his own cup. "It would be rude to keep you waiting any longer."

Isami drew in a slow breath. How much should she tell the Ikoma lord? If Shinzō's assault had been on his orders, Isami would be building her own pyre. And yet, the Lion Clan were paragons of duty, their reputation unsullied by rumor or machinations. Hanbei was one of the direct retainers of the Ikoma Anakazu, daimyo of the Ikoma family, only two steps removed from the Lion Clan Champion, Akodo Arasou himself. Isami could not believe Shinzō's conspiracy could rise so high in the ranks.

She let out her breath, swallowing her doubts. "Lord, I bring grave news concerning one of your commanders, the archivist Ikoma Shinzō."

Hanbei listened quietly as Isami described the events in Stone Willow Valley. Although she explained the deal that had been struck, she left out any mention of Kentarō's maps. Isami had met few Lion lords in her time, and all had been military commanders attached to the imperial legions. Lord Hanbei seemed cut from the same mold, and Isami wagered details about secret surveys and hidden valleys would only complicate the issue.

When she was done, Lord Ikoma leaned forward, seeming to consider her words.

"You spin quite a tale, Lady Miya." He glanced toward the guards outside the pavilion. "Just as Shinzō told me you would."

The bottom dropped from Isami's stomach as one of the guards stepped forward, stripping off his mask and helmet.

"It is as I said, my lord." Although Shinzō's tone was measured, fury glittered in the Ikoma archivist's eyes. "She is in league with the Scorpion."

# CHAPTER FOURTEEN

"We should attempt escape, mistress." Gorobei's voice was barely a whisper.

"To flee will only confirm our guilt." Isami kept her hands hidden in the folds of her kimono to hide the trembling. After being stripped of their weapons and equipment, she and Gorobei had been politely but firmly escorted to a fortified pavilion. Although it possessed all the comforts a noble of Isami's rank could expect, the heavy cedar bars upon the windows and the guards stationed at every exit made her situation very clear.

"Guilt can be expunged," Gorobei replied. "The dead stay dead."

Isami was about to reply, when Lord Ikoma swept in, Shinzō and a half-dozen other guards in tow.

"I apologize for the deception, Lady Miya." Lord Ikoma Hanbei settled onto the dais, straightening the sleeves of his kimono with a practiced flick. "But I desired that Shinzō hear your words before deciding whether to level an accusation." He glanced at the Ikoma archivist, who knelt just below the dais to his right. "Also, I wished to better grasp the situation myself.

"You must understand this puts me in a very difficult

position," Hanbei continued. "Shinzō is my personal archivist. Do I take the word of a retainer of proven loyalty and integrity over that of an emissary of the Otomo?"

"Lord, if I may explain?" Isami asked.

Hanbei gestured for her to continue.

"I was dispatched by Lord Otomo Shinpachi, that is true. But my mission was only to broker an understanding between Scorpion and Lion."

"Yet you failed to mention your connection to the Otomo upon meeting Shinzō." Hanbei's brows met like storm clouds over his deep-set, dark eyes. "Did you not claim to represent the Ministry of Cartography?"

"I am a member of the Ministry."

"But you were sent by Shinpachi."

"Lord Ikoma is correct." Isami struggled to maintain her composure. Despite the formal trappings, the meeting had the air of an inquest. "I wished only to be an impartial arbiter."

"And were you?"

"To the best of my ability, lord."

Although Shinzō remained perfectly still, the Ikoma archivist seemed a bent sapling, momentarily restrained, but ready to lash out. It was clear Shinzō believed Isami, not he, had betrayed the agreement. The realization coiled like a serpent in Isami's chest, tight inside her ribs.

Lord Ikoma seemed to notice the change in his retainer's bearing, and turned to Shinzō frowning. "You wish to contest Lady Miya's version of events?"

"With your permission, lord." Shinzō bowed.

Hanbei glanced between the two of them, then sighed. "By all means."

"You admit acting on Lord Otomo Shinpachi's orders?"

"Yes," Isami said.

"Lord Otomo is highly placed within the Imperial Treasury and an active member of the court." Shinzō looked to Lord Ikoma. "The Scorpion Clan holds many high positions in the courts, including the Imperial Advisor herself, Bayushi Kachiko. Any emissary dispatched by a member of the high court may have been unduly influenced by the Bayushi."

"I hear much supposition. What evidence do you have that my actions benefitted the Scorpion?" Isami felt comfortable replying, as Hanbei had given her leave to speak. "I seem to recall negotiating a compromise agreeable to both you and Lord Keisuke."

"You had me fooled, lady." Anger bled into Shinzō words. "I thought you bargained in good faith, but really it was all a ruse to learn the location of the Lion documents so your Bayushi ally could destroy them."

"The maps are... gone?" Isami rocked back on her heels, the smell of cedar suddenly cloying.

Her surprise seemed to take Shinzō aback. He regarded Isami for several breaths. For a moment, Isami thought her sincerity might have pierced the cloud of outrage and embarrassment that hung over Shinzō. Then, the Ikoma archivist's eyes narrowed.

"I awoke to find the chests smoldering, the documents aflame. There was nothing to be done," Shinzō continued. "Lady Miya was the only one to have access to the maps. Either she revealed their location and Bayushi Keisuke was able to slip an agent into my camp, or the lady herself–"

Lord Ikoma cleared his throat. "Accusations are like blood, impossible to recall once spilled."

Shinzō looked as if he wished to say more, but wisely remained silent.

"We tried peaceful means, but the Scorpion have never shied from attempting to manipulate such to their advantage," Hanbei said. "They mistook our words for weakness." He nodded his head. "Now, we shall show them strength."

"Lord, please." Isami bit back her plea as Hanbei's gaze hardened. She realized he would never believe her, not when Shinzō's account gave him cause to take Stone Willow by force.

"What am I to do with you, Lady Miya?" Hanbei's tone was almost regretful as he looked to Shinzō. "Or you?"

"Lord, the Scorpion may have driven me back, but their position is weak," Shinzō said.

Isami glanced away to hide her surprise. The Lion had been winning when she and Gorobei fled Stone Willow. It seemed impossible to think the few remaining Scorpion samurai had turned the tide.

"They hold the valley, but we have forces across the border. Any Scorpion reinforcements would need to come through Beiden Pass and up the river." Shinzō squared his shoulders. "With a few hundred warriors, I am confident I can drive them from Stone Willow."

"I think you have done quite enough already," Hanbei replied.

"Lord, I could not have known that Bayushi viper had more soldiers hidden in Ikemura." A note of disgust edged Shinzō's words. "Only Scorpion samurai would stoop so low as to disguise themselves as peasants."

The admission hit Isami like a physical weight. No wonder Keisuke had been so confident. He had fooled her too. Isami had spent a morning in Ikemura and sensed nothing amiss. It was unsettling to think some of the peasants who had fawned over her might have been Scorpion warriors. Isami had been confused by the train of people coming from Ikemura as she and Gorobei fled, now she understood they had been warriors hurrying to battle.

"There were one hundred samurai under your command. Only forty returned," Hanbei said. "You failed to secure Stone Willow Valley. Worse, you saw the Lion's only claim on the land turned to ash. The Ikoma are, first and foremost, keepers of the Imperial Histories. No matter the outcome of this conflict, your failure to protect the records has cost our family greatly."

Shinzō pressed his forehead to the floor. "Lord, please take my life in recompense."

"I already have your life." Hanbei rose to stare down at the archivist.

Shinzō offered no reply, only trembled before the disapproving gaze of his lord. There was nothing he could say. Hanbei had as much as cast the archivist from the Ikoma. If Shinzō retained any standing within the family, it would be as an object of pity, an abject lesson to others who might flag in their duty.

Isami had spent days ruminating on Shinzō's betrayal, imagining all the ways she would castigate the traitorous archivist. Now, seeing all her vengeful hopes come to fruition, Isami felt an uncomfortable kinship with Shinzō.

"It seems I must see to this matter myself," Hanbei said. "Lord Akodo has absented himself so as to not give the appearance of open war. But I assure you, there will be a reckoning."

Hanbei turned to Isami. Although his expression remained studiously neutral, the look in his eyes was of a man discovering a day-old corpse on his doorstep.

"There is no evidence linking you to the Scorpion." Turning his back on Isami, Hanbei flicked his fingers in the direction of the main gate. "You are free to leave. But know that I will not forget your part in the destruction of our records. Whatever Lord Otomo promised you, I hope it is worth the cost."

Lord Ikoma strode from the chamber, head high, back stiff.

Isami turned to see Shinzō staring at her. Although propriety forbade them from exchanging words, Isami could almost feel the disgraced archivist's hate, hot as if she stood but a few feet from a bonfire.

Ikoma guards took up position to either side of Isami and Gorobei. It was all Isami could do to keep her legs steady as she rose. She walked from the pavilion, Shinzō's glare like an arrow aimed at her back.

Their possessions were waiting for them at the castle gate, along with provisions and fresh horses.

"Lord Ikoma bids you a speedy return to the capital, Lady Miya." Although the guard's tone was respectful, his words dripped with unstated threat.

They rode from the city as if a horde of oni dogged their steps. Isami had no doubt Hanbei would be true to his word, but deemed it unwise to test the resolve of the Lion Clan. She did not call a halt until the last tower of Sacred Watch Palace had slipped behind the gentle curve of the horizon. Although Isami could not deny her relief at escaping the jaws of the lion, it was tempered by cold certainty.

Shinzō had believed every word he spoke, Isami was sure of it. Which meant Keisuke had somehow used them both.

Isami dismounted near a roadside shrine to the Fortune of Mercy. Little more than a small hut containing a rough wooden carving, it was well kept, with a small pot for burning incense, and a plate on which sat various offerings of fruit and grain. The shrine was situated near a crossroads, the larger traveling east toward Otosan Uchi, the smaller wending south to disappear amidst the low hills ringing the plain.

"I thought he would have our heads for sure, mistress." Gorobei reined up beside her, face flushed from the ride. "Still, it will be nice to return to the capital."

"We are not returning to the capital." Isami glanced back down the road to Sacred Watch Palace, empty but for a few peasants leading an ox-drawn cart and a single mounted messenger in Lion colors. Isami regarded the messenger, but the man seemed intent on the road, spear held high and unthreatening. It seemed Lord Ikoma had not deigned to follow up on his threat by sending a patrol to shepherd them from Lion lands.

Gorobei dismounted. Gathering up both horses' reins, he tied them to a nearby tree before coming to kneel next to Isami.

"You have done all you could, mistress." He watched as she offered incense before the tiny altar. "Not even Lord Otomo could fault your dedication."

"How many will die when the Lion seek to claim Stone Willow Valley by force?" she asked. "Will this lead to war?"

Gorobei glanced away, then back. "That is only for the gods to know."

"I cannot walk away, not when I am the cause."

"If anything, it was Bayushi Keisuke's ambition that set this pyre alight," Gorobei stated.

"And shall *he* be allowed to benefit?" Isami replied. She could never settle accounts with Kazuya, but she could deal with Keisuke. "The Scorpion archives."

"Mistress?"

"He said the Scorpion also retained records related to Stone Willow Valley," Isami replied. "We will find them. We will show them to the Lion Clan."

"But how can you know what they contain, mistress?"

"If they were written by Lord Kentarō, then I know." Isami looked to her bodyguard. Gorobei's hair had pulled loose from its queue to hang around his head, his chin and cheeks rough from days without a shave, but in his eyes, she saw only concern.

Isami drew in a deep breath. If she could not tell her bodyguard, the man who had saved her life, who could she tell?

"There is a secret valley." She glanced to her hands, suddenly nervous. "At least, I believe there is."

Gorobei frowned, eyes narrowing as he considered Isami's words. "And how do you know this, mistress?"

Isami told him.

Gorobei remained quiet for some time after Isami had finished, his expression unreadable. Silence stretched between them, broken only by the plaintive lowing of oxen and the thud of the messenger's hooves upon the packed earth of the road.

Isami sat, discomfited by Gorobei's stillness, but unwilling to say anything further lest the former rōnin think she was mad.

"I believe you." He spoke at last, his words measured. "If such a record exists, then we must retrieve it. The promise of new lands may bring the clans back to the table."

It would not be proper for Isami to show the relief she felt, even to Gorobei. Yet she could not restrain herself from reaching out to clasp his arm.

The former rōnin cocked his head, confused.

"Thank you for believing in me." Isami blinked back tears,

heart seeming to pound with the messenger's hooves as he cantered past them.

"Truth does not require belief," Gorobei replied with a bow. "It only requires–"

The butt of the messenger's spear hammered into Gorobei's temple, dropping the former rōnin like a felled tree.

Isami surged to her feet, already unwinding her surveyor's chain even as the Lion samurai wheeled for another pass. There, in the quick breath between lightning and thunder, she recognized the rider.

"You may have deceived my lord." Ikoma Shinzō leveled his spear. "But you shall not escape justice."

# CHAPTER FIFTEEN

"You are making a mistake!" Isami shouted, as Shinzō kicked his horse into a gallop.

Standing in the road, Isami watched him come, her fear receding like a morning tide as instinct took over. She had trained for this, her teacher at the Miya Dojo running through a thousand, thousand different permutations. Isami had practiced against swords, spears, naginatas, even clubs, her opponents both mounted and unmounted.

The Lion were famed warriors. Isami was sure even their archivists received instruction in martial matters. Even so, she would bet her spyglass Shinzō had never trained against a surveyor's chain.

At the last moment, Isami spun away from the spear thrust. Knowing Shinzō would expect such a maneuver, she dropped low as the Ikoma archivist shifted his aim. The spear tip hissed through the air, close enough for her to feel the wind of its passing on the back of her neck.

Isami twisted, flinging one end of her chain up to loop around the spear haft. The weighted end wrapped around twice before binding fast. Isami braced herself, dragging the spear tip down so it buried in the ground.

With the spear couched for a charge, Shinzō could not release the weapon quick enough. The haft flexed and snapped, catapulting the archivist from his saddle. Unable to halt his fall, Shinzō had the presence of mind to tuck his shoulder as he hit the hard-packed earth of the road. The move turned what would have been a potentially fatal impact into a bone-jarring roll.

Isami hastened to unwrap her chain from the spear haft, but the weighted end had become tangled. Apart from a small dagger it was her only weapon, and she had little inclination to face a raging Lion samurai bare-handed.

With an inarticulate shout, Shinzō pushed to his feet, clawing at the hilt of his sword. He was already charging before the blade hissed free of its scabbard, footsteps loud in Isami's ears as she finally worked her chain from the broken haft.

There was little time for finesse. Blindly, Isami lashed out with her chain, the links catching Shinzō's sword just above the hilt. Unfortunately, the blade was close to the archivist's body, and instead of wrapping about the sword, the weighted end hammered into Shinzō's shoulder, sending him stumbling to the side.

Isami lashed out with the chain's other end, bringing the weight around to crash into Shinzō's helmet. Although the blow sent the archivist staggering back, he swung his sword in a tight arc. Isami was forced to throw herself back to avoid the slash, unable to do more than gather up her chain.

"I am not working with the Scorpion," she said, as Shinzō regained his balance. "I mourn the loss of Kentarō's maps as much as you."

"Lies!" The archivist came on again with a heavy overhand chop.

Isami swatted the blade away with her chain, but Shinzō drew back before she could properly entangle the sword. As the archivist circled, Isami tried another tack.

"Assume you are right, assume I am a Scorpion agent." She spread her arms, letting both ends of the chain hang low, ready to strike. "Why would I go to all the trouble of negotiating a compromise *after* I had reviewed your documents."

"To lull me into complacency so Keisuke could destroy the records." Shinzō's words came almost as a snarl. "I trusted you!"

He came again, feinting high with his blade, then kicking out as Isami swung her chain to deflect the blow. Shinzō's boot caught her just below the knee.

Her shin throbbing, barely able to keep her balance, Isami whipped the other weight directly at Shinzō's face. As she had hoped, the archivist raised his blade to block, and Isami drew back on the chain, checking the blow even as she swung the other end around to deliver a punishing strike to Shinzō's thigh.

With a pained shout, the archivist disengaged, and the two of them limped back, eyeing each other warily.

"I saw your work," Isami said. "Genealogy, history – it was astounding. You unearthed a viable claim from centuries-old records."

"And then I handed it to the Scorpion," Shinzō replied.

"I, too, thought Keisuke bargained in good faith." Isami fought to keep the desperation from her voice. "He tricked us both."

"Perhaps." Shinzō raised his sword. "Perhaps not."

Instead of cutting for Isami's body, he aimed a quick slash at her wrist. Isami snatched her arm back, too slow, the edge of

Shinzō's blade striking the back of her hand. Had the chain not been wrapped around her clenched fist, the blow would have almost certainly taken off Isami's fingers. Instead, it wrenched her arm painfully down, scoring a bloody red line just above her thumb.

Acting on pure reflex, she swung the other end of the chain around as Shinzō drew back for another cut. It caught around the midpoint of the blade, weighted end wrapping several times around the sword. With an injured hand, there was no way Isami could pull the blade from Shinzō's two-fisted grip.

She threw herself back, using her body weight to drag the blade from Shinzō's hands. The archivist's shout became an outraged scream as his blade rattled down amidst the stones lining the roadside.

"It doesn't have to be like this," Isami said between panting breaths. "We can work together, have our revenge against Keisuke."

"I cannot reach Keisuke." Blood speckled Shinzō's teeth, fury lending his face an almost feral aspect.

"But I can," Isami said. "I still bear Lord Otomo's seal. I still speak with his voice."

"Keisuke would simply deny everything." Shinzō drew his dagger. "There is no evidence, not without the records."

"Even so, we could prevent more bloodshed," Isami replied. "There is still a way to press the Lion claim to Stone Willow Valley."

"But Kentarō's records are gone."

"Not all of them." Isami took a step back, both to put more distance between them and to seem less a threat. "Keisuke spoke of more in Journey's End City."

"The City of Lies?" Shinzō gave a dogged shake of his head. "The Scorpion would never give us access."

"Until Lord Otomo revokes his seal, I remain an emissary of the imperial court," Isami said. "Even the Scorpion cannot refuse a direct request."

Shinzō's dagger wavered.

The moment balanced upon a knife's edge. Isami had the advantage over Shinzō, but defeating the Lion samurai would earn her nothing.

Steadying herself, Isami lowered her chain. "If you wish to kill me, do it. But know that with me dies your last chance at redemption."

Shinzō took a step forward, then hesitated. Although his dagger remained pointed at Isami's throat, the anger bled from the archivist's face, his expression reminding Isami of the desperate terror of a fox finally run to ground.

With a groan, Shinzō let the dagger drop. Abruptly, he turned and stalked several paces away before falling to his knees, face buried in his hands.

Isami recognized the archivist's grief as the same species of mad sorrow that had afflicted her after Kazuya burned her maps. Seeing such unfeigned regret, the last of Isami's doubts about the archivist drifted away like smoke upon the breeze.

With the immediate threat passed, she turned away. Wrapping her chain back about her waist, Isami ran to kneel beside Gorobei. The former rōnin lay on his side, right eye swollen, his face covered in blood, an ugly bruise along his cheek and temple testament to the accuracy of Shinzō's strike. Isami knelt to gently roll him over, a hand supporting his injured head. She was relieved to see Gorobei still breathed, even more so when he let out a soft moan, his eyelids flickering.

A shadow fell across them.

Isami glanced back to see Shinzō standing a pace away. He had retrieved his blade and returned it to its sheath. The fear and anger was gone from the archivist's face, replaced by an expression Isami couldn't parse.

"Is he well?"

"That remains to be seen," Isami replied.

Shinzō took a quick step forward. Kneeling to be on Isami's level, he held out a stoppered gourd.

"Water. To clean the wound."

Trying not to flinch at the Lion samurai's nearness, Isami took the proffered gourd. She turned to root around in her satchel, eventually finding the rag she used to clean her instruments. It was far from pristine, but better than blood and road dirt.

"I did not aim to kill." Shinzō looked at his hands as if seeing them for the first time. "But I had never swung a weapon in earnest until a week ago."

"Nor I." Isami did her best to rinse away the worst of the blood. As much of their time was spent away from civilization, apprentice cartographers were required to study basic healing. Fortunately, the cut was small, and already beginning to scab over. Wadded fabric bound with a bit of measuring cord was enough to stop the bleeding, although she did not envy Gorobei the headache he would have upon waking.

"Drills, techniques, practice duels – none of it is quite like the real thing." Shinzō clucked his tongue as if admonishing a small child. "When I woke and found the records gone, all I could hear was blood, all I could see were blades. More than reputation, my life was in those documents. What am I without them?"

Isami looked to the east as if to conjure the image of Otosan Uchi. She wanted to say something, but everything that came to mind seemed trite or insulting. What would she have wanted to hear after having her work stolen, her life destroyed?

She closed her eyes, heartbeat slowly returning to normal. "At the Ministry, I had a friend named Kazuya… at least I thought he was my friend."

It seemed the height of madness for Isami to unburden herself to someone who, mere moments ago, had been intent on killing her. And yet, there was a strange similarity between her and Shinzō's situations. Isami half expected the archivist to be irritated by her tale – that, or amused. Shinzō only listened quietly as Isami recounted the events surrounding Kazuya's theft of her research.

There wasn't much to tell. Isami's confession felt a pitiful thing when weighed against the events of the past few days. Like a beaten dog, she searched for any sign of anger in Shinzō's face, but the Ikoma archivist's expression remained somber, almost thoughtful.

"If you truly are a Scorpion agent, they should treasure you like precious jade."

Isami cocked her head. "I am not sure if you meant that as an insult or a compliment."

"Nor am I."

A moan from Gorobei cut their conversation short.

"Mistress, your arm." His words were slow, but clear.

Isami glanced down to see the hem of her sleeve black with blood from her injured hand.

"It is nothing." She drew her sleeve down to conceal the wound.

"Still, I would see to it." Gorobei pushed up, but Isami laid a hand on his chest.

"Later. For the moment, I would make sure you have suffered no lasting injury."

"What hit me?" Gorobei asked. "It feels like some drunken ogre bounced a stone off my head."

"Shinzō followed us," Isami replied. "But do not worry, I have seen to him."

Gorobei fixed her with his good eye. "If you have slain a samurai in Lion lands, we are in great danger."

"I am far from dead," Shinzō said.

Gorobei scrambled back, hand dropping to his sword hilt.

"There is nothing to fear." Isami caught his arm. "He will be accompanying us to Journey's End City."

Gorobei looked between the two of them, astonishment plain on his battered face.

"For the moment, our goals are the same," Shinzō spoke as if measuring every word. "Know that should I discover you have played me false, not even the elemental spirits themselves could shield you from my retribution."

"It is not my place to know the will of the founding deities." Gorobei shook off Isami's hand to push unsteadily to his feet. "But I have seen you fight, Ikoma. You may want to spend a few more years in the dojo before threatening my charge."

Shinzō stood, color rising to his cheeks. "Seems I know enough to set you on your back, old man."

Isami rose, intending to step between the two, when Gorobei gave a loud laugh.

"I like this one, mistress. I'll have to keep an eye on him." He gestured toward the swollen side of his face. "Two when this heals up."

Shinzō seemed taken aback by the former rōnin's sudden good

humor. For the first time since Isami had met the archivist, she saw a crack in Shinzō's expression; not a smile, but something less than his perennial scowl.

Isami hated to cut the moment short, but every hour that passed brought the Lion and Scorpion Clans closer to open conflict.

"Are you well enough to ride?" she asked Gorobei.

"I've traveled with far worse than this." He grinned.

"Give me a moment to collect my mount." With a nod, Shinzō jogged after his horse, which, after a brief run, was cropping grass in a field a little way from the road.

Gorobei gingerly touched the bruise on his head, winced, and then gave a little chuckle.

"Didn't expect that."

"Neither of us did."

"Still." He nodded at the broken spear, the jumbled footprints across the road. "You seemed to have handled yourself well, mistress. Perhaps I should spend more time unconscious."

Isami laughed despite herself. Embarrassed by the unexpected outburst, she covered her mouth.

Gorobei developed a sudden and intense interest in the roadside shrine, turning away until Isami could collect herself.

"I much prefer you awake and aware," she continued as if nothing had occurred, glancing at Shinzō. "More so now than ever."

Gorobei gave a deep, if somewhat shaky, bow. "Then I shall never sleep again, mistress."

"Do you find something amusing?" Shinzō joined them, his tone wary.

Isami's smile flickered, but Gorobei was quick to breach the awkward silence.

"I was merely regaling Lady Miya with the tale of another time I almost had my skull caved in." Gorobei moved to untie the horses. Handing over Isami's reins with a respectful nod, he turned back to Shinzō. "You are scholar of history. Come, I shall tell you all about it."

The archivist gave Gorobei a suspicious look, but said nothing as they mounted up and turned their horses south toward Beiden Pass and Scorpion lands.

Isami sat back as Gorobei chattered away, not quite believing she had survived the encounter with Shinzō, let alone made an ally of the archivist. She tried to gather some of the confidence with which she had convinced Shinzō to join them, but despite Isami's bold promises, gaining access to the Scorpion archives at Journey's End City would be difficult, if not impossible.

She glanced toward the high road leading back to Otosan Uchi, drawing conviction from her memories of the place. There was nothing for Isami in the capital. Her only choice was to ride forward. And yet, she could not help but feel as a sailor caught in a storm, hands tight on a rigging rope, unsure if it would snap and send her tumbling into the angry sea.

Looking to the road ahead, Isami kicked her horse into a canter.

Whether the rope held or broke, she resolved to hold on until the end.

# CHAPTER SIXTEEN

A cool breeze rolled off the mountains, laden with the promise of autumn. In a few days, perhaps a week, it would begin to grow chill, clouds gathering like herds of oxen, ponderous and heavy. Then would come the stampede – a monsoon, wind and slashing rain. They would just be putting up storm shutters back at the capital, trading out light summer screens for heavier winter ones. Idly, Isami wondered if the rains would reach this far inland.

She, Gorobei, and Shinzō had followed a small trade road around the edge of the Venerable Plain. This far into the Lion heartland, attempting to avoid the guards would draw attention. Had Isami and Gorobei been traveling alone, this would have led to uncomfortable questions, but a few words from Shinzō proved enough to allay suspicions. It helped that the archivist was still attired as a Lion messenger.

Isami shed her Ministry background like a sodden cloak, passing herself off as a Miya herald returning from a mission to the north. Of course, it was a crime to impersonate an imperial envoy, but Isami had learned much from watching her parents during their infrequent visits to Otosan Uchi. If the occasional trickle of guilt worked its way through the cracks in her resolve, it was easily quashed. The lie was in service to preventing conflict between Lion and Scorpion.

Like tributaries flowing to a mighty river, the road gradually curved south, linking up with the wide Merchants' Road that bridged Lion and Crane lands. Several other routes branched from the crossroads. Mostly minor trade roads like the one Isami and the others had been following, they spread across the countryside like the roots of a vast tree, carrying goods from field and village to city and castle town. Within a few weeks, they would flow with peasants bringing the autumn harvest to market.

"We should take the Merchants' Road." They were the first words Shinzō had spoken in hours. Although the Ikoma archivist rode with them, he had made no secret of his continued suspicion, refusing to share meals and maintaining a careful distance from Isami and Gorobei over the last few days.

"The Merchants' Road would add a week to our journey," Isami said.

"Better than ending it prematurely." Shinzō regarded the distant mountains as if an army of hostile warriors crouched amidst the foothills. "The River Road would take us along Stone Willow Valley, right into Scorpion hands."

Isami glanced toward the road, twin anxieties warring within her breast. The remaining Scorpion warriors were a danger, but one eclipsed by her concern Lord Otomo might hear of Isami's failure and rescind his support. Without the threat of courtly censure, Isami would lose what little credibility she had. Word traveled surprisingly quickly in Rokugan, especially important news which could be sent at the speed of gusting wind by priests skilled in entreating spirits of air to bear their missives. If news of Lord Otomo's displeasure reached the Scorpion before Isami did, all she was likely to find waiting in Journey's End City would be a swift escort back to the capital. But she could not tell Shinzō that.

Reaching a decision, Isami tried a different tack. "You said Keisuke's force was small."

"Perhaps three hundred warriors." Shinzō frowned. "I did not have time to count."

"Hardly enough to patrol the entire valley," Isami said. "And his attentions are likely to be on the approaching Lion soldiers."

Shinzō glanced away, jaw tight.

"What say you, Gorobei?"

"I go where you go, mistress." The former rōnin shrugged. "If the Lion forces are already marshaling, it seems as if time is our enemy."

Shinzō gave an irritated grunt. "*Everything* is our enemy."

"We'll skirt the valley, avoid the main roads," Isami said. "My map is yet unfinished, but with it and the imperial survey, I think we can stay clear of trouble."

Shinzō fixed her with an appraising look.

"I trusted your scholarship," Isami said. "Now trust mine."

With a flick of his reins, Shinzō started down the River Road.

"I guess that settles it." Gorobei gave an amused tilt of his head. "Lion samurai – hard as swords and twice as sharp. Now you know why I did my best to avoid them."

As Shinzō was still in earshot, Isami chose not to dignify the former rōnin's remark with a response, although she agreed with him. She turned her own mount to follow the Ikoma archivist. A moment later, she heard the thud of Gorobei's hooves on the road behind her. If he had any other comments, he wisely chose to keep them to himself.

True to its name, the River Road ran alongside Three Sides River. One of the largest waterways in Rokugan, it flowed south from the City of the Rich Frog, girding both Lion and Scorpion lands before curving down toward the Esteemed Palaces of the Crane. Its position between the territory of three great clans had made Three Sides River and its surrounds the site of many skirmishes over the centuries, the most recent being the one Isami had hoped to prevent.

Several hours of hard travel found them overlooking Stone Willow Valley and the mountains beyond. Isami was relieved to find the thin curls of smoke rising from the dale produced by cookfires rather than burning houses. Peasants worked the terraced fields cut into the eastern hillside, sickles flashing in the late afternoon light as they cut and bundled sheaves of rice for drying.

Of the Scorpion soldiers, there was no sign. But based on Shinzō's recounting of the battle, Isami hadn't expected to see any. She cast an eye to the villages as they rounded the valley ridge, careful to keep to the tree line lest any of the peasants be Scorpion agents in disguise.

"It seems the Lion have yet to arrive," Gorobei said.

"Lord Hanbei is a vigilant and methodical commander," Shinzō replied. "When the Lion move, it will be with overwhelming force. We must remain watchful as it is certain he sent scouting parties ahead of the main army."

They dismounted behind the cover of a stand of spreading pine, Shinzō keeping careful lookout while Gorobei watered the horses at a small brook that flowed from higher in the hills. Isami consulted her surveys, little more than a crisscross of footpaths marked with the occasional notation of distance and direction. Without time to properly survey, she had been forced to work by sighting the position of the sun and stars as she and Gorobei had fled north.

"The Scorpion forces are likely concentrated near the northern edge of the valley to block the Lion's approach," she said, as Shinzō moved over to regard the maps.

"It's what I would do." The Ikoma archivist gave a terse nod. "But Keisuke seemed more courtier than general."

"He had enough knowledge of strategy to conceal soldiers in Ikemura," Isami replied.

Shinzō's lips gave a sour twitch, but he nodded in acknowledgment. "It depends on whether he expects reinforcements from the south."

"They would have to come upriver." Isami traced the twisting blue ribbon with one finger. "Days, perhaps weeks."

"Lord Hanbei won't be able to move so many soldiers through rough terrain." Shinzō thrust his chin at the arc of hills that curled north of the valley. "Keisuke will need to hold the lowlands around the river mouth."

"Then we must avoid the villages and keep to the hills as much as possible."

Shinzō grunted his approval of the plan. Isami had barely enough time to massage some feeling back into her aching thighs before Gorobei returned. They ate on the move –vegetables, stale rice, and a few scraps of dried fish. When the ground was level enough, they rode, but otherwise walked, both to conserve the horses' strength and spare the animals from potential injury on the rocky hillside.

Night found them following a footpath that twisted among the wooded foothills. Little more than the occasional patch of grass or barren rock, it seemed barely a trail at all, but between Isami's compass and Gorobei's woodlore, they were able to keep a steady pace.

Despite not seeing another soul for hours, they decided to go without a fire. Even with the early autumn chill, the night was still warm enough. Although Isami begrudged another cold meal, she ate without complaint, spreading her blankets upon a carpet of pine needles to make a soft, albeit prickly, bed.

Gorobei rolled himself in his cloak, and a moment later was snoring softly. Of all the former rōnin's skills, this was perhaps the one Isami most envied. The assorted aches and bruises conjured by weeks on the road seemed to have made a home in her. No sooner had Isami found what seemed a good position, than a new pain would set her shifting again. She looked over to see how Shinzō was faring.

The archivist sat on a coil of exposed roots, lips tight as he worked the straps of his breastplate. Although the messenger armor was far lighter than the heavy kit he had worn for the battle, the Ikoma archivist still seemed to be having trouble removing it.

"Would you like some help?"

Shinzō glanced over, his expression seeming almost nervous in the pallid moonlight. "I am quite capable."

Isami laid back, frowning as the archivist continued to struggle with his armor. After another long minute, she sighed and stood.

"The back straps are the hardest." Moving over, she began to work at one of the knots. "My parents had stories about trying to remove messenger armor in a hurry."

Shinzō flinched at Isami's touch, standing.

"Either I help you or we both lose sleep," Isami said.

Grudgingly, the archivist turned so she could loosen the armor. In a few moments, Shinzō slipped free of the breastplate.

"Thank you." He gave a quick nod. "Although I wore armor on occasion back at the Archives, there was never any call to ride for days in it."

"Gorobei said I would get used to the trail." Isami gave a wry tilt of her head. "He has been wrong about other things too."

Although Shinzō's expression did not so much as flicker, Isami could notice a change in the archivist's bearing. His posture seemed somehow less stiff as he sat upon the ground, working at something within his kimono.

Isami turned away to give Shinzō some privacy, but could not help but glance down as the archivist unwove a wide strip of cloth from around his chest. Having grown up in Otosan Uchi, with its many pools and bath houses, Isami was no stranger to nudity, but the sight of Shinzō's discarded binder still brought a blush of heat to her cheeks.

The Ikoma archivist sat back with a low sigh. When Isami looked back, he had folded the cloth and replaced his kimono.

"Is it difficult?" Isami nodded at the long, folded cloth, then glanced away. It was rude to inquire about such things, but the question had just slipped out.

Shinzō massaged his ribs, wincing. "Sometimes."

"There are some nobles who are like you, but I have not had opportunity to meet them." Isami swallowed, forging ahead. "What is it like?"

"I am what I have always been," Shinzō replied. "Unlike you, the world requires I prove it."

"I am sorry. I meant no insult."

"I am not offended." Shinzō took a slow breath, letting his chest expand. "The Lion cares only that I fulfill my duties to family and clan. No one has called me any other name for a long time, but there are sometimes challenges."

"Like Stone Willow Valley?"

Shinzō leaned back, resting his head against the side of a partially exposed boulder. "That was to be my capstone. The deed that would bear me into the clan's higher ranks – a good marriage, lesser nobles clamoring for me to adopt their children." He gave a sharp laugh. "I told Lord Ikoma I could win it all back without a sword being drawn."

"You nearly did," Isami said softly.

"Nearly counts for nothing." Shinzō turned away.

Isami wanted to say something more, but the moment had passed. Whatever closeness dwelt in that tiny span had fled, carried away like ash on the breeze. Dully, she lay back down upon her blankets, sure that sleep would be a long time coming.

In that, she was wrong.

# CHAPTER SEVENTEEN

The buzz of flies was Isami's first warning something was amiss. A moment later, the wind shifted, carrying the charnel reek of corpses. Isami pressed a hand to her nose, peering into the bushes ahead. They had been picking their way down a wooded switchback, moving slowly lest they dislodge any stones or dirt and thus betray their movements to any who might be watching.

Gorobei saw them first. The former rōnin dropped into a crouch, blade hissing from its scabbard as he scanned the surrounding brush.

Four bodies sprawled in a gulley farther down the hill, limbs splayed as if they had fallen from a great height. Their armor was bare of all ornamentation, the color of their kimonos indistinguishable beneath a thick layer of mud and dried blood. Arrows riddled their bodies, their limbs cut and battered, helmets beaten almost shapeless by heavy, punishing blows.

Isami pressed a hand to her mouth, breathing deep to quell the flutter in her stomach as the true cost of the coming conflict settled on her. She didn't recognize the dead for Lion samurai until Shinzō gave a strangled cry. The Ikoma archivist started forward, but Gorobei raised his blade to bar the way.

"Move aside." Cold fury rimed Shinzō's words.

"Are you in such a hurry to join them?" Gorobei thrust his chin at the path ahead.

Isami followed his gaze. At first, she saw nothing amiss with the thin trail. Gradually, as her eyes focused, she saw the thin cord stretched across the path.

"That would set you quite a tumble," Gorobei said. "And if the fall didn't snap your neck, the stones our Scorpion friends piled up there would finish the job." He nodded to the rocky cliff that rose above the valley.

Shielding her eyes from the afternoon glare, Isami saw a small heap of boulders balanced precariously upon the summit. Restrained by little more than a few twists of rope, it would take little to send them plummeting down to crush the bones of any who had the misfortune to be below.

"How did you know?" she asked.

With a rueful shake of his head, Gorobei stood. "Because it is exactly what I would have done."

"You would murder passersby with trickery?" Shinzō asked.

Gorobei shrugged. "It's far safer than blades."

"Cowards." Shinzō's hands made tight fists at his side, his back straight as a banner pole. "They didn't even burn the bodies."

"'Entice the enemy with falsehoods, turn their strength to weakness'," Isami recited. "'Blind death is swift death. A fire may ravage the land, but it cannot touch the wind.'"

Shinzō turned on her. "You would quote Akodo at me? Having seen this?" He flicked an angry hand at the pile of bodies. "Are we meant to simply move on?"

"What would you have me do?" Isami felt the Ikoma archivist's pain, sharp like a fresh wound, but she could spare no time for the dead, not when the living needed her far more.

"You still bear Lord Otomo's seal. Use it," Shinzō said. "There are imperial messenger posts on the Merchants' Road. Write a missive castigating the Scorpion for destroying the documents and slaughtering Lion scouts."

"We have no proof it was Keisuke who burned the maps." Isami spoke into the mounting storm of Shinzō's anger. She was trying to stop a war, not set the valley aflame. "Until the matter is resolved, this remains Scorpion land. They have a right to defend it."

"I cannot believe you would take that snake Keisuke's side in this."

"You overstep, Ikoma." Isami drew herself up, steady gaze belying the hammering of her heart. "I serve the Empire, not the clans."

For a moment, she thought Shinzō would strike her. Gorobei edged forward, blade at the ready.

"Did you imagine the Scorpion would simply concede the fight?" Isami continued, emboldened by Gorobei's solid presence at her side. She knew it was dangerous to antagonize Shinzō, but these were truths the archivist needed to hear. "Do not forget it was you who drew the first blood."

"Of that, I am painfully aware, Lady Miya." The coolness in Shinzō's tone robbed the title of all respect. His gaze flicked between Isami and Gorobei, as if the archivist were judging his chances. Then, with a disgusted grunt, he turned away.

"It saddens me to see any dead," Isami softened her tone. "But the conflict has grown beyond our ability to stop it. Our only chance lies in Journey's End City."

Shinzō looked down the hillside, shoulders rounding as he regarded the bodies of his fallen comrades. "Can we build them a pyre, at least?"

"Smoke would bring the Scorpion running," Gorobei said.

"We must consider the living before the dead. There is not the time to burn your comrades." Isami knelt to pick up a fist-sized stone. "But perhaps we can bury them."

With a grunt of effort, she pitched the rock downhill. It was an ugly throw, but the cliff was hard to miss. The stone struck just below the summit, unleashing a deluge of boulders and gravel. It was hardly a cairn as had been erected in the ancient days, but the pile of fallen stone would be sufficient to keep predators away.

"That was unwise, mistress," Gorobei said.

"Unwise, but necessary." With a nod to Shinzō, Isami unrolled her map, marking the site with a small circle. "Whoever rules Stone Willow Valley, I shall see they provide these warriors with a proper pyre."

Although the Ikoma archivist returned a stiff bow, his gaze never wavered from the cairn of stones. Isami could well understand the burden of responsibility that weighed upon Shinzō, for it had settled firmly upon her shoulders as well. Had she simply been more dedicated, more clever, more calculating, perhaps none of this would have happened.

"We should leave before the Scorpion investigate the noise," Gorobei said.

They hurried through the narrow ravine, picking their way past the makeshift cairn to where the path joined another switchback that led over the hill. The trees had thinned enough that Isami could see the sky. It stretched overhead, delicate as a woodcut print, thin streamers of cloud swirling against a backdrop the bruised blue of a sullen sea. The setting sun drew long shadows upon the ground, jagged peaks stark against the muddy browns and grays. Three Sides River wound along the foot of the mountains like a ribbon of spilled ink, its banks crowded with the flinty-barked willows from which the valley took its name.

Isami was struck with a deep and abiding urge to set the scene upon paper; not so much a map as an artist's rendering. But she had neither the skills of Master Kageyasu nor the eye of Master Naotora. For Isami, beauty lay in lines and vertices, perfect angles shepherded by the careful interplay of measure and calculation. And yet, for a moment, she understood what Kageyasu saw, maps rendered not as guides or surveys, but objects of wonder, tales of faraway places to be admired and enjoyed.

So lost was Isami in her contemplation of the valley, that she hardly noticed as an arrow flicked across her vision to rattle down amidst the rocks. It was only when her horse shied away from the sudden noise that Isami glanced up, dragging back on her reins as another arrow slashed down from above.

"They're on the boulders above us!" Gorobei turned his horse.

With a shout, Shinzō drew his sword, wheeling his horse as if to charge up the hill, but it took only a glance to see the gravel was far too loose.

"Back to the rocks!" Isami tried desperately to turn her panicked mount as more arrows rained down, but the path was too narrow. One of them sank into the poor beast's flank, and it kicked out, eyes rolling white as it lurched into a panicked gallop.

"Mistress, leap clear!" Gorobei cried.

Isami tried to jump from her horse, but her hands had become tangled in the reins. Although she tried to pull up, the horse only dragged her forward with a pained whinny, hurtling down the rocky path at a breakneck pace.

Back up the trail, Gorobei shouted something, but Isami was unable to make out his words over the clatter of hooves upon stone. She could hear Shinzō as well, unleashing a torrent of raging invectives upon the archers.

Isami tried to glance back, and almost pitched from the saddle as the horse skidded on the loose scree. Her riding skills were put to the test as her mount slid down the embankment in a shower of dirt and gravel. By the Ancestors' grace, somehow Isami managed to keep her seat, leaning low over the neck of her maddened steed as the ground leveled out. After what seemed a terrible eternity, Isami was at last able to coax her horse to a trembling halt.

They stood in a low canyon, sheer walls to either side. Distant shouts echoed from the walls, accompanied by the rattle of hooves, but such had been the directionless speed of her horse's flight that Isami did not know in which route her comrades lay. She drew forth Tadataka's compass from her saddle. Consulting her map and the imperial survey, she was able to get a rough bearing.

Anxiety worked cold fingers between Isami's ribs. There was no sign of the path. Wandering blindly, Isami was as likely to run into Scorpion archers as her comrades. She needed to find a higher vantage point, where Isami's spyglass would offer at least some vantage over her pursuers.

First, she needed to see to her horse.

The arrow had grazed the beast's flank, the wound bloody but shallow. Fortunately, the head was not barbed, so drawing the shaft forth presented less trouble. Standing to the side lest the beast kick or bolt, Isami made soothing sounds as she applied water and some crushed herbs to the wound. Although the horse moved without a limp, she thought it best to walk the beast.

Nightfall found Isami picking her way across a field of fallen boulders. She had moved steadily uphill, but the way was treacherous. It was as if the foothills had simply swallowed her companions and the Scorpion samurai, leaving not the slightest trace of their passing.

Although darkness closed in around her, Isami was loath to light her lantern. When her fourth stumble on loose rock almost resulted in a twisted ankle, she was forced to admit it would be best to find somewhere to wait for morning. Isami had begun ruefully casting about for some marginally comfortable spot when a familiar voice brought her up short.

"Lady Isami." Keisuke rose from behind a nearby outcrop. "It has been far too long."

The Scorpion courtier's eyes were red-rimmed in the lantern light, shaded by dark hollows that gave his face an almost skull-like aspect. Unshaved stubble shadowed the skin around Keisuke's dusty mask, his hair plastered to his head with sweat. He carried a lantern in one hand, helm nestled in the crook of the other. Although there was a sword and dagger belted at his waist, Isami did not give him opportunity to draw them.

She twisted, unwinding a length of chain, weighted ends dangling loose from her clenched fists. The chain was meant to be a weapon of self-defense, but with enough momentum the weights were heavy enough to crack a bare skull.

"Please, I mean you no harm." Keisuke took a shuffling step forward, seeming almost pained by his heavy armor.

"Is that what you told the archers?"

"A regrettable necessity." Keisuke gave an apologetic bob of his head. "I needed to separate you from the others."

"I won't go willingly." Isami scanned the shadows for other Scorpion warriors, back prickling at the thought of hidden watchers. Let them come, she would not be taken, not by the likes of Keisuke.

"I've no plans to escort you anywhere." Keisuke gave a raspy chuckle. "I only wished to talk without that blood-mad Ikoma sticking a blade in my gut. And, frankly, I've never liked the look of your bodyguard. You seemed most likely to give me a fair hearing."

"In that, you are sadly mistaken." Isami swung her chain in a wide arc.

With a startled squawk, Keisuke dove away from the strike.

"I have no time for traitors and thieves." Isami's chain struck sparks from the flinty boulders behind which Keisuke sheltered. Fury filled her, so hot and bright she thought it might burst forth from her chest in a spray of flame. Kazuya was beyond retribution, but she could punish Keisuke for his betrayal, here and now.

"I did not destroy the Ikoma records!" Keisuke shouted.

Rounding the boulder, Isami ignored his feeble denials, chain already lashing down in anticipation of the Scorpion courtier's lunge. But Keisuke only twisted to avoid having his arm broken. He rolled away in a spray of dust, the weights of Isami's chain hammering divots into the rocky ground. One of her swings rebounded from the back of his breastplate, and the courtier went flat as a trodden insect. Pale and gasping, he managed to roll over, gaze seeking Isami's.

She braced herself, chain ready to swing down and end the

traitor's miserable life. Whatever ploy Keisuke planned had failed. His guards were on the way, surely, but Isami vowed she would take the Scorpion courtier with her.

"Look at me!" Keisuke made shields of his hands, his voice raw and terrified. In the light of the fallen lantern, he looked practically haggard. Something in the ragged aspect of his expression gave Isami pause. It was one thing to kill a man in the heat of combat, but quite another to strike down a helpless, pleading foe.

Isami knew Kazuya would have done it in a heartbeat, which is why she stayed her hand.

"Look at me," Keisuke repeated, more softly. "I've lost everything."

"You hold Stone Willow Valley."

"Until Lord Hanbei carves me from it." He shook his head. "I have barely two hundred warriors and Lady Kaede's reinforcements are yet days away."

"You expect sympathy?" Isami asked. "From *me*?"

"Not sympathy, only a moment of your time." He swallowed. "This was not my plan."

Isami felt her upper lip curl, scorn and disgust in equal measure. "We had an accord."

"I would have abided by it, had not that Ikoma madman set my camp ablaze."

"If Shinzō drew blades, it was because of your treachery." Isami practically spat the words. "You could not share the valley, Scorpion. Well, you are welcome to it now. At least until the Lion army arrives."

"Do you think I wanted this?" Keisuke's question was almost a sob. "Lady Kaede sent me to frustrate and slow the negotiations, not to start a war. She was furious when she heard of the battle. Rather than enjoying acclaim back in Journey's End City, I find myself here, on the front lines against the largest army in Rokugan."

Isami took a step back, careful lest the Scorpion courtier attempt some new trick. "You claim you did nothing to the documents?"

"What could I stand to gain by destroying them?" Keisuke met her eyes. "Your compromise was well founded, Lady Isami. It would have earned me Lady Kaede's esteem, especially once I took credit for the idea."

"You would have stolen my work?"

"Only a little." Behind the dirty silk mask, his grin seemed more tired than amused. "It is, after all, what I do."

Isami studied Keisuke's face, searching for deception beneath the dust and grime. For all her misgivings, he seemed a man pushed to the edge of endurance, his face free of all vestiges of the amused detachment he had so carefully cultivated in their previous meetings.

Strangely, Isami found herself starting to believe the little man. She fixed him with an appraising look.

"If you had no hand in destroying the Lion documents, then who did?"

He cocked his head. "Have you considered maybe Shinzō burned them himself?"

"If you believe that, you know nothing of Ikoma Shinzō."

"Perhaps it was an oni, or mischievous yōkai spirit, or an agent of Fu Leng." Keisuke raised a hand as if to placate her. "I am not here to accuse anyone of anything. I only want to set things right."

"And how do you propose to do that, Bayushi?"

"The original agreement, the one you brokered." He spoke quickly, eyes bright in the lamplight. "You must convince Shinzō to honor it."

Isami blinked, frowning at the suggestion. "I think that time has long passed."

"I was listening at the rock fall. I heard you speak in defense of the Scorpion," Keisuke replied. "That was what gave me hope you could be reasoned with."

He stood, slowly, empty hands spread wide. "Despite what you may think, it's clear Shinzō trusts you. If you talk, he will listen."

"Even if I were able to convince him, the original agreement was predicated on the Lion documents," Isami replied. "Which *someone* burned."

"The papers are not a problem," Keisuke said. "There are others."

Isami leaned in, interested despite herself. "In the Scorpion Clan archives?"

Keisuke nodded. "Safe under lock and guard."

"But you said they ceded Stone Willow Valley to the Scorpion Clan."

"I lied." Embarrassment peeked around the edges of his mask. "They support the Lion claim. Which is why I left them in Journey's End City."

It seemed the height of madness to trust Bayushi Keisuke, and yet, Isami found the courtier's weary desperation more convincing than his honeyed words. The Keisuke of their previous meetings was gone, replaced by a man who seemed genuinely regretful, even afraid.

"You will not make it far into Scorpion lands without my help, let alone reach the clan archives." He spoke as if privy to the war within Isami's thoughts.

Isami let out a long sigh, not quite believing she was about to place her trust in Keisuke once more, but the courtier's words had the ring of truth about them. He had had plenty of opportunities to kidnap or kill them, and yet Keisuke had come, seemingly alone, to speak with her. Like it or not, he represented Isami's only real chance. Despite her confident words to Shinzō, she had significant doubts concerning whether Lord Otomo's seal would grant her access to the Scorpion archives.

The lives of hundreds, perhaps thousands, sat balanced upon Isami's next act. If she was mistaken, if she trusted Keisuke only to have him betray her again, all that followed would be Isami's responsibility. In that moment, she understood how Shinzō had felt during their recent altercation – unwilling to believe, but desperate for any chance to salvage the wreckage of his ambitions.

It was not a feeling Isami much enjoyed.

With an irritated grunt, she wound the ends of her chain back around her waist. She turned on her heel and walked over to catch up the bridle of her horse. Drawing her lamp from the pack, Isami struck sparks to light the wick, before beginning to once more pick her way through the fallen boulders.

Stones rattled as Keisuke shifted from foot to foot behind her.

"Well?" Isami glanced back at him. "Aren't you coming?"

# CHAPTER EIGHTEEN

"They are in there." Keisuke nodded at the crest of the hill, where a small bamboo enclosure was flanked by a pair of Scorpion guards. "I gave orders to take your companions alive, but after we lost so many during the Lion attack, my soldiers' faith in me has been somewhat shaken. Captain Masaru has taken charge."

"I thought Masaru was your bodyguard's bodyguard?" Isami asked.

"Lady Kaede knows I am no warrior." Keisuke glanced away. "I was to handle the negotiations, yes. But it is Masaru who commands."

"Then how do you propose to free Gorobei and Shinzō?" Isami shifted to squint at the enclosure, trying to pick out her companions from the shadowy forms within. She considered getting out her spyglass, but feared the glint of metal in the torchlight might give them away. Isami and Keisuke crouched behind a low stand of brush perhaps a hundred yards downhill from the Scorpion camp, but she was under no illusions they would remain hidden for long.

"I believe it was Akodo who said: 'Simple plans are oft best.'" Keisuke made a show of brushing some of the dust from his robes and straightening his armor. "I am going to walk over and order they be freed."

Despite Keisuke's desultory attempts to tidy himself, anxiety creased his forehead, the tension in his face visible around the edges of his mask.

Isami could well understand the Scorpion courtier's concern. Loyalty, duty, and other such high-minded principles made for good warrior tales, but there were many stories of commanders being forcibly removed by their subordinates. Many interpretations of Akodo's Code even argued it was a loyal samurai's responsibility to betray an unfit lord, especially if their actions would bring harm to clan or family.

"Will Masaru's warriors obey?" Isami asked.

"That depends." Keisuke ran a hand through his hair to work out some of the tangles, then tied it back with a twist of silk ribbon.

"On what?"

"On how good a liar I am." Like the straightening of a rumpled sheet, all traces of anxiety fled the Scorpion courtier's face. He stood and began to walk up the hill. After a few steps, he glanced back to where Isami lingered behind the bush.

"Aren't you coming?"

"I don't see how my presence will help matters," she replied.

"It will." He nodded. "Trust me."

"I wish you wouldn't keep saying that."

"Saying what?"

"'Trust me,'" she replied, very much not feeling as if she could.

He considered for a moment. "Trust in my ambitions, at least. It would do me no good to betray you now."

"And when will it do you good?"

He sniffed. "That remains to be seen."

"I am not exactly filled with confidence."

"I shall attempt to free your friends with or without you." He turned away. "But it would be much easier if you came along."

Isami shook her head, her mouth gone unaccountably sour. It was not as if she could win her way into the Scorpion capital alone, and she owed it to Gorobei and Shinzō to at least attempt to free them.

Cursing herself for a fool twice over, Isami followed Keisuke.

"The Scorpion are, in our way, as proud as any Lion lord," he said as they climbed the hill. "But believing oneself clever is not the same as *being* clever."

A brief commotion accompanied their being spotted by the Scorpion guards. Although the sight of Keisuke caused the waiting samurai to lower their blades, they did not sheath them.

"Lord Bayushi." Masaru's bow was perfunctory, at best. The Scorpion samurai wore the same grinning oni mask as he had when Keisuke had tried to bring two guards to the meeting, but the lacquer was chipped and discolored, one curving tusk broken clean off. His armor was in a similar state, torn straps mended, steel glinting through the cracked lacquer of his breastplate.

"Captain Masaru," Keisuke said. "I have captured Lady Miya."

Masaru shifted to regard Isami. "She doesn't appear captured, lord."

"You must forgive Masaru," Keisuke turned to her with a bow, his voice dropping low. "He and my bodyguard were... close. And I am afraid he did not take Okita's death well."

"Perhaps if I were to disarm?" Isami drew her dagger from its sheath and offered it to the guards, hilt first.

"It is not your blade that concerns me." Masaru waved his

sword at the chain wrapped around Isami's waist. "I mean no insult, Lady Miya, but I saw the Lion corpses you left behind."

With a nod, Isami unwound her chain, letting it clatter to the ground. It was not as if the weapon would avail her against so many Scorpion warriors. To tell the truth, after so many others had discounted her skills, Isami was even a bit pleased to be viewed as a threat.

"Now that we have reached an accord…" Keisuke pressed his hands together, his silk mask creasing in a grin as he drew forth a tightly wrapped scroll bearing the Bayushi crest. "This is a missive from Lady Kaede. I am to escort Lady Miya and her companions back to Journey's End City."

"What of us?" Masaru asked.

"You are to retreat into the hills along with such villagers as will join you," Keisuke said. "We cannot keep the Lion forces from Stone Willow Valley. Far better to hold back, so you may strike at their lines from behind when reinforcements arrive."

Although the oni mask hid Masaru's reaction, his stance betrayed naked suspicion. There were mutters from among the other Scorpion samurai, exhausted warriors with little reason to trust their commander.

"You have all served me well." Keisuke's calm affect slipped, regret turning his words rough and raw. "Better than I deserve. I would not see more of your lives lost on the pyre of my failure. It is best I bear this alone so that no ashes stain your reputation."

He met Masaru's gaze. "I should never have been the one to lead you here. My overconfidence, my foolishness, cost the lives of better samurai than I. Let me do what I can to salvage what remains."

The Scorpion captain's eyes narrowed behind the slits in his mask. Slowly, his sword came up, trembling ever so slightly as it pointed at Keisuke's breast. The moment stretched tight as a bowstring, the clearing silent but for the crackle of torches and the distant whicker of horses in the pen.

With a low grunt, Masaru sheathed his blade. "Bring the prisoners."

Keisuke gave a low bow, his poise so perfect that Isami would hardly have believed him a man near breaking.

She watched the Scorpion courtier, concern blossoming in her stomach. Was Keisuke's ragged affect the truth, or merely another façade to hide his real motivations? If not for the weary desperation that bunched the skin at the corner of Keisuke's eyes, she would have thought him in complete control.

"I shall convey our noble guests to Lady Kaede," Keisuke continued. "If you could detail a few samurai to–"

"No." Masaru's reply came like a sword thrust.

"I don't understand." Keisuke frowned. "We will need guards to secure the prisoners and see to our safe travel."

"As you said, lord. Many brave warriors have already been lost to your failures," Masaru replied. "I would not see more lives wasted."

He turned away. "We shall need every blade in the days to come. You shall have to trust Lady Miya's word."

Keisuke looked about to argue, but at that moment, Gorobei and Shinzō were led forth. The former rōnin looked none the worse for wear, his robes dirty but unbloodied. If anything, he seemed to have benefitted from captivity. The bruise covering the right side of his face had faded to a blotchy yellowish green, the swelling around his eye almost gone.

Shinzō, on the other hand…

From the sorry state of the Lion archivist's robes, Isami would not have been surprised to learn he had been dragged behind a horse. Scrapes and abrasions seemed to cover every inch of Shinzō's face and hands. Where Gorobei seemed loosely bound, Shinzō had been hobbled and gagged, his arms tied tightly behind his back in a way that looked painful.

"He would have torn the cage apart had we not tied him tight," Masaru said by way of explanation.

If anything, the bonds seemed to have fanned the flames of the Ikoma archivist's anger. Shinzō's gaze burned hot and bright, undimmed by his condition as it swept over the assembled warriors and came to rest on Keisuke.

With a muffled roar, the Ikoma archivist tore free of his captor's grip, hurling himself bodily at Keisuke. Although Scorpion guards pulled the squirming archivist away, they were not quick enough to prevent Shinzō from delivering a vicious headbutt to his opponent.

Isami glanced at Masaru as the guards dragged Shinzō back. It might have been her imagination, but she detected a glitter of something approaching satisfaction in the Scorpion captain's eyes.

Blood soaked through Keisuke's mask. He cast an anxious glance at Shinzō, then turned to Isami, voice muffled by the hand pressed to his nose.

"*This* is why I thought it better you come along."

Shinzō struggled in the grip of the Scorpion guards, almost pulling one from her feet in his struggle to reach Keisuke. Masaru took two quick steps, laying his sword's edge against Shinzō's throat.

Although the Ikoma archivist went rigid, it was not the

stillness of a beaten foe, but that of an opponent searching for an opening – eyes narrowed, muscles coiled tight. The two stood almost face-to-face, their hatred for one another seeming almost to bend the air between them. A thin runnel of blood crept down Masaru's blade, but Shinzō seemed not to notice, his gaze as sharp as any knife.

Isami looked to Keisuke.

"Masaru, stop." His command was barely above a whisper, imbued with as much force as a courtesan's breathy titter.

"Stop." Isami laid a hand on Masaru's arm. The Scorpion samurai's gaze flicked to her, then back to Shinzō.

"If you murder this man, I can promise more of your comrades will die." Isami tightened her grip on the Scorpion captain. She could hear the hiss of angry breath behind Masaru's mask, feel the fury that lay coiled in his trembling muscles.

With a furious shout, the Scorpion captain turned away, blade slipping back into its sheath. He stood for a long moment, staring into the night, shoulders rising and falling with each heavy breath.

"Take the Ikoma from my sight," Masaru said, at last. "I want all of you gone."

He stalked off into the darkness.

"Release him," Isami said.

The Scorpion samurai looked to Masaru's retreating back, but their captain was little more than a shadow in the flickering torchlight, just another unquiet shade stalking the darkened hills. Isami glanced over her shoulder at Keisuke who, after taking several steps back, gave an accommodating wave.

"Obey Lady Miya."

The Scorpion samurai released Shinzō, backing away as if the

Ikoma archivist was a venomous spider. Isami stepped forward to hook the gag from Shinzō's mouth.

The Ikoma archivist regarded her with naked suspicion. "I cannot believe you would—"

"Save your life?" Isami spoke over him. "I find it difficult to accept as well. And yet, here we are."

"You trust *him* now?" Shinzō thrust his chin at Keisuke. "After all he has done?"

"This was far from my first choice, either," Keisuke replied, taking another cautious step back. "But needs will as needs must."

Isami stepped between them, hoping to break Shinzō's eyeline before he could work himself up again.

She leaned close, voice pitched so only Shinzō could hear. "There is a way to salvage what was lost." She nodded at Keisuke. "He can guarantee us access."

Shinzō drew in a shaky breath. "When we were separated... I thought they had killed you, Lady Miya. Now, I find you with this Scorpion traitor. How am I to trust anything you say?"

"Don't trust my words," Isami replied. "Trust my actions."

She turned to the nearest guard, holding out her hand. "Your dagger, please."

Seeming taken aback, the guard drew her blade, holding it out hilt first.

The bonds on Shinzō's arms and legs parted before the sharp edge of the knife. Once Shinzō was free, Isami returned the blade to its owner. Turning her back on the Ikoma archivist was a calculated risk, but she hoped the display of trust would help calm matters.

When she looked back, Shinzō was rubbing his wrists, his

expression that of a captive tiger who has suddenly found his cage unlocked.

"I have given my word to Keisuke that we will not attempt escape." Isami's lie was more for the benefit of the Scorpion onlookers. "We are to travel south to Journey's End City at Lady Kaede's request. You will come, now."

Shinzō gave her an appraising look, expression wary. The unearned harshness of Shinzō's regard grated across Isami's nerves, but she did her best not to let her anxiety show, keeping her hands at her sides, her expression cold and commanding.

"We will need supplies and fresh horses." She turned to the Scorpion guards. "As fresh as you can manage, at least."

They hesitated until Keisuke gave a soft cough.

"Go on." He waved a hand as if to brush them away. "Wouldn't want to keep Lady Kaede waiting."

Mention of the Scorpion noble's name seemed to unlock whatever twist of obligation had bound the guards, and they moved quickly into the camp.

Isami waited until they had moved a short distance away before turning back to Shinzō.

"I ask nothing but for you to stay your hand until you have heard everything I have to say. Do I have your word?"

"No," Shinzō said. "But you shall have my actions. At least until we are beyond the grasp of the Scorpion."

Isami frowned at the Ikoma archivist. Could nothing be simple?

"It will have to do." Turning away, she motioned for Gorobei to join her.

"Your arrival was unexpected, mistress." He bobbed his head in a rough bow. "Although very, very welcome."

Although the former rōnin's gratitude did much to quiet the roil of anxiety in Isami's breast, she did not allow herself a smile.

"Do you think you can keep Shinzō from killing anyone before I have the chance to talk some sense into him?"

"Probably." Gorobei gave a thoughtful frown. "Although I would have much preferred you left him tied up."

The next ten minutes were some of the most uncomfortable of Isami's life. Shinzō regarded Keisuke as if he were some vile spirit come to torment the living. Although Gorobei kept surreptitious watch on the Ikoma archivist, Isami was left with the strong suspicion that, were Keisuke to utter one word, Shinzō would tear him limb from limb. Fortunately, the Scorpion courtier kept quiet, one hand pinching his nose, head tilted back to stop the flow of blood.

After what seemed an eternity, the guards arrived with fresh horses. Although the saddlebags did not brim with supplies, there was enough to see them beyond the edge of the valley. Isami did not bother to make a point of it. There were towns along the river from where she could find more food. Even if the villagers' stores were barren, hunger was, by far, the least of Isami's concerns at the moment.

"My weapons," Shinzō said.

Ignoring the Ikoma archivist, the lead Scorpion guard nodded to Isami, then extended one hand toward the edge of camp. There, at the edge of the torchlight, Isami could just make out where Gorobei and Shinzō's equipment had been unceremoniously piled.

Isami bent to retrieve her chain. Taking her new horse's bridle with a slight bow of gratitude, she led the animal from camp, hoping the others would follow.

The Scorpion guards watched them go with barely disguised mistrust, hands hovering close to blades as the others retrieved their equipment. Although it was good to have the surveyor's chain belted once more around her waist, Isami was under no illusions about her chances should the Scorpion attack.

Isami half expected Shinzō to simply gallop away, but the Ikoma archivist stayed with them, his expression cold as summer snow.

They moved down the hill in single file. Isami, then Keisuke, Gorobei behind, and Shinzō bringing up the rear. Although they quickly passed beyond the range of Scorpion bowshot, it did nothing to ease the tension in Isami's chest, the feeling of a coming storm, not avoided, only deferred.

Even so, Isami drew some small comfort from the thought that, with all the troubles yet to come, she and her reluctant companions were at least headed in the right direction.

Isami could figure everything else out along the way.

# CHAPTER NINETEEN

"I don't believe you." Shinzō gripped the hilt of his sword, but Isami was grateful to see it remained sheathed for the moment.

"It hardly matters what you believe. The records are there." Keisuke kept his hands well clear of his blades.

"Lady Miya," Shinzō turned to Isami, "this is but another ruse."

"If I wanted you dead," Keisuke replied, "I had but to order Masaru to cut your throat."

Shinzō looked as if he wished to spit. "The Scorpion wishes to lure us into his lair."

"Ah, yes, Journey's End City," Keisuke said with a wry thrust of his chin. "Truly, the Bayushi will shower me with accolades when I present them with an apprentice cartographer and disgraced archivist."

Isami ignored the insult. "What does Keisuke have to gain by taking us to the Scorpion archives?"

"Information," Shinzō spat back. "None know where we are, so no one will speak out if we are tortured for details."

"Details on what exactly?" Keisuke cocked his head. "The finer points of Lion genealogy?" He flicked his fingers at Isami. "How to properly shade riverbanks?"

Gorobei's stifled chuckle earned a glare from Shinzō, but the former rōnin only shook his head.

"He makes a fair point."

"Are you not familiar with the parable of the Scorpion and the Frog?" Shinzō's scowl was as unyielding as granite. "He is a Bayushi, he does not *need* a reason for betrayal. If we trust this man, we shall be dead before winter, mark my words."

"You speak of betrayal, yet the only blade I needed fear was yours." Isami could see from the twitch of Shinzō's frown that her barb had struck home. Isami's already brittle temper began to fracture. Master Tadataka had spoken of moving sand, but Ikoma Shinzō was like a boulder – difficult to shift and impossible to stop once he had begun rolling.

Isami swallowed against the tightness in her throat. She needed to resolve this argument before things ended in blood. There was but one path left to chart.

"If you cannot see reason, then go."

As she had hoped, the suddenness of Isami's command seemed to surprise Shinzō.

"Are you not a scholar? Do you not deal in facts?" Isami took a step toward the archivist, uncomfortably aware he still had a hand on his blade. "We have lain out our arguments. If anger overwhelms your reason, then there is nothing more to say."

"Lady?" Confusion warred with fury in Shinzō's eyes.

"Return to Lord Hanbei, tell him the Scorpion have quit Stone Willow Valley. He will be pleased, I'm sure. Perhaps he will even reinstate some small scrap of your former reputation." Isami made a vague gesture toward the north. "You will have delivered new land to the Lion, at least until Lady Kaede arrives with reinforcements and drenches the valley in blood."

Shinzō opened his mouth, but no words emerged.

"Would you give your life for your clan?" Isami asked. "For the Empire?"

"Without question." Shinzō's reply came before Isami had even finished.

"Then do it," she said. "If this is a trap, you are no more doomed than now. If not, we stand a chance of stopping future bloodshed, perhaps even of preventing a war."

Shinzō bared his teeth, but his gaze was distant, as if the anger were directed inwards.

Isami well understood the feeling. She continued, more softly. "We have failed, all of us, but that does not mean hope is lost."

"You cannot trust him, lady." A note of concern threaded the anger of Shinzō's reply.

"I trust you," Isami replied. "And you tried to kill me." She took a step, now almost face-to-face with the archivist. "*Twice.*"

Shinzō's jaw pulsed, the tendons on his neck standing stark against the flesh. Isami tried to keep her gaze from slipping down to the archivist's blade. It took every bit of resolve, but she managed to hold Shinzō's stare.

After what felt like hours, Shinzō took a step back, head inclined in the slightest of bows.

"The agreement." He glanced over Isami's shoulder to where Keisuke stood on the other side of the clearing. "Will Lady Kaede honor it?"

Isami turned, half-expecting some cutting remark, but Keisuke only looked to his hands.

"I cannot say."

Shinzō stepped around Isami. Although he approached Keisuke, the menace seemed to have fled his bearing.

"That is perhaps the first honest thing you have said to me, Bayushi."

"He stands to lose as much as you," Isami said. "And to gain."

"Enough." Shinzō waved a hand as if brushing away an annoying fly. Isami could not help but realize it was the first time he had released his sword since they left the Scorpion camp.

"You have convinced me, Lady Miya." He turned, pointing at Keisuke. "But do not think I have forgotten what you did. When this is over there will be a reckoning. Of that you can be sure."

"As Lady Sun rises in the east," Keisuke placed a hand over his heart, "so shall I mark my days by the inevitability of your vengeance."

With an irritated grunt, Shinzō turned away to see to his horse.

At last, Isami allowed herself to relax, fatigue and anxiety lapping over her like a rising tide. She took an unsteady step, one hand pressed to her forehead. A moment, and Gorobei was at her side. Catching her elbow in a firm yet gentle grip, he guided her to a fallen log.

"You need water and food, mistress." He produced a gourd and small wrapped bundle from his pack.

"There is no time." Isami shook her head, the move bringing on another wave of dizziness. "I can eat on the trail."

"I am your bodyguard. It is my duty to protect you." Gorobei pressed the food into her hands. "Sometimes even from yourself."

Isami returned a thin smile. She desperately wanted to wave the former rōnin off, to push onwards, the weight of duty like a wind at her back. But to do so would make Isami just like Shinzō, bound so tightly by responsibility that she could not see the path even when it stood clear before her.

So Isami ate. Leaning her back against a tree she let the others do as they wished. It was strange, but in not one of her parents' stories could Isami remember either of them speaking of how grueling travel was. In the tales, they seemed almost to float over the land, remarking on temples, towns, and curious roadside encounters. Somehow, Isami had imagined going to a place was merely a series of interesting sights. Her parents never mentioned the cuts and bruises, the way the cold seeped up from the ground at night, or how, after days of hard riding, Isami's spine felt as if someone had sprinkled the joints with crushed glass.

An hour found her, if not refreshed, then not as likely to topple from her horse, at least. Mounting up, Isami grimly reflected that if the Ancestors ever saw fit to see her named an imperial cartographer, she would work to add a regime of physical fitness to the Ministry curriculum. She imagined herself presiding over a gaggle of young apprentices, shepherding them along a rocky road or over a mountain pass, doing her best not to smile as they tried to conceal the aches and pains of the road. She would be older then, wiser, all the nested anxieties of her current predicament little more than unhappy memories.

That fine thought carried her through the rest of the afternoon.

The River Road led beyond the threat of Masaru's vengeance, but deeper into Scorpion lands. The Spine of the World stretched to their right, high peaks like the heads of ancient giants, lost amidst the clouds. Terraced fields dotted the hills on their left, the occasional tiny village seeming almost lost amidst waves of late season rice and barley. Wind made strange ripples among the stalks – serpentine symbols that seemed to hover just at the edge of comprehension. If they were messages, only the gods could divine their meaning.

Just before evening, Keisuke called a halt, reining up his horse to regard Isami and Shinzō.

"This is as far as you go like that." He thrust his chin at them.

Shinzō seemed about to respond, so Isami spoke first.

"What do you mean?"

"This is Scorpion land." The ghost of a grin played across Keisuke's hollowed features. "I shouldn't need to remind you the Lion are not well regarded. It seems unlikely the Yogo family will grant you the requisite papers to cross our borders."

Shinzō's frown mirrored the downward curve of the setting sun. "I am not some thief, creeping in the night."

"Lest you forget, we are attempting to steal into Journey's End City to abscond with records the clan would very much like to keep sealed," Keisuke replied. "A thief is *exactly* what you are."

The Ikoma archivist leaned back in his saddle, arms crossed. "And what of Lady Isami, the Miya are welcome across the Empire."

"Lord Shinpachi's seal would be sufficient to win passage through Beiden Pass," Keisuke said. "But the arrival of an imperial representative will surely be noted. That could lead to… unwelcome inquiries."

Isami raised a hand before Shinzō could argue. "What do you propose?"

"A change of attire for you and our Lion friend." Keisuke gave a wry tilt of his head. "Something tasteful, but unassuming. Servants, perhaps?"

Shinzō scoffed. "You would like that, Bayushi."

"Would you prefer to play courtesans?" Keisuke raised his hands in mock surrender. "I think only of your reputation. It would be strange for a Bayushi, even one of marginal notoriety such as myself, to travel unaccompanied." He reached inside his robe to withdraw a small sheaf of papers. "And I just happen to carry enough travel documents for a small entourage."

Shinzō looked to Isami. "Once more, he seeks to twist the situation to his advantage."

"It seems to all our advantage." Isami frowned, considering. "What would you propose, Shinzō?"

Shinzō took several long breaths, his expression reminiscent of a man forced to handle excrement. At last, he shook his head.

Isami frowned. It was not the first time she had heard of imperial representatives moving in secret, although such tactics were usually reserved for the Otomo.

"I mislike this charade," Isami said. "I don't know the first thing about being a servant. Beiden Pass is almost week away, it seems likely we will be found out."

"Worry not, Lady Isami, you will only have to play the part for a short while." The Scorpion courtier nodded toward the rushing water. "Three Sides River moves more quickly than horses, and it never tires. There is a town perhaps a half-hour's ride from here. Boats come and go. We could book passage on one traveling downriver and reach Beiden Pass in a few days' time."

"Book passage with what?" Shinzō asked. "Unless you have koku hidden away, Bayushi, we are without funds."

"Even at this moment, we sit upon our means of transport."

"You would sell the horses?" Shinzō asked.

"This close to harvest they will fetch a good price. In a few hours' time we could be ensconced in the cabin of a fine riverboat, wending our way toward Beiden in reasonable comfort."

Isami's heart rose at the thought of not spending another night outside, but it seemed as if Keisuke was not revealing the full scope of his plan.

"You wish to sell our horses to book passage on a boat," she said. "What of the return journey?"

"I am quite confident I can secure new steeds for us in Journey's End City."

"You were also confident you could trick both Shinzō and me into ratifying the Scorpion claims," Isami replied.

"Yes, I was." Keisuke's nod reminded Isami of a duelist acknowledging an opponent's point in a practice bout. Isami steeled herself for another round of verbal sparring, but the Scorpion courtier merely shrugged.

"What would you propose, Lady Miya?"

It was not pleasant for Isami to have her own tactics turned against her. In truth, she had hoped to simply avoid the towns, but even with Gorobei's knowledge of hidden trails it seemed unlikely they could completely escape detection, especially once they reached Beiden Pass. More, the Scorpion had only given them enough supplies for a few days. They would need to resupply, and soon.

Despite her distaste at the means, Isami was forced to admit Keisuke's plan represented their best chance at reaching the archives.

It also meant giving up her one last scrap of control to the Scorpion courtier.

She regarded Keisuke thoughtfully. Amidst the nervous exhaustion she could yet see hints of his former arrogance, but the battle and subsequent flight seemed to have tempered the Scorpion courtier's conceit.

Keisuke had admitted to lying to her, and it seemed impossible he had not had a hand in destroying the Lion records. But if so, why was he so intent on bringing her and Shinzō to Journey's End City? The Scorpion and Lion had already shed blood. Although imperial edicts forbade open war, the clans frequently skirmished without formally marshaling their armies. Like two great waves, the Lion and Scorpion moved inexorably toward conflict.

Tenuous as it was, this was Isami's best hope.

"We will do as Keisuke suggests." Isami held up a hand to forestall any complaints. "But Gorobei shall oversee the arrangements."

"I know these lands, I can get us a better price," Keisuke said.

"I am willing to forgo a bit of comfort if it means I can sleep more soundly."

Keisuke's lips worked for a moment, but he seemed to master whatever protest lay within him. He returned a gracious bow.

"As you desire, lady."

They removed the necessities from their saddlebags, making a small camp beneath the shelter of a limestone overhang. Gorobei set off at a brisk trot, the other horses trailing behind on a lead.

Both Shinzō and Keisuke watched the former rōnin disappear around the bend, concern mirrored in their anxious expressions. Isami found their apprehension oddly reassuring, as if by discomforting her supposed allies she had won some semblance of a victory.

The high trill of a hunting shrike rose above the murky babble of the river. Isami scanned the surrounding trees, but was unable to pick the bird from amongst the deepening shadows. More calls cut the evening, sharp against the regretful tenor of Isami's recollections. She could not help but be reminded of her talk with Master Tadataka.

It had seemed like Isami's choice to accept Lord Otomo's offer, to leave the Ministry and abandon her former master. But what if she was merely a bird acting according to her nature, all her decisions circumscribed by the will of Heaven?

She looked to the sky, lit by barely the thinnest sliver of Lord Moon as he raced across the sky in pursuit of Lady Sun. The gods had always seemed vast, unknowable things to Isami, all humanity swept along by the wind of their passing. Their trials and conflicts had shaped the Empire, the great clans, even the creeping threat of corruption that lay behind the Carpenter Wall. And yet, in that moment, they seemed somehow more understandable, as if they too moved only according to their natures.

Isami gave a soft laugh, she must be truly exhausted if she was attempting to survey the will of the gods. They were not birds, and neither was she. Come what may, Isami would act as she thought best.

And yet, it would be nice, even once, to be presented with better options.

# CHAPTER TWENTY

"*Fortunes' Favor*?" Keisuke regarded the river barge with barely disguised disdain. "More like *Fortunes' Fool*."

"You wished to be inconspicuous," Gorobei replied curtly. "This is inconspicuous."

Isami was forced to agree. The *Fortunes' Favor* was a wide, flat-bottomed barge, square bowed in the old imperial style. In addition to the cargo space below, several large wooden frames filled the barge's deck, each stacked with bales of rice. Sailors were engaged in covering the frames with oilcloth, tying the tarps with ropes run through numerous iron rings secured to the deck.

"Stay behind me," Keisuke continued. "Heads low, hands at your sides. And for the Ancestors' sake, Isami, keep your mouth shut. Shinzō can pass for a servant, but your courtly accent will give us away in a moment."

"I hardly think that's necessary," Isami replied, letting her vowels settle into the low, rolling cadence of river folk. "My parents taught me a number of dialects."

Keisuke gave her a sideways glare.

"Is my inflection really that bad?" Isami looked to Shinzō,

who returned a straight-faced nod. Even Gorobei rubbed the back of his neck, glancing away as Isami turned to him.

Fortunately, Isami was spared further embarrassment by the appearance of a smiling, red-cheeked riverwoman from behind one of the piles of cargo. From her bearing, and the marginally superior quality of her clothes, it was easy to mark her as the owner of the barge.

"Captain Ishi, at your service, lord." She stepped to the top of the gangplank, slipping into a low bow. "It is an unrequited honor to have someone of your august lineage aboard my humble vessel."

"Humble indeed," Keisuke muttered under his breath as he mounted the gangplank.

"I have prepared our stateroom for you and your entourage." Ishi gestured to a ladder that disappeared down into the belly of the barge, her delight at having a noble passenger obvious despite her attempts to maintain a respectful air. "We have not borne such an eminent personage as yourself in some time. Not since Tokagure Yōdō, in fact. Lord Yōdō was transporting some wisteria cuttings from north of the mountains. Truly beautiful blossoms in the foothills, such a delicate purple as to complement even the finest–"

"Captain Ishi," Keisuke interrupted.

"Yes, lord."

"I am fatigued from my journey," he continued. "And I would see my... stateroom."

"My apologies, lord." Ishi led them into the bowels of her barge.

Despite the boat's ponderous exterior, the room was relatively clean and spacious, with planks of polished maple, privacy screens, and several high, covered windows that could be opened to let in light.

Captain Ishi showed them around with the air of a palace courtier displaying a series of fine wall scrolls, explaining the rooms were occupied primarily by wealthy merchants wishing to accompany their goods downriver. Keisuke was only able to deflect her unceasing elaborations by promising to join her for dinner in the captain's mess.

Freed of Ishi's well-meaning attentions, they set to unpacking their meager possessions and arranging the rooms to give the impression of a noble returning home after a long journey. Before long, the *Fortunes' Favor* cast free of the docks, bobbing along the wide current of Three Sides River with surprising speed.

Although Isami had quite enjoyed the initial thrill of masquerading as a servant, the role quickly wore upon her. Keisuke made only such demands as were required of him, but the myriad tasks that seemed to accompany even such mundane occurrences as a visit to the upper decks soon began to wear on Isami.

She would have dearly liked to chart the course of Three Sides River, to better compare it to the imperial maps, but such free time as remained to her was largely given over to eating and sleeping. Within a few days, her hands were chapped and red, her back sore from ducking through the barge's low corridors. Fortunately, the crew kept to themselves, seemingly cowed by Gorobei's threatening glares.

Isami had hoped to discuss their plans, but close confines and thin walls made it almost impossible to speak without being overheard. Nor could she review her maps and calculations for fear of one of Captain Ishi's frequent, unannounced visits. Of all her comrades, only Shinzō seemed to take pleasure in the journey, and that exclusively from the discomfort the captain's unflagging attentions inflicted on Keisuke.

Apart from a few brief stops to load and unload, the *Fortunes' Favor* made good time, wending down the broad channel Three Sides River cut through below the mountains. They passed other barges and riverboats poling their way laboriously upriver. Often such meetings were marked by a shouted exchange of information – mostly grain prices and good markets, but occasional tidbits of gossip. The Scorpion Clan was gathering in Beiden, Lady Kaede herself had come from Journey's End City on a gilded palanquin, accompanied by a host of performers, guards, servants, and wrestlers to preside over the harvest festival. The other captains relayed such varying reports that it was hard to gather any real knowledge of the Scorpion response, but Keisuke seemed unsettled by the news.

"A harvest festival." He shook his head, speaking in a low whisper. "Good cover for moving a large number of warriors without drawing attention."

"Do you think she will contest the Lion forces?" Shinzō asked.

"Without a doubt," Keisuke replied. "The only question is how? To move openly would risk the appearance of war. If Lady Kaede wishes to remove your lord's forces from our lands, she will need some pretext."

"That shouldn't be hard. The Scorpion specialize in pretext," Shinzō responded with a curl of his lip.

"Ah, the fabled Lion rectitude," Keisuke chuckled. "And just how do you think Lord Hanbei justified his occupation? It was not simply your failure, Shinzō. I'm sure he discovered plenty of reports of bandits along the border, unrest in Stone Willow Valley. All better to frame his invasion of our lands as a peacekeeping exercise. Go on, tell me I lie."

Shinzō's hands made tight fists at his side. "We are merely reclaiming what is rightfully ours."

"And how does this bickering help matters?" Isami moved between them before the argument could escalate. Normally, she would have interceded more calmly, but a long afternoon spent airing out the futons had left her temper brittle. "The situation is already dangerous. I cannot have the two of you squabbling at every turn."

"As you wish, lady." Shinzō gave a stiff bow before withdrawing to the other chambers.

"You shall see." Keisuke turned to Isami, his tone steeped in the chill courtesy that passed for disdain among the higher classes. "Lady Kaede will come north, and soon."

His prediction was made reality the very next day. During a stop at one of the many towns dotting high above the wooded banks of Three Sides River, Isami was awoken by shouts from above, the stamp of boots upon the deck planking far different from the barefoot whisper of sailors.

Isami was up in a moment, but a hiss from Gorobei gave her pause. The former rōnin stood beside the door, sword sheathed, his face in shadow.

"What is happening?" Keisuke asked from behind the screens.

"River pirates?" Shinzō ducked below one of the roof beams, sword in hand.

"No." Gorobei cocked his head. "Soldiers."

"How do you know?" Isami asked.

The former rōnin nodded toward the deck above. "No one is screaming."

"If they are local guards, we should present our travel papers," Isami said. "Otherwise it would appear suspicious."

"I am a Bayushi noble riding on a decrepit river barge accompanied by only two servants and a hired guard." Keisuke ran a hand through his hair. "That is already suspicious."

"If it is an inspection, we'll be discovered soon enough," Shinzō said.

Keisuke nodded. "Help me with my robes."

Despite her misgivings, Isami helped to make the Scorpion courtier presentable. Days of travel and Isami's questionable laundering had left his robes frayed and pale, but when Keisuke emerged, the three of them in tow, he moved as if attending a high court function.

His false bravado crumpled like a fallen lantern the moment they climbed on deck.

A dozen Scorpion samurai stood ranged about the barge, spears in hand, arrows nocked to bows. Their leader was arrayed in elaborate armor, helmet replete with the Bayushi crest, his face concealed by a fanged battle mask. Captain Ishi knelt on the deck before him, palms upraised as if in entreaty, although her lips remained pressed together in helpless anger.

"As I said, captain. You will be recompensed for the temporary seizure of your vessel." The Scorpion commander turned to regard the newcomers, his eyes turning from stern to amused behind his mask. "Ah, Lord Keisuke. I did not expect to find you here."

"Captain Yoshio." Keisuke's smile did not reach his eyes. "You should know by now not to *ever* expect me."

"A shame." Yoshio sketched a low bow. "I would have prepared a more suitable welcome." He sighed. "Alas, we are all bound by the will of Heaven. Come, you must be ragged after days in this cramped scow."

"It has been more than suitable." Keisuke glanced at Ishi, who returned a grateful smile. "I would not see its captain or crew unduly harmed. Allow them to continue on their way."

"As you say, lord." At Yoshio's wave, the Scorpion samurai drew back behind the stacks of cargo. With another bow, Yoshio turned to join them.

Isami's breath of relief came too soon. The Scorpion commander paused as if recalling a bit of ephemera.

"One last thing, lord." Yoshio turned, tone suddenly sharp. "Your mother is looking for you."

A boot scraped to Isami's left, and she turned to see a Scorpion samurai, his spear planted firmly on the deck. On her right, she felt Shinzō tense. A muttered curse from Gorobei confirmed Isami's dire suspicions.

They were surrounded.

"What a pleasant surprise," Keisuke spoke quickly. "I was just going to see Lady Kaede."

Isami swallowed her surprise, struggling to maintain a servant's bent posture. She had thought the relationship between Kaede and Keisuke was one of patronage; to learn it was familial explained Keisuke's desire to avoid her.

"Then you would take nothing amiss were my guards and I to accompany you?" Yoshio nodded, and the ring of samurai moved closer. "It would do much to set my mind at ease."

"Of course." Keisuke did an excellent job concealing his nervousness.

They were led from the barge and down onto the docks, there to a small military ship bearing the Scorpion banner.

For all his air of menace, Yoshio proved a good host, providing them with food, drink, and such comforts as to make their stay feel less onerous. Although no one took their weapons, and they were shown all due courtesy, it was clear Keisuke was not free to leave. Fortunately, Yoshio did not seem to take Isami, Shinzō, and Gorobei for anything more than Keisuke's entourage.

It was some time before anyone risked conversation beyond the most trivial. They waited until evening, timing the intervals between the patrolling guards.

"Lady Kaede is your mother?" Isami's whisper was soft, but urgent. The desire to know more overwhelming any concern the guards might overhear.

"Unfortunately." Keisuke's discomfort was plain even in the flickering lamplight. "My father was a clanless poet who wrote some sweet verse about one of her victories in the ring. He went about his way none the wiser, and I suppose Lady Kaede chose to keep me as a souvenir."

"But you bear the Bayushi name," Isami said. By all accounts, Lady Kaede had several children, all with high positions in the Scorpion Clan. Keisuke's status was barely above that of a common court functionary.

"Lady Kaede claimed me as her own, yes," Keisuke replied with a regretful tilt of his head. "There remains no evidence of my mother's dalliance. Although I have never given cause, I suspect her husband and my siblings have always suspected something amiss."

"But why risk her position?" Isami asked. Although many nobles engaged in discreet affairs, if Lady Kaede were discovered to have borne a child out of marriage, it could be cause for censure, even banishment. There were many potions and prayers to ward against such inconvenient outcomes. If Lady Kaede gave birth to Keisuke, it was by choice.

"My mother enjoys family." Keisuke gave a slight shrug. "I did not inquire too deeply into her motives."

"Perhaps you should have," Shinzō replied.

"When my soul ascends to the Realm of Waiting and my deeds are arrayed upon the Wheel of Judgment, I doubt my decision to be born will number among the most regrettable." Although Keisuke's tone was sharp, his words were tinged with resignation.

"You planned all along to betray us to Lady Kaede?" Shinzō's question was a low hiss.

"I planned to avoid her completely, but the situation has changed." Keisuke shifted on his sleeping mat to fix the archivist with a level stare. "That hardly matters now the Scorpion Clan is seizing riverboats. If my mother wished to contest the Lion occupation, what better way to move a large force upriver in secret?"

"I thank you for trusting us with your true parentage, Keisuke." Isami spoke more to silence Shinzō's further questions than out of actual gratitude. It was not as if any of them had the standing to question the choices of a high lady of the Scorpion Clan. Even so, to reveal such scandalous details showed a surprising amount of trust on Keisuke's part. If only Isami could be sure it wasn't calculated to lure her deeper into the courtier's web.

She wished to ask more questions, but the guard had returned. Apparently wary of the whispered conversation, he remained nearby for the remainder of the night.

Morning saw them delivered through Beiden Pass, although certainly not in a manner of their choosing.

# CHAPTER TWENTY-ONE

Isami had never been to Beiden before. From studying maps over the years, she knew the city had changed hands more times than almost any other place in Rokugan. Currently ruled by the Yogo family, it was located southwest of Beiden Pass, the only path through the Spine of the World for many days in either direction. Although the Scorpion currently controlled the city, and by extension the lucrative trade route, the Lion Clan had claimed the network of fortifications overlooking the pass, extracting duties from all those who sought to move from one side to the other.

Gazing up at the high, nested towers on the cliffs above, Isami felt a cold prickle of apprehension. If the conflict spilled beyond Stone Willow Valley, Beiden Pass could very well run red with blood as it had so many times in the past.

She had known the pass was well traveled, boasting merchants from as far away as Dragon and Crab lands. But she was unprepared for the river of humanity flowing through the pass. Not only traders, but scores of peasants, monks, and travelers made their way between the high cliffs. Captain Yoshio offered no comment, ushering them through the various checkpoints with a thin-lipped efficiency that almost approached distaste. The Yogo guards passed them by with barely a nod, proof that Lady Kaede had somehow secured the support of the second largest family in the Scorpion Clan.

The reason for the throngs became clear once they reached Beiden itself. Every street corner seemed to boast a half-dozen performers – singers, jugglers, fire-breathers, even the occasional ritualist conjuring intricate illusions for the delight and amazement of the gathered throngs. The air hung heavy with the smell of spices threaded with sickly sweet scents of spilled sake and pipe smoke. Had it not been for Yoshio's guards, Isami and the others would have been swept up by the sheer mass of people. As it was, the phalanx of Scorpion warriors discouraged all but the most inebriated revelers, and even those were quickly seen off with a desultory cuff from a spear haft.

Lady Bayushi Kaede sat alone upon a makeshift platform erected in some merchant's courtyard, empty but for a few sitting pillows and a number of screens to shield her from the ongoing festivities. Despite the illusion of privacy, the screens did little to muffle the thud of festival drums from the marketplace beyond, nor the drunken songs and occasional bray of laughter from the crowds of villagers that swarmed every street. Although no servants or guards were visible, a cup of steaming sake sat untouched at her side.

She was a large woman, broad-armed and thick-waisted, the red silk of her kimono stretching taut across her shoulders as she turned to regard Isami and the others. Her mask was of black silk embroidered with swirls of gold thread, the pattern seeming to tug at the eye. It covered the lower half of her face, her eyes a pale brown that seemed almost golden in the lamplight.

Although Kaede's hair was mostly gray and her brow creased with age, her bulk was that of a sumo rather than the tepid softness that occasionally descended upon courtiers in their later years. Isami recalled Kaede had been a celebrated wrestler in her day, thrice unseating reigning champions at the Winter Court. Although her last victory occurred when Isami was but a child, it had been the talk of the capital for weeks.

"At last." Although Isami could not see Kaede's lower face beneath the gold-embroidered mask, the relief in her eyes seemed almost genuine. "I had begun to worry."

"Mother." Hands forming a careful triangle on the bamboo mats before him, Keisuke bowed low. Taking up position behind him, Isami and the others quickly followed his example. In addition to food and shelter, Yoshio had thoughtfully supplied them all with clan robes. Although Isami was not quite comfortable in red and black, it was far better than being imprisoned as a potential spy.

"No need for pageantry." Kaede rolled her neck as if working out a cramp. "This is a celebration, after all."

Keisuke straightened. Isami and the others waited a long breath before following his lead, as was proper.

Isami quelled a tremble as Lady Kaede regarded them, sure the Scorpion noble would see through their ruse in an instant, but Kaede's gaze swept past with nary a flicker of suspicion, settling on Yoshio.

"Well done, captain."

"Thank you, lady," Yoshio said. "We found Lord Keisuke in a river barge, alone but for a hired guard and two servants. I thought it best to bring–"

"My apologies," Keisuke interrupted. "You mean one hired

guard, one serving woman, and my valet, Koemon." He glanced at Shinzō. "I know he seems rough about the edges, but the man has a true gift for selecting sashes."

Yoshio regarded Shinzō with barely disguised irritation. The archivist remained completely still, although from propriety or embarrassment, Isami could not say. It was clear Keisuke was merely using the interruption to frustrate Yoshio, but the captain could not interrogate Keisuke's servants without calling the courtier's honesty into question.

"As you say, lord." Reddening behind his mask, the Scorpion captain gave a stiff nod. He turned back, seeming ready to continue, when Lady Kaede fluttered her fingers.

"You may return to your duties, captain." Her voice was sweet, but firm. "With my gratitude."

"Your will, lady." Yoshio made a show of looking around the empty courtyard. "Shall I detail guards?"

"I am quite safe. I assure you."

"Of course." With a final bow, the captain turned on his heel and strode through the gate, his soldiers falling in behind.

Keisuke watched him depart. The delight in the Scorpion courtier's eyes flickered and died as Lady Kaede shifted on her dais.

"You have brought a hungry Lion to our doorstep."

Apprehension prickled along Isami's spine. No Scorpion high noble would consent to have an Ikoma rifle through their clan records. If Kaede knew of Shinzō, their gambit might be over before it truly began.

"Lord Hanbei is not an opponent to be taken lightly," Kaede continued.

Isami let out a slow breath, expression studiously blank. It seemed Keisuke's mother also favored sudden changes in topic.

Keisuke took a quick breath, but before the Scorpion courtier could respond, Lady Kaede continued.

"I do not recognize your servants."

Once more, concern seized Isami's throat in a heavy grip. Whether or not Keisuke had hoped to avoid Lady Kaede, if he planned to betray Isami and Shinzō, now was the perfect opportunity. Although she dearly wished to study Keisuke's reaction, Isami kept her posture straight, her eyes focused on the middle distance, as was proper for a servant.

"Please forgive my rudeness." Keisuke's tone was one of benign civility. "You have already met Koemon. This is Takeshi, my bodyguard, and my body servant–"

"Do you think I care for their names?" Lady Kaede leaned forward, gaze sharp. "Where did they come from?"

"A river town north of Beiden." Keisuke gave an airy wave. "The name escapes me."

"It is not wise to pick up stray dogs. You never know who their true master may be," Kaede replied. "Far better to keep such things within the clan."

"Strange." Keisuke spoke as if discussing the price of barley. "I have oft found the opposite to be true."

Lady Kaede chuckled. "Be that as it may. It might be best you dispose of them before we speak."

"No need." A bead of sweat trickled down the back of Keisuke's neck. "They have been with me for the duration."

"As you wish." Kaede tapped her chin, gaze pinioning Isami and the others before sweeping back to Keisuke. "Now, tell me *everything*."

"It was as you thought, mother," he said. "They had Kentarō's records. I might have yet turned the situation to our favor, but Lord Otomo Shinpachi took a personal interest in the proceedings."

Kaede responded with a very unladylike curse. "That thrice-damned Otomo has been dogging my steps like a hungry ghost. I must have wronged him in a past life to have earned such undying enmity."

Isami found herself leaning forward. She had known Lord Otomo played politics with the great clans, but to hear it put so plainly was fascinating.

"He sent an emissary to oversee the negotiations."

"And take his cut, I'm sure," Kaede scoffed.

"Actually, she proved remarkably resistant to bribes."

Isami wondered how she would have reacted had Keisuke attempted such. Poorly, she supposed. But then again, what had Lord Otomo's offer been if not a bribe? The thought made Isami distinctly uncomfortable.

"That would be in keeping with what we know of Otomo's agents. I'd dearly like to know how the man manages to secure such loyalty on a Second Intendent's stipend." She leaned forward, voice low. "If he is embezzling court funds, he's hidden his trail well."

"Even with the interference, I was able to work out a compromise with the Lion emissary," Keisuke said.

"Then why have I received urgent messages stating Lord Ikoma Hanbei's forces have occupied Stone Willow Valley?"

"There were… complications." Keisuke tensed like a man expecting a blow. "Kentarō's records were destroyed, and the Lion commander seemed to think me responsible."

"Were you?"

"Not to my knowledge." Keisuke gave a penitent shake of his head, gaze flicking surreptitiously to Shinzō. "But that hardly matters now."

Isami realized her hands were bunched in her robe, and relaxed them, feeling surprise and relief in equal measure. Keisuke had not betrayed them, although it was strange both he and his mother feigned ignorance concerning the Lion documents.

Lady Kaede sat back. Expression thoughtful, she cracked her knuckles in a way that seemed like an old habit. Beyond the villa's walls, a burst of delighted laughter and cheers rose from the murky babble, but inside the courtyard, uncomfortable silence reigned.

"So tell me," Kaede said, at last. "Why are you here instead of there?"

"I thought to bring word."

"Then send a messenger."

"Masaru had things well enough in hand," Keisuke replied a little too quickly. "I would have only got in the way."

Kaede watched him, unmoving, her expression that of a fighter sizing up an opponent before a match. Rather than unnerve Keisuke, her cold scrutiny seemed to anger the Scorpion courtier.

There was a tension in the air, a sense of barely restrained fury, of a gate about to burst. Isami dearly wished to intercede, but her accent would give everything away. More, servants were required to remain silent unless called upon, and Keisuke appeared far beyond such niceties.

"I know you sent Masaru to watch me," he said. "As if I could not even manage a simple negotiation."

"And could you?" Kaede's tone was flat as a frozen pond.

Keisuke squeezed his eyes shut, head bowed.

"Then it seems my assumption was correct." Lady Kaede rapped one knuckle on the tray at her side. As if conjured from the night air, a servant hurried from the shadows to kneel by her.

"See my son and his entourage are taken to one of the outlying villas. Provide food, bedding, and whatever else they require."

Isami seized upon the reprieve in Kaede's words. Shifting to glance at the others, she began to rise, hoping to collect Keisuke before the courtier set a burning taper to their plans.

But he would not be managed.

"Did you order Masaru to destroy the Lion records?" Anger twisted Keisuke's question into a jagged accusation. "Was I but another game piece, to be used and discarded?"

Isami swallowed against a throat gone suddenly dry. To interrupt one's lord with such allegations was the height of insolence. Nobles had been stripped of rank, even banished for less. Although he had not betrayed their true mission, Keisuke seemed bent on bringing Kaede's wrath down upon them all.

Isami drifted back to her knees, unable to hide her dismay. Fortunately, the two Scorpion nobles paid no mind.

"It wounds me you would think that." Kaede stared down at Keisuke, her voice heavy with the strain of someone attempting to leash their temper.

"What else am I to think?" he asked. "Cast adrift amidst the clan records. As if by burying me in some dusty archive I might fade into history as well."

"You know not the precariousness of our situation."

"And how was I to learn?" The question had an almost plaintive tone, fury warring with desperation. Keisuke looked away, jaw tight as a coiled serpent. "I thought you were testing me, judging if I was worthy to carry the family name. But there was no test, no judgment… only cruel calculation. What a fool I was to think you believed in me, that I was anything more than a convenient cover for your true ambitions."

Kaede surged to her feet. Crossing the distance to Keisuke in two quick strides, she snatched up the Scorpion courtier by the front of his robes, shaking him like a dog with a rat in its jaws.

The move came so suddenly even Gorobei sat stunned, seemingly forgetting his role as Keisuke's bodyguard.

"There was no judgment. I thought you were ready." Kaede held Keisuke so they were face-to-face. "But if you want to sulk like a child, return to Journey's End City. Another few years in the archives might teach you to guard your tongue better."

As casually as if she were tossing a handful of petals, Kaede set Keisuke tumbling back onto the dirt, his mask torn in the fall.

Isami clenched her fists against the urge to come to Keisuke's defense. Lady Kaede may have spared Keisuke, but Isami was under no illusions about how she would treat a presumptuous servant. Better to remain part of the backdrop than risk becoming the object of a noble's misplaced ire.

Surprisingly, it was Shinzō who moved. Keisuke's fall had left him near the archivist, and he reached out a firm hand – either to steady the courtier or hold him back, Isami could not say.

Lady Kaede towered above them like the statue of some vengeful god. Gone was the fury that had animated the sudden burst of violence, replaced by stony scrutiny, as if Keisuke were a bit of broken crockery she would see swept away.

Keisuke shook free of Shinzō's grip and scrabbled into a sitting position. So sharp were his eyes, Isami thought for a moment he might lunge at his mother. Instead, he bowed low, one hand clutching the torn strap of his mask.

"As you wish, my lady."

Kaede turned away with a disgusted grunt. "We shall speak again when I have finished cleaning up your mess."

Isami moved to help Keisuke to his feet, but the courtier waved her away. Although he limped from the villa, his back remained straight, his head high.

Within three steps of the gate the crowds closed in, a sweaty, shouting press that threatened to drag Isami and her companions apart. Only by clinging to each other's robes were they able to keep from being swept along. Eventually, through shouting and the liberal use of elbows, Gorobei was able to navigate them through the throng. Like the prow of a ship, he cut through the mass of revelers, Isami and the others following in his wake.

At any moment, she expected Scorpion guards to step from the milling crowd, ready to forcibly escort them to less pleasant accommodations, or perhaps to some shadowed back alley. Lady Kaede did not seem like a woman to balk at killing a few nameless servants, if only to teach her son a lesson about defying his betters.

Finally, they reached the relative safety of the outskirts, the trade road curving up along the western side of the Spine of the World.

"Wait here," Keisuke told them, turning toward a nearby Scorpion guard post with a nod of his head.

"What are you doing?" Isami's question sounded plaintive, even to her ears.

"Requisitioning mounts," Keisuke replied. "Unless you wish to walk to Journey's End City?"

"You think they will just give us horses?" Shinzō asked. "After what happened with Lady Kaede?"

"They must." Keisuke cocked his head. "Once I tell them my mother has ordered me home."

Isami blinked. "You goaded her on purpose?"

"She was going to take us north. This seemed the quickest way to reach our destination." Keisuke's self-assured poise was only slightly spoiled by the tremble in his voice. Before Isami could question him further, the Scorpion courtier spun on his heel and hurried off.

Isami shared a look with her companions, not sure if she wanted to flee or sigh with relief.

"To live like that." Shinzō shook his head. "Makes me glad I was born a Lion."

"The Scorpion hold no monopoly on intrigue," Gorobei replied. "Or ambition for that matter. Lion, Scorpion, Imperial, it makes no matter. Integrity is the province of warriors' tales, reality requires far more compromise."

"I have read enough conflicting histories to see the wisdom in those words," Shinzō nodded.

They watched Keisuke disappear into the guard post, contemplative silence lost against the low roar of distant merriment.

Try as she might, Isami could not seem to survey the contours of Keisuke's ambitions. The confrontation with Lady Kaede had seemed real, raw, hardly the product of artifice or acting. She reminded herself that Keisuke was not Kazuya. For all his posturing, he had seen them safely through Beiden Pass and on to Journey's End City.

"Do you still believe he means to betray us?" she asked Shinzō.

It was Gorobei who answered. "If so, he is certainly taking his time about it."

That brought a smile even from Shinzō.

As if summoned, Keisuke emerged from the posthouse, two guards in tow. Catching sight of Isami and others, he beckoned them over.

Expression thoughtful, the Shinzō regarded the Scorpion courtier. "Do you think he planned this all from the beginning?"

Isami sighed, shaking her head.

"I think he would dearly like us to believe he did."

# CHAPTER TWENTY-TWO

From a distance, Journey's End City seemed no different than any other city in the Empire; larger than most, perhaps, but apart from the Scorpion banners flying over the walls it could have been mistaken for any well-appointed provincial capital.

It was only when one drew closer that The City of Lies earned its name.

Miles of rolling fields hemmed the roads, but instead of rice or barley, they were filled with crimson poppies, a sea of blood-red blooms bobbing gently in the southerly breeze. Peasants moved among the rows, backs bent as they tended the delicate flowers. In a few weeks' time the petals would fall, and the harvest would begin.

Isami had known Journey's End City supplied the bulk of the Empire's trade in medicinal opium, but she had never imagined it would be so *much*. The poppy fields seemed to stretch to the horizon.

Scorpion guards waited in the shadow of the wide southern gate, collecting duties on the stream of merchants and travelers flowing into the city. Keisuke's noble bearing coupled with liberal mention of Lady Kaede's name meant Isami and the others were subjected to only the most cursory of inspections before being passed through.

Within the circumference of Journey's End City's thick limestone walls, the city hummed with activity. Merchants lounged beneath shadowed awnings, smoke curling from their pipes as they haggled over the coming crop. It might have been Isami's own suspicion bleeding through, but the people seemed somehow more cautious in their movements, their eyes canny, their conversations guarded.

Although the road was wide, it felt somehow confining. High buildings rose to either side, seeming almost to loom over the street in a way that reminded Isami of a forest canopy. There were few crossroads, but many corners, locals relying on a tangle of alleys and backstreets. It was down one of these that Keisuke led them, barely large enough for their horses to pass. Numerous screens and draperies hung from lines strung above, shadowing the street in pale half-light. Snatches of quiet conversation drifted from corners and shuttered windows, twisted by the strange acoustics of the place so that Isami could place neither words nor source.

Although used to the tight quarters of urban life, Journey's End City discomfited Isami. This seemed doubly true for Shinzō, who rode stiff-backed, one hand resting on the place on his sash where a sword would have hung had valets been permitted to bear such weapons. No doubt, he wished he had not been forced to abandon his blade and armor. This made Isami doubly grateful her billowing Scorpion robes easily concealed her surveyor's chain, tightly bound about her waist. Even Gorobei seemed more on guard, his pinched expression one Isami recognized from when they had fled the Lion soldiers.

Only Keisuke seemed unaffected, appearing to gather the scraps of his tattered confidence as they wended their way deeper into the Scorpion capital.

The city was a surveyor's nightmare. Despite Keisuke's self-assurance, it felt impossible they could navigate the snarl of intersecting backstreets. Keisuke turned corners seemingly at random, alleys doubling back on themselves until it seemed they were traveling in circles. More than once, Isami fought the urge to draw Tadataka's compass to get her bearings.

Just as she had given up hope of ever winning free, Keisuke led them into a wide, tiled plaza. Tall towers ringed the square, the low walls of courtly villas and ministerial courtyards spread between. Everywhere was the crimson and black of the Scorpion Clan, from banners to window screens, to the carefully trimmed maple trees whose leaves had begun to flush a deep, autumnal red.

A forest of manors and ministries had sprung up in the shadow of the Scorpion palace. Individually walled in the Rokugani style, they were connected by streets of pale limestone, servants and functionaries hurrying between, heads low, expressions intent. Here and there, Scorpion guards stood as if cast from lacquered steel, seeming almost inhuman in their armor and war masks. If not for the turning of their heads as Isami and the others rode into the plaza, she might have mistaken them for statues.

Dismounting, Keisuke handed his reins to one of the guards without a word. Perhaps sensing his companion's hesitation, he cleared his throat.

"Take our mounts to the western stables. See they are well cared for."

Isami relinquished her reins with no small measure of trepidation. Though their horses would be next to useless in the city's tight confines, she could not help but feel as if she had been robbed of a means of escape.

Keisuke led them to a tiered stone building. Pausing before the gate, he glanced back at Shinzō.

"Well?"

The Ikoma archivist cocked his head. "Well, what?"

"It would seem odd for me to announce myself." His grin was obvious even behind his mask. "And you are my valet."

Shinzō regarded the Scorpion courtier through narrowed eyes, but the glare did nothing to douse Keisuke's delight. With an irritated grunt, Shinzō pushed by the courtier to hammer a fist upon the gate.

"Open for Lord Bayushi Keisuke, Sub-intendent for Noted Records of the Clan Archives!"

After a bit of shuffling, a small window was thrown open in one of the gates. Although the archivist's face was completely hidden behind a brightly painted tengu mask, her hair was arranged in courtly fashion, held in place by a profusion of lacquered combs.

"Lord Bayushi." Her face disappeared as she bowed, only to pop back into view a moment later. "I had not heard of your return."

"Then all is well," Keisuke nodded. "For I told no one."

There came the distinct sound of bolts being thrown. After a moment, the gate yawned wide, the archivist kneeling just beyond.

"I shall have your rooms prepared."

"No need." Keisuke strolled into the courtyard. "I will not be staying long."

"As you say, lord." The archivist remained bowed, but Isami could not help but note how quickly she hurried away once Keisuke had passed by.

Like many Rokugani manors, the courtyard of the Scorpion Clan Archives was largely given over to gardens and small pavilions. Stands of maple and camelia edged the winding gravel paths, interspersed with beds of poppy, kuroyuri, and red spider lilies. At almost every turn stood a rose bush. Seemingly left to grow wild, they snaked through the flower beds, coiled thorns barely visible through the greenery.

The sight could not help but remind Isami of the Ministry's Scorpion Garden. The last time she had ventured there was when she confronted Kazuya. The memory seemed to open a hollow in Isami's stomach, and she glanced around, hoping to find something, anything to send it flitting away.

The sky above was just edging toward night, shadows lengthening around the garden. There were several outbuildings scattered around the grounds, paths and roofed walkways leading to a large manorial structure at the rear of the courtyard. Just visible through the trees, the lower slope of its roof gables were hung with hundreds of carefully folded papers. At first, Isami took the place for a shrine hung with warding scrolls or good luck charms, but as they drew near, she saw the papers bore neither prayer nor mantra, but were rather covered in small characters as if copied from a book or scroll.

"What are those?" she whispered, gazing up at the hanging pages.

Keisuke grinned. "Records, of a sort."

"You would subject them to the elements?" Shinzō wrinkled his nose.

"They aren't *the* records," Keisuke replied. "Only suggested revisions. When a scholar discovers some new bit of historical ephemera, they are required to write of their finding and display it here for all to see. Those deemed worthy are brought to the archivists, who review the findings, and, if necessary, correct the record in question."

Shinzō made a disgusted sound in the back of his throat. "Only a Scorpion would believe history could be rewritten."

Keisuke chuckled. "Only a Lion would believe it couldn't."

Whatever reply Shinzō meant to voice died as they entered the Scorpion archives.

The smell of books and ancient scrolls enfolded Isami like a quilted robe, all her concerns melting away beneath the quiet rustle of paper and tread of slippered feet. The walls were adorned with the Scorpion crest, the lanterns framed in red and black, the archivists masked, but none of it mattered.

For the first time since she had set foot in Journey's End City, Isami felt at home.

She glanced at Shinzō. The Ikoma archivist regarded the racks of scrolls with a thoughtful expression, eyes bright with interest.

"I am sure it is nothing compared to the Grand Histories," Keisuke said softly.

Shinzō craned his neck to peer into the shadowed recesses of the collection. "It is respectable."

A pair of servants approached, lanterns held high to light the way.

"Thank you, but my own staff shall be sufficient." Keisuke dismissed them with a distracted wave of his hand.

Bowing, Isami and Shinzō relieved the servants of their

lanterns, careful to keep the small flames well away from the racks of ancient scrolls.

Keisuke directed them down a long hall. Screens studded the walls, no doubt leading to research and reading rooms. If Isami closed her eyes, she could almost imagine herself back at the Ministry.

"Keep close, and speak softly," Keisuke murmured. "No doubt word of my return has already spread. There will be meetings, audiences, many questions I would prefer not answer."

"We must move quickly," Isami agreed. "Where are Lord Kentarō's records?"

"Truthfully?" Keisuke winced. "I do not know."

Isami blinked, surprised by the admission. "You said you had them."

"Not personally," he replied. "My clerks prepared reports. I haven't actually seen the original documents."

"Then summon your clerks," Shinzō said.

"And tell them what?" Keisuke cocked his head. "That I am attempting to undermine the war effort and give away territory to our sworn enemies? No, I would much prefer to keep this matter between us."

Isami shook her head, astonished. "What was your plan?"

"I had rather hoped you and Shinzō might be able to find them."

"I catalogue maps," Isami replied. "I wouldn't even begin to know how to search historical records."

"I do," Shinzō said softly.

They looked to the Ikoma archivist.

"I noticed the name plates on the way in." He gave an embarrassed bob of his head. "The records look to be cataloged according to Variegated Seasons Method – a bit archaic, but certainly logical. I should be able to find what we are looking for."

"When acting against the wishes of one's lord, it is best not to deal in half-measures." Keisuke nodded. "Lead the way, Ikoma."

Shinzō raised his lantern, expression focused as he led them into one of the many archival repositories. Running a finger along the row of scroll racks, Shinzō's lips moved silently as he unwove the ancient catalog. Although the storeroom was mostly empty, those few archivists amongst the records watched Shinzō and the others with cold disapproval.

Shinzō paid them no mind, wending amidst the shelves and racks as if returning to his childhood home after a long absence. Like the Ministry Records, the Scorpion Archives were spread across a number of rooms and outbuildings, separated by walkways and high stone walls to prevent the spread of fire.

"If there are any maps, they would be in here." Shinzō nodded to a storeroom door. "Useful for settling any border questions our Lords care to raise."

"Would they not be with Kentarō's other records?" Isami asked.

"The Variegated Seasons Method separates by both imperial reign dates and document type," Shinzō replied with a thin smile. "As I said, a bit archaic."

Nodding, Isami slid the door open. The chamber beyond seemed more storeroom than archive. Although the room was spacious, there was hardly room for the four of them to stand comfortably inside. Piles of discolored scroll cases covered the low table, pillows stacked in one corner to make room for crate upon crate of water-stained books. Several motheaten woven map hangings lay rolled next to the writing desk, a score or more warped banner poles leaning against the rear wall.

Isami brought a hand to her mouth even as Shinzō gave an unbelieving cough.

"It seems the archivists do not think much of cartography." Keisuke craned his neck as if searching for a place to sit. Dust motes swirled in the lantern light, the air sharp with the smell of mildew and neglect.

"It will take hours to find anything in all this," Isami shook her head, appalled by the state of the map room.

"Then we had best start searching." Keisuke moved one of the crates aside, clearing space around the low reading desk. "Help me with these." He held out a scroll case to Shinzō, who regarded it as if the courtier had just offered him a venomous beetle.

"Are you responsible for this?"

Keisuke glanced away. "My duties did not leave me much time for cataloging."

"You are the Sub-Intendant for Notable Records. These seem notable."

Keisuke ignored him, holding the scroll out to Isami. "Help me clear some space."

Together, they shifted most of the assembled detritus toward the far wall. Isami opened several of the window screens, hoping to air out some of the dust, but Keisuke stopped her with an impatient wave.

"Keep those closed, we don't want to attract any more attention."

"Even if the maps are here, we still require the historical record," Shinzō said.

"Then by all means, go." Keisuke fluttered his fingers.

"Aren't you coming?" Shinzō asked.

"My continued presence will only raise more questions," Keisuke replied. "In my tenure, I have never once set foot in the archives proper."

Shinzō stared at the Scorpion courtier.

"You and Keisuke search here. I can accompany Shinzō," Gorobei drew himself into a rough approximation of a belligerent posture, eyes hard and threatening. "I'll glare at any archivist who comes too close."

"Be quick," Keisuke said. "I fear we are on borrowed time."

With a nod, the two departed, leaving Isami and Keisuke in the storeroom.

They worked quietly, Keisuke clearing space and Isami searching through the map scrolls. It was difficult to conceal her scorn. To allow ancient records to fall into such disarray was disgraceful, but such was the fate of many maps. Most archivists treated them with the same casual disdain they would show to a painting or teacup, as if only the written word was worth preserving.

Silence edged in around Isami and Keisuke, tight as a poorly fitted robe. Several times, Isami felt Keisuke was watching her, but when she looked up, he quickly turned away.

Just as the moment became unbearable, Isami broke the quiet. "How will Lady Kaede react to Kentarō's records?"

"That depends." He sucked air through his teeth. "If she ordered Masaru to destroy the first batch, I expect she'll do the same to the second, and us along with it."

"You think your mother would murder us?"

"I know she would," Keisuke replied. "Especially if we are a threat to the clan."

"Can you make her see reason?"

"Perhaps." Keisuke shrugged. "If the agreement Shinzō and I signed becomes public knowledge, it might be enough to drag her to the negotiating table."

"Then that is what we must do." Isami bent back to her task, trying to ignore the questions that weighed upon her mind. For once, the crackling scrolls proved a poor distraction.

"Back at Beiden, when we met your mother. Why didn't you betray us?"

"I might have. Had she asked nicely."

Isami studied the Scorpion courtier. "I don't think so."

"Then you do not know me."

"Perhaps not." Isami sat back, hands folded in her lap. She knew what it was to live in the shadow of one's parents, although her upbringing had suffered more from benign neglect than stifling expectation. Still, it was easy to see how, without Master Tadataka's guidance, she might have become like Keisuke, like Kazuya. She imagined what it would be like to grow up with no one to trust, surrounded by rivals and enemies.

Back at Stone Willow Valley when they had fought, and again when he had confronted Lady Kaede, Isami had seen Keisuke's mask slip. She wished there was something she could say to show him he wasn't alone.

Except, he was.

For all their shared struggles, Isami was yet an agent of Otomo Shinpachi, and Keisuke remained a Scorpion. At the moment, their interests aligned, but it would be foolish of her to think Keisuke would choose her over his clan, or himself.

She spied a familiar seal, rummaging through the scrolls to

draw forth a tattered map. Chest tight, she spread it upon the reading desk. Notes in a memorable hand filled the margins, the expanse crisscrossed by scores of intersecting lines. Perfectly straight, they divided mountain, field, and river into a fractured prism of overlapping triangles, distance and angle carefully recorded along each line.

Isami could not believe her eyes. Numbly, she drew the much-abused imperial survey from her satchel, unrolling it next to the ancient map.

"Did you find Lord Kentarō's survey?" Keisuke leaned in for a better look.

"Better." Isami's voice was a breathless whisper.

Her fingers trailed across the Spine of the World Mountains, settling in Stone Willow Valley where the two characters that formed the cartographer's name were written.

Gyōki.

She unrolled the imperial survey, now seeming little more than a rough sketch compared to the precision of the Gyōki map. Even now, centuries later, she could easily track the curve of the river, the mountain peaks rendered in such exquisite detail Isami felt as if she were gazing at them. She drew forth her own unfinished survey, and the breath caught in her throat.

As rough as her own work was, it matched Gyōki's.

"Isami, what is it?" Keisuke asked. "What have you found?"

She ignored him. The Gyōki map must have belonged to Lord Kentarō and therefore Lady Saihoku. How else would he have learned the cartographic applications of Hui's triangle? Of course Isami and Gyōki's maps would be similar, the triangles needed to be measured from high points to draw a good sightline. The hills and peaks had not changed much in the intervening centuries. Which meant Lord Kentarō's expedition would have followed a recognizable route.

Leaning close, she compared the notes on her map to the expanse of Gyōki's. Although the survey did not reach far enough to include the blank space of Lord Kentarō's "Gilded Scar", Isami was able to mark the curve of the river from whence he departed into the mountains.

Dimly, she heard Keisuke talking, but his questions came as if through water, little more than burbling murmurs against the thunder of Isami's heart.

"The valley," she said. "I can find it."

"What valley? Stone Willow?" Keisuke said. "I don't understand."

Isami gripped his shoulders. "I can *find* it."

"You look about to collapse." Concern colored Keisuke's tone. "Sit down, take a breath."

Isami touched the maps as if to assure herself they were real. In light of the Gyōki map, the imperial survey seemed a terrible joke. The line of the river, the mountains, even the placement of the villages was all wrong, as if the cartographer had ridden by on a cart and simply guessed at the geography.

Isami rolled up her map, slipping it into the front of her robes. There would be time for study later. For now, she wished only to make sure nothing befell the Gyōki map. The paper was brittle and water-stained, liable to fall apart if treated roughly.

She could not wait to show it to Tadataka. This map could not replace the ones Kazuya destroyed, but perhaps it would be enough to earn Isami some small measure of forgiveness. More, it would show the other masters that she indeed honored the work of the ancients.

She was so wrapped up in thoughts of her return to the Ministry she didn't even mark when the door to the storeroom slid open. Only when Keisuke gave a startled grunt did Isami glance up.

She had expected Shinzō and Gorobei. Instead, a pair of Scorpion samurai stood in the hall.

"Lord Bayushi Keisuke." The lead guard gripped her sword hilt. "You are under arrest."

# CHAPTER TWENTY-THREE

"My mother shall hear of this!" Keisuke surged to his feet, hands raised in outrage.

"It was Lady Kaede herself who signed the order." The guards ducked into the room. Although neither had drawn their weapon, both moved with the cool competence of veterans.

Painfully aware of the unstated threat, Isami tried to slip the Gyōki map into her satchel, but a hiss from the nearer guard gave her pause.

Feigning servile politeness, Isami hooked her thumbs around the loop of her chain. She was under no illusions about how well her disguise would stand up to dedicated scrutiny.

Keisuke spluttered. "I will not be subjected to such baseless—"

The lead guard grabbed Keisuke's forearm. In one fluid motion, she twisted it down, dragging the courtier forward even as she spun him about. Keisuke's protest ended in an outraged squawk as the guard wrenched his arm up and behind his back.

Isami took in the scene. Even had she faced the samurai outside of such cramped quarters, Isami would have little chance of emerging victorious against two trained warriors. Still, the dungeons below the Scorpion palace were renowned even among the more ruthless clans. Death by blade was much preferable to the lingering punishments that awaited spies.

Isami stood, flicking out the weighted ends of her surveyor's chain.

The other guard drew his blade. "Stand aside."

"Isami, don't." Keisuke gritted the words between clenched teeth.

Isami flicked one end of her chain up to coil about the man's katana. Dragging down with all her weight, she ripped the blade from the guard's grip.

He recovered quickly. Snatching the wakizashi from his sash, he came in low, the tip of his short sword thrusting toward Isami's gut.

Instinctively, she tried to hop back, but her heel snagged on a crate of books and she crashed backwards, dislodging the banner poles leaning against the rear wall. As they fell, the guard tried to knock the poles aside, but he was off balance from his lunge, and the rain of heavy wooden staves hammered him to the ground.

Isami tried to rise, but it was almost impossible to find her feet amidst the scattered detritus. The downed guard flailed to his knees, knocking over more books and causing the banner poles to roll this way and that. Isami twisted, hoping to snatch up the Gyōki map, but it was buried under a cascade of poles. She threw herself at the pile even as the samurai holding Keisuke dragged the struggling courtier back into the hall.

"Guards!" Her voice rose above the crackle of broken crates and tearing paper.

Isami's heart seemed to seize as an answering cry came from deeper within the archives, the words indistinct, but the meaning clear enough.

Isami pawed at the refuse covering the desk, her breath coming in choked gasps.

The other guard grabbed her ankle and dragged Isami back. She fell hard on her knees, pain shooting up her legs. Isami tried to kick free, but the man's grip was like stone.

His short sword came up.

Isami kicked him in the face, the impact of her heel hard enough to drive the guard's half-mask back into his jaw. His hold relaxed for a moment, and she twisted to grab a stack of crates, toppling it upon the man's helmeted head.

As he tried to rise, Isami finally found her feet. Seizing the end of a broken staff, she brought it down like a club. The swing was ugly, but with Isami's full weight it was enough to send the guard's helmet tumbling free. Her second blow drove him to his belly. He did not attempt to rise after her third.

Teeth gritted against the splinters in her palm, Isami stumbled through the wreckage, hoping to find the map.

"Stay where you are." The other guard had her blade drawn. Keisuke stood as if transfixed, gaze flicking between Isami and the downed samurai.

Commotion from deeper within the building finally resolved into intelligible speech. "*Fire! Fire!*"

As if thrown into clarity by their cries, Isami heard the crackle of burning paper, the smell of smoke suddenly sharp in her nose.

With an angry cry, the guard dragged Keisuke from view. Isami tried to follow, but by the time she waded clear of the room, they had already rounded the corner. She stood in the doorway, jaw tight as she glanced back to the storeroom. The map was buried, but perhaps she could recover it before the fire claimed it, or more guards arrived, or Keisuke was taken from the archives.

Groaning, the guard Isami had clubbed pushed to his feet. Blood matted his hair, spreading down the side of his face like a crimson wing. Amidst the gore, his eyes burned like twin coals.

In them, Isami saw her death.

With a strangled shout, she plunged down the hall, tears stinging her eyes. A pale haze filled the air, billowing from the direction of the main archives. One sleeve pressed to her mouth, Isami hurried toward the entrance, hoping to catch the guard before she dragged Keisuke out into the garden.

Footsteps thudded down a cross-hall. Expecting attack, Isami turned, chain swinging.

She checked the blow as the two shapes resolved into Gorobei and Shinzō. The former rōnin took a quick step back, blade held parallel to his body in a two-handed grip. Shinzō had a scroll under one arm, two books balanced on the other.

"Did you find the maps?" Gorobei asked.

Failure blossoming in her chest, Isami shook her head.

"Where is Keisuke?" Shinzō asked.

"Guards took him." Isami spoke quickly, smoke clawing at her throat.

"I spotted a side door to the garden back down the hall," Gorobei said.

They emerged into the night, coughing in the smoky air. In the firelight, the garden looked like a scene from The Realm of Evil, soot-streaked shadows like damned spirits in the hellish light. Archivists ran along the paths, arms full of scrolls and books salvaged from the hungry blaze. Servants and guards carried buckets of water, while others demolished the walkway leading to the other archives. The gaps had been made to act as firebreaks, and the flames seemed contained to a few outbuildings.

"How did the fire start?" Isami asked.

"I do not know." Shinzō coughed. "I was searching the records while Gorobei stood watch outside."

"I saw nothing," Gorobei nodded. "With everyone running about in such a frenzy. We thought you and Keisuke were in danger."

"We were… are," Isami replied. "The guard who took Keisuke made for the entrance."

"They've probably found other guards, then," Gorobei said. "We should use the fire as cover to escape."

"I won't abandon Keisuke," Isami replied, blinking against the sharp smoke in her eyes.

"He would abandon you, mistress."

"Except he didn't." Isami's voice came harsh from the fumes. She turned toward the entrance.

"We'll be no good to him in a Scorpion dungeon." Gorobei caught her arm. "Mistress, please see reason."

Isami chewed her lip, not willing to simply flee. She looked to Shinzō, but the Ikoma archivist would not meet her eyes.

Isami's companions could not be what they had been before they entered the city.

Like it or not, Keisuke was alone.

As if to torment herself, Isami searched for Keisuke amidst the chaos. She thought she saw him, kneeling in the grass, tears glittering in his eyes as he stared up at the growing inferno. A moment, and he was gone, concealed by the swirling smoke.

They ran, as so many others did. In the confusion, covered in ash and soot, no one stopped them even as they burst from the archive gates and into the broad expanse of the central plaza. All around, Scorpion manors and ministries loomed like tombstones, each promising a different, but no less terrible, demise.

"We should pick a direction," Shinzō said. "Head for the wall, then follow it until we find a gate."

Gorobei shook his head. "You saw the alleys in this cursed place. Not a straight line to be found."

"Blundering around the darkened streets will only land us in the hands of a Scorpion patrol, or worse." Isami didn't even want to imagine the sort of folk who haunted The City of Lies after sundown.

"Well, we cannot simply stand here." Shinzō's voice carried a note of desperation. "The guards will be back once the fire is under control."

Isami glanced at him. "Did you find Lord Kentarō's records?"

"Yes and no." The Ikoma archivist clutched the books and scroll tighter, as if to shield them from harm. "There was nothing by the lord himself, but Lady Saihoku wrote several—"

A dark form hurtled from the shadow along the wall, tackling Shinzō to the tiled stone. They went down in a tangle of limbs. The Ikoma archivist's surprised grunt became a shout of pain as his attacker worked one hand into his hair and slammed his face against the cobbles.

"Traitor! Demon!" Keisuke's features were almost unrecognizable under the layer of soot, twisted into a rictus snarl, his mask hanging loose.

"Keisuke, thank the Ancestors you're safe." Isami took a step forward, but paused as the courtier brandished a dagger at her, blade bright in the reflected firelight.

"It will take more than a low-rank guard to hold me." He bared his teeth, voice rough with anger and smoke. "That was but another test. If my mother truly wanted me imprisoned, they would have never announced themselves."

"I'm sorry, I didn't know."

"Not one step closer, any of you." Keisuke pointed his dagger at Gorobei, who had furtively drawn his katana. "Not until I have dealt with this Ikoma traitor."

Shinzō went still as the courtier pressed the dagger to his throat.

"Are you truly so petty? Or did Lord Hanbei order you to destroy the records?"

"I did not set the fire." Shinzō's words came muffled by the cobbles.

"Do you take me for a fool?" A thin trail of blood crept down Keisuke's blade.

"Why would Shinzō set the fire?" Isami asked, confused. "He wishes to stop this conflict."

"The Lion no doubt already occupy Stone Willow." Keisuke's laugh was a low, ugly thing. "For all her scheming, my mother can't carve them from the valley without risking imperial censure."

He glared down at Shinzō. "What did Hanbei promise you? Higher rank? An archive of your own?"

"Only a Scorpion would–" Shinzō's accusation ended in a low hiss as Keisuke drew the archivist's head back.

Isami stepped forward, hands raised. "Please, wait."

Keisuke seemed not to hear her. "Blame me for destroying the records. Seize the valley. Was that your plan all along?"

"He cannot answer with your blade at his throat," Isami tried to imbue her words with calm despite the tingling rattle of her heart.

"That fire was no accident," Keisuke said. "The Ikoma have always desired a stranglehold on history. What better way than to burn our records?"

"Shinzō saved Lady Saihoku's journals." Isami gestured toward the scroll crumpled beneath the archivist.

"Those that support the Lion claims, no doubt."

"Mistress." Gorobei's warning came low and urgent.

Isami glanced back to see the flames were almost gone, the jagged shadows of armored guards just visible beyond the archive gate.

Isami cursed softly. "Gorobei, you were there. Did Shinzō set the fire?"

The former rōnin gave an embarrassed tilt of his head. "My attentions were focused elsewhere."

"Kill me if you want." Shinzō's words came as a low croak. "But I would *never* knowingly destroy historical records, even Scorpion ones."

"Just like a Lion, to hide behind principle," Keisuke snarled back.

Shinzō ignored him, his gaze seeking out Isami. "Lady, promise you will bear these records north. I may die, but I shall not fail the Lion Cla—"

"Do not speak of noble sacrifice." Keisuke gave the archivist a rough shake. "Your actions give lie to your creed."

Isami stared down at them, mouth working as she tried to dredge something, anything, from the roiling tumult of her thoughts. They had but moments before the guards returned, and Keisuke seemed incapable of listening to reason. He seemed a man teetering upon a precipice.

She could not trust him to be rational, not here, not now – but she *could* trust his ambition.

"There is a hidden valley." Isami's hands made fists in her robe. "In the mountains near Stone Willow."

"What valley?" Keisuke asked. "How do you know this?"

"From the maps, and Lord Kentarō's records."

"The Gilded Scar," Shinzō said. "I thought it but an old man's fancy."

"It is far more than that. I believe it represents the key to ending this conflict."

"Mistress." Gorobei gave her a warning look. "Are you sure you wish to share such knowledge?"

Isami swallowed, nodding. "New land, unsettled and open. Whether it goes to Lion or Scorpion, I care not – only that it stops the war."

"How can I believe you?" Keisuke asked.

"I have never lied to you." Isami's gaze flicked to Shinzō. "Either of you."

Keisuke shifted to regard her, gaze steady, as if searching for some trick.

"I will need both your oaths." Isami drew herself up, desperately trying not to look at the Archive gate. "You will not harm one another, and you will follow my orders."

Keisuke gave a pained grimace, gaze flicking from Isami to Shinzō. Without his mask, Isami realized the Scorpion courtier was about her age, perhaps even younger.

She fixed him with a steady stare. "Decide now, or spend the rest of your life as Lady Kaede's most disappointing son."

As Isami had hoped, her words seemed to stir something in the Scorpion courtier. Although he had tried to hide it, she had seen the rawness in him when he spoke of his mother, the broken determination in his eyes when he thought he had failed.

Keisuke groaned as if he were the one with a blade at his throat.

"May your ghost wander the earth for a thousand years if you play me false." He released the pressure on his blade, standing up quickly before Shinzō could lash out.

The Ikoma archivist pushed to his knees, glaring at Keisuke as he gathered up the crumpled records.

"I would hear you say it," Isami said.

"You have my oath." Shinzō gave a sullen bow. "So long as you do not act against my clan."

"I act, as always, for the good of the Empire." Isami held out her hand. "Now give me the records."

Shinzō regarded Isami as if she had asked for his right leg.

"Keisuke clearly does not trust you with them, and you certainly do not trust him."

Even so, Shinzō balked.

"They are Scorpion records," Keisuke said sharply. "You have no right to carry them."

Looking as if the act caused him physical pain, the Ikoma archivist handed over the books and scroll.

Records in hand, Isami's calm façade fled with the suddenness of a spring rain. Glancing over to see the first guards make their way into the plaza, she turned to Keisuke.

"Now, lead me from this cursed city before your family drags us all to the dungeon."

# CHAPTER TWENTY-FOUR

Beiden seemed a different city in the daylight. Gone were the raucous crowds, the Scorpion soldiers, the performers and prestidigitators drawing throngs at every corner. Paper littered the streets, torn streamers and broken lanterns hanging from eaves and store awnings. The trade city reeled like a drunk recovering from a long night at the tavern, merchants conducting business in the shade, voices unnaturally quiet in the autumn cool.

Few paid any mind to Isami and the others. The calm was a welcome departure from their frenzied flight from Journey's End City, where it had seemed every shadow hid a Scorpion guard. Isami had been grateful to trade her Scorpion robes for merchants' attire and hastily forged travel papers, but even several days' journey hadn't completely quelled her anxieties.

Although the fabric was rough against Isami's skin, the chill breeze off the mountains made her grateful for the extra thickness. Summer broke quickly this far from the sea, the land seeming almost to gather the cold like a blanket. Already the maple trees lining the riverbank had flushed a deep crimson, their color an uncomfortable reminder of the impending violence just a few days upriver.

"Do you think Lady Kaede's forces have reached Stone Willow?" Isami asked Keisuke.

"Certainly," he replied, not even looking at Isami. Keisuke still seemed uncomfortable without his mask, but such sacrifices were necessary if they wished to pass as opium traders. At least Keisuke's sullenness had lessened the bickering between himself and Shinzō. The two had passed the hard ride from Journey's End City in relative silence, their mutual distrust confined to the occasional glare.

Craning her neck, Isami studied the rows of barges, junks, and sampans bobbing at the quay. Although Lady Kaede's push north meant there were few to choose from, it had also left the docks blessedly devoid of Scorpion vessels.

"It seems the Ancestors have not quite abandoned us, mistress." Gorobei drew Isami's attention to a nearby dock.

Isami felt a flush of relief as she recognized the familiar silhouette of the *Fortunes' Favor*.

"No." Keisuke's scowl deepened. "Absolutely not."

"They look ready to cast off." Isami nodded at deck full of baled cloth.

"That scow will never get us to Stone Willow in time."

"We can't afford passage on anything faster," Isami replied. They had been required to return their horses to the guard post at Beiden Pass, and had only a little coin.

"The *Fortunes' Favor* is quicker than it looks." The wisp of a smile curled Shinzō's lips. "And if memory serves, Captain Ishi was quite fond of you."

"It is settled, then," Isami nodded. Ignoring Keisuke's sputtering protests, she strode down the dock.

Captain Ishi stood near one of the mooring lines, judging the river currents with a practiced eye, her tanned brow knotted in concentration.

"Captain, we wish to book passage upriver."

"Can't you see we're full up on cloth, girl? Lady Kaede's roving festival snatched up most of the boats, and with demand for fabric being what it is, we stand to make a fortune at Rich Frog. There's no room for no one or nothing aboard my–" Ishi's scowl melted like morning mist as she turned. "Koyo! We thought those Scorpion louts made off with you. Glad to see you back."

Isami blinked, surprised until she remembered Koyo was the name she had used as Keisuke's servant.

"Y- yes, pleased to see you, captain."

Ishi cocked her head, lips pursed. "Save the poetry for the court. No need to put on airs with me."

Isami reddened, only belated realizing she should have let someone else speak. Even in Otosan Uchi she seldom conversed with the lower castes, and never as an equal. Her courtly dialect would betray her as a noble, and it was too late to feign the river folk's rough brogue.

Fortunately, the captain seemed not to notice Isami's indecision, as the arrival of Keisuke and the others occupied her full attention.

"Noble lord, truly The Fortune of Wealth must smile upon my endeavors to have my path once again cross yours." Ishi's bow was so elaborate as to verge on embarrassing. "To what do I owe such an esteemed pleasure?"

"We require passage north." Keisuke crossed his arms, head low.

"I shall have your quarters cleared in an instant, lord." Ishi turned, already drawing in breath to shout at her crew, but paused as Keisuke laid a hand on her arm.

"Even more than before, we require discretion."

The captain glanced down at Keisuke's hand, her blush almost invisible against the deep tan of her cheeks. "Of course, of course. I shall say nothing until we are underway."

"We are in your debt." Keisuke removed his hand. Although his bow was barely a nod, it might have been an imperial commendation the way Ishi grinned.

"All debts are mine, lord." She seemed to be battling the need to maintain proper decorum. "If not for you, the *Favor* would be upriver with all the others. Now, we are bound for a seller's market."

"Nonetheless, you have my gratitude." Resignation threaded Keisuke's tone.

"Worry not, my lord. I shall see to everything." Oblivious to the courtier's chagrin, Ishi retreated toward the gangplank, bowing with every step.

The moment she was out of sight, Keisuke's pleasant regard shifted like a sea current. He turned to Isami, shaking his head.

"I hope the Ministry takes you back, Lady Miya." He sniffed. "You make for a very poor spy."

With that, Keisuke followed the captain.

Perhaps sensing Isami's consternation, Gorobei leaned in. "I believe he meant that as a compliment."

"Only a Scorpion." Although Shinzō crossed his arms, a strange species of amusement underpinned his usual complaint.

Their journey north on the *Fortunes' Favor* was much more bearable, if only because Captain Ishi kept the crew well clear of their quarters. As cramped as the small below-deck room had been, it was doubly so with bales of tightly wrapped cloth secured to every wall. Even so, Isami rejoiced in shedding her servant's role to spend time reviewing Lady Saihoku's journals. She might not be able to thread the gulf between Scorpion and Lion ambitions, but research was something Isami understood, something she *could* do.

It was too much to hope the records would be a travelogue of Kentarō's expeditions into the Spine of the World, but Saihoku's journals seemed devoid of description, largely consisting of purchases and accounting interspersed with the occasional construction record, shipment manifest, and catalog of goods. In her husband's absence, it seemed Saihoku had thrown herself into administration. Isami considered asking Keisuke to help her with the work in the hopes he might recall some useful bit of information, but the Scorpion courtier's attention was taken up by Captain Ishi.

The riverwoman possessed a singular talent for inserting herself into conversation, seizing upon the flimsiest pretext with a skill many court nobles would envy. Not a day went by when Keisuke was not forced up onto deck to inspect a particularly noteworthy stretch of riverbank; and the captain's flood of dinner invitations meant he was seldom in the cabin until late. Keisuke's slightest complaint was met with a flood of apology so abject as to be endearing, followed, of course, by another invitation.

Isami would have intervened, but Captain Ishi was good to her word, keeping as steady a course as the barge was capable of, driving her crew with the cold ferocity of a flint-eyed drillmaster. Even Keisuke could not deny they were making good time.

If only Lady Saihoku were so accommodating.

In desperation, Isami turned to the imperial survey, combing the swirling, cloud-covered peaks for the merest hint of a landmark or pass. She might as well have spent her time staring at mist. Towns were miles away from where they should be, roads and rivers crossing seemingly at random. Isami spent many an hour cursing the unnamed cartographer.

"You are muttering again." Shinzō ducked under the low ceiling beam to kneel at the edge of the wan circle of lantern light.

"My apologies." Isami rubbed her eyes. "The rigors of history weigh heavily upon me."

"Perhaps I may be of assistance?" Shinzō looked to his hands. "I have spent many years researching Lord Kentarō."

Isami studied the archivist. Although she could not quite believe Shinzō had set fire to the Scorpion archives, she also could not deny Keisuke's suspicions.

"I understand." Apparently mistaking Isami's silence for dismissal, the archivist gave a rigid bow before turning to leave. "I shall not trouble you further."

"What do you know of the Gilded Scar?" Isami inquired of Shinzō's retreating back.

The archivist paused. "Not much, I'm afraid. Lord Kentarō was obsessed with it in his final years. He expended much in the way of clan resources on numerous trips into the mountains, but the Spine of the World is not a forgiving place." Shinzō gave a sad tilt of his head. "Lives were lost, including his. Some say Lady Saihoku was responsible."

"Do you believe that?"

Shinzō turned, his face a morning sky unsure of sun or rain. After a long moment, he blew out a thoughtful sigh. "I do not think so. Bayushi Saihoku was a Scorpion, but she seemed to genuinely care for her husband. It was she who put many of his words to paper. Apparently the currents of Lord Kentarō's mind were difficult to navigate."

Isami sat back, eyes wide. "Lord Kentarō did not write the records?"

"He occasionally scribbled notes in the margins." Shinzō gestured toward the books on Isami's desk. "But they are difficult to decipher, mostly numbers and the odd character. I once thought them some manner of code, but if so, the key died with Lord Kentarō."

"Can you show me some of the notes?" Isami asked.

"Of course." Shinzō edged forward, only to pause short of touching the book. "May I?"

"Gorobei," Isami called.

The former rōnin peeked around the screen. "Yes, mistress."

"If Shinzō attempts to start a fire, kill him."

"Yes, mistress."

"I believe that should be sufficient," Isami nodded. "Now, show me."

Shinzō bent over the book, carefully sifting through the pages. It was as if Isami were seeing the archivist for the first time. Since meeting Shinzō, he had often been animated by anger and disdain, but never excitement. So intent was the Ikoma archivist on the record, it was as if Isami were no longer in the room.

She sat quietly, basking in the reflected glow of a fellow scholar at work.

"Here." Shinzō turned the book so Isami could see. Next to a rambling description of various types of stone to be quarried and shipped was a bit of stray ink.

It was a small thing, easily mistaken for a few errant strokes. Like many ancient writers, Lord Kentarō had a habit of not raising his brush between characters, turning the crabbed notes into a blurry line, but now Isami's attention had been drawn to it, she was able to discern the characters. Like swimmers rising through murky water numbers and words emerged from the chaos.

"Those are directions, distance markers. The stone was being shipped somewhere." Isami forced the words through trembling lips, her throat tight with excitement. Barely able to keep her hands from shaking, she drew forth her map, checking the coordinates using Tadataka's compass.

Realization came like the first breath of spring after a long, harsh winter.

"This location isn't anywhere in Stone Willow." Isami's words were barely a whisper. "It was being taken up into the mountains."

"But why?" Shinzō asked.

"Lady Saihoku was building something," Isami replied. "Something large."

"A hill fort? Perhaps a castle? Why invest so much time and resources?"

"I cannot say." Isami tapped the coordinates, grinning. "But I would bet my chain it is interesting enough to bring Scorpion and Lion to the negotiating table."

# CHAPTER TWENTY-FIVE

The Scorpion camp seemed more parade than army on the march. Pennants and banners flew above tents. Columns of armored samurai moved down the river road, appearing like nothing so much as swarms of black and crimson beetles in their brightly lacquered armor. Others were engaged in weapons drills, to the delight of the peasants crowding the riverbank. The low thrum of festival drums seemed to resonate along the river, threaded by the high skirl of flute and shamisen. Higher ranking Scorpion commanders reclined in shaded pavilions, sipping tea with their followers and assorted hangers-on.

"What is Lady Kaede playing at?" Shinzō asked, eyes narrow and wary.

"My mother is being clever." Keisuke leaned against the railing of the *Fortunes' Favor*, neck craned for a better look. "The Lion might currently occupy Stone Willow, but it is still Scorpion land as far as the Empire is concerned. She is well within her rights to review the clan fiefs."

"She cannot plan to march right into the jaws of the Lion." Isami stared at the camp in unabashed wonder.

"I believe that is exactly what she intends," Keisuke replied.

"Lord Hanbei must either withdraw from the valley or attack an ostensibly peaceful force. No doubt Scorpion emissaries are already laying groundwork in the imperial court to frame any such assault as a declaration of war."

"Will it work?" Isami asked.

"You're the imperial noble." Keisuke cocked his head. "You tell me."

Isami looked away. She had been to court exactly twice, once for her gempuku, and the second when her mother had been awarded an imperial commendation for distinguished service after delivering orders to an embattled Crab Clan garrison.

Isami regarded Keisuke and Shinzō in turn. "There won't be a battle if you can bring Lady Kaede and Lord Hanbei to the Gilded Scar."

"I shall do my utmost." Shinzō rested a hand upon the scroll case thrust through his sash, a twin to the one Keisuke held. In it was a missive requiring both Kaede and Hanbei's attendance at a meeting two days hence. As an imperial representative, such a command was technically within Isami's power once she had affixed Lord Otomo's seal.

Whether or not the Lion and Scorpion lords would deign to accept such orders remained unknown, but by ensuring both lords knew the other had received the same missive, Isami had made the command difficult to ignore.

For once, Keisuke was less sanguine about the prospect of success.

"My mother has never been… indulgent." The Scorpion noble gripped the rail, leaning back to stare at the cloudless sky. "She is more likely to have me whipped than hear anything I have to say."

"Then *convince* her," Isami replied.

"You are sure you know the location of this 'Gilded Scar'?" he asked.

"I do," Isami nodded. Bringing both Scorpion and Lion so close to the hidden valley risked bloody conflict, but it had the potential to put an end to the burgeoning war.

Keisuke's sideways glance did not inspire much confidence. He pushed from the rail, approaching the waiting rowboat like a man walking to his own execution. Isami wanted to call after him, but had nothing more to say.

Captain Ishi waited to help Keisuke down into the rowboat, almost tipping them both into the water when she attempted yet another bow. The Scorpion courtier turned to murmur something to her. Although his words were lost on the wind, the captain's wide grin made the message clear enough.

Ishi knuckled an eye, watching two of her crew row Keisuke toward the Scorpion lines. Only when they reached the bank did Ishi turn away, striding up to Isami and the others.

"Lord Bayushi bid me ferry you upriver." Her rough voice cracked only a little. "You need reveal nothing to me, but I humbly request you do not place my crew in danger."

"We require nothing more than transportation." Isami swallowed against the tightness in her throat, dearly hoping the future would not make a liar of her.

"Then you shall have it." The captain hurried off.

Isami watched Keisuke mount the bank, little more than a speck of crimson and black against the autumn grass. A cadre of samurai hurried down the hill to surround him. After a long moment, they moved up the bank.

"Looks promising," Gorobei said, as Keisuke was lost from view. "They didn't kill him on sight."

The *Fortunes' Favor* rounded a bend in the river and the whole of the Scorpion camp disappeared from view.

The rest of the morning passed in an anxious haze, the call of waterfowl punctuated by the rhythmic splashing of oars as the barge wended upriver. Isami and Shinzō checked and rechecked Lady Saihoku's journals, comparing direction and coordinates against Isami's unfinished map. She would have dearly liked to stop to confirm her measurements, but there was no time. There was never any time.

Only Gorobei seemed untroubled by the impending danger. He sat near the bow, a bit of straw dangling from his lips as he watched the riverbank crawl by.

"How can you remain so calm?" Isami asked during one of her infrequent trips to the deck to stretch her legs.

"I've been dead for years, mistress. Every day is an accounting error in my favor." Gorobei turned to watch two geese scuffle near the riverbank, grinning at the honking, hissing tangle of wings and beaks.

Shaking her head at the former rōnin's morbid serenity, Isami made to descend the ladder to the hold. She was on the second rung when calls of: "*Lion! Lion!*" from the crew on watch made her hop back onto deck.

Up ahead, the river narrowed as it passed a rocky bend. Atop the low cliff on the eastern bank were two mounted warriors. They were lightly armored, and carried the lopsided horse bows common among scouts. Although it was too far for Isami to make out any clan symbol, their helms were crested with the distinctive Lion mane.

"Lord Hanbei must have tasked them to watch the river approach." Gorobei stepped up to squint into the early afternoon sun. "The main camp will be somewhere more defensible."

As they drew closer, Isami saw several more Lion samurai on the bank. They had taken up position behind a rocky escarpment, bows and blades at the ready. A number of horses were tied along the grassy sward behind the bank.

"Whoever planned this knew what they were doing," Gorobei said.

Isami was forced to agree. The Lion had a commanding view of both the river and the valley beyond, and there was no way to approach the position without coming under fire.

"Stow the oars! Show them we're no threat!" Captain Ishi stepped from her quarters, a nervous frown flickering across her tanned features as she met Isami's gaze. "We aren't a threat, are we mistress?"

"I dearly hope not." Isami was about to call for Shinzō when the archivist hurried up on deck. He was clothed in Lion robes, his family crest clearly visible, if somewhat worse for wear.

"I am Ikoma Shinzō." He cupped his hands around his mouth to call across the water. "Personal Archivist to Lord Ikoma Hanbei."

The announcement was met with a flurry of activity from among the scouts, helmets bobbing as they consulted with one another.

"You may wish to change, lady," Shinzō whispered to Isami, who hurried down the ladder into their shared quarters.

Her Miya robes were clean if somewhat faded, a casualty of Isami's questionable laundering. Still, it felt good to cast aside the rough merchant garb, the return of her true name and family somehow cleansing, as if Isami were stepping into a soft towel, fresh from a hot bath.

"Fortunes preserve us. You're an imperial." Captain Ishi

dropped to her hands and knees as Isami climbed back on deck, followed a moment later by those crew able to recognize Isami's family crest.

"To think, I allowed you to wash your own clothes." Ishi practically trembled. "Forgive me, my lady."

"You have given no offense, captain." Isami could not help but smile. "To the contrary, I am in your debt."

The captain did not raise her head. Isami was not sure whether asking Ishi to rise would help or hinder matters.

"Lower a rowboat." Shinzō spared Isami the need to decide. "These scouts can lead me back to the main camp."

"As you wish, lord." The captain pushed to her feet, voice cracking as she called for a boat to be readied.

"Are you sure Lord Hanbei will see you?" Isami glanced up at the rocky shore, discomfited by the hard-eyed stare of so many Lion samurai. "Your last meeting was less than cordial."

"I bear an imperial missive." Shinzō's confident words were belied by a subtle twitch of his brow. "He may not wish to see me, but he cannot deny Lord Otomo."

Shinzō climbed down into the rowboat, taking up a position near the bow as the boat lurched forward, propelled by the sailor's powerful strokes. Isami watched them move toward the earthworks, hands tight on the rail. She dearly hoped Shinzō was correct about her lord. Isami would need more than Hanbei's forbearance for their plan to work.

A small knot of Lion samurai waited on shore. Although none had drawn their blade or nocked an arrow, the warriors' rigid posture and tight-lipped scrutiny was somewhat less than reassuring.

Shinzō stepped into ankle-deep water, striding up the muddy bank as if he were entering a palace gate. Although Isami could not hear what was said, Shinzō exchanged a few terse words with the guard captain, gesturing back toward the *Fortunes' Favor*. The Lion captain regarded the ship with a skeptical air, which elicited another barrage of sharp words from Shinzō.

Finally, with a chop of his hand, the captain turned on his heel, hurrying up the embankment as if seeking to put distance between himself and Shinzō. The other scouts moved to surround the Ikoma archivist. Although they kept a respectful distance, they maintained an unsettling degree of discipline as they began to march up the bank.

Isami held her breath, waiting for the Lion to open fire. But at the crest of the bank, Shinzō turned and waved his arms, gesturing upriver. The move loosened the knot in Isami's throat, and she turned to Captain Ishi.

"They will allow us past."

Although Ishi bowed, Isami could not but notice the doubting frown on the captain's lips. Nonetheless, she ordered the barge forward. As the *Fortunes' Favor* drew within bowshot of the cliff, those sailors not involved in the barge's rigging took pains to hunker behind the larger bales of cotton.

Only when the last Lion helm had disappeared around the riverbend did they emerge from their hiding places.

"By the gods!" Captain Ishi let out a joyful whoop. "That'll be a story worth a few rounds at the Rich Frog teahouses." Glancing back, the captain seemed to realize Isami was still onboard. "My apologies for the shouting, lady."

At Isami's nod, Ishi relaxed.

"Will you be traveling with us upriver?"

"Not far." Isami checked Tadataka's compass, then drew her spyglass to study the nearby peaks.

"Of course, lady." The captain could not quite hide her relief. Honestly, Isami couldn't blame her.

Another hour saw the rocky cliffs on the western shore of Three Sides River gradually giving way to steep, willow-lined banks. Isami examined her map every few minutes, obsessively checking and rechecking the coordinates.

Gorobei's shadow fell over her map. "It is time we disembarked."

Isami looked up, shielding her eyes from the sun. "We won't be near the Gilded Scar for another hour, at least."

"I am not talking about the valley." Gorobei extended his hand to indicate a small circle of tents on the eastern bank.

At first, Isami thought it nothing more than a merchant camp, traders and artisans come down hoping to supply the Lion force. It certainly had the look of camp followers. Even the central pavilion was absent crest or clan color. But although the travelers wore no armor, all carried weapons, moving among the tents with the watchful tread of well-trained warriors.

One came down the bank, a large scroll in hand. She did not speak, only waited for the *Fortunes' Favor* to sail closer. When they were roughly abreast, the woman unrolled the scroll, holding it high.

Raw animal panic gripped Isami's chest, every muscle tensed to flee even though she knew there was nowhere to go.

Upon the scroll was a crest, four serpents arrayed in a circle, each swallowing the other.

It was an emblem Isami knew all too well.

Lord Otomo Shinpachi had come to Stone Willow Valley.

# CHAPTER TWENTY-SIX

Lord Otomo sat like a magistrate preparing to sentence a particularly execrable miscreant. His pinched face held not the slightest echo of mercy, his scowl dark as a broken oath. The walls of the tent were hung with silken murals, autumn landscapes interspersed with scenes copied from famous court painters. Incense burned in a low brazier, filling the air with scents of sandalwood and pine. Although neither of the guards had accompanied them in, Shinpachi was flanked by several servants, heads low, expressions carefully blank.

Even Gorobei's presence, normally reassuring, only compounded Isami's concern. The guards had politely but firmly intimated that Isami wait outside while Gorobei spoke with Lord Otomo. Isami had come to depend on the former rōnin, even think of him as a friend. She hoped he would cast events in a positive light, but it was impossible not to wonder how Gorobei would act in the presence of his true lord.

At least the *Fortunes' Favor* had won free. Although Captain Ishi had offered to accompany Isami ashore, they had both known it was a hollow promise. Ishi and her crew would be little more than irritants to Lord Otomo, who would likely view the presence of a score of unwashed sailors as an affront. So Isami had bid the captain farewell, taking heart that their course carried them far from bloodshed.

Even so, Isami wished she did not have to face Lord Otomo alone.

She dared not rise. Looking up would be to meet Shinpachi's icy glare, to acknowledge how far she had strayed from his orders.

"I despise travel." Lord Otomo finally broke the silence, dispensing with even the barest pleasantries. "It carries certain uncomfortable inevitabilities, even for those of means. To be drawn away from court is an imposition upon my time. To be rudely summoned hundreds of miles from Otosan Uchi is an insult. Especially when such summons are rooted in the incapability of one's retainer to follow even simple instructions."

Isami desperately wanted to defend her decisions, but Lord Otomo had not given her permission to speak. A response, even a well-founded one, would only stoke his ire.

"You were sent to determine the veracity of the Lion Clan's claim, nothing more." A note of venom bled into Shinpachi's tone. "Instead, I find the documents destroyed, the valley in shambles, dozens dead, and two of the most powerful clans in Rokugan sharpening their blades over a worthless fleck of land."

Isami remained bowed, still as stone, letting Lord Otomo's fury part like water around a river rock. She was not the callow girl who had left Otosan Uchi just over a month ago. The anger of an imperial bureaucrat, even one as powerful as Otomo Shinpachi, was nothing compared to the blood and horror that would grip the region once the clans battled in earnest. Keisuke and Shinzō had staked their lives to bring their lords to the negotiating table. What manner of noble would Isami be if she did not do the same?

"Well?" Lord Otomo's question came like a burst of icy wind. "What have you to say for yourself?"

Isami straightened, meeting his eyes for the first time since entering the tent.

"The Lion and Scorpion desire land, position." She opened her satchel, drawing forth her unfinished survey. "I plan to give it to them."

Lord Otomo regarded the map as if it were a bit of flotsam washed up on shore. "As if the clans would ever consent to cede even an inch of territory to their rivals. Are you one of the gods? To conjure land from mist and shadow?"

"The lord is, of course, correct. While I cannot create new land, I *can* locate some that has been overlooked." Isami laid the map flat, carefully turning it so Lord Otomo could see. She indicated the blank stretch southwest of Stone Willow. "Amidst the Spine of the World there is another valley. Long lost, or perhaps never found, I am not sure, but it is there."

The anger drained from Lord Otomo's face, replaced by something colder, if no less unsettling. He tapped one knee with his closed fan, eyes like flecks of shale beneath his narrow brow.

"You of all people should know this region has been thoroughly surveyed," Lord Otomo said. "It may be a provincial backwater, but I hardly think the succession of imperial cartographers who tramped across these foothills would have overlooked something so momentous as an entire valley."

"The way is hidden. Perhaps a pass or mountain trail, Lord Kentarō's records did not speak of the means of entry, only the location." Isami circled the area with a finger. "Near the southern curve of Three Sides River, just at the edge of the cliffs. I have the coordinates and, with a bit of time, I am sure I can find the path."

"I should have known better than to send a cartographer to do a diplomat's job." Otomo flicked his fan in distaste. "This obsession of yours has set two great clans at each other's throats, destroyed priceless records, and offended two powerful daimyo. Now you wish to go traipsing into the wilderness in search of some mythical valley?"

"Lord, it is no legend. When he was lord of this region, Kentarō launched several expeditions. He returned again and again. There is even mention of a castle."

"Your former master obviously indulged such flights of foolishness." The glower seemed etched into Lord Otomo's face. "But I have neither the stomach nor the patience for more nonsense."

"Lord, this could put an end to hostilities." Isami tried to keep her voice level, pressing down the panic that threatened to choke off her plea. She needed to convince Otomo, there was simply no other path forward. "The Lion could retain Stone Willow, while the new valley becomes Scorpion land. It lies to the west of Three Sides River, so that would put an end to the Lion's concerns about Scorpion encroachment. I did not have much time to study Lord Kentarō's records, but if his notes are to be believed, the valley may contain something of great–"

"Enough!" Lord Otomo's fan slapped into the palm of his other hand. "Is it not enough you have dragged two clan samurai down with you? Do not compound this disaster by clutching at clouds."

"Lord, please. I beg of you." Isami's lips buzzed, her head

light as if she had drunk too much sake. "This is the best way to prevent war."

"What do I care if Lion and Scorpion bloody each other over some remote valley?" Shinpachi sniffed. "The Scorpion have been growing too influential of late, they could use a reminder of the Emperor's power. And the Lion have always been keen to test their blades."

Isami's mouth worked, throat tight from the shock of Lord Otomo's admission. "Was it your plan to set them at each other?"

"Only fools have but one plan." Lord Otomo jabbed his fan in her direction. "A true sage turns all eventualities to his advantage."

Isami rocked back on her heels, voice soft. "The valley is there."

But Lord Otomo Shinpachi was not listening.

"Miya Isami, I hereby strip you of rank and title. You are no longer my emissary, you are no longer anything. Your mission is over." He stood, thin lips curling back from teeth the color of old parchment. "Gorobei will see you returned to Otosan Uchi. After that, I hope to never hear your name again."

It was as if Lord Otomo had snatched the bones from Isami. She sagged back, only spared collapse by Gorobei's firm grip upon her arm.

"Come, mistress. It is over."

He bore her from the tent, one arm around Isami's shoulder as she stumbled on legs gone soft as rotten wood. She had thought Lord Otomo would see reason, but like Master Kageyasu, Master Naotora, even Master Tadataka, he thought only in terms of calculation and advantage.

Isami sat outside the tent, hands folded in her lap as Gorobei sent servants for horses and supplies. The meeting with Lord Otomo occupied the whole of her thoughts. They rode from camp as if in a dream.

Again and again, she replayed the conversation, searching for something else she could have said, something she could have done. She and Lord Otomo became as bunraku puppets, set and reset upon each showing, the ending always the same.

Perhaps sensing Isami's thoughts were elsewhere, Gorobei took her reins, leading their horses up and out of Stone Willow Valley. The mountains stood at their back, jagged shadows in the deepening gloom. Isami did not even glance back, for to do so would be to recognize those she had left behind.

Isami's cheeks burned as she considered the long, shameful ride back to Otosan Uchi. Even worse was the pain her disgrace would inflict upon Master Tadataka – if he even consented to see her.

Tadataka had tried to warn her, to shield her from the Otomo, but Isami had blundered into Shinpachi's snare. A yearling deer floundering through the forest on her own, unaware of the dangers behind every tree and bush.

They made a small camp in the curve of a low hill, a stand of goblin pine shielding them from the chill wind. Isami hardly felt the cold, only aware she was shivering, Gorobei's fire unable to thaw the chill that had settled into her bones.

She had been so close. Had Lord Otomo not come, had the records not been burned, had Keisuke and Shinzō listened sooner. Baring her teeth, Isami bunched her hands into fists. Only children blamed others for their failings. She could have validated the Lion claim and been done with it. But, as always, Isami had sought too much, too fast.

"One shovel at a time," she muttered to herself.

"Mistress, I made you some tea." Gorobei set a small tray next to her, two steaming cups and a pot. "Warm yourself while I see to dinner."

Isami nodded her gratitude, taking the nearer cup in her hands. Gorobei's familiar smile had grown sharp in Isami's thoughts, whetted by painful memory. He had saved her life, not once, but twice.

In the end she had failed him as well.

Numbly, she set the tea back on the tray and rummaged in her satchel for her map and the imperial survey. She unrolled them side-by-side on the grass, shadows pooling along the well-worn creases. The urge came to cast her map into the flames. It would serve no one, not now; fitting it join the rest of her work.

She sniffed, her grin almost a snarl. Even now, Isami could not understand the mind of someone who could burn records. Knowing Keisuke and Shinzō as she now did, it seemed impossible either could have set the fires. As much as Keisuke was ruled by his ambitions, burning the documents had done more harm than good. Shinzō's anger was a dark and terrible thing, but it was not petty. Had he wished vengeance upon Keisuke, Shinzō would have simply tried to kill him, much as he had attempted to kill Isami at the roadside shrine.

Perhaps Lady Kaede had ordered Masaru to burn the documents, but Isami did not think her vindictive enough to set fire to the Scorpion archives just to deny her son the opportunity to recover Lady Saihoku's journals.

Isami shivered again, although not from the cold. There was one person she had overlooked.

She glanced at Gorobei, but the former rōnin had his back

turned, squatting by the fire as he tended a small bubbling pot. Not quite knowing why, Isami turned the tea tray so her cup was now closer to Gorobei, and his to her.

"Travel rations leave much to be desired." Gorobei set down a bowl of rice and pickled vegetables in front of Isami. "But at least it's hot."

Isami watched the former rōnin as he moved to retrieve his own bowl. Sitting down across from her, he gestured at the food.

"Troubles are much easier to bear on a full belly."

"I don't think I could eat." Isami pressed a hand to her stomach, furtively gripping the chain wrapped about her waist.

"Tea, then." Gorobei set his bowl down. Picking up both cups, he offered the closer one to Isami.

She took it with what she hoped was a grateful smile, pretending to sip. Gorobei downed his own in a few gulps.

"It's no capital blend, but I work with what I have."

Isami placed her cup on the tray. "Why did you set the fires?"

Gorobei's gaze flicked to her cup, still full. He gave a heavy sigh, the smile bleeding from his face.

"You should have drunk the tea."

# CHAPTER TWENTY-SEVEN

Isami twisted as she rose, a length of chain whipping toward Gorobei's head. He rolled back into a low crouch, a blade in each hand.

"I would have preferred to spare you this." The former rōnin came in low and fast, swords back, his upper body almost parallel to the ground.

Isami checked her swing and pivoted to bring the weight hammering straight down. Without even glancing up, Gorobei stepped from the chain's path. Isami was prepared for the dodge and hurled the other weight straight at the former rōnin's face.

He bent like a windswept reed, the heavy iron swishing past.

She jerked the chain back, too late. Gorobei had already stepped inside the arc of her swing, katana slashing around in a tight circle aimed at her belly.

Isami avoided being disemboweled only by dint of a very undignified hop backwards. Although the ground was relatively level, loose stones and protruding tree roots made for uneven footing. Isami's ankle twisted on a gnarled root, and she was forced to drop to one knee or risk losing her balance completely.

Gorobei was quick to capitalize on the stumble, launching a

downward cut with his katana that almost took Isami's arm off at the elbow.

She snatched her arm back just in time. Teeth gritted with effort she whipped up the dangling chains. By the Fortunes' grace, one loop snagged Gorobei's katana as he raised it for another strike.

Isami heaved with all her might, but rather than attempt to keep hold of his weapon, Gorobei simply released the katana. Given force by Isami's pull, the blade tumbled toward her. She was able to check the flailing weapon only by slapping it from the air with the other end of her chain, leaving them hopelessly tangled.

"Your rope tricks may work on Lion brutes," Gorobei's smile held no warmth, "but I have watched you for weeks."

"Why are you doing this?" Isami tugged at her chains, but they remained frustratingly twisted.

"Because my lord ordered it." Gorobei circled her.

"You are my bodyguard," Isami replied, hating the plaintive note in her voice. "You swore to put my life before yours."

"Until your mission was over. And it is over." Gorobei lunged, his wakizashi cutting the air where Isami's throat had been. She threw herself back, rolling to unwind the now useless chain from around her waist. The motion dragged it across the ground and it hooked one of Gorobei's ankles, pulling the former rōnin off balance. He hopped back to regain his footing.

Isami pushed to her feet, dagger in hand. It seemed a paltry thing when weighed against the experience of a veteran warrior, but she needed to buy time.

"I never took you for a murderer," Isami said.

"We are all murderers, mistress." Gorobei drew his own dagger. "The Lion kill for duty, the Scorpion kill for ambition, the Imperials kill for rank and title. I kill for Lord Otomo."

"But you are a samurai. How could you stoop to poison?"

"That was a kindness." Gorobei thrust his chin at the spilled tea. His blade glinted in the firelight. "*This* will be far more painful."

"Why would Lord Otomo order my death?" Isami retreated before the former rōnin's advance.

"The same reason he ordered me to burn the maps." Gorobei punctuated his statement with a lunge toward Isami. His short sword came too fast for Isami to block. In desperation, she did what her fighting instructor had admonished her never to do – throw her last remaining weapon.

It hit Gorobei's chest hilt first, rebounding to clatter amidst the rocks. He paused, glancing down, then chuckled.

"I don't understand," Isami said.

"Yes, you do. And therein lies the problem." Gorobei swung high with his wakizashi. As Isami ducked the slash, he pivoted to hammer a fist into her cheek. The blow sent her sprawling back onto the stony earth, rocks and roots jabbing painfully into her back as she tried to roll to her feet.

Gorobei's kick caught Isami squarely in the stomach, driving the wind from her. She scrabbled at the earth, hands hooked into claws as she gasped and wheezed like a plague victim.

"Such a promising scholar, from an imperial family." Gorobei kicked her again. "Burdened by the shame of failure, Miya Isami fled into the night, where she met an unfortunate demise."

He knelt next to her. "Perhaps she fell into a ravine, or was consumed by wild beasts, or slain by bandits, it hardly matters. There will be much speculation, I'm sure, although none will ever find your body. Would you like to offer up a prayer?" He waved his blade at her throat. "Or shall I make this quick?"

"Traitor." Isami ground the words between clenched teeth,

willing her arms to move. Her limbs might as well have been carved from rock, fingers twitching as she dragged in a wracking breath.

"The only traitor here is you," Gorobei shrugged. "You should have done as Lord Otomo ordered."

"He is nothing more than a murderer." Isami tried to fill her lungs, but the air seemed too thin. "Like you."

"Alas, the night grows short, and I have much to do." Gorobei worked a hand into Isami's hair, dragging her head back to expose her throat. "Quick it is."

Isami beat at him with numb hands, but he swept her blows aside like dangling cobwebs.

Gorobei pressed the blade to her neck. "If it makes any difference, I did enjoy our time together."

The wakizashi slipped from his hand. Frowning, he bent to retrieve it, but his fingers seemed unable to close about the hilt. Confusion flickered across his face, turning to genuine fear as he lost his balance and slumped back.

Isami gripped his wrist, dragging his now slack hand from her hair. Drawing in great, whooping breaths she sat up and pushed him from her. Gorobei tried to catch himself, only to wobble on suddenly nerveless arms and land face-first in the dirt.

"Isami, what have you done?" His words came muffled as he flopped upon the ground like a landed fish.

"You shouldn't have drunk the tea." Wincing, she pushed to her feet.

"But … it was in your cup."

"I turned the tray." Retrieving Gorobei's blade, she moved well out of the former rōnin's reach. "What is Lord Otomo's plan?"

"I could tell you, but it would be a lie."

"Was anything you said the truth?" Isami asked. "Were you even a rōnin?"

"The story I told... of the mountain village." Gorobei tried to swallow, coughed. "The peasants had hired a handful of rōnin, not hardly enough. We killed them, the villagers, too. When Lord Otomo arrived with a contingent of imperial samurai, we thought ourselves doomed." These last words came slow, Gorobei's voice slurring as the poison took hold. "He saw something in us, I suppose. Something useful."

"There are more of you?"

Gorobei's only response was a hoarse chuckle.

"Why murder me? Why bring Lion and Scorpion to the brink of war?" Isami almost shouted the last question, but Gorobei was beyond answering.

Eyes fixed on the middle distance, he gave one last hitching breath and fell still. The accounting of his life balanced, at last.

Isami regarded the prone form of her erstwhile bodyguard for a long moment. He had been Shinpachi's creature all along, every kindness, every calming word calculated to bring him closer to his lord's goal. Ever the fool, Isami had unwittingly aided Gorobei in his task. She thought Lord Otomo only maneuvered to weaken the great clans, but his plans spread much deeper. Lord Kentarō's maps, Lady Saihoku's journals. It seemed so clear now.

Otomo Shinpachi did not want the hidden valley found.

Even the imperial surveys took on a corrupt light. It would have been difficult, but not impossible, especially for one so highly placed – a bribe to the right copy clerk, an accident concerning the original.

Isami's thoughts spun with dire possibilities. She had assumed Kazuya's choking death was an unfortunate accident. Could Lord

Otomo have ordered his own nephew's murder? If so, Isami would never again be safe, not so long as she knew about the Gilded Scar.

Cold realization gripped her heart. Keisuke and Shinzō were also privy to the secret. If Lord Otomo had been willing to kill Kazuya, it would be nothing to order the deaths of an inconvenient archivist and disgraced Scorpion courtier.

Breath coming quick, Isami retrieved her chain, unwinding it from Gorobei's blade to wrap about her once more. She prodded her former bodyguard with the sword, hard.

Convinced Gorobei was well and truly dead, Isami searched through his possessions, almost crying out in relief as she found Lord Otomo's seal. Although he had taken Isami's, as the lord's emissary, she had hoped Gorobei would yet bear one.

Gathering up their supplies, Isami helped herself to Gorobei's string of coins and traveling cloak. After packing the horses' saddlebags, she turned back along the road. Lord Otomo traveled in secret, surrounded by retainers dressed as common warriors. It seemed impossible he was not already working to dispose of Keisuke and Shinzō.

Isami kicked her horse into a gallop without a care for the dark road ahead. The crescent moon slipped behind the clouds, the air alive with the call of crickets and the last of the summer cicadas. There would have been a time, not long ago, she would have stopped to admire the evening, but the gentle breeze seemed only to belie the urgency of her mission.

Shinzō and Keisuke had risked their lives for Isami.

It was only right she do the same for them.

# CHAPTER TWENTY-EIGHT

The Lion guard was a small man, long-faced with a nose so thin it almost seemed to disappear when he faced Isami straight on. He shifted from one foot to the other, casting a glance back toward camp.

"Apologies, Lady Miya." He bowed for perhaps the dozenth time since Isami had come pounding up to the gate. "Sergeant Taka is on his way."

Isami gave the man her most imperious glare. "To stand in the way of a Miya is to bar the Emperor's voice."

It was a gross exaggeration, but Isami's pronouncement had the desired effect. The guard swayed as if caught by a strong wind, knuckles whitening on the haft of his spear. A low-ranked ashigaru, Isami would bet her chain he had never met an imperial noble before, let alone one professing to carry urgent news.

Isami's plan, such as it was, seemed to be working. By sketching the outline of the Lion fortifications against her map of Stone Willow Valley, she had located the most remote entrance, little more than a gap in the earthworks plugged by a wagon fitted with wooden planks on the outer side. Far downwind and downriver of the command tents, it was the place most likely to house the latrine pits, and so draw sentries of the lowest rank. The acrid odor on the breeze was welcome confirmation of her hopes.

The guard's single companion had gone sprinting off to fetch their sergeant as soon as Isami had announced herself, leaving this poor wretch to ward the gate alone. Isami had not announced herself as an imperial herald, only given her family name and allowed the guards to draw their own conclusions.

The Lion samurai might have been a terror on the battlefield, but against the stone-faced contempt of an imperial noble, he was practically unarmed.

"I should not divulge this." Isami leaned from her saddle, voice pitched to a conspiratorial whisper. "But the message I carry is of dire import to Lord Otomo Shinpachi."

"Forgive my impertinence, lady, but we must wait until Sergeant Taka arrives."

"That is regrettable." Isami's frown was not just for show. "I bear another missive. Some notes copied from the Grand Histories, entrusted to me while I passed through Sacred Watch Palace. They were compiled at the behest of Lord Hanbei's personal archivist, Ikoma Shinzō I believe his name was?"

"I must once again beg your pardon, noble lady. Ikoma Shinzō has been removed from his post. He awaits Lord Hanbei's judgment."

"And where is Lord Hanbei?"

The guard stiffened. "I cannot say, lady."

Isami nodded. Most likely, Hanbei was combing the surrounding hills for Masaru and his band. The Ikoma lord did not seem the type of man to leave enemies at his back.

"If I tarry long, it could spell dire tidings for the Empire." Another truth, if presented somewhat obliquely. Employing a trick she had learned from Keisuke, Isami softened her tone, leaning forward as if to take the man into her confidence. "I need only a few moments with Ikoma Shinzō. Once my message is delivered, I will depart the camp immediately."

The guard cast a forlorn look over his shoulder, as if to conjure his superior through desperation alone.

"On my word as a Miya, I shall not stray from my task."

As she had hoped, reference to duty lit a fire in the guard's eyes. Although a mere ashigaru, he was yet a Lion. As heralds and surveyors, the Miya were well liked, their reputation for honesty and benevolence far exceeding their meagre standing among the imperial families. To call Isami's word into question would be to cast doubt upon the nobility itself.

"If you wish, I shall draft a missive to this effect," Isami continued. "You may present it to your superior when he arrives."

"That will not be necessary, lady." The guard turned to put a shoulder to the wagon, moving it from the gate.

"You have my gratitude." With a nod, Isami guided her horse through the gap. "Where is Ikoma Shinzō?"

"Near the command tents." He gestured up the narrow path. "Continue straight on until you see the Ikoma banners, there will be guards to direct you."

He began another bow, but Isami was already cantering away. She did not enjoy misleading loyal samurai, but such subterfuge was necessary when lives hung in the balance. As if drawn from the mists of her recollection, Gorobei's words came creeping back into Isami's thoughts.

*Integrity is the province of warriors' tales, reality requires far more compromise.*

Isami reassured herself that she was acting out of necessity, to protect her comrades and the Empire. Even so, the deception left an uncomfortable sourness in the back of her throat.

She rode through camp, trying to keep her pace brisk but relaxed. The path was deserted save for the occasional guard, the tents full of sleeping Lion samurai. Isami kept her face turned away in hopes she would not be recognized. The Fortunes had smiled upon her thus far, but luck could only last so long.

"You there!" The call came from Isami's right. Her heart sank as she turned to recognize Captain Kihei. Armored, but helmetless, his smile seemed genuine, but there was a guarded wariness in his eyes.

"Lady Miya." Kihei bowed low, gaze never leaving Isami. "What brings you to the Lion camp?"

Isami exhaled her held breath, a stroke of luck. News of Isami's disgrace had apparently not yet spread.

"I am here to retrieve Ikoma Shinzō." Dipping a hand into her satchel, Isami produced Lord Otomo's sigil. She did not dare announce herself as Shinpachi's emissary, but hopefully the captain would draw his own conclusions.

"I fear Ikoma Shinzō is being held under guard."

"Then I must speak to Lord Hanbei to see about his release." Isami would have never attempted such a bluff had she not known Hanbei was not in camp.

"The Lord is… out." The captain gave an embarrassed nod.

"And yet, I must see Shinzō."

"That is, unfortunately, impossible."

"What has occurred?" Isami kept her voice level despite concern Otomo had already dealt with Shinzō.

"The archivist has committed several breaches of protocol, ignoring orders and absenting himself without leave. We are holding him until the matter concerning Stone Willow Valley is settled."

"Then I relieve you of that task," Isami replied. "Shinzō shall depart camp under my watchful eye. Upon his return, Lord Hanbei may take the matter up with Lord Otomo."

The captain studied Isami for a long moment, but there was little he could do. Isami far outranked a samurai, even a captain. In the absence of Lord Hanbei, Kihei was compelled to follow imperial orders.

"Lady, if you would but consent to wait–"

"Lord Otomo is not known for his patience."

"As you say, mistress." With a nod, Kihei turned toward one of the nearby tents.

Isami dismounted to follow, keeping her pace steady although her heart threatened to crawl up her throat.

Nodding to the guard, Captain Kihei parted the tent flap, gesturing Isami inside. She had barely crossed the threshold before he was off, no doubt hurrying to find someone of sufficient rank to prevent Isami removing Shinzō from camp.

The inside of the tent was bare but for a sleeping mat, a small bronze lamp, and a tray of food. Ikoma Shinzō lay upon the mat, not even turning as Isami entered. A servant in dun-colored robes knelt in the shadows near the rear wall, forehead pressed to the floor the moment he saw Isami's family crest.

"Shinzō," Isami called softly.

The archivist turned, his expression shifting from resigned to genuinely pained. "I delivered your missive to Lord Hanbei. He was furious."

"We shall speak of that later," Isami replied, gaze flicking to the food. "Have you eaten or drunk anything since arriving here?"

"Some water from the communal barrel." Shinzō gave a doleful shake of his head. "My stomach has been tied in knots."

"Good." She knelt to grasp his arm, leaning close. "We must depart."

"Why?"

"Lord Otomo knows of the hidden valley. He has always known," Isami said.

Shinzō gazed up at her. "I don't understand."

"Gorobei tried to murder me." Isami tugged at the archivist. "It was he who burned Lord Kentarō's records, and who set fire to the Scorpion archives."

"Impossible." Shinzō tried to pull away. "Keisuke burned the records."

"There is no time to argue." Irritation at Shinzō's stubbornness colored Isami's tone. "Otomo wishes to keep the valley a secret, and he is willing to start a war to do so."

Shinzō seemed about to reply. Before he could, movement from the rear of the tent caught both their attention. Isami turned, inwardly cursing herself. In her haste, she had fallen back into old habits, treating servants as little more than shadows.

As the man slipped beneath the canvas wall, his face caught the dim light for the first time.

In that moment, Isami recognized him as one of Lord Otomo's followers. She lunged after him, but the man was already gone, his shadow growing on the tent wall as he sprinted away.

"Lady Miya has assaulted the guards!" The man's calls were

answered by the shouts of Lion samurai. "She seeks to flee camp with the traitor Ikoma Shinzō!"

Lies notwithstanding, the servant's cries were certain to bring unwelcome attention. Isami tugged Shinzō toward the entrance.

"Please, you must trust me."

The archivist gave an agonized moan, hesitating just before the tent flap. "Lord Hanbei will have me hanged as a common criminal. My name will be stricken from the histories."

Isami turned to meet Shinzō's gaze. "This is more important than any of our names."

The admonition seemed to harden something within the archivist. With a quick nod, he followed Isami out into the camp. Fortunately, the horses were still outside, drinking from the trough where Isami had left them.

She swung up into the saddle as Shinzō mounted Gorobei's horse. Isami kicked her mount into a gallop, heading back down the rise toward the gate where she had entered. Behind them, shouts rose above the pounding hooves. Glancing back, she saw spears and bows, and leaned lower along her mount's back, praying that the archers would not fire for fear of hitting their own.

The Ancestors must have heard Isami's plea, as no arrows came winging from the firelit gloom. Ahead, the wagon blocked the makeshift gate, the lone ashigaru squinting into the shadows as Shinzō and Isami galloped toward him.

The wagon was too big to jump, so Isami slowed her mount. Discreetly unwinding her chain, she gathered long loops in both hands.

"Scorpion soldiers are attacking the camp!"

It was a bald lie, but one that caused enough confusion

for her to draw close to the guard. She hurled one end of the chain, the weight striking the surprised ashigaru squarely in the breastplate. As he stumbled back, Isami twisted in the saddle and released the coiled chain in her left hand. Using her height and momentum, she brought the length slashing down to entangle the guard's legs.

"Shinzō, the gate!" Holding tightly onto her chain, Isami urged her horse forward. The move snatched the ashigaru's feet from under him. He toppled with a stunned grunt, spear tumbling from his hands. Isami dragged the unfortunate man for a few yards before he was able to twist free of the chain.

Dismounting to kick the blocks from under the wagon's wheels, Shinzō put his shoulder to the wagon.

"I am truly sorry!" Isami shouted, as the ashigaru wobbled to his feet, short sword in hand. Snarling, he took an unsteady step toward her, and she urged her mount through the small opening Shinzō had cleared and out into the night.

They galloped away from camp. Although it was tempting to veer into the woods, the night remained dark enough to make the footing treacherous, so Isami judged it better to keep to the road than risk one of their mounts breaking a leg.

The air whipped by, Isami's wild exhalations steaming in the late evening chill. She heard no sounds of immediate pursuit, but knew it would be some time before they halted. A strange feeling of exaltation seized Isami.

It seemed impossible, but she had managed to bluff her way in and out of the Lion camp. Even so, her excitement was tempered by the knowledge of more challenges yet to come. If rescuing Shinzō had been difficult, Isami shivered to think of how she might win her way into the Scorpion camp. It seemed unlikely that the guards would believe similar lies. She would need to find some other way to reach her friend, but at the moment, Isami could think of nothing.

Although Isami had survived Gorobei's attempt on her life and rescued Shinzō from another, she did not think Lord Otomo would ever relent.

Only fools made but one plan.

# CHAPTER TWENTY-NINE

Isami swept the Scorpion camp with her spyglass, making sure to keep the early morning sun behind her so the lens did not catch the light and reveal their hiding spot. Although the parade retained its festive atmosphere, Isami could not help but notice steel behind the silk. Scorpion samurai patrolled the length of the procession, armor hung with festival swatches. The near shore of Three Sides River was full of painted boats, but many sailors moved with the careful alertness of warriors on campaign rather than the broad swagger of river folk.

Isami might have overlooked even this, had not she and Shinzō passed the remains of several small clashes on their journey south. Although the bodies had been burned by the victors, signs of conflict were obvious in the rust brown bloodstains upon the grass, the hacked foliage, and the occasional arrow sticking from a tree. It was clear, despite the celebratory mood, Lady Kaede had no intention of being taken unawares.

"Do you see him?" Shinzō edged closer, squinting down into camp.

Isami shook her head. She had selected the low, bush-covered rise because it provided a good vantage on the Scorpion procession. Even with the spyglass, both the distance and milling crowds were proving troublesome. While she was easily able to spot Lady Kaede's palanquin, Keisuke remained frustratingly hidden.

"And if you do find him?" Shinzō asked.

It was a fair question, one Isami had been considering since they fled the Lion camp. Sweat beaded on Isami's upper lip, hands tightening around the spyglass. It had taken them the better part of the night to reach the Scorpion lines, and although the parade moved more slowly than two riders, Isami judged Lady Kaede would reach Lord Hanbei's forces in two, perhaps three days. Based on the skirmishing already taking place, the conflict was liable to be bloody.

So wrapped up was she in morbid calculations, Isami's glass swept across the riverbank twice before she noticed Keisuke. The Scorpion courtier sat upon a stretch of flattened grass, aimlessly tossing stones into the current. He seemed to ignore all around him, nor did any of the guards appear to be paying him much mind. Even so, appearances could oft be deceiving among the Scorpion.

"Wait here." Wrapping herself in Gorobei's traveling cloak, Isami stood to pick her way down the rise.

"Where are you going?" Shinzō asked.

"To purchase some clothes that won't get you killed on sight."

There were a number of hawkers following the procession, selling everything from bean cakes to festival streamers. Roughening her voice as much as possible, Isami purchased two brightly colored capes from an elderly woman with beads woven into her hair.

Isami had expected Shinzō to balk at the tawdry clothes, but to his credit, the Ikoma archivist donned the patchy blue-and-yellow cape without complaint.

"My reputation already lies in the muck of Three Sides River," Shinzō shrugged. "What is one more indignity?"

Isami and Shinzō left the horses tied amidst a stand of willow. The meandering throngs of peasants may have given any Lion attackers pause, but they made slipping along the edges of the parade relatively easy. Appearing like nothing so much as two low-rent courtesans, they were able to skirt the riverbank almost to where Keisuke sat.

"Care for some company, lord?" Bowing low, Isami approached Keisuke.

"Don't you people have someone else to annoy?" the Scorpion courtier snapped back. Glancing over, his angry expression became a look of surprise.

"Isami?"

"My peasant accent must be getting better." She smiled back.

"What are you doing here?"

"It would take quite some time to explain." Isami held a hand to her face, tittering as if Keisuke had offered some romantic blandishment. "Only know your life is in danger if you don't come with us."

"My life is *always* in danger." Keisuke rocked back, chuckling. "Mother must have a half-dozen guards keeping an eye on me."

"I saw no one."

"You wouldn't." He gave a helpless wave of his hands. "Lady Kaede may not respect me, but she does like to keep her children safe."

Isami frowned. "So, she won't come to the meeting."

"Oh, she will," Keisuke replied. "Mother would never pass up a chance to gauge an opponent in person." He glanced at Shinzō. "Will Lord Hanbei be in attendance?"

"In force." The Ikoma archivist returned a stiff nod. Seeming to catch himself, he relaxed a bit, offering a pained smile. "It seems I must apologize."

Keisuke seemed genuinely surprised. "For what?"

"For starting a war," Shinzō said.

Keisuke sucked air through his teeth, eyes widening as he regarded Isami. "This I need to hear."

"In time." Isami sidled closer, placing a hand on Keisuke's knee. "First, we need to flee the camp."

"What of the boats?" Shinzō asked.

"Half of them are full of mother's warriors, the other half drunken sailors."

"Can you tell the difference?" Isami asked.

Keisuke gave a sly glance toward the river. "I can try."

Standing, he put an arm around Isami, then nodded to Shinzō. "Shout at me."

"What?"

"You're either a courtesan or protection." Keisuke gave Isami's shoulders a squeeze. "And I am being *very* forward with your charge."

Shinzō blinked in surprise.

"We have to make this convincing." Isami simpered as if Keisuke had said something witty.

Shinzō reddened. "What do I say?"

"It hardly matters," Keisuke replied. "No one can hear you except us."

Shinzō gave a quick nod, then raised his hands in mock outrage. "I misjudged you, Scorpion!"

"How so?" Keisuke pointed to his own face, as if surprised to be addressed by a commoner.

"I now know you did not start the fire!" Shinzō paced back and forth, gesturing at Isami and Keisuke in turn. "We were all manipulated by Lord Otomo. He attempted to have Isami murdered, and now we fear he may seek your life as well!"

Keisuke released Isami to take a step toward Shinzō. "Why would he do such a thing?"

"To weaken the clans." Shinzō raised a fist, shaking it below the courtier's chin. "Isami believes Lord Otomo wishes to keep the Gilded Scar a secret. It was Gorobei who burned my records, and yours."

Isami noticed several of the crowd surreptitiously moving closer, but before they could intervene Keisuke raised his hands, palms flat, fingers spread. "Then it seems I owe you an apology as well."

They stood for a long moment, red-faced and panting, almost nose-to-nose with one another.

"Apology accepted." Shinzō took a step back.

"Likewise." With a mocking bow, Keisuke produced a strand of coins, pressing them into Shinzō's hands.

"What's this?" Shinzō asked.

"Payment." Keisuke's gaze flicked suggestively toward Isami.

"Oh… yes, of course." Shinzō stuffed the coins down the front of his robe. Taking a step back, he looked to both Isami and Keisuke in turn. "Now what do we do?"

"Now," the Scorpion courtier's masked grin positively dripped with smugness, "we find a boat."

The vessel Keisuke ended up selecting seemed hardly worthy of the title of watercraft. Fortunately, its dubious crew were out enjoying the festivities, leaving one disheveled sailor to mind the boat. From the look of him, he had spent the last several days in various states of intoxication, and it took quite a bit of hammering on the bow to rouse him from his stupor.

When at last he appeared, blinking in the sunlight, hair matted to one side of his head, Keisuke flourished a string of coins below his nose, promising them as payment for a brief jaunt across the river. Together with Isami's simpering smiles and Shinzō's stone-faced silence, it took almost no time to convince the riverman they were simply out to enjoy a private excursion away from prying eyes.

Despite the questionable state of his vessel, the sailor was quick to fit the oars and cast away the line. It seemed Keisuke had chosen well. If the man were a Scorpion agent in disguise, he had long ago disappeared into the role. So unsettling was the squint-eyed leer with which he favored Isami, Shinzō had to order the man to row facing away from her.

The current quickly took the boat, and within a half hour they found themselves across Three Sides River. Keisuke promised the man another handful of coins if he would retrieve them. Even though they had no intention of returning to camp, Isami understood it would appear suspicious if they did not plan for such an eventuality.

With a bow and wink to Isami, the sailor bent his back to the oars, soon moving out of earshot.

"That was distasteful," Shinzō said.

Isami could only nod.

"But effective." Keisuke nodded at the retreating boat. "They'll come looking for me soon enough, but this should give us a good start."

"I wish we could have brought the horses," Shinzō said. "It will be a long walk to the Gilded Scar."

Isami squinted up at the mountains, ranging the peaks against the course of the river. She drew forth her survey and Tadataka's geomantic compass, turning to fix direction and position. Smiling, Isami recalled this particular bend from Gyōki's map, a shielded curve in the shadow of one of the larger mountains. Despite the ache in her legs, Isami's heart was light with the promise of finally proving the existence of Lord Kentarō's valley. Glancing up to judge the position of the sun, she chewed her lip, mind working through distance calculations.

"A day on foot." She cocked her head, considering. "Perhaps longer if the ground becomes difficult, but if we stick to the riverbank, it should be relatively traversable."

"Will we make it before my mother and Lord Hanbei?" Keisuke asked.

"We shall have to," Isami replied. Matters might turn deadly if the Scorpion and Lion forces arrived at the valley entrance without Isami to mediate. And she did not even wish to conscience what might occur if Lord Otomo descended upon the negotiations.

Isami sighed – the path ahead might be fraught, but she had survived thus far. She had come to walk the land, to measure and map, to survey and square. Amidst all the struggles, she had longed to return to such simple and forthright endeavors. Geography did not change its mind, it had no ambition, no clever stratagems or sudden betrayals. It did not lie. It did not pretend to be something it was not.

Clouds might obscure the future, but, for the moment, skies were clear.

# CHAPTER THIRTY

Wind plucked at Isami's hair. She had long ago given up attempting to keep it in check, settling for a leather thong that kept most of it from sticking to her sweat-slicked cheeks. Although the foothills of the Spine of the World were but children compared to the high peaks beyond, there was nothing in the way of trails, forcing Isami and her companions to press through crackling brush and cling to tree roots as they traversed the treacherous inclines. Fortunately, the coolness of the day turned what would have been an unbearable climb into one that was merely arduous.

More than once, Isami found herself wishing for Gorobei's pathfinding talents. Each time, the longing was accompanied by a sting of shame at having been manipulated so easily. And yet, even knowing Gorobei's kindnesses had been rooted in cruel calculation, Isami could not simply discard her feelings.

Whatever his motives, Gorobei had saved her life. It felt like a betrayal to grieve for him, but try as she might, Isami could not figure the wages of such dire accounting.

"We should have taken our chances on the river," Keisuke muttered after a loose stone turned under his foot, pitching him forward into the mud.

Shinzō stooped to give the courtier a hand. "If Lord Hanbei's scouts discovered us, I doubt even you could have talked your way free."

"How much farther?" Keisuke asked.

With a grunt of effort, Isami levered herself up onto a shelf of bedrock. Although the cliff was small, it projected far enough for her to win free of the trees that covered most of the lower reaches. With compass and spyglass, she was able to fix their position at a few hours' ride south of the Lion camp across the river. If Lady Kaede's forces continued north, they would reach the Lion lines some time tomorrow afternoon.

Despite Keisuke and Shinzō's assurances, Isami could not quite bring herself to believe both Kaede and Hanbei would consent to negotiations. If they followed Isami's request, and Lord Otomo did not interfere, this evening would see contingents from both Lion and Scorpion cross the river somewhere near the mouth of Lord Kentarō's hidden valley.

That is, if Isami could locate it.

She checked her survey for perhaps the dozenth time, even going so far as to consult the imperial map. Although useless, it provided some hint of where not to search.

Puffing, Keisuke climbed up to join her. "I thought you and Shinzō discovered the coordinates in Lady Saihoku's journals?"

"We did." Isami peered through the spyglass, then made a few more notes in her book. "But the map they were based on burned with the others."

"The geography could not have changed so much." Shinzō sat down with a grateful sigh. Uncorking his gourd, he took several long swallows.

"I know the distances," Isami replied. "I just don't know where they were measured from."

Spying a ridge of broken stone, Isami felt her breath quicken. There, just along the rise, stood a canted camphor tree. Swathed in moss, it seemed a powerful, ancient thing, stately enough to be possessed of spirit itself. If only they had a ritualist or monk, it might have been possible to commune with the spirits of the tree. Isami had never much talent for magical matters, even the most basic transcriptions of arcane theory left her mind in knots. The thoughts of spirits did not walk the same paths as mortals, logic and calculation as foreign to them as more numinous matters were to scholars like Isami.

The camphor would have been far smaller centuries ago. Isami could see twisted stumps along the mountain, the remains of trees felled by wind and lightning. Over the long years the camphor's companions had fallen away, leaving it to reign unopposed over this stretch of rocky ground.

"Shinzō, didn't Kentarō mention a grove of camphor trees?"

"They rested there." The archivist nodded. "He remarked how peaceful it felt."

With a nod, Isami packed up her equipment and lowered herself from the boulder. Without a word, Shinzō followed.

"I thought we might rest for a bit," Keisuke said. When neither Isami or Shinzō replied, he levered himself up with an exaggerated groan and hopped down after.

The trees thinned as they ascended, undergrowth giving way as the soil became rockier. For the first time in hours, Isami was able to see Three Sides River below, a stony escarpment leading down into the channel. Although there was no sign of movement yet, in a few hours' time the bank would be alive with ships as Lord Hanbei and Lady Kaede answered Isami's summons.

They were all breathing heavily by the time they reached the camphor tree.

"I can see why no one would come here," Keisuke said between breathless gasps.

Shinzō leaned over, steadying himself on the tree, his face flushed.

Isami looked around, seeing nothing apart from loose stone and more forested hills stretching in either direction. There was nothing here.

It might have been the exertion or elevation, but she felt fit to collapse, the ragged beat of her heart a doleful counterpoint to the furious churning of her thoughts. They could not simply wander through the mountains. Even without the approaching negotiations, these cliffs were known to be the haunt of bandits, beasts, and all manner of unnatural things.

She tried to calm herself, but could not find even a whisper of stillness. Isami needed to regain her bearings; compass, spyglass, calculation – they had never failed her. Numbly, she rummaged in her satchel, eyes squeezed shut against the tears that threatened to ruin what remained of her composure.

"Isami." Shinzō's call snapped her head up like a thunderclap.

She turned to see the archivist pointing at a patch of rocky ground. Although the wood had long rotted away, gaps amidst the boulders showed where fallen trees had once stood.

Isami shook her head, confused.

"Look at the stone."

She peered at the jagged boulders, worn by wind and rain, the echoes of broken edges just barely visible. At first, they looked to have been part of a larger cliff, broken by tree roots and ice, but as Isami studied them, she began to notice irregularities –

beveled edges, breaks too straight to have been caused by nature.

"They're cut." As if waking from a dream, Isami's surroundings became clear. "This was a quarry."

Shinzō's smile was relieved. "And where there is a quarry…"

"There, on that flat stone," Keisuke shouted, hurrying along what Isami now saw was the remnants of a gravel path. "Some manner of mark."

Isami joined him, peering down at the ancient symbols etched into the stone.

"It's a measuring point. And there is another." She indicated another some ten paces distant. "This is a baseline."

Pulling forth Lady Saihoku's journal from her satchel, she thumbed the crackling pages to find the notation, checking the coordinates and direction against her compass.

"They match." Isami's voice seemed to come from far away. Carefully, she bent to mark the angle indicated in the book, then hurried over to do the same at the other side of the baseline. Using her spyglass, she traced each to where they intersected.

Her legs felt weak, arms as loose as a puppet's as she raised a finger to indicate a narrow defile farther down the other side of the cliff.

"There."

They ran down the hill, tripping over stones and loose gravel. High cliffs rose to either side, draped with vines and hanging wisteria. Throat tight with excitement, she would have hurled herself forward, heedless of what lay ahead, had Keisuke not put a hand on her shoulder.

He thrust his chin at the path ahead, at rock mixed with sandy dirt, far finer than the stony grit farther up the hillside. In it was the print of a single sandaled foot.

"Someone has passed this way." Shinzō reached up to thumb a vine, its end cleanly severed.

"We must proceed carefully," Isami said.

"It would be better to turn back," Shinzō frowned. "Fetch Lord Hanbei and Lady Kaede."

"And have them kill each other trying to reach here?" Keisuke asked.

"We cannot face them without seeing the valley for ourselves," Isami said. "Not after we have come so far."

Shinzō looked from one to the other, then gave a slow nod. "Lead on, lady."

What began as a small break between cliffs, soon opened wide enough to allow two palanquins to pass side-by-side. Even so, Isami kept the shadowed overhang beneath the bluff, as if the curtain of hanging vines might shield them from danger. It curled around a stone outcrop. The thin trickle of water from farther up the mountain had carved channels into the rock, layer upon layer of shale like the spines of books stacked along the cliff. Although the path itself twisted like a snake on sand, it remained broad and flat enough that passage was relatively easy.

"Lord Kentarō must have brought the stone through here," Isami said, eliciting a grunt of affirmation from Shinzō. "Although why he would want to build a castle in such a remote place I cannot say."

"Perhaps he wished to push the bounds of the Empire," Shinzō said.

"More likely there is something here worth protecting," Keisuke replied, peering ahead.

The Scorpion courtier's supposition was proven right as the

rock walls widened further, falling away to lay open the valley beyond.

It was smaller than Stone Willow, no more than a few miles long. Framed by distant, snow-capped mountains, it was shielded from wind and weather by high cliffs on all sides. The center held a thin lake, its waters the dark, rich blue that came only from channels cut deep into ancient stone. Grassy hills filled the lower reaches, giving way to trees; reds, yellows, and golds giving the vale an almost festive air. But it was not the scenery that drew Isami's eye, rather the thin tail of smoke that crept from the near slope.

At first, she thought it a village, but the huts were too rude, and while the cliffside was excavated there were no terraced fields cut into the stone. Perhaps a dozen small caves yawned from the rock, an irregular, but steady stream of people moving in and out. A number of wooden sluices stretched down the slope, reaching almost to the lake below. They looked to be fed by water diverted from uphill, several small wheels powering machinery Isami could not see.

"What are they doing?" Shinzō asked.

"It's a mine," Keisuke replied with a thin smile. "My family has several similar operations along the western side of the Spine of the World. Mother once toyed with the idea of exiling me to one."

"Not similar to this, I hope." Isami peered through her spyglass. "Those workers are wearing chains. And I can see guards – armed, but with no colors or family crests."

"Rōnin?" Keisuke asked.

"Former bandits." Isami swallowed against the tightness in her throat. "Like Gorobei."

"What are they mining?" Shinzō asked.

"They look to be dumping sacks of rock into the sluices," Isami replied.

"Now we know why Lord Otomo wanted to keep this valley a secret." Keisuke let out a low whistle. "They're mining gold."

"The Gilded Scar." Shinzō spoke the name like a prayer.

"It's heavy, but easy to hide. Even a few pounds would fetch a fine price in the capital," Keisuke said. "Plenty of money for bribes and agents. My mother will be delighted to discover the source of Lord Otomo's mysterious wealth."

"We should return to the river." Isami glanced at the sky. The mine explained Lord Otomo's desire for secrecy, but, for the moment, blood weighed more heavily on her mind than gold. "The Lion and Scorpion contingents will be arriving soon."

"Otomo will not be pleased," Shinzō said.

"I hardly see how that is our concern," Keisuke replied with a smile. "A working gold mine is more than enough to balance the scales between our clans. All that remains is to determine who retains Stone Willow and who–"

The arrow hit Keisuke just above the elbow. If he had not already been turning, it would have taken him in the ribs. He glanced down at the shaft as if unsure of its provenance, lips forming a small, astonished circle.

Isami had enough time to take a step back, one hand rising to muffle her surprised gasp.

Then the arrows came slashing down.

# CHAPTER THIRTY-ONE

"Down!" Shinzō tackled Keisuke as more shafts followed the first.

Isami ducked behind a column of rock, thinking they had been spotted by hidden guards, only to almost catch a barbed arrow in the stomach. She flinched aside just in time, and it rattled off into the rocks below, but not before she saw movement among the ivy back along the path.

Isami threw herself flat, crawling to where Shinzō and Keisuke lay.

"Otomo." She spat the word like a curse.

"The old goblin must have followed us," Keisuke gritted out from between clenched teeth. Blood darkened the crimson of his robe, his hand pressed tight to the wound, shaft protruding from between trembling fingers.

Another arrow hissed overhead, followed by the sound of running feet from up the path.

"They'll be on us soon." Shinzō hazarded a glance. "I count at least six."

Isami tensed at the dire news. Even if Otomo's warriors were former bandits, they had the advantage in numbers and position, and the noise of combat was likely to bring reinforcements from the valley.

Shinzō met her questioning gaze. "Akodo once said: 'When faced with a superior foe, time and distance can be allies.'"

"The Scorpion have a similar saying," Keisuke shifted with a pained grunt. "When a Lion advises you to run. *Run.*"

At Isami's nod, they half-sprinted, half-tumbled down the hill, kicking up plumes of loose dirt and gravel in their headlong flight. Although the cloud of dust would certainly catch the attention of the guards at the mine, it spoiled the aim of Lord Otomo's archers.

They hit the tree line at a stumbling run. Branches whipped across Isami's face and upraised hands, the sounds of her companions crashing through the brush punctuated by distant shouts from the pass behind. Remembering what little Gorobei had told her of evading pursuit, Isami led them on a wild course, careening along a wooded rise only to leap down into the icy flow of a mountain stream as it wended its way toward the lake. Although the knee-deep water would conceal their passage, Isami was under no illusion she could avoid a dedicated search.

"I can't keep this up." Keisuke collapsed with a breathless groan on the riverbank, face pale and teeth chattering.

Shinzō waded over to him, kneeling to inspect his wound. Keisuke hissed as he pried his fingers from around the shaft.

"You're fortunate. The arrow went clean through," Shinzō said.

He returned a wan smile. "If I were truly lucky, it would have hit you instead."

Shinzō gave the courtier an irritated cuff. "Find something to bite down on."

While Shinzō worked on Keisuke, Isami scanned the hill behind. She could detect no movement, nor could she hear anything beyond the rustle of squirrels amidst the limbs and the occasional wren from high in the trees. If the bandits were half as talented trackers as Gorobei, the silence meant nothing.

Despite Akodo's words, time was not Isami's ally. Lord Hanbei and Lady Kaede would soon arrive to find the negotiation site empty. Isami cringed to think of the two bullish nobles coming face-to-face with no one to mediate.

There would be blood, of that she was sure.

If only there was a way to draw the Lion and Scorpion to the valley, some way to signal them.

Desperation made a hard fist in her stomach. There might be other ways out of the Gilded Scar, but Otomo would not be so foolish as to leave them unguarded. The only true option was to find some place defensible and sell their lives as dearly as possible.

Otomo's ruffians might know this valley, but they had not mapped it.

Ignoring Keisuke's pained moans, Isami splashed up onto the bank to rummage through her satchel. Although water had soaked into the bottom, the oilcloth wrappings had kept the papers relatively dry. Spreading her survey upon the grass, Isami carefully marked the valley entrance, then added the coordinates from Kentarō's notes. The trees were too dense to see the pass, even with her spyglass, but Isami was able to fix on one of the surrounding mountains, a sharp snow-covered peak she had noted from the entrance.

"What are you doing?" Shinzō's shadow fell across her map.

"Finding us a place to hide." Isami glanced back to see Keisuke spread upon the grass, eyes closed, his arm bound with a strip of cloth torn from Shinzō's robes.

"He's only playacting," Shinzō said.

"Are you a healer now?" Keisuke asked without opening his eyes.

"I've read treatises on the subject," Shinzō sniffed. "Enough to know Lord Otomo's bandits will murder us long before that wound festers."

"Perhaps." Isami bent close, using the spine of a book to sketch straight lines upon the map.

"Can you find another way out?" Shinzō asked.

"No, but I may know of somewhere we can go." Isami checked Tadataka's compass, then made a few more marks upon the paper. "The castle Lady Saihoku's journals spoke of."

Shinzō shook his head. "Otomo's guards have been here for years. They must have found it by now."

"If they knew where to look." Isami marked the intersection of several lines, then rechecked her calculations. "Saihoku's notes show the stone was taken to the west side of the valley, the mine is on the east."

"Even if you are correct, how will that avail us anything?"

Isami bent to her work. To be fair, she hadn't thought that far ahead.

"We've followed Lady Miya this far. I say we find the castle." Keisuke pushed to his feet with a grunt of pain. "At the very least, it should make for a pretty place to die."

Shinzō let out a short bark of laughter. "Now you are thinking like a Lion."

Isami charted the path as best she could, fear of pursuit warring with her desire to stop to fix their position. Together with spyglass and compass, she was able to guide them around the edge of the lake, keeping to the trees to avoid being spotted. The afternoon sun reflected from the water, shouts drifting down from above as Lord Otomo's warriors scoured the mountainside. If anything, the calls seemed almost jovial, like children hunting eels through the shallows.

After a few minutes, the land began to rise once more, gradually growing steeper as they neared the other side of the valley. Keisuke stumbled on an exposed root, his grunt becoming a cry of pain as he flung his injured arm out to break his fall. Shinzō was quick to help him, slipping an arm around the courtier's shoulder despite his protests. He waved off Isami's aid with a tight-lipped grimace.

"See to the path, mapmaker."

She rechecked her lines. Sighting along the hillside, she was excited to see a flat stone just ahead. About knee height, it was mostly overgrown with moss and ivy. Isami bent to clear the brush away the undergrowth, arms prickling as she tore at the vines. As if to mock her efforts, a shout sounded from down the hill.

Shinzō's blade hissed from its scabbard. "They've seen us."

Isami brushed the last of the moss away, almost crying out with relief as she saw the faint characters etched into the stone's surface.

Painfully aware of the snapping brush and excited calls of their pursuers, Isami checked the coordinates against her map. As always, she sought refuge in calculation, focusing on numbers rather than the approaching bandits.

A sigh of relief slipped between her pursed lips as she was able to fix their position. Together with the marker near the valley entrance she was able to draw a clear line across the lake, creating the baseline of Gyōki's Triangle. Hands trembling, she checked the angle measurements against Tadataka's compass, fixing her spyglass on the point where the two sides of the imaginary triangle met.

It looked to be a stretch of nondescript hillside, perhaps a quarter-mile distant, nothing to distinguish it from the rest of the valley.

"This way." Despite her misgivings, Isami lurched to her feet, gesturing to Shinzō and Keisuke.

Abandoning all pretense of stealth, they waded into the undergrowth, Shinzō slashing leaves and loose branches to clear the way for Keisuke. Although the Scorpion courtier's shoulders hunched tight with pain, he offered no complaint as they stumbled along the hillside.

One of the bandits called after them, her voice high and mocking. This set her companions into loud brays of mirth, their cackling laughter reminding Isami of crows tussling over an old kill.

Breath catching in her throat, Isami shambled into the small clearing. She cast desperately about for signs of ancient construction.

An arrow rustled through the foliage to lodge in the bole of a nearby tree. Without a word, Isami and the others scrambled up the incline, more shafts winging their way through the underbrush behind. Wild whoops and laughter echoed from the stones, the afternoon sun drawing out the bandits' shadows until they appeared like nothing so much as a horde of capering demons.

Ahead, the cliff face rose sheer and foreboding, impenetrable as the Carpenter Wall. Isami fell against the cool stone. Panting, she scanned the surrounds for any sign of a break in the rocks. Panic blossomed in her chest as the steel flashed among the trees below, bandits dodging from tree to tree. They were cautious now, perhaps unsure if any of their quarry possessed a bow, but that would fade. Soon enough, they would come for blood.

"Over here, look!" Keisuke's voice was pitched just above a whisper. Isami followed his outthrust hand to see the slightest shadow on the rock face. Even in clear sunlight it appeared little more than a jagged crack snaking up the side of the cliff, but as Isami craned her neck, she began to notice small, regular deviations along the length.

"Ancestors preserve us." Shinzō shook his head in wonder. "It's a stair."

Shielded by boulders at the base of the cliff, the stone steps had been expertly carved to match the natural curve of the stone. Even with Isami and the others barely a dozen paces away, the stair was almost invisible against the rock.

Taking care to shelter behind the boulders, they hurried to the base. Isami led the way, Keisuke behind, with Shinzō bringing up the rear, blade bared. Blessedly, the stairs curved around the jagged cliff face, shielding them from the bandits' view.

Carved from granite bedrock and protected from wind and rain by overhanging cliffs, the stairs had suffered only the most minor wear over the intervening years. At any other time, Isami would have stopped to marvel at the sheer artistry of their construction, ancient masons directed by Lord Kentarō's expert design and Lady Saihoku's oversight.

They ascended quickly, laughing shouts from below turning

at first confused, then angry. Isami allowed herself a small smile at this. The bandits would come soon enough, but for now it felt good to have frustrated their pursuers.

They rounded the cliff to find a narrow, yet deep hollow carved into the rock. The artificial tunnel faced west, away from the valley, and would have been impossible to spot unless one were looking down from the mountains beyond. Its interior had been excavated, marks of pick and hammer clearly visible on the stone. Perhaps thirty paces long, the tunnel had a slight upward curve to keep out the elements while still allowing the setting sun to illuminate the interior.

Isami paused as the tunnel widened, staring open-mouthed at the cavern beyond. She had expected a mountain fortress in the old imperial style, or perhaps some manner of temple to the Fortunes.

What stood before her was not a castle, but a tomb.

In keeping with the care that had gone into its concealment, the tomb was elaborately designed. Pillars of worked stone flanked the entrance, bracing a number of heavy beams that supported the low, peaked roof. Flaking paint was all that remained of what must have been a breathtaking mural, twisting shadows hinting at the form of palaces, ancestors, and celestial dragons.

"I cannot believe it still stands." Awe colored Shinzō's tone. "Truly a work of genius. Hidden all these years."

"I believe Lady Saihoku had a hand in that." Keisuke nodded toward a series of dusty mounds scattered across the cavern.

At first, Isami thought them to be some manner of ritual offering, but as she regarded the piles the late afternoon sunlight glimmered on the pale white of ancient bone.

"The workers." Shinzō squatted to inspect one of the mounds, his voice tight and disgusted. "She had them all murdered."

"What better way to keep a secret?" Keisuke asked.

"What better way to make unquiet spirits?" Shinzō replied.

Isami ignored the exchange, her eye caught by a glimmer of bronze from within the tomb's entrance. While there were crypts and burial vaults within the temple precincts of Otosan Uchi, they were usually small affairs, housing only ashes and ancestor plaques. The grand tombs of the ancient days had fallen out of favor after the dread blood sorcerer Iuchiban had reanimated the honored dead to serve in his vile army. The Hantei emperors had declared all bodies must be burned, and while the Ancestors were still venerated, ritual had largely replaced edifice.

Isami mounted the low stone steps leading up to the tomb. A pair of statues warded the entrance, green verdigris bleeding from their somber expressions. Armed with sword and polearm, they wore the square, woven armor of ancient warriors. So lifelike were their poses, Isami half expected them to leap to bar her way, but they remained blessedly still as she slipped past and into the tomb.

The barest hint of sunlight filtered through the latticed windows, casting scaffolded shadows upon the dozens of screens and hangings which adorned the walls. Squinting in the gloom, Isami almost lost her breath as she recognized the faint outline of mountains and rivers, the whole sketched with a network of intersecting lines, precise as a spider's web.

She ran to the nearest, careful not to touch lest the ancient parchment turn to dust in her hand. At any other time of day, the maps would have been unreadable without a lamp, but the sliver of late afternoon light provided enough illumination to discern faint coordinates and directions.

"It's all here." Isami's words sounded choked, even to her. She walked among the maps, hardly daring even to breathe. "The Gilded Scar, Stone Willow Valley, the mountains beyond."

She traced the flow of Three Sides River along the Spine of the World, its sinuous curves rendered more precisely than any imperial map. She moved from screen to screen, staring at each as if to commit its contents to memory. Isami could have spent years cataloguing the tomb's interior, but there was no time. There was never any time.

"Isami, they come." Shinzō's call dragged Isami from the warmth of interrupted dream. The Ikoma archivist strode into the tomb, and stopped, mouth open. Keisuke followed, eyes wide as he stared at the rear of the structure.

Isami followed his gaze, seeing Lord Kentarō's sarcophagus for the first time.

It lay in a small alcove, surrounded by braziers, candles, and hanging prayer strips. But it was not the adornments that drew the eye, but the coffin itself, which was covered in solid gold.

Isami ran a hand through her hair, not quite believing the scene before her.

"Lady Saihoku spared no expense." Keisuke drifted toward the coffin, one hand outstretched as if afraid it would turn to mist.

"To lay untouched for so long." Shinzō shook his head, seemingly unmoved by the opulence.

Keisuke winced at the echo of sandaled feet upon stone. "A few moments and we shall join him."

"We must meet them at the entrance." Shinzō drew his sword.

"The stairs are narrow, and their sword arms will be against the cliff."

The hiss of Shinzō's blade clearing its scabbard made Isami flinch. It seemed a cruel jest they should come so far only to be cut down by a band of ruffians. Isami imagined them laughing over her corpse, rough fingers tearing though ancient parchment screens, scraping the gold from Lord Kentarō's coffin.

Numbly, she followed her companions out into the cavern. If only Isami or one of the others were a priest, to pass a warning along the whispered breeze or through the bones of the earth. Scorpion and Lion would bleed each other as they had a thousand times before, unaware of Otomo's manipulation.

Thought of Shinpachi made Isami want to kick down the mountain herself. Once they were dead, he would scuttle back to Otosan Uchi like some goblin spider, another sack of ill-gotten gold in hand.

Isami's fate settled upon her like a funeral shroud, thin as gossamer, but inescapable. She had always thought she would be afraid when the moment came, but all that rose from the whirling gyre of her thoughts was a vague sense of sorrow.

Not for herself, but for her companions.

Among the many regrets that haunted Isami, leading Keisuke and Shinzō here was the one that cut deepest. Although Isami wasn't sure she could count either as a friend, they deserved better than a bloody death, their bodies left to rot alongside Kentarō's bones, unburned and unmourned.

The thought came not with sadness, but a flicker of realization. Isami glanced back toward the shrine, the shadow of an idea taking form. At first, she rebelled against the notion, but against her reticence, a desperate plan began to emerge.

Throat tight, she rooted around inside her satchel.

"You don't happen to have a lion dog in there?" Keisuke asked. "Honestly, I'd settle for any guardian spirit."

Isami drew forth Gorobei's flint and match cord, the same he had almost certainly used to set the Scorpion archives aflame. She turned to mount the tomb steps, tread heavy with the weight of what must be done.

"Please forgive me." She bowed before the entrance. The match cord caught quickly, the dry wood of the temple screens even faster.

"Isami! Have you been possessed?" Keisuke ran to her side as the first yellow-gold flames began to lick at the temple columns.

Isami raised an arm to bar Keisuke from putting out the flames. He glanced back to Shinzō as if for support, but the archivist only watched, light from the spreading fire casting his pained expression in harsh relief.

Slowly, Shinzō met Isami's eyes and nodded.

"This is madness." Keisuke looked between the two of them. "What are you doing?"

Isami's voice was steady as she met the courtier's disbelieving stare.

"We are sending a message."

# CHAPTER THIRTY-TWO

Shrieking like a hungry ghost, the bandit twisted his blade to lock Shinzō's, shoving the snarling archivist against the cliff face as two other attackers slipped by. They stepped over the bodies of the three bandits Shinzō had already felled to advance up the narrow stairs.

Isami moved from the shadow of the cavern entrance. She had unwound her chain from about her waist, lest one of the bandits become tangled and drag her from the cliff. The extra length allowed for more reach. She brought her chain swinging around in a wide arc out into the open air.

The bandit didn't notice the heavy weight until it smashed into his helmet. He stumbled back, stunned, arms flailing as he teetered on the outer edge of the stair. The man's companion grabbed his wrist, and Isami dragged her chain back for a heavy overhand swing.

Still holding his companion, the second bandit raised his sword, but Isami had let the chain play out farther than necessary, the blade catching the chain perhaps a foot from the end. As it wrapped about the blade, Isami wrenched back, sending the bandit lurching forward. Releasing his comrade, he threw out a hand to check his fall.

Isami tried to draw back her chain, but the bandit gripped his blade like a drowning man. Stumbling up the stairs, he caught Isami about the waist and bore her to the ground. She sought to drive a finger into his eye, only to have her hand slapped aside.

The bandit's punch smashed her head against the cavern floor.

Isami's arms went limp and wooden, her vision curling up at the edges like burning paper. The bandit grabbed the front of her robes and slammed her back again. Flames danced across Isami's eyes, bright as festival lanterns in the smoky gloom. The bandit seemed a demon from myth, a vengeful fiend wreathed in dust and ash, his cruel blade held high.

A shadow rose behind him. At first, Isami thought it a trick of the smoke until the shape leaned forward to trace a crimson line across the bandit's throat.

With a wet cough, the man released Isami to clap a hand to his neck, but he might as well have been trying to stem the tide. She kicked free of the bandit's weakening hold, scrabbling back on her elbows.

Keisuke relieved the dying man of his sword. Soot smudged the Scorpion courtier's forehead, his eyes red, a heavy length of cloth wrapped about his lower face to cut out the smoke.

A shout drew their attention to the stair below. Shadows struggled, blades flashing amidst clouds of roiling smoke. With a cry of pain, one fell away.

Blinking against the stinging haze, Isami snatched up her chain. Her lungs felt full of jagged nettles. The hungry blaze snatched the sweat from her cheeks and singed the edges of her robes.

Shinzō stumbled through the haze. The archivist was bleeding from a cut on his scalp, sword arm pressed close to his chest. He carried his blade in his off hand, the edge chipped and blemished from hard use. With a pained grunt, Shinzō dropped to his knees beside them.

"They have withdrawn for the moment."

"We can't stay." Keisuke's voice came rough.

"Otomo's bandits will kill us if we leave." Isami blinked back stinging tears, heat from the burning temple like a fresh brand pressed to her cheek. The smoke was becoming too thick, even near the ground.

Keisuke bobbed his head. "Blades or flames, which would you prefer?"

"Quicker to leap from the cliff," Shinzō said.

"And give up so easily?" Keisuke's quip devolved into a coughing fit.

Isami let out a low curse. It was certain death to remain in the cavern, but she was unwilling to allow Lord Otomo the satisfaction of watching them cut to pieces.

"We should take the stairs down," Shinzō said. "It is clear of the smoke, and Otomo's archers will not be able to spot us until we round the cliff face."

Jaw tight, Isami nodded.

The three of them crawled toward the pale smudge of light. It pained Isami to have set Lord Kentarō's tomb aflame, but their only chance lay in the Scorpion or Lion spotting the plume of dark smoke. Lord Otomo must have grasped Isami's gamble, as he had sent several sorties of bandits up the stairs to winnow them out.

Out in the air, Isami was able to breathe again. She scrubbed a hand across her stinging eyes, head still throbbing from where the bandit had dashed it against the stone.

Frail as wizened monks, the three of them descended as far as they dared. Hugging the edge of the cliff they were shielded from arrows, but Shinzō looked on the verge of collapse, and Keisuke was pale enough to pass for a corpse. Jaw tight, Isami slipped by Shinzō to stand first upon the stairs.

The Lion archivist gave a cough of protest, but seemed to lack the wind for words.

Isami waved him back. "I brought you both here. The least I can do is give you time to catch your breath."

Shinzō took a slow step, then seemed to think better of it. Collapsing back upon the stairs, he lay panting, gaze fixed upon the evening sky, his words almost too soft to hear:

> "*Mountains in dark ink.*
> *We are naught but autumn clouds,*
> *writ upon the page.*"

Isami glanced at Keisuke, who nodded.

"As good a death poem as we deserve."

That brought the barest flicker of a smile to Isami's lips. Even now, the Scorpion courtier couldn't bring himself to compliment his former enemy. A rumble from below snapped her attention back to the stairs. Not the staccato slap of running feet, it was lower, louder, seeming to resonate deep within Isami's chest.

"The Fortunes weep," Keisuke said weakly. "Can those thrice-cursed demons not give us a moment of peace?"

"That is not Otomo." With effort, Shinzō pushed to his feet, head cocked. "Those are war drums."

Isami shuffled down the stairs. Shinzō caught her arm as she rounded the cliff, ready to snatch her from the path of any arrows, but the Ikoma archivists' grip fell away as they beheld the valley beyond.

The late afternoon sun glimmered upon a sea of lacquered plate, the tawny gold of Lion battle flags as they streamed from the narrow entrance like ants from a kicked hive. On the opposite slope the deep crimson of Scorpion warriors spread like autumn leaves. Spear and sword blades flashed, ripples of light spreading like sun upon crashing waves.

"Lord Hanbei and Lady Kaede must have seen the smoke." Isami felt torn. Lord Otomo's secret was out, but at what cost?

"They're going to kill each other." Shinzō's voice came heavy with hopeless sorrow.

Fingers numb with emotion, Isami wrapped her chain once more around her waist, and drew forth her battered spyglass. Scorpion samurai spread like blood along the southern slope of the valley, the Lion forces a thick ribbon of gold along the northern hillside as they descended toward the valley floor. If either had seen the mining camp, they gave no sign, attention wholly focused upon their enemy.

"We must get down there," Isami said.

"Otomo's bandits may still be waiting for us," Shinzō said.

Isami took a deep breath, wincing at the pain in her ribs. "If we don't talk to your lords now, all is lost."

"They were willing to shed blood over Stone Willow," Keisuke said. "Imagine what they will do when they discover the Gilded Scar."

Isami steadied herself before cautiously descending the remaining stairs, expecting at any moment to feel the cold bite of steel. But if bandits yet lingered at the base of the cliff, they held their fire.

"Thank the heavens for cowards." Keisuke gave a wry tilt of his head. The move seemed to disorient him, and he sagged back against the cliff face.

Carefully, Isami and Shinzō helped Keisuke to stand. Threading their arms under the courtier's shoulders, they limped down the hill. The breeze shifted, hints of smoke among the rich tang of dry leaves.

Scorpion and Lion formed into rough battle lines on opposing hills just north of the lake, perhaps a hundred paces of rocky grass separating them. Isami was both heartened and distraught to see the forces were of roughly equivalent size – a core of spear, sword, and archers warded by riders on the flanks. The battle would be bloody, but at least it wouldn't be a slaughter.

"We must get between them." Isami gritted her teeth, pushing toward the open space.

"Even odds all we'll receive for our trouble is an arrow in the eye," Keisuke said.

"They'll likely ride us down," Shinzō replied. "If they notice us at all."

Banners snapping, the clan forces began to advance to the thunder of drums. They moved slowly at first, little more than a shuffling walk, dressing lines and forming ranks. Two mounted parties rode forth, Kaede and Hanbei at their head. If Isami could not find a path between them in the next few moments, it would be far too late.

"Remain here." Isami let Keisuke lean onto a mossy boulder. "I will see to the negotiations."

"Not alone, you won't." The firmness in the Scorpion courtier's voice was largely spoiled by the fact he seemed unable to focus his eyes.

"I will come." Shinzō took a limping step forward, arm curled to his chest, face ashen.

"I can't be seen to be taking sides." Isami turned away. "This is my task. It has *always* been mine."

Shinzō called after her, words lost against the clattering roar of the advancing forces. Using Tadataka's compass like a walking staff, Isami picked her way down the rocky hill. In her haste, a rock turned under her foot, sending her tumbling down the sharp incline in a spray of dirt and gravel.

She would have broken her neck if not for the grassy sward below. As it was, Isami had barely clambered to her feet before a forest of spears was pointed in her direction.

"Halt, by order of the Emperor!" She turned, brandishing Lord Otomo's seal like an ancient relic.

"Lady Miya?" The hedge of Lion spears parted to reveal Lord Ikoma Hanbei. Mounted atop a dun-colored stallion, he wore a heavy suit of armor, gold-flecked lacquer glinting like fireflies in the fading light. With a grunt of distaste, Hanbei removed his helmet, pointing his war fan at Isami.

"What is the meaning of this?"

"I wondered much the same." A woman's voice rose among the Scorpion lines.

Lady Kaede had traded her festival robes for a set of articulated plate, its deep-red lacquer embellished with hundreds of tiny golden scorpions. Her mask was blackened steel, almost insectile in aspect, with wide, sharp jaws and silvery mesh over the eye holes.

The two lords glared at one another over the thin strip of grass.

"Lords, I have called you here today to negotiate a truce."

Lord Hanbei slapped his war fan against his saddle, expression hard as a castle wall. "You steal into my camp on false pretenses, abduct one of my retainers, and *now* you wish to talk?"

"You have far exceeded your mandate, Lady Miya." Something akin to mirth glinted in Kaede's eyes. "Assuming that is your true name."

"If you would allow me to explain, lords." Isami tried to keep the desperation from her words. "This valley is–"

"Step aside." Lord Hanbei spoke like a magistrate passing sentence. "This is a clan matter."

"I must concur," Lady Kaede said. "Return to Otosan Uchi and inform Lord Otomo this dispute will be settled presently."

"We cannot be responsible for your safety if you remain," Hanbei said.

"Kill us all, then." The words were weak, but clear. Isami turned to see Keisuke and Shinzō hobbling down the hill. It was the Lion archivist who had spoken, but the Scorpion courtier bobbed his head in agreement. They drew abreast of Isami, standing to either side.

Lord Hanbei drew back as if scalded, seeming at a loss for words.

"Keisuke, come here." Lady Kaede pounded a fist against the wood of her palanquin.

The Scorpion courtier pushed free of Shinzō, almost collapsing into a bow. "Please, listen to Lady Isami."

It was Lord Hanbei who spoke. "We are far past words."

"If you wish to remain here," Lady Kaede's gaze did not waver, "you may die with the rest."

"There is no need for death." A new voice called from the far edge of the lines.

Isami turned with the others, no less surprised as Lord Otomo Shinpachi rode down the hill surrounded by a circle of guards in imperial colors. He came at a slow trot, as if bound for a garden viewing rather than a battle.

"Thank you for your noble service, Miya Isami." Lord Otomo glanced down as he rode past, the smile on his pinched face sharp as a drawn blade. "I shall handle matters from here."

# CHAPTER THIRTY-THREE

Isami didn't even realize she had bitten her tongue until the sharp, coppery tang of blood filled her mouth. Of all the things she expected to see, Lord Otomo Shinpachi sitting in conference with the Bayushi and Ikoma lords ranked up among the divine siblings returning to Rokugan. Questions blazed through her thoughts, but her lips seemed unwilling to respond, even as Lord Otomo invited the assembled lords back to his tent.

Dully, she limped behind the procession, unable to believe the brazenness with which Shinpachi comported himself. Rather than flee as Isami expected, he acted as if he had brought Lion and Scorpion to the Gilded Scar. There was nothing Isami could say or do.

She had, after all, used Otomo's name and seal every step of the way.

Isami glanced at Shinzō, but the Ikoma archivist was on his knees, forehead pressed to the dirt. Keisuke had also knelt, although Isami guessed his seeming deference owed more to blood loss than respect.

Unaccountably, Lord Otomo seemed pleased to see her.

"With the valley overrun, we thought you had run afoul of

ruffians." He gave a respectful tilt of his head toward Isami. "Had I known the danger, I would have never sent you ahead."

"It appears your agents are more resourceful than you imagine, lord." Lady Kaede regarded Shinpachi through heavy-lidded eyes, as if she expected him to suddenly burst into flames.

Shinpachi replied with a modest wave of his hand. "Lady Miya is the one who volunteered to scout ahead."

"It seems we owe both of you our thanks." Kaede leaned forward as if to study Isami's face. "The Bayushi, in particular. I fear my son might have made out far worse without your intercession on his behalf."

Keisuke muttered something, making motions as if to stand.

Isami spoke first. "You are too kind, Lady Bayushi, but Keisuke has done much to commend himself."

"I believe the archivists at Journey's End City would disagree." Kaede flicked her fingers as if to brush away an annoying insect. "But who am I to argue with the savior of the day?"

"Indeed." Lord Hanbei's frown deepened as his gaze shifted to Shinzō. "I had reports you… retrieved my archivist from camp."

"Yes, lord." Isami's thoughts were wave-tossed flotsam. It was all she could do to maintain some semblance of composure. Shinpachi was going to kill her, that much was certain, but perhaps there was a way to save Keisuke and Shinzō.

The Ikoma lord's scowl seemed etched from gray basalt. "I am not in the habit of losing retainers."

Isami tried to reply, but could find no words. She had entered the Lion camp under false pretenses and made off with the lord's personal archivist. That Shinzō had come willingly was beside the point. Her gaze flicked to Lord Otomo, who was watching her like a lizard waiting for a fly to blunder close enough to snap up.

As she met his eyes, something seemed to harden in Isami's chest. If Shinpachi wished to pretend he remained her lord and patron, she would sharpen his lie into a dagger.

"I must apologize for the deception, but I was acting under Lord Otomo's orders." Isami bowed low. "Ikoma Shinzō's knowledge and expertise were vital to discovering the Gilded Scar, and with the issue of Stone Willow Valley coming to a head, there was no time to wait for your return, Lord Ikoma."

"Is this true, Lord Otomo?" Hanbei asked.

"Regrettably, yes." Shinpachi spoke without even the slightest hesitation. "Please accept my sincerest regrets for circumventing your command."

"You are forgiven, of course." Hanbei shifted as if discomfited by Lord Otomo's contrition. "Let us not speak of this matter again."

"And so must I apologize for the actions of Ikoma Shinzō and Bayushi Keisuke," Isami spoke quickly, wondering how far she might press her luck. "Any seeming disloyalty or questionable behavior was at my behest. True samurai, they have endured shame and disgrace for the good of the Empire."

At last, momentary hesitation sent a crack through Shinpachi's calm façade. His throat bobbed, then he gave a quick nod.

"Indeed. Quite commendable."

"Lord, if I might request one small boon?" Isami fought to keep her voice humble, surprised no one else could hear the hammering of her heart.

"If it is in my power to grant." Shinpachi raised a hand, palm up.

"I know you had intended to do so, but would you allow me

to deliver the imperial commendation to Ikoma Shinzō and Bayushi Keisuke?"

Although Shinzō did not raise his face, Isami could see the archivist's shoulders tighten. By contrast, Keisuke's wild grin was visible even behind his mask. Isami half-thought the Scorpion courtier might break out in a mad titter.

Lord Otomo spoke through gritted teeth. "How could I deny such an honor to those who so richly deserve it?"

Isami turned to her companions. "There will be a formal ceremony later, of course. For now, on behalf of Emperor Hantei XXXVIII, please accept the appreciation of a grateful Empire. You have done great service to both your clans and to Rokugan. I hereby name you Shōsoige – lesser initial rank, lower grade; deserving of such praise and honor commensurate with such an exalted position."

Contrary to Isami's elaborate pronouncement, the titles were quite minor. Lacking land, stipend, or any true authority, they were often given to minor court functionaries who had earned the favor of some high aristocrat. In granting such boons however, Isami had forced Lord Otomo to tacitly acknowledge Keisuke and Shinzō acted under his auspices. All of the weight now fell upon him alone.

"Well done, my son." Lady Kaede's mask shifted as she smiled. "A small conflagration is nothing compared to the enduring luster of imperial regard. It seems I shall have to find more fitting work for you."

"I thank you, lady." Although Keisuke spoke to Kaede, his eyes were on Isami.

Not to be outdone, Lord Hanbei gave Shinzō a gruff nod. "You are, of course, reinstated as my personal archivist. Upon our return to Sacred Watch Palace, we shall discuss such additional responsibilities as are attendant to your new rank."

Shinzō drew in a slow breath, the coiled tension leaving the archivist's stance for the first time since Isami had met him.

Two samurai bulled through the tent flap. Although one wore Scorpion crimson and the other Lion gold, their faces were uniformly flushed, shoulders rising and falling with each hurried breath. Both immediately dropped to their knees as if they had rehearsed the move.

Bowing low to their respective lords, they gave their reports, each acting as if the opposite was not present.

Amidst the competing voices, Isami was able to glean that the bandits had fled into the hills, leaving the captured villagers behind. While the Lion held the mining camp and its surrounds, the Scorpion forces had taken up position on the hillside, securing the valley approach.

Silence filled the tent, each lord discreetly watching the others as they reflected on how best to broach the topic which weighed upon everyone's mind.

Isami looked to Lord Otomo, but the older man simply sat back upon his heels, a thoughtful glimmer in his eyes as he studied Kaede and Hanbei. With a word he could condemn further bloodshed, but Isami knew he would say nothing.

"It seems we find ourselves once again at an impasse," Lady Kaede spoke first. Although her war mask concealed all expression, her voice carried an almost mocking tone.

"The Lion were first into this valley," Lord Ikoma replied.

"And yet you cannot leave it without my blessing." Kaede cocked her head, one hand extended as if to bestow a benediction upon her foe.

"I could remove you," Hanbei replied.

"You could try."

Although no one moved, there was an unmistakable change in the air; a tightening of posture, a sharpening of intent that seemed to darken the space between the Lion and Scorpion contingents like a storm rolling off the sea.

"Stone Willow and all its surrounds are ours." Lord Ikoma's declaration fell like an executioner's blade.

Lady Bayushi laughed. "Then I shall endeavor to see your ashes buried here."

Now the others moved, hands slipping to blades, poise shifting from respectful to threatening as each lord's followers prepared to leap into battle.

Both Kaede and Hanbei glanced to Lord Otomo, but Shinpachi seemed engrossed by the golden chrysanthemum flowers embroidered on his fan.

"Lords, if I may trouble you for a moment?" Isami's voice broke, but she forged on. "I have no wish to undermine any ongoing negotiations, but I fear the dispensation of the valley has already been decided."

"You *dare*." Hanbei reacted as if Isami had slapped him, jaw tight, eyes burning bright as festival lanterns.

Kaede raised a calming hand. "I think we should hear what Lady Miya has to say. If Lord Otomo consents, of course."

Shinpachi fixed Isami with a sharp look. She could see he dearly wished to object, but could not do so without appearing rude, given the praise he had just lavished upon her. After a long moment, he folded his hands.

"Please, Lady Miya, continue."

Rooting through her satchel, Isami retrieved the agreement

Keisuke and Shinzō signed prior to the burning of Lord Kentarō's records. Although the scroll was battered, the writing remained quite legible.

The assembled nobles sat quietly as Isami read the treaty aloud.

"That carries no weight." Hanbei was the first to speak. "I did not sign."

Kaede nodded. "I must agree with my esteemed colleague."

"Forgive my confusion, lords." Isami was glad to be kneeling, elsewise her knees might have given way. "Were Ikoma Shinzō and Bayushi Keisuke not your representatives?"

"They were, yes," Hanbei replied, discomfort obvious in his bearing.

"Keisuke and Shinzō's circumstances have changed," Kaede added.

"Indeed, lords. They have received imperial commendations." Isami fought to keep her hands from curling into fists, her back straight as a banner pole.

Kaede and Hanbei exchanged an appraising glance before turning to Lord Otomo.

He cleared his throat, tone polite, but cold as snowmelt. "Lady Miya is correct save in one regard – the treaty applies only to Stone Willow Valley. As such, the dispensation of this new territory remains unclear."

"With respect, Lord Otomo; as written, the treaty encompasses all Lord Ikoma Kentarō and Lady Bayushi Saihoku's former domain," Isami replied. "They claimed this valley as well. Lord Kentarō was even buried in it."

"But who owns it *now*?" Hanbei seemed but moments away from drawing his blade.

"It has been a long journey for us all." Kaede's tone carried a note of warning. "Speak quickly, Lady Miya, before what remains of my patience slips away."

"My sincerest apologies. The treaty stipulates the Lion gain control of all land represented on the imperial map." Isami drew the scroll from her satchel, spreading it upon the ground for all to see. "Whereas the Scorpion would claim such new territory as was uncovered by my survey of the region."

Shinpachi shook his head. "It is my understanding you did not have the opportunity to survey Stone Willow."

"Lord Otomo is, of course, correct. I did not survey that valley." Isami reached once more into her satchel. "But I did survey this one."

The assembled lords regarded her map of the Gilded Scar, frowning down at the web of lines connecting mountain to lake to mining camp. It was a poor representation, barely a sketch, but none could deny it *was* a map.

Hands tight in the sleeves of her robes, Isami prayed to the elemental spirits, the Fortunes, the ancestors, to any spirit that would listen – please let sense outweigh the clans' need for blood.

Lady Kaede shook her head, chuckling. "This seems a fine agreement."

It was clear she recognized the value of a working gold mine.

Lord Hanbei favored the Scorpion with a wary scowl, as if searching for some snare within the arrangement. Although the treaty denied the Lion the riches of the Gilded Scar, it also removed the Scorpion from the eastern bank of Three Sides River while providing them access to the valley via the river.

At last, the Ikoma lord gave a low grunt. "A Lion's oath is as strong as our blades."

Isami felt her stomach unclench, only to seize up once more as her gaze fell upon Shinpachi.

The Otomo lord sat as if listening to a poetry recital, eyes distant, the barest hint of a smile upon his thin lips. In any other circumstance, Isami would have mistaken the look for regard, perhaps even respect; but it was impossible not to suspect Shinpachi's amusement boded ill for Isami and the clans.

"It is good that the Emperor's servants do not shed blood needlessly. This treaty is well founded." He gave the slightest of nods. "I am grateful for Lady Miya's diligent efforts on behalf of the Empire."

"As are we." Lady Kaede inclined her head. "And to you, Lord Otomo."

"Your foresight has spared the lives of many brave warriors," Lord Hanbei added. "My clan is in your debt."

As one, the Scorpion and Lion lords bowed to Lord Otomo Shinpachi.

Despite her reservations, Isami could not but join them.

"I only act as the Emperor wills." Lord Otomo acknowledged the obeisance with a grateful wave.

It felt as if Isami's chest were full of birds, light and airy, tiny wingbeats brushing against her ribs. She could hardly believe the clans had agreed, let alone Lord Otomo. And yet, Isami only had to glance to her left to see unshed tears glittering in Shinzō's eyes, Keisuke's grin so wide it stretched the edges of his silken mask.

Isami's joy withered the moment Shinpachi spoke.

"Alas, matters have kept me abroad for far too long." He stood, flicking back the long sleeves of his robe. "It is time I returned to court."

Shinpachi's gaze pinioned Isami like a thrown spear. "Lady Miya, I look forward to a detailed report on our journey home."

He swept from the tent like a triumphant general, head held high, a tail of guards and servants threading between the Scorpion and Lion.

Isami knew only death awaited her on the road to Otosan Uchi.

Even so, she had no choice but to follow.

# CHAPTER THIRTY-FOUR

"You should flee." Keisuke spoke in an urgent whisper. "I'll conceal your escape. Surely there is someone in Otosan Uchi who can protect you."

"Shinpachi will never allow me to slip from his grasp." Isami glanced at the two guards in imperial colors standing a few paces away. Although Shinpachi was required to give her time to write Keisuke and Shinzō's commendations, he seemed loath to waste any more. It had been all Isami could do to steal a few moments to bid farewell to her friends.

"I will speak to my mother," Keisuke continued as if he hadn't heard. "She can request you finish surveying the Gilded Scar."

"Lady Kaede is already in Shinpachi's debt," Isami replied. "I doubt she desires to sink deeper into the mire of obligation on my behalf."

He shook his head stubbornly. "Even my mother must recognize you have done the Scorpion a great service. Come to Journey's End City, I will hide you myself."

"You would see us both shamed and ruined."

Keisuke laid a hand upon her arm. "I will not allow that two-tongued goblin to simply steal you away."

"You will, because you must," Isami replied, strangely calm now she had almost reached the end of her journey.

Keisuke looked plaintively toward Shinzō, who had been watching the exchange with a thoughtful expression. "Talk some sense into her."

"Your path leads through Lion lands," Shinzō spoke slowly, every word carefully measured. "I shall ensure Lord Hanbei sends an honor guard to accompany you."

Isami said, "Even were they to walk me by the hand back to Otosan Uchi, I am at Shinpachi's mercy the moment I pass into the inner city."

Shinzō gave a slow nod, pressing a clenched fist to his chest in a warrior's salute. "Then I shall avenge you."

"You will do nothing of the sort," Isami replied. "Avenge me by fulfilling your ambitions. Remember me by serving the Empire."

"That's it, then?" Keisuke looked between them both. "After everything, you're simply giving up?"

Isami could find no reply. She looked to the sky, dark now, the edges of clouds just visible around a waning sliver of moon.

Keisuke gave an angry grunt, turning away. "If you wish to die, then I shall not stand in your way."

"Keisuke, wait." Isami drew a pair of scrolls from her satchel. "I put your commendation in writing. Also, there is a letter from me."

A glimmer of helpless sorrow broke through the Scorpion courtier's anger. For a moment, he seemed about to speak, but then only shook his head, regarding Isami as if trying to commit her to memory. He took the scrolls from her. Gripping them tight enough to crumple the paper, Keisuke stalked off, shoulders hunched.

Isami watched him go, resignation sinking into her bones.

"Do not judge Keisuke too harshly," Shinzō shook his head. "He still believes the world should be better than it is."

Isami smiled. "It would be quite the irony if I condemned others for that particular fault."

"It pains me to leave you this way," Shinzō said.

Isami gripped the archivist's shoulder, drawing him into a close embrace. Shinzō tensed, shifting his weight almost as if to toss Isami to the ground. After a moment, he relaxed, patting Isami awkwardly on the back.

After they broke apart, Shinzō drew his katana from his sash, sheath and all. "Take my blade, at least."

Isami pressed it back toward him. "I wouldn't know what to do with it."

"I shall do all I can to see Otomo faces justice." Shinzō dropped into a low bow.

"I know you will." Isami held out two scrolls.

The Ikoma archivist took the proffered letters, and with one disdainful last look at the Otomo guards, spun on his heel and strode off as if he marched in formation.

Isami did not blame her friends for their reactions. She hoped with time they might even forgive her. Only the elemental spirits knew whether Shinzō or Keisuke would achieve their ambitions. All Isami could do was see they did not suffer for aiding her.

"Lady Miya." One of the Otomo guards stepped to her side. "Your palanquin awaits."

She glanced back at the Gilded Scar. Moonlight glittered on still waters, tree branches gently swaying in the slightest of breezes. Campfires dotted the slopes, torches like bobbing fireflies. The flames showed dancing shadows – some were kidnapped villagers freed from bondage, others samurai celebrating a victory. Although Scorpion and Lion remained separate, here and there Isami spotted a flash of red among the tawny yellow, or the glimmer of gold bobbing in a sea of deep crimson. Tomorrow, there would be posturing and plotting as the clans once again sought to advance their position, but Isami could take satisfaction in the fact none would die tonight, at least.

Four bearers knelt beside the box-like palanquin, wearing only light shirts despite the chill. Of Shinpachi there was no sign, but Isami could see the thin ribbon of the lord's procession beginning to wind its way up the hill.

Opening the screen, she ducked inside, reclining on the silken pillows as the palanquin lurched into motion. Someone had thoughtfully set out a tray of fruits and pickled vegetables along with a small decanter of barley tea.

Isami did not touch the food. There might be nothing she could do to stop Lord Otomo from murdering her, but she had no desire to simply hand over her life.

A half hour saw them passing through the narrow defile that led from the Gilded Scar. Isami could see very little through the gaps in the wood of her palanquin, but was still gratified to know she had been right about the valley, if little else.

They traveled all night, crossing Three Sides River on a large, flat-bottomed ferry, then following the road up through Stone Willow Valley. Word had spread, and in every village the imperial procession was greeted with bows, cheers, and gifts of food. Although the procession made frequent stops for rest and refreshment, Isami took nothing she did not see others eat first.

Isami's bearers were replaced many times, as were her guards. The countryside was beautiful, trees girded in red and gold finery, arrayed as if for a court function. The air was chill, but had yet to yield to winter's cruel bite. Everywhere, smiling peasants danced around bonfires and swirling festival lanterns, celebrating the final fruits of a bountiful harvest.

The autumn magnificence was lost on Isami, her attentions worn thin as old leather. Every moment, she expected the knife to fall. Every night, she slipped into a fitful doze, never expecting to awake.

And still, her death did not come.

The guards and servants remained polite, yet distant. Of Shinpachi, she saw nothing at all. Although the lord traveled with the procession, he remained in his palanquin during the day. Each evening, he would retire to a fine pavilion, erected by servants who had hurried ahead of the main body to see everything was set to the lord's specifications.

To keep from going mad with worry, Isami charted the roads they traveled. The march stopped often enough for her to survey the surrounding territory and take frequent bearings with Tadataka's compass.

Isami did her best to force down the sharp pang of guilt that pierced her thoughts each time she used the geomantic relic. She had hoped to return to Otosan Uchi a hero, now it seemed she would not return at all.

On the sixth night, Shinpachi finally summoned her.

Isami started awake, dagger ready, the other hand tight on her chain. The fire had died to embers, but in the sullen glow Isami could just make out an armored samurai. He stood at attention, arms at his side, features little more than a blur of shadow.

"Lord Otomo requests you attend him." The guard's respectful phrasing was belied by the flatness of his tone.

Drawing in a deep breath, Isami stood. The guard turned on his heel and marched into the woods, away from the direction of Otomo's pavilion.

Isami hesitated, torn between resignation and the need to survive. She had expected poison, perhaps a concealed blade, not to be hacked apart by some bandit in imperial colors.

Truthfully, it was a bit galling.

Unwinding her chain, Isami walked into the darkened woods.

The guard led her deep into the trees, the night sky little more than a thin ribbon overhead. The sounds of camp faded into the gentle hum of crickets and autumn frogs, campfires no brighter than the misty stars above.

Ahead, Isami saw a flicker of light. She tensed, expecting it to signal her end, but the glow gradually resolved into a number of lanterns hung amidst the branches.

The trees parted to reveal a small clearing. In it were spread several thick mats, folded blankets arrayed to ward off the chill. A coal brazier sat in the center, tended by a kneeling servant, while another saw to the preparation of tea and bean cakes.

Lord Otomo Shinpachi sat upon one of the raised mats, draped in a heavy blanket.

"You must forgive this informality, but these are matters best discussed away from curious ears." He accepted a steaming cup of tea. "I find the cold slips into my bones more easily these days."

Isami raised her chain in a defensive posture as she surveyed the shadows for waiting assassins. With a bow, the guard who had led her to the clearing turned and departed.

"Do not fear." Lord Otomo tilted his head at the pair of

kneeling servants. "These are my personal aides, they are trustworthy and discreet."

"It is not *their* reliability that concerns me," Isami replied coolly.

One corner of Shinpachi's mouth twitched with something that could have easily been irritation or amusement.

"I thought the remote setting might ease your concerns."

"It also happens to be far enough from camp that none will hear my cries for help."

"It does have that to commend it too." This time, Shinpachi definitely grinned. "Please, have a seat, enjoy some tea."

Isami did not move.

"If I were going to kill you, I certainly wouldn't do it myself."

Isami fixed him with a level stare. "If the last several months have taught me anything, it's that you aren't afraid to dirty your hands."

"Oh, you have grown sharp, haven't you?" Shinpachi took a long sip, then sighed. "Remain standing if you wish, it only adds to your discomfort."

A hot bolt of anger shot up Isami's spine. She took a step forward. "Does my distress amuse you?"

"Vengeance is a liability reserved for the small-minded." Shinpachi's smile did not reach his eyes. "Your suffering means nothing to me."

"Then why not end it?"

The grin slipped from his face. If anything, Shinpachi seemed genuinely startled. "I would rather smash an imperial vase than destroy such a useful agent."

"Useful?" Isami almost spit the word.

"I admit, you cost me a substantial source of income, as well as the life of an exceptional murderer." He clucked his tongue. "But such things are of little consequence when weighed against the prestige I will receive for preventing war between the Scorpion and Lion. Not to mention, you have secured me the gratitude of two powerful clan lords."

Isami stared at the Otomo lord. Unbidden, the memory of their last meeting rose in her mind.

"Only fools make plans," she said. "A true sage turns all eventualities to his advantage."

"Indeed!" Shinpachi raised his cup as if to salute her. "I underestimated you, Miya Isami. It is a mistake I shall not repeat in our future dealings."

"Have you been possessed by a demon?" Isami asked, surprised. "How could you ever expect me to serve you?"

Otomo seemed unperturbed. "You see but a small portion of the map. Storm clouds gather across the Empire, the clans grow too strong. Lion and Unicorn seek to bludgeon the court into submission while Crane and Scorpion play deadly games over tea. Dragon and Phoenix delve into things best left hidden. The Crab bleed in endless war while lesser clans circle like vultures." Shinpachi rolled his neck. "You may not agree with my methods, Lady Miya, but never doubt I serve the Empire."

Isami could but shake her head. "You lie well, Lord Otomo."

"I do many things well."

"Thievery and murder among them."

"Repudiate me if you wish," Shinpachi shrugged. "But keep your hatred close, lest it reflect poorly on your reputation. As far as anyone knows, I remain your patron."

"And what if I tell others how long you concealed a gold mine for your own benefit?"

"Tell whom? With what proof?" One of Shinpachi's thin eyebrows made a perfect arch above his darkly glittering eye. "Gorobei destroyed all record of the hidden valley, and you destroyed Gorobei."

"What of the captured bandits?"

"Do I seem foolish enough to have ever visited the Gilded Scar?" Shinpachi replied coolly. "Everything was put in place through agents such as Gorobei, all of whom need no longer trouble your thoughts."

"But you hadn't considered Lord Kentarō's maps."

"How was I to know some mad Ikoma lord had built his tomb there?" Otomo replied. "An oversight, now rectified."

"Rectified?" Isami drew in an angry breath. "You murdered your own nephew."

"That was unfortunate, yes." Lord Otomo frowned. "Kazuya was taken before his time. It would pain my heart to reopen the investigation, especially if new evidence were to implicate one of Kazuya's former friends – a woman with whom he had close dealings, one whom he betrayed, one who was even seen slipping into his quarters just after his death. Quite unfortunate indeed, although not for me."

Isami's knuckles whitened on her chain.

Lord Otomo's gaze flicked to his servants, who both straightened, drawing daggers from their robes. The blades glittered like spilled oil, steel sheened with something Isami was sure would quickly dispatch her to the Realm of Waiting.

Isami silently judged the distance to Lord Otomo. With the Ancestors' favor she might be able to send one of the steel weights crashing into Shinpachi's head. Although far from frail, he was not a young man, a blow like that might be enough to end him.

"You would throw your life away over a petty grudge?" Lord Otomo asked.

Isami studied him through slitted eyes. The harm he had inflicted, on her, on her comrades, on the Lion and Scorpion – all of it to protect a single forgotten mine. Shinpachi was far cannier than Kazuya, but at the root of things, they were the same – arrogant and self-important, blinded by the delusion they acted for the Empire.

For all his lies, at least Gorobei had not hidden behind flimsy justifications.

Shinpachi might be an imperial noble, but he was a slave to his ambitions, his greed. Every move, every word, every reaction was carefully calculated to advance his goals. He was gripped by neither joy nor anger. Yet, in removing emotion, he had rendered himself predictable.

Like surveying lines, Shinpachi's motivations became clear to Isami. He would act in his own interest, without preference, without rancor. Discovering his plan was merely a matter of measurement and calculation, and Lord Otomo had given Isami all the tools she needed. Now that she knew Shinpachi's destination, divining his thoughts was just a matter of finding the right path.

Isami might not be able to chart the clouds, but she understood maps.

"You will not harm me." She lowered her chain.

He gave a thin smile. "Will I not?"

A flick of his fingers sent the two servants scuttling forward.

Isami watched them come, hoping she had measured right. If Lord Otomo truly wished her dead, he would not have wasted breath with discussion.

Their blades stopped a hair's breadth from her throat, sharpened tips so close Isami did not dare move lest they open a vein.

"A fine display, but wasted on me," she said, careful not to swallow. "Perhaps you could have explained away my death when I was a failed scholar, but now there will be uncomfortable questions if my body is found."

"And who said it will ever be found?"

"You are my patron. I am under your protection," Isami replied. "It would reflect even more poorly upon you should I simply disappear."

"Perhaps now." He tapped his chin thoughtfully. "But I am a patient man."

"And yet, it would still bring unfortunate consequences."

"Oh, how so?"

"Upon my departure I gave letters to Ikoma Shinzō and Bayushi Keisuke." Isami willed her breath to slow. The first was true, but now she ventured into the realm of fabrication. "They detail, in depth, every aspect of your operation in the Gilded Scar – the kidnappings, the banditry, the murders, all of it."

"Again, I would ask, what proof can you provide."

Isami smiled. "The court might require evidence of your crime, but the clans… Lord Hanbei is suspicious by nature, and Lady Kaede, well, I believe we both know how delighted she would be to receive such information, proof or no."

"So, it is to be blackmail?"

"Hardly." Isami took a step back, relaxing marginally when the servants did not follow. "If I die, they are to present the letters to their lords."

"And if I kill your comrades?"

"You would murder an imperial noble and two highly placed clan samurai." Isami cocked her head. "Now who is nursing a petty grudge?"

Lord Otomo's laugh was the rusty screech of a startled crow. He set his cup down to wipe an amused tear from one eye, then gestured to one of the servants, who edged forward to place a small, lacquered box at Isami's feet.

"What is this?"

"My letter of support," he replied. "Assuming you still wish to retake your imperial cartographer's evaluation."

Apprehensively, Isami nudged it open with her foot. Inside was a beautifully embellished scroll bearing Lord Otomo's personal seal.

"Use it or not. It makes no matter to me." Shinpachi stood, straightening his robes. "As your patron, all I ask is that you serve the Empire as best you can."

Isami met his eyes. "Would that I could make the same request of you."

"You are like an archer who aims at the sun, surprised when her arrows fall back to earth. Take care you are not pinioned, Lady Miya." With the slightest of bows, Otomo Shinpachi strode into the shadows. After a moment, his servants followed, eyes still on Isami as they backed into the darkness.

Isami waited until the last crackling footfall had faded before sagging against a nearby tree. The tears came then, hot as fire upon her cheeks. She knelt, face cradled in her hands, anger and relief boiling within her, bright and terrifying by turns.

A sudden burst of laughter broke through the tears. Isami was surprised at first, but the laugh came again, bubbling up through the cracks in her roiling emotions. Like a swimmer surfacing after a long dive, she took a great whooping breath of air, then descended into a fit of mirth. Back against the tree, she drummed her heels against the ground, cackling like a madwoman as the events of the last few months crashed down upon her.

It was a long time before Isami rose. When she did it was with dry cheeks and narrowed eyes, her jaw tight as a clenched fist. Carefully, she gathered up her chain, taking care to put her hair and robes back in order.

Through the tree limbs above, the stars shone bright in a cloudless sky, bits of silver-white glass cast into waters dark and still as a reflecting pool. The night closed in around Isami, and she breathed deeply of the crisp autumn air, her mind calming for perhaps the first time in months.

She availed herself of one of the lanterns and turned back toward camp. Lord Otomo had said he would not underestimate her again, but he had already made another mistake.

He had left Isami alive.

# EPILOGUE

"Highly unusual." Master Naotora held Lord Otomo's letter at arms' length. After a moment squinting at the words, she set the scroll down, regarding Isami with the slightest of smiles. "But I would expect nothing less from you, Lady Miya."

"I am honored Lord Otomo finds my humble works worthy of commendation." Isami touched her forehead to the woven mats. "And I pray to the Ancestors the august masters of the Ministry of Cartography will see fit to overlook my past imprudence when reviewing my candidacy."

"Your flaunting of decorum was insulting and unprecedented," Master Doji Kageyasu favored Isami with a sharp scowl. A moment later, his expression softened. "But you have shown willingness to atone for your transgressions."

Isami hid the smile that threatened to shatter her composure. Her presentation to the committee had even been selected to cater to Master Kageyasu's tastes – a replication of Doji Tadatsune's *Road Most High*. Although Isami had spent the last few months surveying the coastal road, she had taken pains to hide the measurements behind stylized landmarks and artistic embellishments in the Doji style.

"Your conduct has shown marked improvement, Lady Miya. Also, it seems you have amassed some powerful allies." Scrolls rustled under Master Naotora's liver-spotted hands. "Just this morning I received missives from no less than Lady Bayushi Kaede and Lord Ikoma Hanbei expressing support for your candidacy."

"It is cause for concern when the Lion and Scorpion speak as one," Kageyasu frowned down at the letters. "But only a fool would ignore them."

Isami released the breath she had been holding. Worried the implications might unsettle the Crane Master, she had worked to ensure the scrolls did not arrive until just before her evaluation. To Isami's delight, they had also included mention of Keisuke and Shinzō, both of whom seemed to be flourishing in their new roles. Isami had exchanged letters with both, filled with banal pleasantries and comments on the season. That Lord Otomo read every one was certain, but Shinpachi could puzzle over hidden meanings. The words did not matter, the missives' only purpose was to ensure she and her friends yet lived.

"I agree this bears watching." Master Naotora's creaky voice drew Isami from her thoughts. "But I can find no fault with Lady Miya's work."

Master Kageyasu studied Isami for a long moment. "Nor I."

"I see no reason not to approve her candidacy," Master Naotora continued.

Isami blinked against the tears that suddenly blurred her vision.

"On a *provisional* basis," Kageyasu added.

"Indeed." Naotora gave a slow nod. "Two years probationary

period, her rank to be immediately revoked should any more…
inconsistencies come to light. What say you, Master Tadataka?"

Although no longer Isami's master, and thus permitted to
speak, Master Tadataka had remained silent through the entire
proceedings, shoulders straight, robes in perfect array, eyes fixed
on a point slightly beyond Isami, as if he were lost in thought.

His gaze shifted to Isami for the first time. She had expected
anger, sorrow, but Tadataka's expression betrayed nothing save
cool civility, as if she were a stranger.

His throat bobbed once, then he gave a brisk nod. "That is
acceptable."

It should have been a moment of purest joy, the culmination
of everything Isami had suffered for these long months. And yet,
her heart held only ashes, chilled by Tadataka's stern regard.

"Then it is agreed," Master Naotora said. "Lady Miya Isami,
I hereby confer upon you the title of Imperial Cartographer of
the Eighth Rank, entitled to all honors and powers inherent to
such position."

Isami bowed to each master in turn, Tadataka's gaze like a
chill hand gripped tight around her heart.

The ceremony concluded, Tadataka rose and departed, two
servants hurrying to lift the tail of his trailing formal robes.

"I look forward to toasting your successes, Lady Miya."
Kageyasu raised a welcoming hand.

"I hope to give you much cause for celebration, master."

With a smile and nod, Kageyasu left, leaving Isami with
Naotora.

The old master rose, waving for servants to collect the
scattered scrolls. Instead of departing, she took a few slow steps
toward Isami, then paused to pat her on the shoulder.

"Tadataka will come around. Especially once he realizes you slipped a survey past Master Kageyasu's artistic sensibilities." Naotora gave a rusty chuckle as Isami stiffened. "It is not often I am provided with the opportunity to tweak the Doji's nose."

With another pat, Naotora turned away. "I shall be watching your career with interest."

Isami gave a grateful nod to conceal the flicker of apprehension that tickled along her spine.

Master Naotora would not be the only one watching her.

Word traveled fast in the ministry. Outside, Isami received congratulations from other cartographers moving through the garden, but Isami could only think of how quickly they had distanced themselves after her failed evaluation. She returned each bow and murmured compliment, searching the faces of her new colleagues for hints of what they sought to gain through association with her. Apart from Kazuya, Isami had had few friends among the copy clerks and archivists.

A celebration had been prepared in one of the Ministry villas. Grilled sea bream, miso soup, rice, and roast vegetables, along with warm sake to ward off the late autumn cold. Isami ate and drank sparingly, speaking only enough to continue conversations. She should cultivate new contacts, but the only person she wished to speak with was not in attendance.

It was long past dark before Isami could politely excuse herself. Lamps lit the Ministry Gardens; trees, shrubs, and beds carefully pruned in expectation of the coming winter. The air curled like smoke from Isami's lungs, sharp and cold.

Not a single lantern burned outside Master Tadataka's manor, the darkened interior cold and silent as a tomb.

Isami paused at the entrance stairs. If Tadataka were in

attendance, there would be servants, guards, but Isami waited several long breaths and detected not even the faintest glimmer of movement.

"I sent them all away." Master Tadataka was a shadow among shadows, recognizable only by his voice. "I did not wish them to see."

Isami mounted the stairs, step by trembling step. It was hard for her to swallow, her mouth dry as the Burning Sands.

Tadataka waited for her in the entrance chamber. The light of her lantern revealed a pile of quilted robes, unadorned but for the occasional embroidered pine. Tadataka sat on a woven blanket, hunched over a low coal brazier. His gray hair hung loose, his hands cupped for warmth.

Isami paused in the doorway, struck by the dissimilarities between this and their last meeting. Then, Tadataka had seemed in control of the situation. Now, the man before her appeared mournful, almost lost.

Isami drew in a shaky breath, but Tadataka spoke before she did.

"I am sorry for doubting you." He closed his eyes as if the words caused him pain. "I thought I was protecting you, but my concerns were simply another cage."

Tadataka's words slipped through Isami's ears. She had come expecting to throw herself upon her former master's mercy. Instead, he was the one asking for forgiveness.

Two quick steps, and she knelt next to the brazier. "You have nothing to apologize for, master."

He gave a breathless chuckle. "I hardly deserve such a title, driving you into the clutches of Otomo Shinpachi. They say there were skirmishes."

"Several," Isami replied.

He lifted his head, tears glittering on his cheeks like spilled silver. "Were you harmed?"

"I am fine." She reached over to brush the hair from his face. "All is well."

"You have never been a very good liar." He raised one thin hand, patting hers.

"I may surprise you." Isami was not surprised to find herself crying as well. They sat for a long moment, all silent but for the gentle creak of wind against the shutters.

"After how we parted," he said, at last, "I did not think you wished to see me."

"I thought the same," Isami replied. "But I need your guidance more than ever."

Tadataka straightened. "Are you in danger?"

"No." She bit her lip. "Yes."

Isami let out a slow sigh. It was hard not to view everything through a lens of suspicion. She had been scarred – by Kazuya, by Lord Otomo, by Gorobei. It was tempting to see the world as Lord Otomo did, to think all others thought only in terms of how they might gain advantage from a situation, a relationship, a murder.

But there were yet good people in the Empire, people like Keisuke, like Shinzō. Lord Otomo thought he had outmaneuvered Isami, that she would have no recourse save to follow his commands. He thought his will a mountain, massive, unmovable. In truth, it was but a storm cloud, full of thunder and fury, but ultimately helpless before the everchanging sky.

Tadataka had been more than Isami's master, her patron, he had been a solid compass with which to chart the course of her life. And that was something people like Lord Otomo would never understand.

She reached into her sash. Drawing forth Tadataka's geomantic compass, she held it out to him.

He pressed it back toward her. "You have put it to far better use than I ever did."

Isami hesitated. Tadataka was no longer her master, and yet she did not know what else to call him.

"Thank you, father." Her voice was barely a whisper, and yet it seemed to fill the whole of the chamber. Her parents would always have a place in Isami's heart, but blood was no substitute for word and deed.

"Daughter." The rightness of Tadataka's reply seemed to resonate within Isami's very bones.

He leaned forward to coax life from the smoldering coals. "Tell me everything."

So Isami did.

When she had finished, Tadataka sat back, shaking his head. "You have made a powerful enemy."

"Indeed." Isami could not help but grin. It was as if she had been wearing a suit of ill-fitting armor these past few months, only to suddenly breathe freely once more.

"Lord Otomo Shinpachi is a dragon on the rise," Tadataka said. "It is not wise to vex him further."

"Is it not worse to simply stand by, knowing what we now know?"

"I have done so my whole life," Tadataka said ruefully. "To my shame and discredit." He seemed to straighten, head coming up, eyes bright and determined. "But no longer. You may rely upon me."

"I always have."

"Even so." Tadataka gave an anxious tilt of his head. "The road ahead is likely to end in our deaths."

"All roads eventually end in death."

Tadataka gave a somber nod, but Isami could already see the old master's reservations beginning to surface. For one such as Tadataka, who had lived his life avoiding the snares of ambition, challenging one so powerful and unscrupulous must seem a truly daunting task.

The answer came, popping from Isami's memory like the solution to a particularly vexing calculation.

She may not have the words to convince her former master, but he did.

"After I failed my first evaluation, do you remember what you said to me?"

Tadataka frowned, considering. "I said many things."

Isami met his eyes. "Lord Otomo may seem like a mountain – a grand thing, imposing, sharp, and obstinate. In truth, he is more like a stone garden; carefully cultivated, perhaps, but ultimately composed of rocks and sand. And what is the best way to move sand?"

"One shovel at a time," he replied.

"Not so." Isami leaned in, drawing her adopted father into a tight hug. She pressed her face into his hair and breathed deep of the comforting smells of sandalwood and sharp nettle tea.

"The best way to move sand is with help."

# ABOUT THE AUTHOR

By day, EVAN DICKEN studies old Japanese maps and crunches numbers for all manner of fascinating research at the Ohio State University. By night, he does neither of these things. His work has most recently appeared in *Analog*, *Beneath Ceaseless Skies*, and *Strange Horizons*, and he has stories forthcoming from Black Library and Rampant Loon Press.

*evandicken.com*
*twitter.com/evandicken*

Enter Rokugan, a realm of warring samurai clans – filled with honor, battle, magic and demons. Fight for the Emperor, usurp rival clans, and earn glory for your family.

 **EDGE** STUDIO

Explore an epic fantasy world with Fantasy Flight Games.
**fantasyflightgames.com**

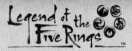

## Legend of the Five Rings™

**Curse of Honor**

CAN HONOR SAVE A LOST SON?

DAVID ANNANDALE

At the edges of the Rokugani Empire, brave warriors defend its borders from demonic threats, while battle and political intrigue divide the Great Clans in their quest for glory and advantage.

**The Night Parade of 100 Demons**

MARIE BRENNAN

BESTSELLING AUTHOR OF THE MEMOIRS OF LADY TRENT

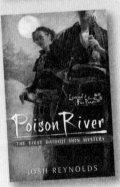

**Poison River**

THE FIRST DAIDOJI SHIN MYSTERY

JOSH REYNOLDS

Follow dilettante detective, Daidoji Shin, and his samurai bodyguard as they solve murders and mysteries amid the machinations of the Clans.

**Death's Kiss**

A DAIDOJI SHIN MYSTERY

JOSH REYNOLDS

**THE GREAT CLANS OF ROKUGAN**

KATRINA OSTRANDER • ROBERT DENTON III
MARI MURDOCK • DANIEL LOVAT CLARK

The Great Clan novellas of Rokugan return, collected in omnibus editions for the first time, with brand new tales of the Lion and Crane Clans.

**THE GREAT CLANS OF ROKUGAN**

ROBERT DENTON III • MARIE BRENNAN
D.G. LADEROUTE

ACONYTEBOOKS.COM

# ARKHAM HORROR™

*Riveting pulp adventure as unknowable horrors threaten to tear our reality apart.*

*A barnstorming movie star exposes frightful horrors, a mad Surrealist tears open the boundaries between worlds, crawling terrors lie deep in the jungle, dark incantations fracture reality... explore the uncanny realms of Arkham, and beyond.*

# DESCENT
## LEGENDS OF THE DARK™

**Epic fantasy of heroes and monsters in the perilous realms of Terrinoth.**

*A reluctant trio are forced to investigate a mysterious city, but in doing so find themselves fighting a demonic atrocity, and a holy warrior is the only hope of salvation from a brutal demonic invasion...*

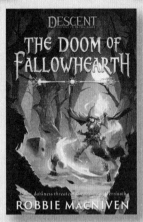

*Three legendary figures reunite to solve a mystery but instead uncover treachery and dark sorcery.*

# EXPLORE AMAZING NEW WORLDS

ACONYTEBOOKS.COM

# WORLD EXPANDING FICTION

## *Do you have them all?*

### ARKHAM HORROR
- ☐ *Wrath of N'kai* by Josh Reynolds
- ☐ *The Last Ritual* by S A Sidor
- ☐ *Mask of Silver* by Rosemary Jones
- ☐ *Litany of Dreams* by Ari Marmell
- ☐ *The Devourer Below* ed Charlotte Llewelyn-Wells
- ☐ *Dark Origins, The Collected Novellas Vol 1*
- ☐ *Cult of the Spider Queen* by S A Sidor
- ☐ *The Deadly Grimoire* by Rosemary Jones
  *(coming soon)*

### DESCENT
- ☐ *The Doom of Fallowhearth* by Robbie MacNiven
- ☐ *The Shield of Daqan* by David Guymer
- ☐ *The Gates of Thelgrim* by Robbie MacNiven
- ☐ *Zachareth* by Robbie MacNiven *(coming soon)*

### KEYFORGE
- ☐ *Tales from the Crucible* ed Charlotte Llewelyn-Wells
- ☐ *The Qubit Zirconium* by M Darusha Wehm

### LEGEND OF THE FIVE RINGS
- ☐ *Curse of Honor* by David Annandale
- ☐ *Poison River* by Josh Reynolds
- ☐ *The Night Parade of 100 Demons* by Marie Brennan
- ☐ *Death's Kiss* by Josh Reynolds
- ☐ *The Great Clans of Rokugan, The Collected Novellas Vol 1*
- ☑ *To Chart the Clouds* by Evan Dicken

### PANDEMIC
- ☐ *Patient Zero* by Amanda Bridgeman

### TERRAFORMING MARS
- ☐ *In the Shadow of Deimos* by Jane Killick

### TWILIGHT IMPERIUM
- ☐ *The Fractured Void* by Tim Pratt
- ☐ *The Necropolis Empire* by Tim Pratt

### ZOMBICIDE
- ☐ *Last Resort* by Josh Reynolds
- ☐ *Planet Havoc* by Tim Waggoner *(coming soon)*

## EXPLORE OUR WORLD EXPANDING FICTION

ACONYTEBOOKS.COM
@ACONYTEBOOKS
ACONYTEBOOKS.COM/NEWSLETTER